THE DUMARI CHRONICLES: YEAR TWO

THE DUMARI CHRONICLES

YEAR TWO

by

ANNE PATRICE BROWN

iUniverse, Inc.
New York Bloomington

The Dumari Chronicles: Year Two

iUniverse books may be ordered through booksellers or by contacting:

iUniverse
1663 Liberty Drive
Bloomington, IN 47403
www.iuniverse.com
1-800-Authors (1-800-288-4677)

ISBN: 978-1-4401-0991-1 (pbk)
ISBN: 978-1-4401-0992-8 (ebk)

Printed in the United States of America

iUniverse rev. date: 12/02/2008.

ALSO BY ANNE PATRICE BROWN

The Dumari Chronicles: Year One

Be Sure You Get My Best Side

Special thanks to:

Debbie - my Cape Cod tour guide
Michael - my "officially unofficial" editor
and as always
Christopher - for supporting my habit

Contents

Hey, you're back! Cool!

Bet you hated how I ended the first book — leaving you hanging like that. One of the tricks of the trade. LOL. Don't worry, you'll find out more in this one. Can't tell you how much though. Gotta keep the suspense going, ya know?

So, have you figured out which one of us turns out to be the Dumari yet? What about Alex and Morty? Know who they are? And did you absolutely HATE me at the beginning? Can't say as I blame you. I was SUCH a pain back then! But hey, I had "issues". Hell, who am I kidding, I was just a pain!

Needless to say, I've done a fair amount of growing up since then. Even Braidy admits I'm actually part human these days — now that's what I call a compliment!

What? What did you say? Who's Braidy?! What's a Dumari?! Are you telling me you haven't even gotten around to reading *Year One* yet?! Well! The nerve!

LOL — don't worry, I'm just kidding. I know how it goes — you were planning to read it but you got called into work that night, you had to wash your hair, your dog ate the first three chapters...yadda, yadda, yadda. Well, at least you're here now. Guess I'd better get you up to speed, though, or you'll be kinda lost. Time for a quick synopsis:

My twin cousins (Brody the Geek and Braidy the Blond Goddess) and I (Moira the Magnificent...*teehee*) were kidnapped one summer by this ugly old hag named Lorena Lewis. She was working for two ignorant evil wizards named Alex and Morty — more on them later. She took us to New York City and locked us up in a filthy attic (Braidy and I had a fight). Thanks to some brilliant thinking by yours truly, we managed to escape. Great. Just one problem — we were lost, we had almost no money, Braidy and I had another fight, somebody knocked out the phone service in New York (my money's on Alex) so we couldn't call home, and ol' Lorena sent a couple of goons named Paul and Pete after us. Okay, that's actually five problems. Never was good at math...

So why did they do this, you ask? Simple — they thought one of us was the new Dumari. Oops! I forgot — you don't know what the Dumari is because you didn't read the book...that'll teach you to procrastinate. All right, all right, I'll tell you...the Dumari is a particularly powerful witch or wizard. There can be only one alive at any given time in history and sometimes there isn't any at all...

What's that? Oh man! Didn't I tell you? I'm a witch. That's right — a real, honest-to-God witch. No, not one of those freaky old biddies like you see little kids dressing up as on Halloween. We're not like that at all. In fact, we're just like everyone else. We're young, we're old, we're short, we're tall, we're pretty, we're ugly...we're absolutely, totally normal. We just have this...gift. Or maybe I should call it a talent. And no, we don't use wands. We don't brew up potions by the light of the full moon. We don't even have to mutter a bunch of nonsense words. We just...do it. Magic, that is. Just like some people can sing and some can cook and some can hit homeruns.

Now, where was I? Oh, yeah...the Dumari. Okay, traditionally the Dumari is believed to be not only incredibly magical, but immensely good and selfless. Not necessarily a saint (although one or two have gotten close), but someone who genuinely wants to use their powers for the good of everyone. However (knew there had to be a catch, didn't ya), rumor has it that if this Dumari kid is subjected to evil influences before he or she becomes an adult, all that goodness can go right out the window. Hmmmm...I guess that could happen to any kid, couldn't it. But when it happens to a kid who has phenomenal cosmic power, things can get kinda ugly. You get the picture...

So, this Alex guy wanted to kidnap the Dumari in order to make use of all that super-duper magic for his own nefarious purposes. By the way, he was quite a magically powerful dude himself. But like most people who have a lot, he wanted more. Did I mention that in those days I hated magic and anything to do with it? I didn't want to be a witch. I hadn't done any magic in years. Needless to say, my loathing of witchcraft only served to make the entire scenario even more ignorant, in my opinion.

Anyway, there we were, me and the Bobsey twins, wandering around New York City, hungry, tired, scared (Braidy and I were arguing again)...and the lovely Pete and Paul were still chasing us all over Queens. Not exactly my idea of a fun time. Luckily, we managed to hook up with some friendly magicals who helped us hitch a ride back to Boston (yep, you guessed it, another argument). We were less than a block from my house when Alex's cronies reared their ugly heads once more, threw us into the back of a van, and took off with us. By that time, I was getting pretty fed up with those jerks. But since there were more of them — and they were bigger than us — we couldn't do much about it. We spent the next couple of days, tied up and gagged, being dragged from one hiding place to another all over Boston as they tried to throw our family off the scent (one bright note: since we were gagged, Braidy and I couldn't argue any more! LOL).

As you've probably already guessed, we were eventually rescued. This really hot guy named Russ (LOTS more on him later!) turned up totally by chance at the old house we were being held at and got into a fight with the dorks guarding us. I mean an all-out, no-holds-barred magical battle. Pretty impressive stuff. His dad was my mom's boss, so one quick call to him and the cavalry was on the way. The folks arrived on the scene, the bad guys made tracks, and the adventure was finally over. For the time being...

Chapter One:

A Change Of Scenery

"I'm not going!"

"Oh yes, you are!"

"Oh no, I'm not! And you can't make me!"

Andrew rolled his eyes at Ainsley. "Here we go again!" he muttered, making his young daughter giggle. The two of them were doing their best to keep their heads down and stay out of the way as Renatta and Moira battled it out in the kitchen. Andrew was beginning to think that the breakfast room was nowhere near far enough away from the line of fire.

"Moira, please! Let's not go through this again!"

"But it's ignorant! It's totally ignorant! You just make this decision on the spur of the moment, without even considering how I might feel, and BAM! my whole world is turned upside down! You can't do that to me! It's not fair!"

"It wasn't like that! I told you, Andrew and I discussed this for weeks! We thought long and hard about how it would affect each and every one of us!"

"And then decided to do just what you wanted and to hell with the rest of us!"

"THAT'S ENOUGH!" Andrew shouted as he stood up and strode into the kitchen. Renatta and Moira both stared at him, their mouths open in shock.

"Andrew!" Renatta gasped. "I've never heard you yell like that!"

Andrew ignored his wife. Backing Moira up against the refrigerator door, he glared down at his stepdaughter, his eyes shooting sparks.

"Now, you listen to me, young lady," he began. "Your mother had every intention of turning this promotion down at first, just for yours and Ainsley's sakes. She didn't want to uproot either of you, make you change schools, everything. But I insisted..."

"You insis...!" Moira attempted to interrupt, but Andrew talked right over her.

"...that she at least give it serious consideration. Your mother has worked long and hard to get where she is in her career. She might never get another chance like this. Managing her own bank branch — a brand new branch, I might add — is a wonderful opportunity. You should be proud of her. I know I am — very proud. And it's quite a testament to her abilities that Desmond Baines is showing that much confidence in her. He's practically given her carte blanche with the operation. It'll be like being her own boss."

"I know that," Moira said, slightly deflated. "And I am proud of her." A look of pleased surprise crossed Renatta's face. "It's just that — well, we're gonna have to move! I'll have to change schools and everything. What about my friends? What about my life?"

"The Cape isn't that far away, Moira," Renatta pointed out. "Granted, you and Ainsley will have to change schools, but you won't be that far from your friends. Now that you're driving, it should be easy to get together with them on the weekends."

"But I won't see Lucia every day, like I do now."

"You can still talk to her on the phone every evening."

"You talk to her on the phone every evening now," Andrew stated. "Never have figured that one out. You see her all day at school, and then you're on the phone for at least two hours every night. Why is that?"

"So they can discuss what happened during the day, Daddy," Ainsley explained patiently, in that superior tone women have used for generations when their men are being typically dense about the obvious.

"Huh?"

"It's a girl thing, dear," Renatta smiled and patted Andrew condescendingly on the shoulder . "You wouldn't understand."

"Got that right!" he muttered. "The thing is, Moira, it's simply too good an opportunity for your mom to pass up. Besides, we'll be living right on the ocean, just like you've always wanted. That has to count for something."

"Yeah, I guess so," Moira mumbled, her head bowed dejectedly. She glanced up sharply at Andrew. "Can my room overlook the ocean?"

"Sure! You can have the room at the back corner. And I'll even add in a nice big bay window — with window seat — looking straight out over the Atlantic."

"Cool!"

"But, Daddy," Ainsley appeared a bit worried, "you said my room overlooked the ocean."

"And what about our room?" Renatta put her two cents' worth in. "I thought you promised we'd have an ocean view. I'm not going to live that close to the Atlantic and not be able to wake up to it every morning, Andrew!" All three women advanced on the grossly outnumbered Andrew, determined looks on every face. Andrew backed up helplessly, his hands in the air in surrender.

"Okay! Okay! I'll...I'll just rearrange the plans a bit and put all the bedrooms at the back of the house!"

"How can you do that?" Moira snorted. "That doesn't make any sense!"

"Yeah, Dad," Ainsley said, "that would look stupid."

"Do you doubt my architectural abilities?!" Andrew attempted to sound insulted, but it didn't work. "I'll figure it out. Somehow," he whispered that last word to himself — and made a hasty exit. Renatta laughed softly as she watched him depart. Turning back to her daughters, she sighed.

"Moira...?"

"I know, I know!" Moira agreed reluctantly. "If you guys move, I have to move. I guess it won't be all bad. It's just that...aw, Mom, it's my senior year! I was really looking forward to it!"

"I know, sweetheart." Renatta wrapped an arm around Moira's shoulders and squeezed tight. "I'm sorry. Believe me, I wish the timing had been different, too."

"Can I at least finish out this year at my old school?"

"Of course! The house won't be ready until the end of June at the earliest. Andrew is still fine-tuning the blueprints. We probably won't be moving until after your birthday."

"So what are you going to do about getting to work every day until then?" Ainsley asked.

"Oh, that reminds me!" Renatta took both girls by the hand. "Until we move, I'll probably stay in Orleans during the week, and come home only on the weekends. So I'll need the two of you to hold down the fort around here. Can you do that for me?"

"What do you mean — hold down the fort?" Moira asked, her eyes narrowed in suspicion.

"You know — keep the house clean, do the laundry, make sure the three of you get a hot meal every evening, and..."

"And...?"

"Behave yourselves!" Renatta stared pointedly at Moira.

"I always behave myself!" Moira's attempt at an innocent look failed miserably. Ainsley giggled as their mother raised an eyebrow at her older daughter. "Mother, you doubt me?!"

"Yes!"

"But...!"

"No hanging out at the Mall after school, no boys in the house without Andrew's supervision..."

"As if!" Moira muttered.

"...make sure you do your homework — on time, that is! — don't spend all your free time on the phone or the internet or watching soaps..."

"This deal is getting worse by the minute!" Moira grumbled under her breath. She held up both hands in surrender. "Okay, Mom, okay! I promise I'll be a perfect little angel while you're gone. Just remember, this was your idea, not mine."

"Understood."

"We are going to live right on the beach? You promise?"

"Right on the beach," Renatta assured her. "We actually bought the lot several years ago with the thought of perhaps someday building a vacation home on it. It's a beautiful location — barely a block from your Aunt Caroline..."

"OH GOD!" Moira clapped a hand to her forehead. "I'd almost forgotten! I'm gonna have to go to school with Princess Braidy! How could you do this to me?!" She stormed out of the kitchen and up the stairs to her room.

"Maybe you shouldn't have reminded her of that, Mom," Ainsley stated blandly.

Renatta gave her daughter a dirty look, causing Ainsley to dissolve into giggles once more. A moment later, Renatta smiled in response.

"So, are you okay with this?" Renatta asked.

"Yeah," Ainsley replied, her face pensive. "I mean, sure, I'm gonna miss my friends a lot. But it's not like we're moving across the country. And I am excited about living right on the ocean. Do you really think Dad will be able to give all of us an ocean view?"

"I'm sure he'll try his best." Renatta smiled.

* * * * *

February 12

Can you believe this?! I knew things were going too good!

Okay, so maybe everything wasn't going so great, but school was pretty decent. My grades haven't been bad and I really like my writing class. Mr. Panopolis is so cool! — for a teacher, that is. And joining Chorale has turned out to be a lot more fun than I ever thought it could be. I mean, Lucia and I just thought it would be a big joke, being in a singing club with a bunch of geeks. I figured we'd never manage to sing anything — we'd be laughing too hard. But I really enjoy it! I had no idea Luce had such a good singing voice. And I'm actually looking forward to doing that duet with her at the spring concert. I can't believe Miss Hill agreed to it. She's usually so gay — making us do all that old crap, like Handel and Beethoven and — gag me! — Rodgers &

Hammerstein! It totally blew me away when she said that she likes Stopgap, and that *Winding Upwards* is one of her favorite songs. If we do a good job with it at the concert, she might let us sing it at graduation as well. I guess there's hope for her yet!

But, God, what a bite! This could be the one — and only! — time Lucia and I will get to perform together! Why does this kind of stuff always happen to me?! Okay, so maybe it doesn't always happen to just me. After all, Ainsley has to leave her school and her friends, too. But it's easier for her. She's only thirteen. She'd be starting a new school in a little over a year anyway, when she finished junior high and went on to high school. Although, I guess it is almost as bad to have to change schools for eighth grade as it is for senior year. Almost...

I mean, don't get me wrong. I really am happy for Mom — and proud of her, like I said. I just wish we didn't have to move. Why couldn't Mr. Baines have made Mom manager of the Quincy branch? That old fossil, Mr. Vaughn, has been running the place since the Ice Age. I keep expecting to walk in someday and find him sitting behind his desk, petrified in his chair! He's got to be ready for retirement soon. Wouldn't it have made more sense for Mom to take over for him? But when has anything to do with the business world ever made sense?! When has ANYTHING ever made sense?! Like guys —

Okay, so I saw Russ Baines at the Christmas party, and he was nice enough. Talked to me for a while, got me a Coke. But he never called me! Okay, just that once last summer.

But never since. And not since Christmas, either. I really thought, when he called me on my birthday —

Aw, who am I kidding? He was just being polite — a gentleman. A guy like him — older, mature, handsome (sort of), self-assured — he could have any girl he wants. He's a college man, for christ's sake! Why would he bother with a freaky-looking little chick like me? It's just — that day we met — when he helped rescue us — I really thought we connected. And then when he called just to check up on me, to make sure I was doing okay — my mistake. Like every other guy I know, he's probably dating some cheerleader with blond hair and blue eyes and great push-'em-ups. Besides, he's rich. I mean, we're not exactly poor, but Russell Baines is R-I-C-H, RICH! His dad's gotta be a multi-millionaire — at least. All those banks he owns, and hotels, and who knows what else. Russ'll probably end up with some debutante type from New York, or even some pseudo-royal chick from England or Sweden or something. They still have a royal family in Sweden, don't they?

Anyway, thinking about him is a waste of my time. I have as much of a chance with Russ Baines as I did with ever even meeting Ben Branson. Man, what a geek I was, crushing on him! A soap star! How pathetic is that! I'm so glad I've outgrown that phase! Besides, he wasn't even that good an actor. Of course, once he'd take his shirt off — which was practically every time he was in a scene — I'd forget all about his bad acting! LOL!

I guess it's okay to fantasize a little now and then. But it sure would be nice to have the real thing for a change. Why can't any guy like me just for me? Nobody at school has shown any interest. Devon hasn't brought anybody home from college, like I thought he would. And when I change schools next fall, everybody will compare me with Little Miss Braidy, the Blond Goddess, and I'll have even less of a chance than I do now. It's just not fair!

Oh well. No use whining about it. I can't change anything, so just get over it. Maybe someday somebody will learn to appreciate me. And in the meantime, I've got good friends, like Lucia & Leslie — except I won't have them soon! We have to move!

I DON'T WANT TO MOVE!!!!!!!

Okay, a part of me does. I have always wanted to live right on the beach and wake up every morning to the sound of the ocean. But there's ocean in Quincy, too. Well, harbor at least. Close enough.

Why does life have to be so complicated? I mean, some people seem to have it made — money, looks, brains. Everything falls right into their laps. But then there's the rest of us losers. Seems like no matter what I do, things never quite turn out the way I hoped they would. Man, wouldn't it be nice to just be able to coast through life, everybody liking me, everything going MY way? I know, I know! Ain't gonna happen. I can just hear Grandma Meredith saying it now: 'Trials build character.' Yeah, well, I think I have enough character already...

* * * * *

"You're kidding me, right? Moira Fitzgerald, our annoying cousin..."

"Our totally psycho cousin!" Brody put in.

"...is going to be transferring to Orleans High next year?! Our senior year?! The one I've been looking forward to for years?!" Braidy's voice grew steadily louder and higher pitched as her anger built. "Why?!"

"Because they're moving here," Caroline said calmly, doing her best to head off her daughter's tantrum. "I told you Aunt Renatta has been named manager for the new Cape Cod branch of the bank."

"Yeah, but we thought she'd just commute or something," Brody said. He, too, was somewhat less than enthusiastic about having to deal with Moira's presence on a daily basis. She was okay in small doses, but all day, every day? Not exactly his idea of the perfect scenario, either.

"That's a bit far to drive each day, don't you think? Especially with hydrogen prices going higher every week. Besides, your aunt doesn't want to spend that much time away from her family. She'd have to leave the house long before the girls left for school, and she'd be lucky to get back home before eight o'clock every evening. No, once she decided to accept the position, it was obvious that they'd have to move. It's going to be enough of a strain, staying here during the week, and only being home on the weekends until the new house is ready."

"What about Uncle Andrew?" Brody put in. "What about his job?"

"He's decided to go freelance," their mother told them. "He's wanted to for years, and now is the perfect opportunity. He's putting in an office on the ground floor of their new house and will be working from home."

"Wow! That's cool!" Brody whistled in appreciation.

"Yeah, that's great," Braidy agreed, "but it still doesn't solve our problem. What are we supposed to do about Moira, Mom? All our friends think she's a freak. Understandably, I might add."

"I thought you were getting along better with her," Caroline said. "Since last summer."

"A little bit, yeah," Braidy admitted, somewhat reluctantly. "At least, enough to tolerate her at family stuff. But all the time? At school and everything? Oh, Mom!"

"Look, kids," Caroline sighed, somewhat exasperated, "no one expects you and your friends to hang out with the girl on a regular basis. Just introduce her around a bit, help her find her feet for the first few days. She'll make her own way after that, I'm sure." With that, the front doorbell of the Bed & Breakfast chimed. "That must be the delivery truck with those antique chairs I bought last week. Finish up the kitchen for me, will you?" She made a hasty retreat.

"Can you believe this?" Braidy groused as she waved the last of the lunch dishes into the dishwasher and slammed the door.

"Jeremy's gonna hit the roof when I tell him. He hates Moira!"

"With good reason! I'll never forget the way she dissed him last summer. And right in front of the whole gang!"

"Yeah, well, I guess we're just gonna have to grit our teeth and make the best of it. Besides, she hasn't been anywhere near as bad as she used to be, before...you know...New York." Brody blushed slightly. By unspoken mutual agreement, the twins never referred to their adventures of the previous summer. It had not been exactly the most pleasant experience for them. But now, nearly a year later, the fear and horror had faded somewhat. At times it almost seemed as if it hadn't even happened, or had only been a dream. But neither one of them ever forgot it, either. It was not an easy thing to talk about.

Braidy looked out of the window, avoiding her brother's eyes. "Yeah, I know. It's just...well...it's Moira, you know?"

Brody laughed sharply. "Believe me, sis, I know! I know!" He leaned back against the counter while Braidy took the dishrag into the breakfast room and had it wipe down the table. Upon her return, the lovely young blond had a resigned look in her eyes.

"You're right, of course," she said, tossing the rag into the sink. She snapped her fingers and the dishwasher began to hum. "We'll just have to deal with it. There's nothing we can do to change it."

"Yeah. And chances are, Moira's no more thrilled about the situation than we are. She's not gonna want to hang out with us, either. It's a big school. We'll probably never see her. Maybe just in a class or two."

"Just my luck, she'll end up assigned to every one of my classes," Braidy muttered disgustedly.

Brody grinned as he patted his sister on the shoulder.

* * * * *

"He's gonna what?!!!"

Russell Baines pulled the phone away from his ear. Dan's screech had nearly punctured his eardrum.

"Take it easy, dude!" Russ tried to calm his friend. "What's the big deal?"

"Your dad is gonna run for mayor of Boston, and you don't think it's a big deal? What planet are you from?!"

"Lots of people run for political office. Dad's got some good ideas. I think he'd make a great mayor." Russ sounded slightly ticked. He'd expected his best friend to be excited, not appalled. Of course, he wasn't about to admit to his own apprehensions concerning Desmond's decision.

"It's not that I don't think your dad couldn't do the job, man," Dan apologized. "It's just that...well...you know what political campaigns are like. They're dirty, nasty, crooked....the list goes on and on. Mom has always said we can be anything we want to be, as long as it's honest... which automatically excludes used car salesman, lawyer, or politician. And she wasn't kidding!"

"Yeah, I know," Russ reluctantly agreed. "But it's something he really wants to do. He thinks he can make a difference. And I'm going to help him any way I can."

"What about school?"

"The campaign won't really get going until this summer. It might be a little tricky next fall, with the election in November, but I'll manage. Besides, Callista will be doing most of the legwork. She's planning to work for Dad full time. Sort of an unofficial campaign manager. I'll just be a glorified gofer."

"She is?" Russ could hear Dan's voice brighten. He sighed. Would his friend ever get over his hopeless crush on the beautiful Callista? Probably not. "Maybe I could help out, too. You know — stuff envelopes, answer phones, kiss babes..."

"Dude...that's babies, not babes."

"You kiss what you want, I'll kiss what I want!" Dan laughed. "Hey, we still on for Tuesday?"

"Yeah! I'm looking forward to it. I haven't been to a playoff game in ages."

"The Bruins have been playing so much better the past few weeks, we may be going to the Stanley Cup after all. The way they were choking back in January, I had my doubts."

"You and me, both! Man, I'd love to see the Cup come back to Boston! It's been, what, seven years since the last time?"

"Too long, man. Way too long. Hey, couldn't you do something? You know, wiggle your nose...waggle your ears..."

"No way, dude. Not allowed. That kind of interference would send me straight to the penalty box — for life!" Russ grinned.

"Bummer! Oh well, just a thought. You wanna grab a bite to eat before we go, or plan on eating at the Garden?"

"My last class doesn't end till five. We'd better plan on eating there."

"Sounds good. The game starts at 7:05, so I'll pick you up about six-fifteen, okay?"

"Sure. See ya then, Dan."

Russ hung up the receiver.

"An' just what is that young scallawag tryin' ta talk ye inta doin' this time?" Mrs. O'Malley asked as she bent down to check the roast cooking in the oven.

"Nothing, Mrs. O'Malley," Russ assured her. "Dan was just kidding around."

"Na doubt." The Baines housekeeper sounded skeptical.

"Honest! Dan knows I would never use magic for the wrong purposes."

"Is that so, now?" Mrs. O'Malley snapped her fingers. The oven door popped open. With a wave of her hand, the rack slid out. Another wave and the baster flew through the air, sucked up some of the meat juices, and gently squirted them over the top of the roast. Satisfied, Mrs. O'Malley waved the rack back into the oven and the door slammed shut. She turned to face Russ, her hands on her hips. The baster hung suspended in mid-air, forgotten for the moment. "An' what abut when he talked ye inta changin' his algebra grade from a D ta a B...or th' time he had ye fix his da's car when he ran inta that mailbox...or when..."

"Okay! Okay!" Russ held both hands up in surrender. "I give! There have been a few times that I used magic to help him out. But those were all personal things. They really only affected Dan and me. Or some of his family. And they knew nothing about it. He knows I would never even consider using my abilities against others. C'mon, Mrs. O'Malley, you know Dan as well as you know me. He's a good guy. He just likes to kid around a bit."

"A bit!" Mrs. O'Malley exclaimed. "That lad would try th' patience o' Blessed Saint Bridget herself." Her tone was sharp, but Russ thought he detected a small smile hovering around the old woman's lips. "How his poor mother has put up wi' him all these years, I dinna...och, saints preserve us!" she exclaimed, noticing the dripping baster at last. As she rushed to clean up the mess, calling on all the Irish saints to witness her absentmindedness — and making no bones about her own opinion of herself — Russ made a hasty exit. He smiled to himself as he walked toward the living room of the penthouse. He knew from long experience that Margaret O'Malley was all bark and very little bite. The feisty old Irish woman had been with their family since Callista had been born; cooking, cleaning, scolding. And loving. Russ knew she thought of them as her family. Her husband had died many years earlier, leaving her alone and childless. But the lack of children of her own had only served to strengthen her devotion to the Baines family. When Athena Baines first became sick, Mrs. O'Malley had insisted on being the one to nurse her. During those last horrible weeks, she had done everything for Athena; feeding her, bathing her, reading to her. And it was her strong arms that had cradled Russ when his mother had finally died, stroking his hair and wiping his tears. When Desmond decided to sell their home and buy the penthouse several years later, fourteen-year-old Russ had refused to move until Mrs. O'Malley agreed to come along as well. As far as he was concerned, she was part of the family. And that was that.

Russ stretched out on the living room sofa, his long legs dangling over the edge, and closed his eyes. A short nap, until supper was ready, seemed perfectly in order. Studying for his Physics exam could wait. Unfortunately, sleep eluded him. Dan's initial reaction to his father's political ambitions had bothered Russ more than he'd been willing to admit. He knew only too well that Dan had backed off not because his apprehensions had eased, but because he'd been distracted by the news that Callista would be working on the campaign as well. Russ's own concerns were easily a match for his friend's doubts. There was something about a magical in government that bothered Russ. Not that he thought his father would ever use his magical abilities to take advantage of his non-magical constituents — provided he was elected in the first place. It was simply the principle of the matter. The potential for abuse was too tempting.

Russ wished he could talk to Desmond about his feelings, but he was afraid of offending his father's sensibilities. He'd tried to discuss the situation with Callista, but that had been a waste of time. As far as Russ's sister was concerned, their father could do no wrong. If Desmond thought it was a good idea, then it must be. And Mrs. O'Malley made a point of never involving herself in the family squabbles — quite wisely. So Russ was alone with his disquiet.

As he lay on the sofa, his arm thrown across his eyes, his thoughts bouncing back and forth, the face of a girl slipped into his mind's eye. A girl with short, spiky orange hair, bright green eyes and a rather saucy smile on her lips. Suddenly, Russ felt an overwhelming desire to talk to Moira Fitzgerald. Instinctively he knew that Moira wasn't the type of girl to pull her punches. She'd tell him exactly what she thought of Desmond's political ambitions, in no uncertain terms. Sitting up, he headed for the phone in the den, then pulled up short at the door, embarrassment washing over him. When he'd last seen Moira, at the bank Christmas party last December, she'd been somewhat less than friendly. In fact, she'd looked at him with a distinctly accusing glare in her eyes. Not sure what it was he had supposedly done wrong, Russ had made small talk for a few minutes, then beat a cowardly retreat, murmuring something about having to mingle. He'd gotten the distinct impression that he'd reneged on a promise he'd made to the girl — but what that promise was, he had no idea. He'd neither seen nor spoken to Moira since.

Russ sighed, running his hand through his hair. There was no way he could call Moira now, after all this time, as if they were old friends, and pour his heart out to her. They barely knew each other. And he still felt an unexplainable and totally unreasonable guilt where Moira was concerned — for what imagined transgression, he had no clue. No, best not to open that can of worms. He'd simply have to trust his father to do the right thing. Desmond had never let him down before.

"Supper's ready!" Mrs. O'Malley called from the dining room. Pushing his uneasiness to the back of his mind, Russ joined the family for the evening meal.

Chapter Two:

Endings...And Beginnings

"Last week of school! Yaaaaah!!! We're almost Seniors!!!"

"Yeah, last week! Whoopee!" Moira grumbled.

"What's up, Moira?" Justin asked with a grin. "You gonna miss getting up at six every morning? Or is it Mr. Crane and his Roman Empire lectures you're pining for?"

"No, stupid!" Moira punched the skinny Oriental boy in the arm. "It's you guys I'm gonna miss, dork! I'm not coming back here next year, remember?"

"Oh, yeah, I almost forgot. Bummer!"

Moira and her four closest friends were hanging out at their favorite lunch table — the one nearest to the windows and farthest from the lunch line. Moira, Justin and Lucia were on one side of the table, while Taylor — a nice-looking, slightly heavyset boy with light brown hair and hazel eyes — and Leslie — a petite black girl with very short, very curly black hair and large sparkling brown eyes — faced them from the other side. It was their first study period on Monday. Only four more days of school left.

"We're gonna miss ya, Moira," Leslie said quietly.

"Yeah, it won't be the same without your ugly mug around," Taylor added.

"Gee, thanks!" Moira scowled at him.

"Too bad you can't commute next year," Justin commented.

"Yeah! Couldn't you just drive in every day?" Leslie visibly brightened at the thought. "It's senior year."

"Two hours each way? You kidding?" Moira shook her head sadly. "Naw, no way, folks. Even if my mom would agree to it — which she wouldn't, by the way — that's just too much time on the road. When would I do my homework?"

"Homework?" Justin grinned at her. "You actually do homework?"

"Only when I'm forced to," Moira grinned back.

"I thought you were allergic to the stuff!"

"Yeah, doesn't it make you break out in hives or something?" Taylor joined in.

"Yep! Nasty rash, all over!"

"Kinda like the one on Taylor's face, right?" Justin snickered.

Taylor threw a cold french fry across the table at his friend as the girls burst into giggles.

"No food fights on my watch, boys," Mr. Panopolis warned with a smile as he walked by.

"It just jumped right out of my fingers...honest!" Taylor grinned up at the English teacher. Mr. Panopolis was popular with everyone in the school, but in particular with the kids in the upper grades. Tough, but fair, he gave everyone an equal chance. He treated them like adults, working them hard, rewarding their efforts not only with well-earned grades, but with praise as well. Because he treated them with respect, they gladly returned the favor. He was Moira's favorite teacher. She was going to miss him badly.

"Moira, do you have a minute?" Mr. Panopolis asked, beckoning with his hand.

"Sure, Mr. Panopolis." Moira stood up and followed the English teacher to the other side of the cafeteria. Glancing back at her friends, she shrugged her shoulders in bewilderment. Mr. Panopolis had already returned their last assignment to them the previous Friday — Moira had received an A — and informed them that they would spend the last week of school on fun, creative projects. They had spent their class that morning acting out scenes from a collection of Mother Goose rhymes. Moira and Taylor had had a blast pretending to be Jack and Jill, bucket and all. Of course, Mr. Panopolis allowed them a great deal of liberty with the original plot. In the kids' version, "Jack's" head was broken, not when he fell down the hill, but when "Jill" knocked him over the head with the bucket, after finding out that he'd been seeing "Little Bo Peep" (portrayed rather poorly by Amber Birch, the head cheerleader) on the other side of the well. They'd had the entire class roaring with laughter. Mr. Panopolis had jokingly told Moira she should consider a career as a soap opera actress. She was a shoe-in as the next Susan Lucci.

"What's up, Mr. P?"

"I've heard you won't be coming back here next year, Moira," Mr. Panopolis began.

"Yeah. We're moving to the Cape. My mom got a big promotion. She's gonna be managing the new bank branch out there," Moira told him, sadly but proudly.

"That's great! You must be very proud of her," he smiled. "But I'm sure it's hard on you, having to leave all your friends."

"Yeah, well, life sucks." She blushed, lowering her head. "Sorry."

"That's all right, Moira. I understand. Sometimes it does. Listen, the reason I wanted to talk to you was to strongly recommend that you continue writing." Moira's head jerked up. "You have some real talent. Granted, it's raw and somewhat immature at the moment, but there is definitely true promise in your work. The best way to learn how to write is to keep writing — every day, if possible. Even if it's only a few sentences, a paragraph or two. Keep at it. You may just have what it takes to make a career out of it. If you want to, that is."

"I do!" Moira breathed, her eyes shining. "I love writing! I keep a journal and write in it every day!"

"Then go for it," he encouraged her. "Just remember, like anything else, becoming a successful author takes more than just talent. It takes determination, and a lot of hard work. I think you have the talent, I know you have the determination — the hard work is up to you. And don't be discouraged. Many a best-selling author had their work rejected dozens of times before they found the right publisher. Just keep at it, keep the ideas flowing, stay focused, and you'll make it. Oh, and when you start applying to colleges next fall, give me a yell. I'd be glad to write you a recommendation."

"Thank you, Mr. P!" Moira beamed up at him. "I'll do that! And thanks for the advice. I promise I'll stick with it."

Mr. Panopolis put his hand on Moira's shoulder. "I'm going to miss you next year, Moira," he admitted with a sad smile."Things will be rather dull around here without you to liven things up." Moira shrugged her shoulders, embarrassed. "You've been quite a challenge. You've angered me at times, frustrated me, annoyed me. There were even times I wanted to take you by the shoulders and shake you silly!" he laughed. "But you were never boring!"

Moira's brief flash of anger quickly changed to amusement and she joined in his laughter. "I'm gonna miss you too, Mr. P."

"Take care, Moira," he held out his hand. "Best of luck."

"Thank you, sir." Moira shook his hand firmly. As she turned to rejoin her friends, he called to her.

"Don't forget to let me know about the colleges, okay? And keep up with your journal!"

Moira waved her hand in acknowledgment and plopped back down in her chair.

"What did he want?" Lucia asked.

"Somebody must have told him I'm not coming back next year," Moira said. "He wanted to say goodbye and wish me luck." Surprised to feel a lump in her throat, Moira studiously stared out of the window. She wasn't going to let her friends see her cry. Especially the boys. They thought she was tough, tough enough to handle anything. She wasn't about to destroy her image now. She cleared her throat.

"So! What are we gonna do this weekend?"

As the others began discussing various plans, Lucia surreptitiously reached over and squeezed Moira's hand, giving her best friend an encouraging smile. Moira returned the smile and the squeeze, her heart full.

* * * * *

"Ainsley! Hey, wait up!"

Ainsley turned at the sound of Jason Hick's voice and blushed prettily. Jason was the most popular boy in her class. He was tall for his age, slender, athletic — and incredibly nice. Most of the girls had crushes on him — including Ainsley. She quickly attempted to arrange her face in what she hoped was a pleasant, but disinterested expression as Jason approached.

"What's up, Jason?"

"I...um...I'm going this way, too." A rather obvious statement, seeing as the walkway between the middle school and high school buildings was the shortest way to the school buses. Jason blushed. "I thought maybe we could walk together." Jason stared at the toes of his tennis shoes as he spoke, apparently succumbing to a sudden attack of shyness. Ainsley couldn't believe it. Jason Hicks was shy?! With her?! Her heart made a sudden bound upward into her throat.

"Sure, no problem," she managed to say, hoping her voice didn't sound as shaky as she felt.

The two young teens walked in silence for a while, both of them frantically trying to think of something clever to say. Finally, Jason gave up and simply said the first thing that came to mind.

"So when do you move?"

"The first week of July," Ainsley told him. "Mom and Dad want to be moved in by the Fourth."

"You excited?"

"A little, I guess." Ainsley pondered the question. "I mean, it'll be cool living right on the ocean. Our back yard is the beach. And we'll be right down the street from my aunt and uncle. They're really fun. But I'm gonna miss everyone here. A lot."

"I'll miss you, too," Jason murmured so softly, Ainsley wasn't sure she'd heard him correctly.

"You...you will?" she whispered, her eyes shining.

"Um...yeah....yeah..." Jason's shoes were once again of immense interest to him. "I mean...you're smart....and you're really nice...and... and..." grasping his courage with both hands, the love-struck young boy leaned close and whispered in Ainsley's ear, "....I think you're the prettiest girl in the whole school."

Having made his declaration, Jason squared his shoulders and stared straight into Ainsley's eyes, as if daring her to laugh. But Ainsley had no desire to laugh, unless perhaps with delight. She'd fantasized about this moment so many times over the past few months, she could hardly believe her dreams had actually come true. Oddly, she no longer felt the least bit shy or nervous. A strange calm washed over her, along with an unusual, but pleasant tingling in her fingers and toes. She smiled gently into Jason's eyes.

"I like you, too, Jason," she said softly.

The boy's face lit up. "You...you do?" Ainsley nodded. Glancing around quickly to ascertain if they were being observed, her admirer grasped Ainsley by the hand and pulled her around the corner of the school building. Momentarily awkward again, he gazed down at her, squeezing her hand convulsively. Ainsley gave his hand an encouraging return squeeze and waited for the most important moment of her life to occur. It took Jason several agonizingly long seconds to wrench up his courage, but eventually he leaned a tiny bit closer. Ainsley closed her eyes and instinctively rose up on her tiptoes, her lips puckered slightly in anticipation. Jason eagerly met her halfway, and Ainsley found herself reveling in the utterly new sensations of her very first kiss.

* * * * *

Moira, Lucia and Justin were walking to the bus stop when Lucia pointed toward the wall of the middle school ahead of them.

"Moira, isn't that Ainsley? With that tall blond boy? Kissing?"

"Ainsley? Kissing a boy? No way, Luce! She's still just a kid." Moira laughed, then looked again. She stopped dead in her tracks. "Holy...! It is Ainsley! Why, that little....!"

"That's Jason Hicks!" Lucia exclaimed

"Who's Jason Hicks?" Justin asked.

"Just the hottest boy in the entire middle school. He's just finishing seventh grade, but I've heard that even some of the freshman girls are after him. This is quite a coup for our little Ainsley. Didn't think she had it in her."

"She doesn't!" Moira hissed through gritted teeth.

"What's wrong, Moira?" Justin teased. "Jealous 'cause your little sister's getting some, and you're not?"

"Go sit on a tack and rotate, will ya?" Moira snapped, stomping away in the opposite direction.

"Our bus is this way!" Justin yelled, chuckling when Moira replied with a silent, but extremely succinct hand gesture. "Guess she'd rather walk home today."

"Leave her be, Justin," Lucia said. "She's going through a rough time right now."

"Yeah, who isn't!" Justin replied as they reached their bus. "I ain't getting any either!"

* * * * *

May 23

Can you believe this?! Ainsley has a boyfriend?! That goofy, geeky, skinny little redhead has got the most popular boy in her class — the most popular boy in the entire middle school — drooling over her?!

LIFE IS NOT FAIR!!!!!!

Not that I'm jealous or anything like that! Who cares if the little witch has some dork hanging all over her. I have better things to do with my time.

WHO AM I KIDDING?!! I WANT A BOYFRIEND!!

Geez, I've never even been kissed! How pathetic is that! My thirteen-year-old baby sister knows how it feels to be kissed and I don't! Not for real, anyway. This is one area in which dreams definitely do NOT qualify as life experience! And that quick peck Brody gave me when we were about five doesn't count either. Not only were we way too young to have any idea what we were doing, HE'S MY FRICKIN' COUSIN! And it was only on the cheek, anyway. Hardly worth stopping the presses, gang.

Maybe I should just walk up to some total stranger and plant one on him, see how it feels. I can always say that I'm a writer and need to do research for a new book I'm planning to write. *The Male Libido: How To Attract A Man In Five Seconds Or Less.* Yeah, right!

I should hate her. I DO hate her! No, I don't. Yes, I do! Oh, hell....

"Moira?" Ainsley's voice floated through the door of Moira's bedroom. "Can I come in?"

Shoving her journal into her desk drawer, Moira reached over to flip the lock. Ainsley stepped in and closed the door behind her, flopping down on the bed and pulling up her legs, Indian style. Pretending disinterest, Moira leaned back in her chair, her arms crossed on her chest.

"What's up, chit?"

Ainsley was trying her best to seem nonchalant, but with eyes shining and a secret smile playing across her lips, her success was minimal. Moira snorted quietly to herself, disgusted. But whether her disgust was directed at her sister or herself, she wasn't exactly sure.

"Oh, nothing, nothing much," Ainsley said, staring at her fingers, which she was twisting nervously. She jumped up suddenly and moved to the window. "Jason Hicks walked me to the bus today after school," she said over her shoulder, avoiding Moira's eyes. "He happened to be walking that way and thought he'd keep me company."

"Yeah? That was real gentlemanly of him," Moira replied sarcastically. "Jason Hicks, you said? Isn't he that dork all the girls in your class have been crushing on?"

"Could be. I don't keep up with that nonsense." Moira couldn't help but smile a little. Ainsley was such a pathetic liar. She'd been talking of nothing but the Hicks boy for weeks. "And he's not a dork," Ainsley whispered. Moira's smile became a grimace. "He's smart, and nice, and really cute, and..." Spinning around and dropping to her knees at Moira's side, Ainsley gazed up at her older sister, her face alight, her words tumbling over themselves in her eagerness. "...and he likes me, Moira! He likes ME! He told me, today, just after school. He...he kissed me! And it felt really nice!" The expression on Ainsley's face made Moira's stomach tighten with envy. "Why didn't you tell me how nice kissing is?"

"Yeah, well, I figured you'd find out for yourself eventually," Moira muttered, pretending a sudden interest in her mousepad. "So, he was okay at it? Not too hard, not too slurpy? No teeth? Watch out for braces, kid. They can be murder! I remember this one guy, in fifth grade...."

"Oh, Moira! Jason got his braces off ages ago!" Ainsley giggled. "It was more than okay. It was wonderful!" she sighed.

"Yeah, it looked like he knew what he was doing."

"It was incredible! He was..." Ainsley stopped, Moira's words suddenly registering. "What do you mean, 'it looked like'?"

Moira shrugged. "We saw you. On our way to the bus. Lucia and Justin and me."

"You saw us?!" Ainsley squeaked.

"Well, yeah!" Moira laughed at the horrified look on her sister's face. "You were standing right out in the open, making *beeyouteeful* mouth music. Everybody could see you."

"Everybody?!" Ainsley's face had turned bright red. "Oh no! Moira, what am I going to do?"

"Do? About what?"

"They'll all tease me tomorrow!"

"Yeah, probably. So what?"

"But...the other girls! They're going to hate me! Especially Adrianna! She's been bragging about how Jason always talks to her at church on Sundays. We all thought for sure he was going to ask her to go out with him. What am I going to say to her?"

"Nothing."

"But..."

"Look, Ainsley, this is nobody's business but yours and Hickey Boy. If the other girls are jealous, that's their problem. The guy made his choice — they'll just have to live with it. Besides, she'll get her chance."

There was a moment of silence, then Ainsley asked quietly, "What do you mean, Moira?"

"Oh...um..." Moira hesitated, her conscience battling with her jealousy. Jealousy won. "Just that boys that age, they're pretty fickle. Jump from one girl to the next all the time. He'll probably be swapping spit with good ol' Adrianna in a few weeks. Especially since we're gonna be moving. You won't be around to keep an eye on him — not that that usually stops them."

"But..." Ainsley's eyes filled with tears, "...Jason isn't like that. He likes me, he really likes me! I know he does!"

Moira laughed sarcastically. "Give me a break, kid! They're ALL like that! Take it from one who's been there — don't waste your time getting all misty-eyed over this guy. Just get what you want from him and move on. That's what they do. In fact, that's probably all he wanted from you in the first place. Figured he'd better fit you into his schedule before we move."

"You're wrong!" Ainsley whispered.

"Look, chit, I'm sure this...what's his name? Jacob?"

"Jason."

"Yeah, that's it. Jason. Anyway, I'm sure this Jason is the hottest thing since Orlando Bloom in *Die For Me*. And I'm sure he's a real nice kid. Just be realistic, is all. Don't expect too much. Guys don't have the longest attention spans, ya know what I mean? He thinks he likes you now, but once we're in Cape Cod, and he's here, he'll start thinking that one girl's pretty much like any other, and find someone else to occupy his time."

"That's a horrible thing to say! Jason is sweet, and nice, and smart, and...and..."

Moira threw her hands up in the air in mock exasperation. "Fine, whatever! It's your funeral. Just don't say I didn't warn you."

Ainsley stood up slowly, wiping her eyes. In the doorway, she turned and fixed her sister with an accusing stare.

"You know what I think? I think you're jealous. You don't have a boyfriend, and now I do, so you're jealous."

"Why, you little...!" Moira sprang to her feet.

"Braidy's right. Nobody wants to be with you because you're mean, Moira. You're just plain mean!" With that declaration, Ainsley turned on her heel and left the room.

Rage bubbling through her, Moira jerked her hand through the air as if slapping Ainsley's face. The door slammed shut of its own accord. Stunned by her unintended use of magic, Moira stood staring at the door for several minutes, breathing hard. Finally, she slumped back down in the chair and pulled her journal out of the drawer...

...She's got a lot of nerve! Coming in here, braggin' on her boyfriend, and then insulting me like that! I AM NOT MEAN!!!! I'm simply being realistic. And who the hell cares what Braidy thinks, anyway?! What does she know?! Mean! She's the one who's mean! Flaunting herself in front of everybody, acting like the perfect little lady in front of the grups, then turning her nose up and treating me like the poor red-headed stepchild when none of the adults are around. Mean! I'll give her mean!

And as for Ainsley...I was just trying to help. The poor little chit is so naive, she's bound to get her heart broken. I was only trying to warn her....

Aw, hell! Who am I kidding? I AM jealous — jealous as hell! I guess I shouldn't have dissed her new squeeze so hard. Maybe he is an okay kid. Maybe he really does like her. I mean, I guess she is kinda cute, in a dorky sort of way. And she's pathetically sticky sweet — guys like that. Don't ask me why.

What the hell! Who cares! It's her problem, not mine. And no, I will not go and apologize to her. What for? I was simply teaching her some of the facts of life. Lots of guys ARE like that! I could just let her figure it out for herself, but I was concerned enough for her well-being to give her some sisterly advice. Why should I apologize for that?!

Concerned, hell! What do I care what happens to the little chit?!

She's my sister! Of course I care!

No, I don't! She's a pain! She just insulted me!

But she didn't really mean it. She was upset....hurt....She came to me all excited, and all I could do was try to burst her bubble. That WAS kinda nasty of me....I mean....

Oh, SHUT UP!!!!

* * * * *

"It's good to have you home, Devon," Renatta commented at supper two days later. "We've missed you."

"Yeah, we're just a nice normal little family again," Moira said, crossing her eyes.

"Nice to see some things haven't changed," Devon stated dryly, giving Moira a sharp glance, tempered with a fond grin. He'd missed his irascible younger sister. He'd missed them all. As exciting as college life was, as noisy and chaotic as living in a dorm had been, there was no one quite like Moira for livening things up. The food on campus was much better than he'd expected, but it didn't begin to compare to his mom's cooking; not even his advisor could match Andrew for simple wisdoms; he'd even found himself pining a little for Ainsley's dogged devotion. Although he had to admit, the little girl wasn't such a "little girl" anymore. She'd done some serious growing up since he'd been home at Christmas. She was beginning to look like a young lady. It was a bit disconcerting.

"So how did your exams go?" Andrew asked.

"Not bad," Devon told him, spearing a forkful of lasagna. "I doubt I'll be getting straight A's, but I think I held my own. Spanish was a breeze, but Physics was a bitch...sorry, Mom." He glanced at his mother out of the corner of his eye, a sheepish grin on his face. "Living in the dorm doesn't make for the best of parlor manners."

"Apology accepted," Renatta smiled understandingly. "Ainsley, pretend you didn't hear that."

"Please, mother," Ainsley looked at Renatta pityingly. "It's not like I haven't heard the word before. Adrianna Dupre called me one yesterday."

"She did?!"

"What for?!"

"Why, that little...!"

"What'd you say back to her, kid?" Moira asked, grinning.

"I just told her it takes one to know one," Ainsley stated matter-of-factly, popping a green bean into her mouth, a smug expression on her face.

"Ainsley!"

"You did?!"

"Way to go!" Devon praised her, grinning. "That's what I call grace under fire."

"Why did she call you that?" Andrew asked, suspicious. "What did you do?"

"Oh...um..." Ainsley blushed, staring at the table. "Nothing, Daddy. Nothing in particular. She's just....she's not a very nice girl, that's all."

"Hmmm..." Andrew didn't look like he believed his daughter, but wisely decided to change the subject. "So, what are your plans for the summer, Devon?"

"Working at the paper, as usual. Mr. Wilson said he might let me cover the regatta this year."

"Cool!" Moira exclaimed. "Can I go with you?"

"Maybe," Devon said, looking Moira up and down. "It depends."

"On what?"

"On how much it's worth to you," he grinned. "I'm broke. I figure a free trip to the regatta is worth...oh....at least fifty."

"Fifty! Not exactly free, dork!"

"Nothing is free these days, dear sister."

"Hmmmph!" Moira grunted in disgust, giving her brother a dirty look. Devon merely laughed.

"Vy 'a way," Devon said around a mouthful of food a moment later. There was a loud gulping sound as he swallowed. "I hope you don't mind, Mom. I asked Jonathan Crenshaw to spend the Fourth with us at the new house."

"Who?" Andrew asked.

"I told you about him. He's in the Journalism School, too. Planning to be a TV news anchor. He's from Chicago, but he's not going home for the summer. He got an apprenticeship at Channel Seven, that little PBS station out of Hyannis, so he's staying there instead. He's been hired to help out with their summer pledge drive. I thought you might like to meet him."

"I certainly would," Renatta stated. "You've talked about him so much the past couple of months, I feel as if I know him already."

"He's really cool!" Devon enthused. "Knows a ton about reporting. He's the one who convinced me to learn all I can about live action as well as still photography — expand my horizons. Can't hurt, anyway."

"Why does he want to be on TV?" Ainsley asked.

"Well, as Jonathan says it, he's not brave enough to be a war correspondent, not smart enough to be a newspaper reporter, not artistic enough to be a photographer, and not stupid enough to be a sportscaster. So that leaves anchorman." Devon laughed.

"That wasn't a very nice thing to say about sportscasters," Renatta commented as Andrew joined in Devon's laughter.

"Jonathan said it, Mom," Devon protested, "not me! Besides, he's definitely got the looks for it — TV anchor, I mean."

"He does?" Moira perked up visibly.

"Down, girl," Devon warned her with a smile. "He's twenty-one already — way too old for you."

"I'm seventeen," Moira reminded her brother indignantly. "Well, almost."

"Devon's right," Andrew stated calmly. "Twenty-one is much too old for you, young lady."

"Great!" Moira muttered under her breath. "The one guy my dear brother brings home from college, and he's off limits."

"Anyway," Devon continued, "I hope that's okay with you guys. I thought he'd enjoy some home cooking for a change."

"It's fine with me, Devon," Renatta said. "There's always such a crowd at your Aunt Caroline's for the Fourth, one more mouth won't matter. Just warn him in advance — I may enlist him to help with the unpacking while he's here."

"Hey, Dev," Moira jumped in, " you gonna come see Lucia and me sing tomorrow?"

"What are you two doing? Entering a karaoke contest?" he teased.

"No! It's graduation! We're singing our duet again! I told you about it!"

"I know, I know!" he grinned. "I'll be there, don't worry."

* * * * *

"...And as the days drift by,
Filled with memories
Of chance and choices,
Truth and lies,
Hopes and failures,
Laughs and cries,
We find ourselves forever
Winding upwards."

Applause burst forth as the final notes drifted away. Moira and Lucia, eyes shining, bowed to the crowd in the high school auditorium and returned to their places among the choir. A quick glance to the back of the hall showed Moira her own family, standing against the wall, clapping harder than anyone else. Devon gave her a "thumbs up" sign, along with a big grin. Letting out a big sigh of relief, she reached over and squeezed Lucia's hand.

Chapter Three:

Bubble, Bubble, Boys And Trouble

"Thank you all for coming here today," Desmond's deep voice floated over the crowd milling about the Commons, grabbing their attention. The speakers crackled a little as the sound engineer adjusted the volume on the elaborate mixing board. Desmond continued. "My name is Desmond Baines, and I'd like to be your next mayor." He was interrupted by cheers, as several well-placed supporters waved "Baines for Mayor" signs over their heads. Russ noted the Channel Ten News truck parked nearby. It looked like his dad would make the eleven o'clock broadcast.

Russ was standing on the makeshift stage directly behind his father, Callista beside her brother, smiling proudly, her eyes on Desmond. Dan was placed in the front row of spectators, gazing up at Callista, a mixture of rapture and agony evident on his face. The poster he was supposed to be holding aloft was hanging limply from his hand, forgotten. Gazing out over the crowd, Russ recognized a few other faces; people from the bank, friends from their old neighborhood, some of his father's business associates.

"Boston is at a crossroads, my friends, as is our entire country," Desmond declared. "One path will lead us forward, toward an even brighter tomorrow, through the rest of the twenty-first century and on into the twenty-second. The other will take us nowhere, leave us stumbling and stagnating, wallowing in the mistakes of the past, unable to see the future. But which one is which? What path should we choose? It is going to take some truly hard-working, dedicated men and women to get the job done. I believe I am the person to help Boston choose the right path, for today and for tomorrow. But I can't do it alone. I need your help..." Desmond pointed directly at Dan, who started guiltily and quickly raised his poster aloft. "...And yours..." Desmond reached his hand out to a pretty young coed several yards back. "... And yours!" Spreading his arms wide, the new candidate looked as if he would encompass the entire crowd in his grasp. He smiled widely as the applause rose, washing over the few people standing on the stage behind him. For some unknown reason, Russ shivered.

"Thank you, thank you!" Desmond continued to smile complacently until the clapping and cheering subsided. "The task is at hand, my fellow Bostonians. We must put our shoulders to the wheel and get the job done, not only for ourselves, but for our children, and our children's children, as well. Together, we can change the world!" More cheering and waving of signs occurred. The cameraman from Channel Ten panned over the crowd and zoomed in on the pretty coed. "I have asked you all here today to officially announce my candidacy for mayor of the great city of Boston!"

The cheering and clapping burst out again, even louder this time. Russ shook his head in silent amusement. It wasn't as if his father's plans had been any great secret — as evidenced by the many posters, buttons and t-shirts scattered throughout the crowd. Most of those present knew why they were here. But many of the spectators acted as if Desmond's announcement was totally unexpected. As if they'd been trying to talk him into running for mayor for ages and he had finally, reluctantly, given in. He supposed it stemmed from a desire on everyone's part to feel important, as if they were critical to the operation. In a way, their acclaim was stroking not only Desmond's ego, but their own. Russ himself couldn't help but get caught up in the waves of excitement and anticipation washing over the crowd. At this moment, all his doubts and misgivings seemed like nothing more than undue pessimism. Everything would be great. Desmond would win the election handily, and he'd turn out to be the best mayor Boston had ever known.

"I won't take up any more of your valuable time today, folks," Desmond continued when the applause had died down somewhat. "But if at any time during the next five months, you find yourself with an empty afternoon or two, feel free to stop by and lend a hand. I'm sure my daughter will manage to find something for you to do." There was scattered laughter as Callista made a face at her father. "After all, she's kept me busy for years!" More laughter and clapping as Callista hugged her father. Russ privately raised an eyebrow — his sister was not known for her displays of affection, public or private. Although the moment probably appeared quite spontaneous to everyone else, Russ knew it had to have been staged in advance. His stomach squirmed slightly, and all his earlier apprehensions rushed back. He tried his best to ignore them.

"Once again, thank you for being here today. I look forward to seeing you at the polls in November." The cheering swelled momentarily, then faded away as Desmond turned and walked down the steps of the stage. The sound engineer cued up some canned music as Russ's father began to work the crowd; smiling, shaking hands, waving to familiar faces farther away.

Watching his father, Russ had to hand it to him. The man knew how to connect with people. He exuded strength and a calm intelligence that left people feeling reassured and confident in his ability. Perhaps everything would turn out all right. But for some reason, that nagging ache deep down in Russ's stomach simply wouldn't go away.

"That went well, I thought," Callista commented, her habitual haughty expression of disdain back in place. "Father certainly can be convincing when he wants to be."

Russ gave his sister a sardonic glance. "Are you saying he didn't believe in what he said? That it was...what...political mumbo-jumbo?"

"Oh, please, Russell!" Callista laughed, a low, sarcastic, mirthless sound. " 'Boston is at a crossroads' — 'We must put our shoulders to the wheel'. Standard psychobabble."

"I thought you supported Dad in this!" Russ said, surprised. Callista had appeared to be one hundred percent behind Desmond whenever the subject had come up for discussion.

"Of course I do, Russell." Callista refused to use her brother's nickname. She felt it wasn't dignified enough. "I simply find it rather pathetic — the nonsense people in this country expect their politicians to spout on a regular basis. We're always at a crossroads. Nothing has changed from four years ago. Or forty years ago. Hopefully, once Father has been elected, we'll be able to rectify that."

"What do you mean?"

"Simply that Father and I have serious plans — plans that will change the future of this city, and this country, forever. It is time someone took charge and accomplished a few things."

"Father and you? What are...." Russ was interrupted by the approach of his best friend, poster still in hand.

"Great speech, man!" Dan enthused. "Hello, Callista." The young black man blushed, suddenly shy. Callista ignored him.

"I'd best see if Father needs me," she said, waving vaguely as she walked off of the stage. Russ sighed in exasperation as Dan's eyes followed her through the crowd.

"Man, she looks great," Dan enthused. "Doesn't she look great?"

"Yeah, great," Russ mumbled, shaking his head. Oh, well. "C'mon, man, I'm dying of thirst. Let's go get something to drink." Tugging on Dan's arm, Russ managed to drag his friend free of Callista's gravitational pull and in the direction of a nearby deli.

* * * * *

"So, how's this gig working out?" Justin asked Taylor as he, Lucia, and Moira took their seats at a table near the large front window of the Beacon Street Bistro. Taylor had started working at the restaurant two weeks before, thanks to Leslie's recommendation. Leslie had been working there as a waitress for almost a year. She gave her friends a quick wave from the back of the room, where she was waiting on another table.

"Not too bad," Taylor told them as he handed them menus. "The pay is pretty lousy, but the tips aren't bad. And the food's really good. Can't stand the boss, but his wife is a knock-out!"

"Yeah?" Justin perked up visibly as Moira grinned at Lucia. "She around?"

"Over there," Taylor pointed toward the bar. "The tall redhead."

"Sweet!" Justin let out a soft wolf whistle. "With scenery like that to look at, who needs tips!"

"Yeah, well, she ain't here every day," Taylor informed his friend. "And I gotta pay for my car insurance somehow."

"Oh, yeah...right!"

"So you guys gonna order something, or what?"

"Give us a chance to check out the menu, will ya?" Lucia laughed at him.

"Oh, yeah, sure," Taylor grinned. "Guess I'm a little nervous. This is my first day on my own. I've been following Leslie around up till now."

"Dude," Moira stated blandly, "you've been following that girl around for years."

"Yeah, man, when you gonna work up the nerve to ask her out?"

"Will you pipe down!" Taylor shushed them. "She might hear you!"

"She's all the way across the room, dork!" Moira laughed.

"She has excellent hearing!" Taylor grumbled. The other three only laughed harder. "Just order something, will ya! The boss is giving me dirty looks!"

"Okay, okay. Don't get your wand in a knot." Moira glanced down the list of menu items. "Bring me....bring me half a club sandwich with the house salad and an iced tea."

"I'll have the tuna on whole wheat — no chips — and a Diet Coke," Lucia ordered.

"Gimme the mushroom swiss burger — medium, extra cheese — with fries and a regular Coke. None of that nasty diet stuff for me. Oh," Justin added as an afterthought, "and one of those big honking pieces of cheese cake. With strawberries and whipped cream. In fact, bring that first." He grinned at the girls.

"Gotcha. Anything else?" Taylor asked as he finished keying their order into his handheld and sent it back to the kitchen.

"That's not enough?" Moira raised her eyebrows. Taylor waved over his shoulder as he went to get their drinks. Moira leaned across the table toward Justin. "You planning to try out for the football team or something?"

"No. Why?"

"You're sure eating like one of those nano-brains."

"I'm a growing boy," Justin replied smugly.

"Yeah, the question is, you growing upwards — or outwards?" Moira chuckled.

"Oh please! Like he has anything to worry about!" Lucia pointed out the obvious. "He's skinny as a rail, and always has been. He turns sideways, you can't even see him."

"Please! Don't rub it in!" Moira grumbled.

"Hey, aren't you Moira Fitzgerald?" a voice asked from the table behind them. Moira turned around.

"Who wants to know?" Her eyes widened involuntarily as she recognized the boys sitting behind them. They were all members of the school football team. Moira gulped.

"I'm Brad. Brad Mulligan. We had Algebra II together this year, remember?"

"Um...yeah...sure. Nice to see ya, Brad." Moira started to turn back around, hoping to end the conversation, but Brad was apparently the persistent type. He pulled his own chair closer, leaning on the back of Moira's. Moira exchanged a glance with Lucia and Justin, partly worried, partly amused.

"Yeah. I had to take the stupid class over. Flunked it Junior year. I mean, like, when am I ever gonna use that stuff again, ya know? I'm not planning to be some nerdy rocket scientist, or something."

"Fancy that!" Justin whispered to Lucia, who tried desperately to hide her giggles. Moira glared at the pair of them.

"Anyway," Brad continued, oblivious to Justin and Lucia's amusement, "I just wanted to tell you, you sounded real good at graduation. Singing, I mean. I like that song."

"You like Stopgap?" Moira actually looked at him for the first time.

"Yeah, they're not bad. At least, I like some of their stuff. But Grannie's Complaint is my favorite."

"No kidding! They're my favorite, too!"

"Yeah? What d'ya know! They're coming in concert this Saturday."

"I know!" Moira moaned. "I really wanted to go! But it sold out so fast!"

"I got tickets," Brad grinned. "Two."

"Hey," Justin whispered in Lucia's ear, "he can count!" Lucia's giggles got the better of her once again, but this time Moira didn't notice.

"No way!" she exclaimed, turning around completely to face the bulky football player. "You are so lucky! Who're you going with?"

"I was gonna take my girlfriend," Brad said, "but we broke up last week. She doesn't much care for Grannie's Complaint anyway. Hey...!" his eyes lit up. "You wanna go with me?"

"Who? Me?" Moira pointed at herself, taken totally by surprise.

"Yeah. You said you like 'em, right?"

"Um...yeah....but....how much are the tickets?" she asked hesitantly. She had planned to sit in the cheap seats herself. Something told her Brad wouldn't have settled for the ozone level.

"Don't worry about that," Brad waved his hand dismissively. "My treat."

"Thanks!" Moira's face was a study in confusion — mostly delighted by the opportunity to see her favorite band, but also rather flustered by the suddenness of the invitation.

"I'll pick you up around seven." Brad stood up as his friends deserted their table, having paid the check. "You live over on Shore Drive, by the harbor, right?"

"Yeah...um...Number Twelve," Moira told him, her head swivelling to follow him as he walked toward the door.

"Great! See ya Saturday!" Brad waved as he ran to catch up with the others in his group.

Moira, Lucia and Justin sat in silence for several moments, then all three of them burst into laughter at the same moment.

"Can you believe it?!" Moira gasped, trying to catch her breath.

"Our little Moira," Justin teased, wiping a fake tear from the corner of his eye, "going on her first date. And with a nano-brained football player, no less! They grow up so fast!"

"It's not a date, stupid!" Moira slapped his arm.

"It sure as hell is, Moira," Justin laughed.

"No, it's not!" Moira insisted.

"Then what is it?"

"It's a....it's a...." A look of shock came over her face. "Oh God, what if it is? What do I say? What do I do? I barely know the dork!" Justin laughed even harder. Taylor chose that moment to return with their drinks.

"What's so funny?"

"Moira's got a date for Saturday night," Lucia told him, trying not to laugh. But it was difficult. The horrified expression on Moira's face was absolutely priceless.

"No way!" Taylor gasped.

"Yeah," Justin managed to choke out. "And with Brad Mulligan, no less."

"Who's he?"

"One of the football players. He just graduated."

"One of the footb....!" Taylor's face turned bright red. "Moira's dating a stinking jock?!" He almost dropped Lucia's drink, he was so shocked.

"I am NOT dating him!" Moira insisted, regaining her aplomb. "It's just a concert."

"He's picking you up," Lucia pointed out, "and he's paying for the ticket. That sorta makes it a date."

"Oh God! What have I done?!" Moira groaned, hiding her face in her hands.

* * * * *

"Hey, I thought you were dying of thirst," Dan said as Russ suddenly steered him away from the door of the deli.

"Yeah...um...that place is too...too crowded," Russ stammered as he walked quickly down the street, Dan in tow.

"It was half empty!"

"Well then, it's...it's too pretentious. The Beacon Street Bistro — give me a break! It's a deli, call it a deli."

"What? What do you care? You had no problem with it a minute ago."

"So I changed my mind! So shoot me!"

"What's up with you, man?"

"Okay, look," Russ stopped and turned to face his friend. "There was a girl in there I didn't want to see. That is, I'd kinda like to see her, but I'm pretty sure she doesn't want to see me, okay? So let's just go somewhere else."

"Who?" Dan craned his neck, trying to see in the window of the Bistro.

"The one sitting at the front table," Russ told him reluctantly.

"The Hispanic girl? She's cute!"

"No, not her. The other one. With the blue hair."

Dan started to laugh. "You're joking, right? You suddenly develop a thing for turquoise porcupines?"

"Don't laugh!" Russ punched Dan in the shoulder. "Moira's okay. She's just....she's just a free spirit, that's all."

"Yeah, right!" Dan looked at Moira again, squinting his eyes to see her better. "Moira, huh? Wait a minute!" He snapped his fingers as his memory caught up. "That isn't that girl from last summer, is it? One of the ones we rescued at the Denby mansion?"

"As a matter of fact," Russ stared at the sidewalk, his cheeks slowly turning red, "it is. Her name's Moira Fitzgerald. Her mom works for my dad."

"You've been holding out on me, dude," Dan grinned. "Never even mentioned her."

"There wasn't anything to mention. I called her once, a couple of weeks after the thing at Denby's, then I saw her at the bank Christmas party."

"So what's the big deal, then?"

"Let's just say the temperature at the party was icier inside than it was outside. She was definitely not full of the holiday spirit. At least, not toward me."

"Why?"

"I'm not sure. But for some reason, I felt like I'd let her down somehow. Don't ask how, I haven't a clue."

"Girls! They refuse to tell us what's wrong, but still get all pissed when we can't figure it out for ourselves. What do they think we are, stinking mind readers?"

"Yeah, pretty much."

The two friends joined the line at an outdoor Starbuck's kiosk.

"I'm confused, though," Dan continued the conversation.

"So what else is new?" Russ teased him.

"Ha, ha. Very funny. Since when are you the comic?" Dan smirked. "No, I mean, okay, so this Moira's apparently something less than thrilled with you. So what? What do you care? You've only seen the chick, what, twice? Three times, tops?"

"Twice. And one phone call."

"So why are you letting it eat at you?"

"That's the thing, Dan," Russ admitted, running his hand through his hair. "I'm not sure why it bothers me. It just does. I'll go for weeks without even thinking about her, and then suddenly she pops into my head. And I can't get her out for days."

Dan raised an eyebrow. "Freaky, man." They paid for their drinks and headed back to the Common. "Moira's a magical, right?"

"Yeah. So?"

"Maybe she's bewitched you somehow. Used a love potion on you or something."

"Yeah, right!" Russ scoffed.

"No, I'm serious, dude! I bet she stole a lock of your hair and brewed it up at the dark of the moon with some bat wings and newt tails and lizard lips...or whatever it is you Merlin types use and..." Dan's grin grew larger and larger.

"How many times do I have to tell you, dork?" Russ shook his head in mock exasperation. "We don't work like that!"

"Sure. That's what you say. But all the experts say otherwise."

"Experts?"

"Yeah! You know — the Brothers Grimm, Anne Rice..."

"She did vampires, man, not witches," Russ pointed out. Dan ignored him.

"...J.K. Rowling, Shakespeare..." Dan hunched his back and crooked one hand in the air. "Bubble, bubble, boil and grumble..." he rasped in a high-pitched, squeaky voice.

"That's 'double, double, toil and trouble...', you moron," Russ grinned.

"See! You *do* know about that stuff! I knew you were holding out on me, man!"

"Whatever!" Russ rolled his eyes, laughing. "Think what you want. Moira Fitzgerald has not brewed up a love potion to use on me. I'm not in love with her — I just — hell, I don't know! She just gets to me, ya know?"

"Do I ever!" Dan breathed as they approached the now smaller crowd still milling around Desmond — and Callista. He wandered toward the beautiful young woman, Russ and his dilemma forgotten. Russ watched his friend sadly, then sighed. He turned to face Beacon Street, a troubled frown creasing his brow.

* * * * *

June 12

WHAT HAVE I DONE?!!!!!!

I can't go out with a football jock! That goes against every principle I hold dear! What am I gonna do?!!!

Okay, girl, deep breaths. Get a grip. It's a concert — not a date. You're just hitching a ride, that's all. No biggie. You go to the concert, enjoy the show, and when he drops you off, politely shake his hand, thank him — end of story, right? Just two friends — acquaintances — spending a few innocent hours together along with about twenty thousand other screaming teenagers. Nothing remotely romantic about that, is there? Of course not! Justin's looking at it all wrong. Brad was simply being considerate — knew I like the band, didn't want to waste the ticket. And besides, I don't consider it a date. Not even remotely.

But what if HE thinks it's a date? Aw, hell!

Okay, look at this from a practical point of view. What would be so awful? He's not bad looking — granted, he's got that neck-as-thick-as-his-head thing going for him — but his face is okay. Not too beat up. Of course, he's about seven feet tall, so I'm gonna look like a hobbit next to him. And what if he wants to kiss me? He'll have to get on his knees to reach me! Or pick me up! Oh God, what a laugh!

Hey, though — if I can talk him into letting me sit on his shoulders, I'll have a great view of the band. Best seat in the house.

You know, this could be fun. I mean, okay, he's not exactly the brightest star in the universe, but he seems nice enough. Harmless, anyway. And he is sorta cute. In a Cro-Magnon kind of way. And I REALLY want to see Grannie's Complaint.

It's gonna be fine. The concert will be great, Brad will be lots of fun, I'll have a fantastic time. Yeah, I know. Now I just have to convince myself of that....

* * * * *

"I'm really sorry, Moira," Andrew said that evening just before the eleven o'clock news started. "I tried to snag some comp tickets to that concert you wanted to go to this weekend, but someone else in the office beat me to it. Seems to be the hottest show in town."

"Yeah, it is," Moira smiled, "but that's okay. I'm going anyway. I forgot to tell you."

"You are?"

"Yeah. A guy from school had an extra ticket. He's asked me to go with him."

"Who?" Ainsley asked suspiciously.

"Brad Mulligan," Moira told her, a bit reluctantly. The two sisters had remained cool toward each other ever since the "Jason Hicks Incident", as Moira thought of it. She wasn't quite sure how Ainsley would react to this new development in her older sister's love life.

"The football player?!" Ainsley squealed. Andrew raised an eyebrow. "You hate football players!"

"Yeah, well, I don't plan on marrying him, chit," Moira stated, trying to look cool. "I'm just hitching a ride with him, okay?"

"How much is the ticket?" Andrew asked.

"Um...he didn't say," Moira mumbled.

"Then how do you know you'll be able to afford it? Moira..." A warning tone crept into Andrew's voice as suspicion dawned.

"He...um...he said it would be his treat." Moira blushed as both Andrew and Ainsley continued to stare at her.

"So..." Andrew finally said, "it is a date."

"Um....yeah....kinda...I guess." A small smile hovered around Moira's lips.

"Well, then." Andrew managed to hide his own smile. "Is he a gentleman?"

"Were you a gentleman when you were eighteen?" Moira grinned at her stepfather.

"I most certainly was," Andrew stated pompously. "And you can confirm that with your mother. Is this boy picking you up here?"

"Yeah. He said he'd be here around seven."

"Good. I'd like to meet him."

"Andrew," Moira warned, "if you dare ask him what his intentions are, I'll...I'll...."

"You'll what?" Andrew grinned at her.

"I'll throw something at you!" she declared. "I swear I will!"

Andrew laughed. "Oooh, I'm scared!"

"Hey," Ainsley interrupted, "isn't that Mr. Baines?" She pointed toward the television screen. The other two swivelled around to look.

"It certainly is," Andrew replied, frowning slightly. "What's he doing on the news?"

"You don't think there was a problem at Mom's bank, do you?" Moira asked, her face concerned. "Turn it up, Ainsley."

Ainsley wiggled her finger and the volume increased drastically.

"...but for our children, and our children's children as well. Together, we can change the world! I have asked you all here today to officially announce my candidacy for mayor of the great city of Boston!"

"Holy...!" Moira whispered.

"Well, what do you know!" Andrew shook his head, a slight smile on his face. "I had a feeling..."

"I wonder what Mom thinks of this," Moira mused.

"But..." Ainsley hesitated, "Mr. Baines is a magical, isn't he, Dad?"

"Yeah, that's right!" Moira said. "I thought magicals weren't allowed to run for political office."

"There's no law that says we can't," Andrew explained, "it's just not exactly encouraged. The potential for abuse — intended or otherwise — would be too great."

"So how come Mr. Baines gets to do it?" Moira asked. Staring at Desmond's smiling face on the TV screen, she couldn't help but be reminded of his son. Moira scowled. "How come he gets to break the rules?"

"I told you, Moira, he's not breaking any rules. It's just...well...I don't know. Desmond's a good man; strong, intelligent, hard-working. He knows the risks involved. I'm sure he'll be careful."

"Hmmm...." Moira didn't appear convinced.

"I don't like it," Ainsley suddenly stated.

"What, punkin?" her father asked.

"Mr. Baines, running for mayor. Why would he do that?"

"Probably because he feels he can do a good job for the city."

"But how? I mean, what if he uses magic while he's in office — or even to win the election in the first place?"

"I doubt he'd do that."

"How do you know, Dad?" Ainsley looked at Andrew sharply. "How well do you know him, really?"

"Your mother has worked for him for years..."

"Yeah, but how well do you know him?" Moira repeated her sister's question, crossing her arms over her chest.

"I know he did everything he could to help us find you kids last summer," Andrew stated quietly. "That alone puts him pretty high on my list. Besides," he added in a lighter tone, "who's to say he'll even win? We're probably arguing about something that isn't going to happen. Look, girls, Desmond Baines is a man of principles and integrity. I'm sure he has only the best motives in mind."

"I sure hope so," Moira murmured to herself, " 'cause if he doesn't, all hell could break loose."

Chapter Four:

Car Problems

"MOM! HAVE YOU SEEN MY PURPLE SHIRT?!"

"Which one?" Renatta called up the stairs.

"WHICH ONE! MY FAVORITE ONE! THE ONE WITH THE SEQUINED SCORPION ON THE FRONT! Which one!" Moira muttered to herself as she rummaged frantically through her closet. "As if she doesn't know. Where the hell is that damn thing?!"

It was 6:07, Saturday evening. Brad Mulligan was due to pick Moira up in less than an hour and her nerves were definitely getting the better of her. Still in her bathrobe after a hot shower that had none of the calming effect it was intended for, Moira feverishly searched for her missing shirt. She hadn't done her hair or her makeup yet. A black leather mini-skirt lay on the bed, along with a pair of purple lace leggings and her black leather jacket, her trademark hiking boots tossed haphazardly on the floor below.

"Where did you see it last?" Renatta's voice floated up from downstairs.

"RIGHT HERE, IN MY CLOSET! BUT IT'S NOT HERE NOW!"

"Can't you wear something else?" Andrew asked as he passed Moira's bedroom door. Moira paused in her search just long enough to shoot a scathing look over her shoulder at him. Wisely, Andrew continued on his way.

"What's up with her?" he whispered to Renatta as they passed on the stairs.

"It's her first official date, Andrew," Renatta reminded him. "She's nervous."

"I didn't think she even liked the boy."

"That, my dear, is beside the point." Renatta smiled at Andrew's bewilderment and headed for Moira's room.

"MOM!!!" A distinct note of panic had crept into Moira's voice.

"I'm right here." Renatta stepped into the room, refraining from comment on the clothes that were strewn all over the floor.

"He's gonna be here in forty-five minutes, and I haven't even started on my hair yet!"

"Calm down, Moira." Renatta placed her hands on her daughter's shoulders and steered her toward the bathroom. "Go do your hair and makeup. I'll find your shirt."

Moira stomped into the bathroom and began working gel into her bright pink spikes. Applying mascara and eye liner were particularly challenging with her hands shaking so badly, but somehow she managed. She was just finishing off her lipstick when Renatta poked her head through the doorway.

"I'm sorry, sweetheart," she said, "I can't find your shirt anywhere."

"Damn it, Mom! It was in my closet yesterday! I know it was!" Moira slammed her fist against the sink counter in frustration. "Where did that stupid shirt go?!" There was a sudden loud bang and a squeal from Ainsley's room, followed by several more bangs and bumps. Moira and her mother both jumped, Renatta turning toward the sound as Moira stuck her head out into the hallway. To their combined amazement, the missing shirt came floating down the hall to them. Reflexively, Moira reached out and grabbed it. Totally bewildered, they both walked to the door of Ainsley's bedroom.

Ainsley was crouched in the middle of her bed, her arms flung protectively over her head. Her closet door was swinging wildly and every one of her dresser drawers were laying upside down on the floor, clothes scattered everywhere.

"What's going on?" Renatta asked, suspicion beginning to dawn.

Ainsley peaked out from under her arms. "I'm sorry," she whispered, tears in her eyes. "I took the shirt. I hid it in one of my drawers."

"Why, you little...!" Moira advanced on her little sister, her eyes flashing. "WHAT DID YOU DO THAT FOR?!"

"BECAUSE YOU DESERVED IT!" Ainsley shouted back, her eyes flashing in return. "Besides, what do you care? You're only going out with this guy because you want to go to the concert so bad. You don't even like him!"

"How do you know?! Maybe I do like him! Or maybe, I might like him once I get to know him! But that's totally beside the point anyway! YOU STOLE MY SHIRT!" Moira's hands were shaking again, but this time with anger. "AND WHAT DO YOU MEAN, I DESERVED IT?! WHAT DID I DO TO YOU, CHIT?!"

"Moira!" Renatta tried to interrupt the argument, but her daughters completely ignored her.

"YOU RUINED EVERYTHING!" Ainsley was crying in earnest by this time. "ALL THAT AWFUL STUFF YOU SAID ABOUT JASON!"

"WHAT ARE YOU TALKING ABOUT?! JASON WHO?!'

"YOU KNOW PERFECTLY WELL WHO! JASON HICKS, THAT'S WHO!"

"Jason Hicks?" Renatta was even more bewildered. "What's he got to do with this?"

"Who's Jason Hicks?" Andrew asked, coming up behind his wife. Renatta shushed him with a wave of her hand.

"So I told you what to expect from the Hickster, so what?" Moira tried to feign nonchalance, but the bright red spots on her cheeks gave her away. "Is it my fault he lived down to my expectations?"

"That's not what happened," Ainsley sobbed. "I didn't want to believe you — I tried NOT to believe you. But you stuck the idea in my head and it made me act so suspicious and jealous that he....he...." Crying as if her heart would break, Ainsley flung herself face down on her bed. "He...broke...up...with...me......(hiccup).....yesterday...at.... at....the park! He...he said...I'd changed.... that I....wasn't...as nice.... as he'd thought....I was....that I....I was.....acting like..... acting like.... YOU!" Ainsley pointed an accusing finger at her sister. "I've never.... been....so insulted...in my ....life!"

"Broke up with you?" Renatta said angrily. "What do you mean, he broke up with you? What was there to break up?"

"They were going together, Mom," Moira muttered shamefacedly.

"Going together!" Renatta echoed, aghast. "Ainsley Marie Collins, how dare you! You're only thirteen!"

"WHO IS JASON HICKS?!!!" Andrew demanded at the top of his voice.

"Only the cutest...sweetest...most popular...(hiccup)...boy...in my class," Ainsley told him, her sobs easing somewhat. "He told me he liked me the last week of school. Every girl in my class wanted to go out with him. Even some of the older girls wanted to. But he wanted to be with ME. And Moira ruined it for me!" The tears took over once again as she buried her face in her pillow.

"I...! I....!" Moira tried to come up with a scathing reply, but for once, she was at a loss. "I didn't mean....! Oh, hell!" She plopped down on the bed beside her sister, her shoulders slumped. "I'm sorry, Ainsley," Moira murmured, reaching out to tentatively pat the sobbing girl on the back. "I didn't think you'd listen to me. Nobody else does. I was just messing with you."

"Still....it was....it was....a lousy thing to say..." Ainsley raised her head slightly. "And now everything's....totally screwed up. Jason hates me!"

"Aw, c'mon kid. Nobody hates you. It's ME they hate! You said it yourself — the Hickster broke up with you because you were acting like me. If you'd been acting like yourself, he'd've been head over heels in love by now."

"But you said..." Ainsley twisted around to stare at Moira accusingly.

"Forget what I said, kid," Moira hastened to interrupt, shooting a surreptitious glance at her parents, still standing frozen in the doorway. "I was just jealous, I admit it. You had a boyfriend and I didn't."

"So you made sure it wouldn't last," Ainsley accused, her tone flat.

"Hell, I had no idea you'd actually believe me! That's not my fault! Besides," she added in an undertone, "some boys are like that. You know, the love 'em and leave 'em types. I figured, forewarned is forearmed. But you're the one who decided to turn all jealous and clingy. I never told you to do that." She paused, staring at her hands. "Look, I'll go to his house tomorrow and talk to him. Tell him it was all my fault, that I put you up to it, that you're nothing like me..."

"NO!" Ainsley gasped, her eyes round. "That would only make it worse! Besides," she added, resigned, "it's too late. He's started going with Adrianna already."

"Adrianna Dupre?" Moira scoffed. "Well, if he's stupid enough to settle for that cow when he could have had you, then he's not worth crying over anyway."

Ainsley sniffed and wiped her cheeks. "Yeah, I guess."

The front doorbell rang.

"Oh, God!" Moira exclaimed, jumping to her feet. "I'm not even dressed!"

"I'll get the door, Moira," Andrew offered. "Take your time. I'll keep him entertained." There was a wicked gleam in his eye and a mischievous smile on his lips as he turned for the stairs.

"Andrew...!" Moira warned, running after him. "Don't you dare...!" Her bedroom door slammed shut behind her. Andrew chuckled.

Renatta sat on the bed next to her youngest child.

"You okay, sweetie?"

"Yeah, sorta." Ainsley fiddled with the bedspread, not looking at her mother.

"You know, you are too young to date yet."

"I know, Mom. We weren't dating...exactly...just kinda hanging out together. Nothing formal. It's just...." Ainsley finally looked up, tears welling once again. "....I really liked him, Mom! I really did!"

"I know, sweetheart," Renatta reached out and took her daughter into her arms, patting her comfortingly on the back. "You'll just have to chock it up to experience. And you can learn a valuable lesson from it."

"What?" Ainsley sniffed.

"To trust your own judgement," Renatta told her, smiling gently. "Value the advice of others, of course, but make up your own mind.

Don't let someone else make it up for you. Especially if that someone is Moira," Renatta grinned, eliciting a small smile from Ainsley.

"You got that right, Mom!" Ainsley breathed a fervent sigh and hugged her mother tight.

* * * * *

"Nice trick, that," Andrew commented later that evening, as he and Renatta were relaxing in the living room.

"What's that, dear?"

"Summoning Moira's shirt from where Ainsley had hidden it. How did you know she had taken it?"

"I didn't," Renatta admitted. "Nor did I summon it. I thought maybe you had."

"Me?! No way! I was too busy staying out of the way." He grinned.

"But if you didn't summon it..." Renatta mused, "and I know I didn't....who did?"

"Ainsley?"

"Why would she have done that?" Renatta raised her eyebrows skeptically. "I greatly doubt she intended to confess unless she was caught red-handed."

"Then who...?"

The truth dawned on both of them at the same time.

"MOIRA?!" they both gasped the word, their eyes wide with shock. Andrew slowly shook his head.

"No way! There's no way! She'd never...!"

"Not deliberately, perhaps..." Renatta murmured. "But...."

"What?"

"Moira was very emotional right then — and you know it's harder to control our talents when our emotions are erratic — and she slammed her fist down on the sink counter just before the shirt came flying down the hall toward us, so maybe..."

"Well, I suppose stranger things have happened. By the way, who is this Jason Hicks?"

"Oh, just a boy in Ainsley's class."

"Did he hurt her?" Andrew's eyes glinted. "Because if he did, I'll.... I'll..."

"You'll what, Andrew?" Renatta asked with a small smile. "Beat up a thirteen-year-old boy? Besides, it wasn't so much that he hurt her. It was more that she hurt herself."

"Hmpf!" Andrew snorted.

"We can't protect Ainsley from everything. You know that," Renatta sighed. "She has to live her own life, make her own mistakes...just like the rest of us. All we can do is hope we've given her a good foundation, toss in a little advice now and then, and help her pick up the pieces if it all falls apart."

"I just hate seeing my little girl unhappy, is all," Andrew said.

"I know. Me too." Renatta leaned over and kissed him. "She'll be all right. She's a strong person."

* * * * *

"So...um....I thought we'd start out getting a bite to eat, then maybe we can catch a movie, or something." Brody smiled nervously. "That sound okay?"

"Sure!" his date replied as she hooked her seatbelt. She giggled, glancing at Brody from the corner of her eye. "You know, I was really surprised when you asked me out, Brody."

"Yeah?" Brody put the car in reverse and backed out of the Dalton's driveway. As they pulled away from the curb, he surreptitiously appraised the girl sitting next to him in the front seat. Jan was wearing a soft pink sundress sprinkled with tiny yellow flowers, jeweled flipflops on her slender feet. Her dark blond hair was pulled back into a tight French braid. Her bare arms and legs were lightly tanned, and her makeup was tasteful and subdued. Classy, he thought to himself, and definitely pretty! He began to wonder why he hadn't asked her out before. "Why were you surprised?"

"Because," she giggled again. "I've been friends with Braidy for ages, and you never showed any interest before now."

"Well," he shrugged, "you never showed any interest in me, either."

"Oh, I make it a policy never to make the first move," Jan stated. "If you do, the guy just ends up taking you for granted."

"I wouldn't!" Brody insisted, braking for a stoplight. "Not a pretty girl like you!" Jan giggled at the compliment. "Naw, I just figured you thought I was a dork — like most of Braidy's friends seem to."

"Well, you can be kinda geeky sometimes," Jan mused, oblivious to Brody's discomfort at her painful honesty, "and it's really a shame you have to wear those awful glasses....but I always thought you were nice...and funny...and....well....kinda cute."

Brody brightened visibly. "You think I'm cute?"

"Well...yeah..." Jan giggled. "I mean, now that your hair's gotten longer. I didn't like it much when you had it cut short. You looked about twelve."

"Then I'll be sure to keep it long," Brody declared, "just for you." He smiled over at her as the light changed. She giggled. Again.

There was an awkward pause for several blocks. Brody wanted to say something funny — or witty — or insightful — but nothing came to mind.

"So where are we going to eat?" Jan asked after several minutes of silence.

"There's a great new Indian restaurant that just opened up on Tonset Road, overlooking the cove. My family ate there last weekend." He paused, then asked, "Do you like Indian food?"

"I guess," Jan said absentmindedly. "I've never had it."

"Oh, it's fantastic!" Brody enthused. "Kinda hot, but you can ask the chef to tone it down, if you want."

"Well, I sure don't want it to burn my mouth," she said, "but I don't want to eat it cold, either."

Brody frowned, puzzled by her statement. Then realization dawned. He laughed. "Oh, yeah! Funny! No, I meant spicy hot, not temperature hot."

"Oh!" Jan giggled. Brody was beginning to think the giggling was a bit overdone. Then it was her turn to look perplexed. "I didn't know Indians used a lot of spices in their cooking."

"Oh, yeah! Loads! Curry, pepper, paprika..."

"But didn't they just eat a lot of corn and buffalo meat? Maybe some deer and fish? I didn't think they even had curry. Or paprika. Salt and pepper, maybe...Oh, and tomatoes! I read somewhere that they grew tomatoes!"

Once again, it took a moment for Brody to realize what Jan was talking about. Then it dawned on him — she was referring to Native Americans. He started to laugh at her joke, but stopped abruptly when he noticed the expression of innocent bewilderment on her face. She had no clue what he'd meant by "Indian".

"No, Jan," he said gently, "I meant East Indian. From the country of India." She still looked lost. "You know, in Asia? Near China? And Thailand?" No light bulbs appeared. He tried again. "Gandhi and Hindustani and Rudyard Kipling? Mother Theresa and telemarketers and..."

"Oh!" Jan's face brightened, then she wrinkled her nose. "My mom HATES telemarketers! They always call during dinner. And she says she can hardly understand them, 'cause they're all from other countries and have these really thick accents...But I don't understand — how can they get our phone number when they're from Africa, or China, or India....OH!" Jan blushed, giggling once again. "That's the Indians you were talking about! Sorry. Hey, there's a new Indian restaurant in town! Right on Tonset Road, by the cove. We ate there last week. It's called... The Hindi...I think." Her puzzled expression returned. "But that can't be right, can it? I mean, if it's an Indian restaurant, wouldn't it be called The Indi? Anyway, it was really good! Kinda spicy, but okay. I had something called biri...biri...biriyani. Yeah, that was it! There were these great big shrimp in it — I think they're called prans, or prowns, or something like that — and rice, and tomatoes, and onion. It was yumbo!" *Yumbo?! What the hell is yumbo?!* "Hey, we should eat there! You'd probably like it, since you know so much about India..."

As Jan continued to prattle on, her words punctuated by the all-too frequent giggle, Brody sighed. It was going to be a long evening.

* * * * *

"...Take me, break me!
Chew me up and spit me out!
Are we havin' fun yet?
I hate you, I prate you!
I wanna make you give me
Everything you've got!
Don't love me,
I ain't your type!
The government sucks,
The world sucks,

Everything sucks!
Why are we even here?
Why are we even frickin' here?
Yeeeeeaaaaaahhhh!
Yeeeeeaaaaaahhhh!"

The lead singer of Grannie's Complaint — in extremely tight black leather pants, his bare chest streaked with sweat — screamed the last few lines of the final encore of the night into his wireless mike, as the guitarist frantically pounded out the ending riff. Mouths open, heads thrown back, the entire band nearly went into convulsions as they reached the last chord. The drummer hit the bass and both toms simultaneously as hard as he could, right on cue. The stage went black. There was a split second of silence, then the auditorium filled with the roar of twenty-eight thousand teenagers — give or take a few hundred — voicing their approval.

Moira jumped up and down on her seat, clapping and screaming at the top of her lungs. Her eardrums were numb from the fifty thousand watts of sound that had been pounding against them for the past three hours, her throat was hoarse from all the screaming she'd done, her hands were swollen and sore from clapping — she was ecstatic. This was exactly how a concert should be!

Brad gave her a hand down off of the chair.

"What a slammin' show that was!" Moira enthused as they slowly made their way to the parking lot. "Thanks for bringing me, Brad. I owe you one!"

"Yeah!" he grinned down at her. "Hey, why don't you climb on my back? Don't wanna lose you in this crowd."

"Good idea!" Moira laughed as he crouched down and she clambered up onto his back. She wrapped her arms around his neck and Brad grabbed her legs, pulling them forward around his waist.

Standing up slowly, he settled her more comfortably, then barreled his way to the doors of the auditorium.

"This work?" Brad called to her over his shoulder.

"You bet! There's even a breeze up here!" Moira giggled, shocking herself. When had she ever giggled?! Was she — oh, horrors! — actually flirting? Suddenly, her palms felt sweaty and she became extremely aware of the rippling pectorals beneath his shirt. She decided it would be best to stay silent for a while.

"You sure are a tiny little thing," Brad commented as they made their way across the parking lot. "I doubt you weigh as much as my pads and gear."

"Thank you," Moira mumbled, trying desperately to keep her face turned away from his neck. She didn't want Brad getting any ideas, after all. This was just a friendly little outing — or was it?

"And you don't even stand as high as my shoulder. In fact," he laughed, "the only time tonight I could look you straight in the eye was when you were standing on that chair."

"Yeah...um...I'm sorta the runt of the family," Moira replied, clearing her throat. "My brother Devon's six foot, my mom's about 5'7"....even my little sister is as tall as me now. Just the way it goes. But, hey, at least I never have to duck when going through doorways."

Brad laughed again. "Good way to look at it. I hit my head all the time. Here we are."

Brad let go of Moira's legs and she slid down onto the ground next to his vintage Corvette. It was bright blue with a tan interior and in pristine condition.

"By the way," Moira asked as she climbed into the passenger side, "how'd you manage to afford such a sweet ride?"

"My old man bought it for me," Brad explained. "Bribe."

"Bribe?"

"Yeah. I walked in on him and his hot new secretary one day. He bought me the car so I'd keep my mouth shut. Mom found out anyway and kicked him out. He married the little chit before the ink was dry on the divorce papers. So I got a hot car and a hot stepmom."

"Walked in on....? Oh!" Moira blushed as she realized what he meant. "That must have been pretty embarrassing."

"I guess. For him anyway. I kinda enjoyed it myself."

"You did?"

"Yeah!" Brad laughed. "Like I said, she's HOT!"

Moira rolled her eyes. Typical! "Yeah, whatever!"

"Dad buys me lots of stuff these days," Brad continued. "Pretty much anything I want. Guilt offerings. It's his way of making up for spending so little time with me these days. He's the one who got me the tickets for tonight."

Moira began to feel distinctly uncomfortable. Absentee fathers were not exactly her favorite subject. She hadn't seen or heard from her own father, Stuart Fitzgerald, in more than four years. Quickly, she changed the subject.

"So, where are you going to college?"

The rest of the ride home was filled with Brad's recital of the trials and tribulations of college football scholarships. Moira let him ramble on, murmuring sympathetically from time to time. She actually caught only about one word in ten. Football was not high on her priority list. In no time, they were pulling up in front of Number Twelve Shore Drive.

"Listen, Brad, thanks a lo...*mmmm*!"

Brad had reached across the car with his long arms and dragged Moira toward him, silencing her with a hard, wet kiss. He was squeezing her so tightly, she could hardly breathe. The gearshift was digging into her stomach rather painfully. His large, soft lips completely covered

Moira's mouth, sucking on her lips in what he apparently believed to be a seductive motion. Moira found it more distracting than anything — once she recovered from her initial shock, that is. Her first impulse had been to push him away — or giggle — but then she thought, *what the hell?* Wriggling one arm free, she slipped it around his neck and gave herself up to the kiss.

Big mistake. Unduly encouraged by her response, Brad grabbed Moira's bottom with both hands, lifted her over the gear stick, and right onto his lap. Before Moira had any chance to react, he released the seat. She suddenly found herself lying on top of him, the driver's seat reclined flat beneath them, held in a death grip as Brad's extremely large hands roamed freely. She managed to wrench her mouth away from his.

"What the hell are you doing?!" Moira gasped.

"Shut up, girl," Brad muttered, grabbing her head and pulling it down toward his once again. It felt as if a leech had attached itself to her lips. Then he thrust his tongue between her teeth — and Moira hit the roof.

For a small girl, Moira had a lot of strength, and she made use of it. She frantically began kicking her legs, catching Brad with the hard toe of her hiking boots on his feet, shins, knees. Yelling in pain, he released her head. Moira sat up on his stomach and proceeded to slap and punch every part of his upper body she could reach.

"YOU STUPID, IGNORANT, EVIL, FRICKIN'....!" she yelled, punching him with each word.

"HEY! STOP! WHAT THE....!" Brad tried to cover his face with his arms, stunned by her attack.

"WHAT THE HELL KINDA CHIT DO YOU THINK I AM, DORK?! I OUGHTA...." With that, Moira slipped past his defenses and landed a right upper cut directly on his chin.

"OWWWWWW!!!!! ARE YOU CRAZY?! GET OFF ME!"

"GLADLY!" Reaching down, Moira found the door handle. The door sprang open and she tumbled out onto the ground, landing on her bottom with a thump.

"YOU JERK!" she screamed at him. "HOW DARE YOU?!"

"YOU'RE THE ONE WHO SAID YOU OWED ME!" Returning the seat to its usual upright position, and rubbing his chin, Brad revved up the engine.

"I WAS SPEAKING FIGURATIVELY, FREAK, NOT LITERALLY! NOBODY TREATS ME LIKE THAT!"

"Who would want to, you witch!" He threw her purse out the door, slammed it shut and spun away from the curb.

Moira jumped up, fists clenched, and kicked the mailbox post.

"YOU...YOU...YOU WALKING SPHINCTER MUSCLE!!!!" she shouted after him, punching one fist up into the air. With that, the engine of Brad's Corvette sputtered and died. The car rolled to a stop. He cranked the key angrily — with no success.

"HA!" Moira grinned triumphantly and marched up to the front door, where her mother, stepfather, and older brother stood waiting, mouths open in shock.

"Moira," Renatta said, "are you...are you okay?"

"Fine, Mom. Why?" Moira put on her trademark innocent act.

"We heard you yelling."

"Oh, that. It was nothing. A simple difference of opinion. I handled it."

Renatta and Andrew exchanged dubious glances. Brad's curses floated through the night air as he continued to fight with his uncooperative ignition.

"How...how was the concert?" Andrew asked hesitantly.

"Great! One of the best." Moira yawned. "I'm pretty tired. Think I'll go to bed. 'Night all!" And up the stairs she pranced.

Renatta and Andrew exchanged another glance. Andrew shrugged his shoulders, Renatta sighed and both parents wisely returned to the family room.

" 'Walking sphincter muscle'," Devon murmured, laughing softly. "Good one, Moira. Gotta remember that one."

* * * * *

June 26

Can you believe that jerk! He's got a lot of nerve! He may be used to treating those pathetic little cheerleader girlfriends of his like that, but not me! Nobody takes advantage of me!

He wasn't even that hot, anyway.

Oh, well. At least the concert was good. No, not good — GREAT! Man, my ears are still numb! Grannie's Complaint is, without a doubt, the BEST — the BITCHIN'EST — the COOLEST band ever! I don't even mind the drummer's long hair. I mean, you know I don't usually go for long, stringy hair, but Christopher Williams is soooo hot! Broad shoulders, great pecs, tight little...well, you know. LOL! And it's not like it's dirty or greasy — his hair, I mean, not his...you know.

Oh man, here I go again! Getting all worked up over some guy I'll never even meet — and who wouldn't even acknowledge my existence if I was standing two inches in front of his face! I'm frickin' invisible to guys like that! The ones worth having, that is.

I wonder if I made Brad's car engine die. Man, I hope so! Serves him right. Hope he had to hike it all the way home, the loser. What a creep!

You know, it's guys like him give the rest of 'em a bad name. I mean, I know guys have a much more active libido than girls — although I confess there's times when I have my doubts about that! Like when I'm watching a really hot love scene on one of my soap operas. They sure can make me wriggle! They really get into it! Makes you wonder just how realistic they have to get. I know, the actors always say that it's "just acting", but it sure looks pretty real to me!

What was I saying? Oh yeah — Brad gives other guys a bad name. Take Justin and Taylor, for example. They're okay, for guys. Taylor's had the hots for Leslie ever since Junior High, but he'd never do something like that. Hell, he can't even work up the nerve to ask her out, much less make a move on her. And Justin's cool that way, too. I wonder why some guys are so nice about girls and stuff, and other guys are such Neanderthals. Go figure.

Oh well. At least I've finally been kissed by a guy — okay, by a mental midget, but hey, beggars can't be choosers...

Moira yawned hugely...

Time for bed. Nighty-nite...

Chapter Five:

Four Men And A Truck

"Mom, what box are my books in?"

"Sweetheart, I can't find the checkbook."

"What happened to my good boots?"

"Mom...?"

"Renatta..."

"MOTHER...!"

Renatta locked herself in the bathroom. "I'm never moving again!" she muttered through clenched teeth.

* * * * *

"So, he actually had his hands on your..."

"Right on it!" Moira interrupted. "The stupid dork actually thought that I would give it to him on our first date." She handed Leslie several books. "Stick 'em in that box over there. By the window."

Moira's friends had come over to help with the last minute packing and loading up. The girls were taking the opportunity to rehash the events of Moira's disastrous date one more time.

"I love that you actually punched him!" Leslie crowed.

"Right on the chin!" Moira smiled triumphantly.

"I wonder why his car died like that?" Lucia mused as she emptied a dresser drawer full of t-shirts.

"Oh...um..." Moira ducked her head into the closet. "Who knows? Good timing?"

"I call it poetic justice," Leslie declared, sealing a box with packing tape. "There, that one's full!"

"You girls about done in here?" Andrew stuck his head through the doorway.

"Make sure Moira has all her stuff out of the bathroom, Andrew!" Renatta's voice floated up from downstairs.

"Have you got all your stuff..."

"Already done, dude," Moira grinned, patting a cosmetic bag lying on her bed.

"Good." Andrew headed toward Ainsley's room to check on her progress. "Your mom is leaving in fifteen minutes," he called back over his shoulder.

"Fifteen minutes!" Moira exclaimed. "Hell! We've gotta move it!"

The three girls became a whirlwind of activity as they emptied drawers, filled boxes, ran into each other several times in their haste to finish the job, and finally completed their task. Moira snapped shut the last suitcase just as the movers arrived at the bedroom door, dolly in tow.

"What goes from here, miss?" the older of the two asked.

"Everything, of course!" Moira told him, rolling her eyes.

"Out of the way, then," he instructed, waving his hands at the girls.

Moira grabbed her overnight bag. She and her friends headed downstairs as the movers began loading boxes onto the dolly. A few minutes later, they could hear the thump of the dolly wheels as the men made their way down the stairs and out the front door. Moira's heart sank a little with each thump.

In the rush to get everything packed in time, she'd managed to forget what all the activity was leading to. But suddenly, it hit her. No longer would she see her two best friends every day. No longer would Boston be a short twenty minute drive away. No longer would she be hanging out at the Commons or the Mall, comparing notes in class, sharing lunches and homework with the same kids she'd known since Kindergarten. Her breath caught in her throat as tears filled her eyes. Living on the beach didn't seemed like such a good trade-off, after all.

Silently, the three girls walked to the car. Moira tossed her bag into the back, then turned and looked up at the house she'd lived in since she was five years old. Lucia and Leslie, sensing Moira's mood, watched her in silence. Eventually, Moira shrugged her shoulders.

"Hell!" she muttered under her breath. "It's just a house. Four walls and a roof. What the hell do I care?" She convinced no one, herself least of all.

Renatta came out of the back door, followed by Ainsley, both of them carrying a suitcase and several tote bags each.

"Got everything, Moira?" her mother asked as she finished loading the trunk. Ainsley jumped into the back seat. Renatta gave Lucia and Leslie each a quick hug.

"Thanks for all the help, girls," she said. "We'll see you soon." She climbed behind the steering wheel and started the engine. "Let's go, Moira. We have to be at the new house before the phone company gets there, or our phone won't get turned on."

Moira turned to her friends.

"I'll call you tonight with the new number," Moira told them. The girls embraced each other, all three at once, in one tight group hug.

Moira sniffled a little as she pulled away. "You're coming down on the Fourth, right?"

"You bet!"

"Wouldn't miss it!"

Lucia and Leslie were sniffling themselves as they saw Moira into the front passenger seat.

"Goodbye Mrs. Collins! Goodbye Ainsley!"

"See you in a couple of days, girls."

Renatta backed out of the driveway and slowly pulled away. Moira turned in her seat for one last look, gazing earnestly at her friends until the car turned the corner.

Lucia and Leslie stood silent for a moment. Then Leslie sighed.

"I'm gonna miss that crazy chit."

"Yeah." Lucia's voice choked a little on her tears. Leslie put her arm around Lucia's shoulders and gave her a squeeze.

"C'mon, girl," she said. "Let's go home."

The two girls walked slowly down the sidewalk, arm in arm.

* * * * *

"Top o' th' mornin' to ye, Mrs. O'Malley," Dan greeted the housekeeper in a strong Irish accent.

"An' jist what devilry brings ye around sa early in th' day?" Mrs. O'Malley demanded, stepping back to let the young man inside the Baines penthouse.

"You've got to stop being so suspicious, Mrs. O'Malley," Dan grinned at her. "You always expect the worst."

"Tha's only because I ken ye sa well," the housekeeper said, grinning right back at him. "Russ is in his room." She headed back to the kitchen, leaving Dan to find his own way.

Dan glanced toward the living room and came to an abrupt halt. Callista was seated on the sofa looking through a fashion magazine, her long slender legs stretched out in front of her, one shapely arm draped across the back cushions. She glanced up.

"Mor...morning....Ca...Callista..." Dan stuttered.

"Good morning, Daniel," she replied in her soft, suggestive voice. A chill ran down Dan's spine at the sound.

"How...how are you?" Mentally, he was slapping himself silly for letting her get to him like that. What was it about Callista Baines that instantly turned him into a bumbling school boy?

"I'm fine," she replied, shifting her legs and patting the sofa cushion next to her. Dan stared at her in stunned silence for a moment, then hurriedly took her up on her offer, sitting as close as he dared. "So, what are you and Russell planning for the day?"

"We...um..." Dan cleared his throat and tried again. "We're going out on the Sea Mist." He sat hunched forward, his hands clasped tightly between his knees. This was the closest he'd ever been to the object of his affections. Her leg was only inches from his. His palms felt clammy.

"Lovely day for it," Callista commented, leaning closer to him. "I wish I could join you."

"Could...could you?" Dan asked, and nearly squeaked as her thigh brushed against his. "I'd love to have you. A-a-along, that is," he added hastily, his face growing hot.

"I'm afraid not," she sighed. "I'm spending the day at headquarters. We have two new interns I need to train."

"Need some help?" Dan asked eagerly. "I could come down, give you a hand."

Callista moved closer still, laying her hand on Dan's knee. He jumped. "I thought you were going sailing with Russell," she said, her voice low and seductive, her breath tickling his ear.

"Yeah...um...I...well..." Dan stammered. He worked up the nerve to look into her eyes. "I'm sure Russ wouldn't mind if I cancelled on him. Good cause, and all," he murmured, their lips almost touching. His heart pounding, Dan leaned ever so slightly forward, his eyes closed, his lips pursed for the anticipated — and long-awaited — first kiss.

His mouth met nothing but air. Callista moved back and stood up.

"I wouldn't want you to disappoint Russell like that," she said as she walked to the door. "I'm certain you boys will have a lovely time. Ta!"

Her tinkling laugh floated back to him, her emphasis on "boys" making her meaning all too clear. Dan slumped forward with a deep sigh, disgusted with himself for falling for her game.

"You're an idiot, Dan Brooks," he muttered to himself as he headed for Russ's bedroom. "A beautiful, sexy woman like that can have any guy she wants. Why would she waste her time on a loser like you?"

* * * * *

"Have you made contact yet?"

"No, sir, but I expect to in a couple of days."

"On the Fourth?"

"Yes. They're having a barbecue. I've been invited."

"Excellent! Large crowd, casual setting — perfect opportunity."

"My thoughts exactly, sir. Sir..."

"Yes?"

"Are you sure it's her?"

"Why do you ask?"

"It's just...I would hate to waste any more time on the wrong one. The fiasco last summer has put us drastically behind schedule."

"Don't worry. She's still young enough to be susceptible to suggestion. Her talents will not be fully formed for another year, yet."

"But are you sure, sir? Not that I question your judgement..."

"Of course not. I understand perfectly. And yes, I'm as certain as I can be — without actually seeing the Mark on her, that is. That will be the final confirmation."

"Behind the ear, right? Under the hairline?"

"Yes. It is your job to find the Mark and confirm her identity..."

"Yes, sir. I know that..."

"And then bring her to me. I'll take it from there."

"What will you do?"

There was a long pause.

"Persuade her."

The younger man laughed softly — and coldly. His mentor continued.

"You're certain that the Fitzgerald boy suspects nothing?"

"Not a thing. He has no idea that I'm a magical. The subject hasn't even come up. Although..."

"What?"

"Well...he said something rather odd the other day. It may mean nothing, but it caught my attention."

"What was it?"

"Something about feeling like an outsider his whole life, even within his own family — especially within his own family. And how it drives him crazy that his sister won't use the talent she was born with. Didn't you say Moira Fitzgerald refuses to use magic?"

"That's what Morty told me."

"It made me wonder — gave me the impression that Devon resents the fact that he's not a magical, like the rest of them. Might be something we could use."

"Could be...I'll file it away for future reference. Right now, all we need Devon Fitzgerald for is access to his lovely young cousin, the prim and proper Miss Attison. After you've established yourself with her, he's expendable, in my opinion."

"Right." The younger man stood up. "Is that all, sir?"

"For now. Let me know how it goes on Thursday."

"Yes, sir."

"Jonathan..."

"Yes, sir?"

"Don't disappoint me."

* * * * *

Russ and Dan tacked north from Boston Harbor. A brisk wind pushed them forward at a good clip, cooling the sweat they'd worked up while setting the mainsail and jib. The Sea Mist was a Dart-class catamaran, sailed single-handed without the jib, and intended as a two man craft with the jib in place. The two friends settled themselves on the trampoline of the catamaran, the mainsheet traveller firmly in Dan's hand, Russ positioned at the tiller, both looking forward to an exhilarating, but uneventful afternoon. The silence stretched companionably, broken by nothing but the sound of the waves washing over the bow of the Sea Mist and the call of a lone seagull overhead.

"Saw Callista this morning," Dan broke Russ's reverie, his voice raised to carry over the wind and the water.

"Yeah?"

"She was in the living room when I got to your house. I invited her to come along, but she said she had to go by your dad's campaign headquarters."

Russ picked up on the tension in Dan's voice, and sighed. Something told him Callista had been playing with the young black man — again. Russ loved his sister, of course, but he had no illusions about her attitude toward Dan — or toward men in general. Callista was not exactly warm-hearted. Russ wished Dan could see that. Not wishing to embarrass his friend, Russ refrained from comment.

"Yeah, she's been there a lot lately. I go by a couple of times a week, see if I can help out any, but mostly I just try to stay out of the way. Callista sets her mind on something, she's a force to be reckoned with."

"Yeah." Dan gazed out over the ocean. This time the silence between them was awkward, but Russ wasn't quite sure how to break it tactfully. Eventually, Dan did the job for him.

"So, you still worried about your dad running for public office?"

"Yeah, maybe." Russ ran a hand through his hair. "Hell, I don't know! I guess I'm not sure what to think. I mean, I know my dad's a good guy. I'm sure he'd do a good job, and all. It's just..."

"The magic thing," Dan finished for him.

"Yeah. Don't get me wrong — Dad would never deliberately abuse his powers, not for his own benefit, anyway. But what if..." Russ's voice trailed off.

"What if...?"

Russ sighed. "What if he thought he could do some good? By bending the rules, I mean. What if he does win the election, and something comes up where if he used magic, he could make things better for everyone? Loads better?"

"Would that be such a bad thing?" Dan queried.

"Yes!" Russ stated emphatically. "Okay, maybe not in that particular instance. But it would open up a whole can of worms, you know? He starts out by using magic to help people, but like any power, it can gradually become corrupted, without him even realizing it. Or," he continued quickly, before Dan could respond, "somebody with less scruples realizes Dad's powers and takes advantage of them. Tries to manipulate him somehow."

"Your dad is not easily manipulated, man," Dan pointed out.

"True. But it can happen, even with the best of intentions. I just don't like the possibilities. It's something magicals have always worried about. That's why we have a council — to keep an eye on things, make sure nobody's getting too big for his britches — like Nero did."

"Emperor Nero?! He was a magical?!" Dan exclaimed.

"Hell, yes! How else would a pimply little weasel like that have managed to take control of the Roman Empire — the biggest, most powerful empire the world has ever known — when he was only sixteen?"

"Yeah, but man, your dad is nothing like Nero was."

"I didn't say he was. The problem is, in some twisted way, Nero probably thought he was doing the right thing as well. He intended to increase Rome's power and prestige — instead, his reign, and the chaos after it, resulted in a major economic mess and a civil war."

"Yeah, well, nonmagicals make those kind of mistakes, too."

Russ smiled slightly. "I know that, dude. It's a common human failing. It' s just that magicals can cause a lot more damage."

"Good point." Dan frowned. "So what do you do?"

"Do?"

"About your dad."

"I don't know, Dan." Russ sighed again. "Support him, help him. And keep a close eye on things, I guess."

"And if he does abuse the power, what then?" Dan asked him. "What can you do about it?"

"Report him to the Council, I suppose." Russ sounded less than thrilled about the prospect.

"Could you really do that? Turn your own father in?" Dan stared at his friend.

"I don't know, man," Russ closed his eyes. "I just don't know."

* * * * *

The sun was setting as the movers hauled the last of the boxes into the Collins' new house at Number One Pochet Road that evening. Renatta tiredly directed them toward Andrew's office, then collapsed into the big armchair in the living room. It had been a long day. And they weren't finished yet. Luckily, Andrew had had the foresight to reserve a rental truck for the next day. It was amazing how many things hadn't fit into the moving van. And then there was the unpacking. She groaned at the thought.

Renatta listened vaguely as Andrew settled their account with the movers, not really paying much attention. She must have dozed off, because the next thing she knew, her sister was gently shaking her shoulder.

"Wake up, sis," Caroline said softly. "The Welcoming Committee has arrived."

The sisters embraced, then Renatta greeted her niece and nephew. Phil was in the front hall, talking with Andrew.

"Everything moved in?" Caroline asked. "Take that stuff to the kitchen, kids."

"We'll get it warmed up, okay?" Braidy suggested.

"What is it?" Renatta asked.

"Your supper," Caroline told her as the twins headed for the kitchen, casseroles in hand. "I knew the last thing you'd want to do tonight was cook, and after the long day you've all had, you deserve better than burgers or pizza. So Braidy and I whipped up a little something for you."

"Thank you!" Renatta gave Caroline another hug. "You're a life-saver!"

Caroline laughed. "Don't say that until you've tasted it."

"Oh, yeah, you're such a lousy cook," Renatta grinned at her. "I'd almost forgotten."

"Welcome to the neighborhood," Phil said as he entered the room. He bent over to give his sister-in-law a peck on the cheek.

"Thanks, Phil," Renatta kissed him back.

"So, what's for supper?" Andrew asked.

"It's a surprise," Caroline teased.

"Well, I'm hungry enough to eat a horse," Andrew stated. "Whatever you cooked up, it's bound to taste good to me."

"I'm not sure that's a compliment," Caroline said, one eyebrow cocked, "but I'll let it slide. This time."

They all laughed and headed for the kitchen.

"GIRLS!" Andrew shouted up the front stairs. "SUPPER'S ON!"

* * * * *

July 2

Phew! Home sweet home!

What a day! I never knew moving was such a pain in the tush. I mean, we even hired professional movers (one of whom was totally hot, by the way) and it was still a day from hell. I thought they were supposed to do all the work. What were we paying them for, anyway? But there were tons of little things that they wouldn't do, or couldn't do, or Mom didn't want them to do, or something else totally lame. Andrew and Dev figure it will take most of tomorrow for them to get the rest of the stuff here. And then we get to start unpacking — horrors!

I gotta say Andrew really came through for me. This room is slammin'! Way at the top of the house, the whole floor to myself, my own bathroom, those little — whatdayacallem? — dormer windows, that's it! With window seats, I might add. And best of all, the bitchin'est view of the ocean! Total privacy, plenty of room to hang with my friends (when I get some, that is!). It's so quiet up here, it feels like I'm all alone. I love it! Kinda like having my own place. With room service. LOL. Almost makes up for having to leave Lucia and Leslie. I can't wait for them to see it on Thursday.

Saying goodbye was a lot harder than I thought it would be. STOP! Don't go there, girl! You promised yourself — no more moaning! What's done is done. You just gotta move on from here. And it's not like you won't see them ever again. They're both gonna be here in two days. AND Taylor and Justin, too. It's like Mom said — we all drive now. We'll get together lots of times. And since we're all planning to go to Boston U, within a year we'll be living right on top of each other again. I wish Lucia could talk her dad into letting her live in the dorm, but at least Les and me will be able to room together. And in the meantime, with all this room up here, they can spend the night whenever we want.

PJ Party!!! Yeah!!!

I'm really gonna miss them, though. And starting at a new school...

NO, NO, NO!!!!!

I've decided to turn over a new leaf and only dwell on the positives from now on. Hey, ya know what? That hottie moving guy knows where I live. Maybe he'll come by sometime, see how I'm settling in. LOL! I wish!

He was really friendly, though. When he brought my desk up, he teased me about having my room way up here — called me Rapunzel. Yeah, like!

Hey, a girl can dream, can't she? No law against that...

"Moira!" Ainsley's voice floated up the stairs. "Supper's ready!"
"COMING!" Moira yelled down...

...Gotta go! Chow time! Man, I'm starving...!

* * * * *

"Did I tell you..." Caroline said as she dished out generous helpings of apple cobbler for dessert, "Desmond Baines has bought the old Griffin place?"

"The Griffin place..." Andrew frowned. "Where's that?"

"Just the other side of Beach Road," Phil told him, spooning up a big bite of cobbler. "Barely half a mile from here."

Moira hid her hands in her lap, willing them to stop shaking. What did it matter to her if Russell Baines would be living half a mile down the beach? What was he to her? A casual acquaintance, nothing more.

"Yeah, right!" she muttered under her breath, disgusted with herself. Why could just the thought of him still send her spinning? She gave herself a hard pinch and shoved a spoonful of cobbler into her mouth. It tasted like sawdust.

"I thought Mr. Baines had to live in Boston," Ainsley said, "if he wants to be mayor, doesn't he?"

"He'll still be living in Boston, sweetheart," her mother explained. "I'm sure this is just a vacation home for him — a place to get away to, now and then."

"Must be awful rich," Ainsley continued, "having two houses."

"He has more than two houses, punkin," Andrew smiled at her. "Not that it's any of our business. Caroline, this cobbler is delicious. You've outdone yourself."

"Actually, Braidy made the cobbler."

Moira forced herself to swallow it anyway. Brody grinned at her from across the table. She did her best to ignore him.

"What is Desmond's son's name?" Caroline suddenly asked. "The one that helped the kids last summer? Richard? Ronald?"

"Russell, Mother," Braidy told her, giving Moira a quick glance. Her cousin stared back at her, her face blank. Braidy shrugged.

"Russell! That's right! Nice young man. I wonder if we'll be seeing him around any."

"Desmond has a daughter, as well," Renatta commented. "Callista. She'd be in her early twenties by now. I haven't seen her in years."

"She was quite beautiful, as I recall," Andrew stated. "Exotic, even."

"Yeah?" Brody's attention was fully engaged. "What'd she look like?"

"Long white-blond hair," Andrew ticked off the lovely Miss Baines's attributes for his nephew, "slender, tall. Looked like one of those

European supermodels. Exquisite face — porcelain skin, perfect teeth, high cheekbones. And the most unusual eyes! Long thick eyelashes, perfectly arched brows...”

“What color were they?” Brody asked breathlessly, his eyes shiny with anticipated lust.

“Violet.”

“No way!”

“Yep!” his uncle assured him, grinning.

“I’ve never seen a girl with violet eyes! She must be...has to be...” Brody sighed, rendered speechless by the thought.

“I had no idea Callista Baines made such a lasting impression on you, my dear,” Renatta said blandly, giving her husband a warning look.

“Oh...um...I...uh...” Andrew stammered, exchanging a knowing glance with his brother-in-law, who was hiding a smile behind his hand, “I have a good memory for faces, sweetie. You know that.”

“Nice out!” Phil murmured, grinning down at his dessert plate.

“Good thing Devon won’t be here tonight,” Moira commented casually, gazing innocently at Andrew. “At least you’ll have a bed to sleep in.”

Everyone burst out laughing.

“Okay, I give!” Andrew held up his hands in surrender. “I’m sorry, love. But you’ve gotta admit, the girl is absolutely gorgeous.”

“Yeah, buddy!” Brody crowed.

“She’s too old for you, young man!” his aunt admonished him. “And as for you...” she wagged a finger at her husband. “Oh, hell. You’re right. She is gorgeous! Just don’t get carried away, you hear me?”

Andrew laughed, draping his arm around Renatta’s shoulder. Leaning closer, he kissed her hard. “Don’t worry, punkin, she’s hardly my type.”

"And don't you get any ideas either, mister!" Caroline glared at Phil.

"Who? Me?" Phil tried to look innocent, and failed miserably.

"Chances are the kids won't be around much anyway," Renatta commented. "As I said, Callista has to be at least twenty by now. All grown up and out on her own. And isn't Russ in college now?"

"He started last year," Moira mumbled, her head lowered.

"What was that, Moira?"

"He was a freshman this past year. At the Massachusetts College of Art. He's going to be an artist," she said in a loud defiant tone, as if daring anyone to question her information.

The others stared at her for a moment in surprise, then wisely let it go.

"Well!" Phil finally broke the silence. "I think we'd better get out of here and head home. Let you folks get some rest."

As the others said goodbye, Moira slipped upstairs...

WHAT ARE THE FRICKIN' ODDS?????!!!!!!!!!

Chapter Six:

Hotdogs And Sparklers

The early morning sun peeked through the curtains and splashed a streak of light across the wooden floorboards, onto the bed, and right into Moira's eyes. She muttered in her sleep and turned over, pulling the sheet up over her tousled head. But it was no good. She was awake, whether she wanted to be or not.

Reluctantly, Moira opened one eye and gazed blearily at her alarm clock.

"Seven-fifteen!" she groaned, rolling onto her back. "Nuts!" She stretched, her spine cracking as she twisted the kinks out of it. "I've got to get some blinds on these windows! And soon!"

Sitting up, she tucked her feet into a pair of fuzzy pink slippers and padded her way to the bathroom. Maybe a shower would help.

Twenty minutes later, Moira stared at her face in the mirror, her hair still damp, a thick towel wrapped around her. She attacked a large zit on her forehead, then got rid of a few blackheads that had made an appearance on her nose. She doused both areas liberally with astringent lotion, wincing slightly at the sting. She stared at herself again.

"Why of course, Mr. Hottie Moving Guy!" she mouthed, batting her eyelashes. "I'd be delighted to go to dinner and a movie with you!" She laughed at herself. "Yeah, right!" Her expression shifted, her eyes narrowing slightly. "Russ? Russell Baines? The name rings a bell... Oh yes, I remember you now! You're that *boy* I spoke with at the bank Christmas party — was it last year, or the year before?" She laughed again, trying to sound mature and sexy. "I'm afraid I've lost track. You know how it is. So many men, so little time." Moira stuck her tongue out at her reflection, then turned her back and went into the bedroom to get dressed.

After pulling on her shorts and t-shirt, Moira looked around for her flip-flops. Spotting them across the room, she took a step, then stopped.

"I shouldn't...I could...But I swore...Ah, c'mon! What harm would it do?...Don't go there, girl...Just this once. Just for fun...You're gonna regret this, and you know it...It's just a pair of flip-flops...Yeah, that's how it starts — first shoes, then a book, then before you know it, you're turning on the TV without using the remote, and they've sucked you right in...Oh, shut up!"

Scowling, Moira snapped her fingers. The flip-flops skittered across the floor, stopping right in front of her bare feet. She smiled to herself.

"Nice to know I've still got it," she said. With that, one of the shoes flipped up into the air and landed on the bed, upside down. "Well, sort of," she mumbled, her smile going rather crooked. She slipped her toes into the shoe still on the floor and reached for the other one. It rolled into the middle of the bed. Moira's eyes grew wide.

"No way!" she breathed. Slowly, she knelt on the bed and leaned over, her hand outstretched. The flip-flop slid across the covers and perched on the very edge of the bed, balanced precariously. "This is psycho!" She dove for the shoe. It jumped off of the bed back onto the floor and zigzagged over to the wall. Moira lay still for a moment, breathing hard. "Okay, I'm officially freaked out now," she whispered. "What the hell have I done?"

Carefully, Moira climbed off of the bed and crouched low, holding her hand out to the recalcitrant flip-flop. "Come here, shoey, shoey, shoey." She stopped and shook her head in disbelief. "If the gang could see me right now, they'd think I was mental. And they'd be right!" Standing up, she walked to the wall, determination in every step. The flip-flop skated across the floorboards to the other side of the room.

"Now you're making me mad!" Moira growled as she ran after her shoe. Throwing herself headlong, she grabbed the flip-flop with both hands. It wriggled back and forth, fighting her, finally slipping through her fingers and flying under the bed.

"That does it!" Moira shouted, slamming her hands on the floor. She dove for the bottom of the bed, only to have the flip-flop shoot out from under it and hit her right in the nose. "OUCH!" The shoe dropped to the floor in front of her, apparently subdued at last. "Ha, ha! Very funny!" she grumbled as she jammed it onto her foot and stood up.

"You okay up here?" Renatta asked as she climbed the stairs from the second floor, still in her bathrobe. "I heard shouting."

"Just peachy!" Moira grumbled, rubbing her nose. Renatta gave her an odd look.

"You're up early," she said.

"Yeah, the sun woke me up," Moira told her. "Mom, can I get some blinds on these windows? The sun comes right in and wakes me up every morning."

"I don't see why not. We'll go to Home Decor tomorrow and pick some up. You'll need to measure the openings so we know what size to get. But first, breakfast. I'll have it ready in ten minutes." She headed back downstairs. "And don't forget, we're expected at your aunt's by two o'clock."

"Great!" Moira grumbled. "Another day with the Bobsey twins. Something else to look forward to." She grimaced at her flip-flop, then followed her mother downstairs.

* * * * *

The beach was packed with people; families with children running in every direction, young couples holding hands, girls in skimpy bikinis sunbathing on the hot sand while their male counterpoints stared appreciatively. Most of them were obviously tourists. The locals knew from long experience to avoid the beach on national holidays. But Phil and Caroline's annual Fourth of July barbecue had become a family institution. Dealing with the crowd was a part of the fun.

Moira didn't necessarily agree.

She did, however, look forward to the hotdogs and burgers Phil would be grilling in mass quantities later in the day. Uncle Phil definitely had a special touch when it came to cooking outdoors. And nobody could match Grandma Meredith's potato salad.

"Oh, well," she sighed to herself, as yet another beach ball sailed through the air to land in her lap. "At least the chow will be good." She handed the ball to the grubby little boy who came to claim it.

"Thanks, lady!" he shouted as he ran back to his friends.

Moira chuckled to herself. No one had ever called her "lady" before.

"Yeah, well, I guess to a six-year-old, I'm ancient!" she thought, grinning.

"Moira!" Renatta's voice floated down from the deck.

Twisting around, Moira shaded her eyes and looked toward the house. An instant later, she jumped to her feet and ran toward the group heading her way. Laughing, nearly crying, she flung herself into Lucia's arms. The two girls did a short happy dance on the sand. Then it was Leslie's turn, while Justin and Taylor looked on, grinning from ear to ear. Moira turned toward the two boys, giving them a joint hug, tightly wrapping an arm around each of their necks. They hugged her back, Taylor's cheeks turning slightly red.

"Guess that means you're happy to see us," Justin said, stepping back. He grinned at his friend, obviously glad to see her as well.

"Yeah, well, I was just worried we'd end up with loads of leftovers," Moira grinned back, giving Justin a light punch on the arm. "Mom and Aunt Caroline have enough food to feed an army!"

"Great!" both boys exclaimed.

"Where is it?" Justin asked, looking around for any evidence of the promised feast.

"There's snacks and stuff up on the deck," Moira told them, pointing toward the house. "The barbecue won't be until later. Uncle Phil hasn't even started cooking yet."

Taylor groaned. "I'm starving!"

"So what else is new?" Leslie teased him, her eyes warm. Taylor blushed again and directed his gaze out toward the ocean, studiously avoiding his friends' smiles. Moira and Lucia exchanged a knowing glance.

"C'mon," Moira said, tugging on Leslie's arm. "I'll introduce you." She steered them up to the deck of the Bed and Breakfast. "Aunt Caroline, Grandma....these are my friends — Lucia, Leslie, Justin, Taylor."

The teens murmured their hello's as the adults smiled in welcome.

"Thanks for letting us come to the party, Mrs. Attison," Leslie said.

"No problem," Caroline replied. "The more, the merrier! You hungry? Help yourselves!" she gestured to a folding table laden with chips, cheese, crackers, fresh fruit and vegetables, and several types of homemade cookies. "We have plenty."

"You haven't seen how much these two can eat, Caroline!" Renatta laughed, pointing at Justin and Taylor. "You may revise your opinion after seeing them in action."

"I represent that remark, Mrs. Collins!" Justin protested as he grabbed a handful of chips. Just then, Brody came out from the house.

"Hello!" he said brightly. His eyes lighted on Lucia and he stopped dead in his tracks. "Whoa!" he breathed.

Moira rolled her eyes. "This is my dorky cousin, Brody." Brody tore his gaze from Lucia's face long enough to glare at Moira. "Justin, Taylor, Leslie, Lucia..." she pointed to each in turn. Brody reached his hand out to Lucia.

"Moira's told me so much about you," he smiled, his bright blue eyes gleaming. Lucia blushed, smiling back. She placed her hand in his.

"Hello," she said softly. Brody continued to stare at the lovely girl, apparently enthralled. His mother and grandmother exchanged glances.

"Here we go again!" Caroline murmured, grinning.

"You've told him so much about her!" Justin complained in Moira's ear. "What are we... dung pellets?"

"Pulleez!" Moira shook her head, reaching over to pull Lucia's hand away from Brody's. "He's just being a dork! As usual! Just ignore him. I always do." She laughed at the scowl on Brody's face as she led the way back onto the sand. "So what's been going on since I left?"

"It's only been two days, Moir," Leslie pointed out.

"You know nothing much ever happens in Quincy," Taylor added.

"Not like here," Lucia murmured, glancing back toward the house. Brody stood on the deck, leaning against the railing, his eyes glued to her. She blushed again, ducking her head shyly and looking away. Moira stared at her best friend, shocked.

"You're joking, right?" she said. "Brody?! What have you been smoking, girl?!"

"He's cute, Moira!" Lucia said softly.

"He's a dork!"

"A little, maybe. But a cute dork!" Lucia insisted. The others laughed. "I thought you said he wore glasses and had really bad zits."

"He got contacts about a week ago," Moira told her. "And my aunt has been taking him to a dermatologist. It's really helping clear up his face." Moira took Lucia by the hand. "But, Luce... Brody? You can do better than him!"

"What's so bad about Brody?" Leslie asked.

"Yeah. Theemed nife enough 'oo me," Justin commented around a mouthful of cookie.

"And Luce is right...he is kinda cute," Leslie added appraisingly.

Taylor's face darkened. "He's not *that* cute!" he muttered, his eyes on his shoes.

Moira stared at her friends in surprise. "He's....he's just....he's Brody, that's all! He's my cousin!"

"So?"

"Hell, I don't know! All right, it's your funeral. Just don't say I didn't warn you!"

Lucia grinned at her flustered friend. "I'm not planning to marry him, silly!"

"God, I hope not!"

* * * * *

"Nice place you got here, Mr. Baines."

"Thank you, Dan!" Desmond shook hands with his son's friend. "I love living in the city, but I find it necessary to return to Nature from time to time. It is pleasant to have a quiet retreat nearby."

The next-door neighbors chose that moment to turn their stereo up full blast. Desmond grinned sheepishly as Dan and Russ laughed.

"Well, in theory, anyway."

"Couldn't have a better location," Dan commented, gazing out of the picture window in the living room. "Right on the beach."

"That's the main reason I bought it," Desmond said. "The sound of the ocean is so soothing, especially at night. Russ, have you shown Dan your room?"

"Yes, sir," Russ replied. "I gave him the full tour. We were just about to head outside, do a little beach combing."

"Excellent idea. It's such a beautiful day. Perhaps I'll join you, if that would be all right?" Desmond smiled. "Just let me change my shoes."

"Sure, Dad," Russ said. "We'll wait on the deck."

The two young men wandered outside. Dan threw himself into a deck chair while Russ perched on the railing, staring out at the ocean.

"Sweet digs, man," Dan commented after several moments of companionable silence.

"You said it," Russ agreed. "Wish we could live here full time."

Desmond stepped out from the house. "Ready?"

"Sure thing."

They walked down the steps of the deck and wandered across the beach aimlessly, casually observing the mass of people inhabiting the sand. A group of twenty-somethings were engrossed in a heated game of beach volleyball; a little girl was crying as her mother reprimanded her older brother, a ruined sand castle mute testament to the cause of the tears; a teenage couple were making out on a beach towel, totally oblivious to the world around them.

"Ah, young love," Desmond remarked wryly.

"Get a room, pal!" Dan muttered under his breath, tearing his eyes away from the osculating pair. "How's the campaign going, Mr. Baines?"

"Busy," Desmond said, leaning down to pick up a seashell. "I've been making the rounds of the various civic organizations — trying to get my name out there."

"I would have thought most people in Boston already knew who you were," Dan said.

"In the business community, yes, Dan," Desmond told him. "But the average resident has never heard of me. Winning an election is twenty-five percent luck, twenty-five percent ability and fifty percent name recognition. I've always been fairly lucky, I like to think I have some ability..." he grinned at the two boys.

"A little, perhaps" Russ teased his father.

"...but unless people know who I am," Desmond continued, clapping his son on the back, "I won't stand a chance. Running for office is a job in itself. I'm very fortunate to have Russ and Callista to assist me."

"Will...um..." Dan cleared his throat, trying to sound nonchalant, "will Callista be joining us today?"

"No. She flew down to the island for the week. At my insistence," Desmond added. "She's been working so hard, I felt she needed a good rest."

"Of course." Russ thought Dan managed to hide his disappointment well.

They walked on in silence for some time, eventually coming to Pochet Road.

"An employee of mine recently built a house somewhere along here," Desmond commented upon noticing the street sign.

"Who's that, Dad?" Russ asked.

"Renatta Collins. She's heading the new branch for me. You remember her, Russ. Her daughter was one of those youngsters you two helped rescue last summer."

Dan looked puzzled.

"Moira," Russ whispered to him. Dan's face cleared.

"The turquoise porcupine?" he whispered back, grinning. Russ scowled.

"Wouldn't mind stopping in to say hello," Desmond said. "Do you mind, boys?"

"Um...well..." Russ stammered.

"No problem, Mr. Baines," Dan answered for him. "Lead on!"

"Thanks a lot!" Russ muttered as his father moved ahead of them momentarily.

"You gotta face the girl sometime," Dan pointed out. "Might as well get it over with. Besides, there's safety in numbers," he added with a grin, waving in the direction of the crowd milling around them.

"Something tells me that won't make any difference at all!" Russ groaned. Dan's grin broadened.

"What's the matter, dude? Afraid of a little bitty thing like her?"

"You bet I am! She may be small, but she's mighty!"

Dan burst out laughing as they followed Desmond to the new Collins residence.

* * * * *

"So there I was," Jonathan Crenshaw told his audience, "at the very top of the tower, nothing below me but a whole lot of empty space, clinging to the scaffolding like a scared cat, afraid to move so much as an inch..."

"You must have been terrified!" Ainsley gasped.

"Well, I wasn't exactly jumping for joy," Jonathan grinned at her.

"What happened?" Brody asked.

"One of my friends ran for help. It seemed to take hours, but it was probably only minutes later that the fire department got there. They raised their ladder and brought me down, safe and sound. Until, that is, my mom got hold of me!" He laughed. "Man, did she give it to me good! After a big hug, of course...I couldn't sit for a week!"

The others joined in his laughter.

"Did you learn your lesson?" Caroline asked with a twinkle in her eye.

"Of course not!" Jonathan said, grinning. "How many eight-year-old boys do you know that ever learn from experience! Besides, I was suddenly the coolest kid in the neighborhood. Not only had I climbed the outside of the old electrical tower, but I'd gotten to ride on the fire truck ladder! My friends were so jealous!"

The men laughed even harder, while the women just shook their heads. Braidy gazed out over the ocean, pretending a nonchalance she was far from feeling. Something about Jonathan Crenshaw was definitely getting to her. It wasn't simple attraction, although that was certainly a big part of her emotional turmoil. No, it was more than that. Much more. He made her uncomfortable, but she couldn't say how. Or why.

Jonathan Crenshaw had been the perfect guest since he'd arrived with Devon earlier in the day. Pleasant, polite, accommodating. He was obviously intelligent, quite articulate, and very entertaining. His stories had kept them enthralled for most of the afternoon. Everyone else seemed to enjoy his company immensely. Even Moira was being pleasant to him. So why were there knots in Braidy's stomach? And why was it so difficult to meet his gaze? He made her feel awkward and gawky, like a love-struck adolescent. But he also made her nervous. Anxious, almost. She'd never reacted to any guy this way before. What was wrong with her? She shook her head as if to clear it and turned back toward Jonathan, determined not to let her discomfort show. He was paying no attention to her. That only made matters worse.

"I'll get those, Mr. Attison," Jonathan said as he jumped up and took a large platter of hamburgers and hotdogs from Phil, who was just finishing up at the grill. "Mmmmm! Those smell good enough to eat!"

"I certainly hope so, Jonathan," Braidy's father grinned at the young man, "or this crowd may just grill me!" Both men laughed companionably as Jonathan placed the meat on the large folding table he and Devon had set up on the sand. "CHOW TIME!" Phil yelled, waving his hands at the various family members and friends scattered across the beach and the deck. A dozen people came running from all directions. Meredith walked out of the house carrying a huge plastic bowl.

"Here's the potato salad," she said.

"I'll take that, Grandma," Braidy said, reaching for the bowl. As she set it on the table, her shoulder brushed against Jonathan's arm. A shiver ran through her.

"Excuse me," she murmured, pulling away quickly.

"No harm done," he said, not even looking at her. Sudden anger flared up inside of Braidy. She was not accustomed to being ignored by the opposite sex. Turning her back, she flounced down to the end of the table, determined to give Mr. Crenshaw a wide berth.

"You okay?" Brody asked as he sat down next to his twin.

"Just peachy!" Braidy replied, her scowl belying her words. Brody opened his mouth to continue questioning her when Lucia wandered across his field of vision. All other thoughts immediately flew from his mind.

No one had time to do more than take a bite or two when Renatta suddenly stood up.

"Desmond!" she cried, a big smile lighting up her face. Andrew joined her in greeting their friend. Moira glanced up, spotted Russ standing next to his father, and did her best to make herself as small as possible.

"You remember my son, Russ? And his friend, Dan Brooks?"

"Join us, won't you?" Caroline said. "Brody, get some more chairs..."

"Not necessary," Desmond insisted. "We have some steaks marinating back at the house. I just wanted to stop by and welcome you to the neighborhood, Renatta."

"You too!" she replied, laughing. "I think you beat us by only a day or two!" The adults continued to exchange chitchat as Russ and Dan gravitated toward the younger crowd.

"Hey, man," Brody shook hands with Dan. "Good to see ya. Russ..."

"Hi. Braidy, Moira. How are you?"

"Fine," said Braidy. Moira mumbled something that resembled a response, her eyes glued to her plate, her cheeks blazing red. Dan and Russ exchanged a look.

"So, what's up?" Dan asked, sitting down next to Braidy. As he engaged the others in small talk, Russ moved closer to Moira. She jumped up.

"Where you going?" Justin asked her, surprised.

"I...um...I need a drink," she said as she turned toward the house.

"Mind if I join you?" Russ asked. "I could use something cold." Not waiting for Moira's reply, he walked to the deck steps. Moira hesitated a moment, then shrugged her shoulders and followed him.

"Get me another Coke, will ya?" Justin called out.

Russ leaned down and opened the cooler, holding the lid for Moira as she fished out two soda cans.

"What do you want?"

Russ jumped slightly, a bit taken aback by her forthrightness.

"I...um...well....I just...I thought maybe we could talk...."

Moira stared up at him for a moment, then a slow smile crept across her face. "I meant, what do you want to drink?"

Russ turned bright red, then broke into a grin of his own. Moira's breath caught in her chest as his face was transformed by his amazing smile. Laughing a little at himself, he scratched his neck.

"Coke is fine," he said. Moira reached for another can, then straightened, handing it to him. Russ let the lid of the cooler drop back into place. "Moira..." he hesitated.

"Yeah?" Moira looked up at him, one eyebrow raised.

Russ cleared his throat. "I did want to talk to you."

"What...what about?" Moira fiddled with the can tab, her own cheeks turning pink again.

"Did I....did I...do something...or not do something...or say something....?" he paused, not even sure what he was trying to ask her.

"What do you mean?" She continued to avoid his eyes by gazing out over the ocean.

"It's just....well...last summer...when we first met..." Russ stammered, "I thought we kinda hit it off..."

"You did?" Moira's gaze snapped back to him, her eyes wide.

"Yeah, sort of. And I really enjoyed talking to you on the phone that night..."

"Then why didn't you call me again?" Moira demanded. She squeezed the two soda cans tight, her pulse racing.

"I...I meant to..." Russ said, light beginning to dawn, "but somehow I never got around to it. And then school started...College is way harder than I'd anticipated. I barely had time to sleep or eat, much less anything else. You...you wanted me to call you?"

"Well, yeah!" Moira stated, giving him her best 'D'uh!' glare. "I enjoyed talking to you, too! I thought, maybe, we could be...you know...friends...or something..." she ended lamely, desperately wishing she could use the cold cans to take some of the heat from her face. The expression in Russ's deep blue eyes wasn't helping matters any. If he looked at her like that much longer, Moira was convinced she'd just melt right there.

"Me, too!" Russ said softly. "But the way you acted at the Christmas party, I figured you didn't want anything to do with me. I was going to invite you to go to Dan's house with me on New Year's Eve, but I thought you'd just turn me down."

"Oh!" Moira whispered, staring down at her feet. Mentally kicking herself for her stupidity, she tried to think of something witty to say, to make up for her childish behavior at the party, but no ideas came. After a long, awkward pause, Russ continued.

"Anyway, I really did intend to keep in touch, Moira. I hope you can forgive me for not doing a better job of it."

"Yeah, sure," she mumbled.

"So..." Russ said after another long pause, "are we friends now?"

"Sure, I guess," Moira said softly. "Yeah, we're friends."

"Good!"

"If you bother to call me, that is!" she grinned, her usual feistiness reasserting itself.

"It's a deal!" Russ held out his hand. Moira juggled the two soda cans awkwardly, finally tucking one under her arm in order to shake his hand. They both laughed, pleased with each other and themselves.

"Hey!" Justin yelled. "Where's my drink?"

"I'm coming! I'm coming!" Moira yelled back. "What d'ya think I am, dude? Your slave, or something?"

Moira and Russ returned to the table. She quickly introduced him to her friends.

"And this is my brother, Devon, and his friend, Jonathan Crenshaw."

Russ shook hands all around. He turned back to Jonathan.

"Have we met before?" he asked.

Jonathan shook his head slowly. "No, I don't think so."

Russ shrugged his shoulders. "Just my imagination, I guess. So what are you going into?"

"Journalism," Jonathan told him. "Television, I hope."

"Cool!"

"Devon's going to be a photo journalist," Moira said proudly. "He's really good. He's been working at the Boston Globe the past two summers."

"Just as an intern, sis," Devon said, smiling at her praise. "Moira told us you're an artist?"

Russ shot a quick glance at Moira. She was blushing again. So she was interested! "Yeah, watercolor, mostly. But I like sculpture, as well."

"I don't think I'd have the patience," Jonathan commented. "I need to see immediate results. That's why I like television. You tape it, you watch it, it's...."

"And who is this?" Desmond interrupted, walking up and offering his hand to Jonathan.

"Jonathan Crenshaw, future anchorman," Jonathan grinned.

Desmond laughed as they shook hands. "That's what I like to see, a young man — or woman — who knows exactly what he wants. Pleasure to meet you, Jonathan. Desmond Baines."

"Yes, I know, sir. Saw you on the news a few weeks ago. How's the campaign coming along?"

"Not bad, not bad. We can always use more help, though."

"Maybe I'll stop by...lend a hand..."

Moira was surprised by the expression on Russ's face as his father and Jonathan continued to discuss the ins and outs of the political process. She caught his eye, her eyebrows raised. He shrugged his shoulders and gave her a sheepish grin.

"Well, fellas," Desmond said, cutting the conversation short, "we'd better head back, get those steaks on the grill. All this delicious food is making my stomach growl!" he laughed.

"Are you sure you won't stay?" Matthew asked.

"I made apple pie..." Priscilla tempted them. Dan groaned.

"Thank you, Priscilla, but no. Let's get moving, boys."

"You're welcome to join us for the fireworks later," Phil said as Dan reluctantly stood up.

"We might do that. Thank you!" Desmond waved to them all as he headed down the beach.

"Save us some of that apple pie, will ya?" Russ whispered to Moira. She grinned in reply.

"I'll do my best."

"See ya!"

"Bye!"

Russ turned to wave one last time. Moira, one hand on her hips, the other at the side of her face miming a telephone handset, mouthed the words, "Call me!" Russ smiled and winked as he followed his father across the sand.

* * * * *

July 4

WOW! What a slammin' Fourth this was!

It was so great to see the gang again. I know, it's only been a few days, but it seemed like forever! I guess distance does have something to do with it. Knowing that I couldn't just run down the street to see Lucia like I always have made it feel like I hadn't been with her in ages!

What's with her and Brody, though! Yuch! And why was that other chick — Jan, the space cadet — so weepy all through the fireworks? She kept looking over at Brody like he was her long lost love or something! LOL Could it be my dorky cousin is turning into some sort of Casanova or something? Now, that would be freaky!

That Jonathan guy seems nice enough. A little bit full of himself, but not too bad. And he is pretty cute and kinda funny. Devon thinks he's the greatest. Not my type, though. I've always preferred guys with really dark hair. His is a little too light for my tastes. He'll make a great TV anchorman, though. He's got the looks, the personality, the ego. A bit short, but camera angles can probably fix that. And he sure knows how to tell a story. Weird to think I'll probably see him on the *Nightly News* some day. Hey, then I can finally claim to know somebody famous! Cool!

The fireworks were incredible. Andrew and Uncle Phil really outdid themselves this year. If I didn't know better, I'd say Andrew threw in a little magic to wrench things up a bit. I wonder why everybody always says, "ooh" and "aah" when watching fireworks? Is there some unwritten contract that says we have to? LOL

All right! All right! Yes, I know — I'm avoiding the subject. But the last time I wrote about him, I didn't hear from him in months! I don't want to jinx it again! Maybe if I don't mention his name — just his eyes, his smile, his hair, his muscles.... *shiver* Way better than any fireworks!

I can't believe he felt bad about letting me down! What a gentleman. I mean, really, there was no reason for him to call me again. It was just my overactive imagination that got me going. And it was pretty immature of me to act the way I did at the Christmas party last year. And pretty stupid, too! Just think - we might have had all this time to get to know each other if I hadn't been such a dork! Argh! What an idiot I am sometimes! Oh well, I'll just have to make up for lost time.

Wait a minute. What if all he wants is to be friends? Just

friends? Oh man! That would be such a bummer! I bet he does — he didn't ask me out, did he? He just said he'd call. I mean, he didn't even hold my hand or anything during the fireworks, and he was sitting right next to me the whole time. Crap! There goes my overactive imagination again! I've practically got us married already and he's just thinking of a nice conversation!

Why do I do this to myself?! When am I gonna learn? Guys don't think the way girls do. We're always plotting and planning — and they can't think any farther than the next meal! LOL Okay, maybe they're a little better than that — but not much! Not when it comes to relationships, anyway.

Okay, girl — slow, deep breaths. Be realistic about this. Take it one day at a time. Get to know the guy, let the friendship develop first. Then, who knows? Other things might develop too. You never know. Don't expect too much, but keep your options open. Yeah, that sounds like an excellent policy! Very good, Moira! I'm proud of you!

I bet Russ is a way better kisser than that stupid Brad was. Man, he was soooo bad at it! Not like I got anything to compare it to — hey, what if that's how it's supposed to feel? Eeuww! Wet and sloppy? Naw, it's gotta be better than that! When they do it in the movies it doesn't look all nasty. And Mom sure seems to like it when Andrew kisses her — and she's a complete neat freak. She wouldn't like it sloppy, would she?

I have simply got to get more experience, that's all there is to it.

The question is — how? I start walking up to guys and laying one on them, people will think I'm crazy — like they don't already. It is a thought, though....

Oh yeah, that would go over like a lead balloon! Mom would have me committed! No, I'll just have to wait for them to come to me. Well, for HIM to come to me, that is.

Who am I kidding — I'd settle for just about anybody right now! Except for nano-brained Brad, that is. But it sure would be nice if it was Russ...

* * * * *

"Mission accomplished."

"Yes. Excellent work." Alex smiled. "When are you seeing her again?"

"Possibly at the regatta," Jonathan replied. "Devon mentioned that they might be attending this year."

"What do you mean, possibly? Haven't you set a date with her?"

"No sir."

"Why not? You know we're on a tight schedule!"

"I know that, sir, but I can't rush this," Jonathan said. "Braidy Attison is the type of girl that is used to male adoration. She'd dismiss me instantly if I acted like all her other admirers. No, I have to play this just right."

"How do you mean?"

"Make her want me. Make her think she has to have me."

"And how do you intend to do that?" Alex asked his young protegé.

"By ignoring her."

"Ignoring her?!" Alex gasped. "What on earth...! And how is that going to help you get close to her?"

"As I said, sir," Jonathan explained, "Braidy is used to being the center of attention, at least where the male of the species is concerned. The fact that I barely even gave her a glance all day has got to be driving her crazy right now. It's an insult to her vanity. She'll do everything she can to get her hooks in me, just to prove that she can."

"It might work," Alex mused. "Just don't draw it out too long, you hear me? I want her safely under my wing as soon as possible. We have a lot of work to do, and it's bound to take some time to persuade her to my way of thinking."

"Don't worry, sir." It was Jonathan's turn to smile. "I'll have her eating out of my hand in no time."

Chapter Seven:

A Day At The Races

The morning of the annual Head Island Regatta started out overcast and drizzling, but by the time the race was scheduled to start at ten, the rain had stopped and the clouds were breaking up, promising a hot afternoon.

Braidy woke up with a start shortly after eight o'clock. It took her several moments to recognize where she was. The dream she'd been immersed in had been so vivid, so realistic, it had left her totally disorientated...

She was walking down the beach in the moonlight, barefoot, dressed in a long, silky gown that floated around her in the ocean breeze. Her hair was hanging loose over her shoulders. Some distance ahead, a man stood with his back to her. She moved slowly toward him. Even though she couldn't see his face, instinctively she knew who he was.

When she reached him, she stretched out her hand and touched his shoulder. He turned, the moonlight shining on his handsome face, highlighting his light brown hair. He smiled.

"Braidy, my love," Jonathan said, taking her into his arms.

Braidy raised her face to him, twining her arms around his neck as he kissed her. With that, Braidy realized that they were now on the Tout À l'Heure, in the middle of the ocean, sailing, sailing, sailing. Jonathan laid her down in the bow of the boat and began to make love to her...

And then she woke, trembling, the heat of his hands still on her skin.

Braidy insisted to herself that the extra time she took with her makeup that morning had nothing to do with the fact that she might see Jonathan Crenshaw at the regatta.

"What do I care about him?" she muttered to herself as she changed shirts for the third time. "He means nothing to me. He's practically a stranger." That assertion was belied by her dream, the memory of which she couldn't escape. "Besides, there's going to be thousands of people there. The chances of running into one particular guy are minuscule, right? Right!"

She slammed her closet door, exasperated with herself. Why was she letting Jonathan get to her? He'd barely acknowledged her existence. There were plenty of other boys interested in going out with her. Why waste a single thought on someone who hadn't given her a second glance? She shook her head as hard as she could, trying to shake the memory of him — and the dream — out of her brain. It didn't work.

As the family drove to the marina, Braidy could feel Brody staring at her. She avoided his gaze, afraid he'd read her mind if she faced him, something she definitely didn't want happening. Her inexplicable obsession with Jonathan Crenshaw was something she had every intention of keeping to herself. Forever, if possible. She desperately hoped that seeing him again would cure her — that she'd realize he was actually very plain-looking — ugly even — that he smelled funny, or had bad teeth, or...something. Anything that might put her off and end this strange fascination with this virtual stranger. Before she made a complete fool of herself.

* * * * *

Moira, on the other hand, wasn't bothering to hide her excitement concerning the day's possibilities. Russ would definitely be there — he and his dad were entered in the race — and she would definitely see him. He'd called her once since the Fourth — just to chat — and they'd run into each other at the supermarket in town. In the frozen foods section. They'd had a good laugh over that, teasing each other about the old cliché. Moira had thought, for just a moment, that Russ might finally ask her for a date, but it hadn't happened. Maybe he was shy, maybe he wasn't sure about how she felt...the reasons didn't matter. He'd been happy to see her, enjoyed talking with her, seemed reluctant to end the conversation. There was definitely hope.

Moira was determined to settle things between them at the regatta. She was going to get Russ Baines to ask her out today. Even if she had to put the words in his mouth herself.

Devon pulled into a parking spot reserved for the press, waving his press badge at the security guard as he jumped out, his camera draped around his neck, his bag slung over his shoulder.

"C'mon, sis, get a move on," he called to Moira as he walked with long-legged strides toward the harbor. "I've gotta get some shots of the entrants before the race starts."

"I'm coming! I'm coming!" Moira shouted back, trying to catch up.

Devon soon outstripped her. Moira followed as quickly as she could, her short legs no match for his long limbs. Luckily, her brother was tall, so she was able to see his head over the many spectators milling all along the shoreline, jostling for the best view. Suddenly,

Devon stopped, giving Moira the opportunity to catch up. As she got closer, weaving in and out of the crowd, she realized he was talking to someone. Her heart pounding, she approached, a ready smile on her lips, only to discover that her brother's companion was his friend, Jonathan Crenshaw. Her smile disappeared, disappointment flowing through her, making her stomach tighten. She was hoping Devon had found Russ. Oh well, she'd just have to wait a little longer.

"Hello, Moira," Jonathan said as she joined the two young men.

"'Lo," she replied, less than enthusiastically. She stood up on her tiptoes, scanning the crowd as best she could. Devon grinned and exchanged a glance with his friend, who appeared both puzzled and amused by Moira's actions.

"Looking for someone?" he asked.

"What? Oh...um...no...no one in particular, that is," she stuttered, turning red. She turned on Devon. "Aren't you supposed to be down by the boats, taking pictures?"

"Oh, yeah! C'mon, Jonathan, I'll get ya in close, get a great view!"

Devon grabbed Moira by the hand and pulled her along with him as he made his way to the docks, Jonathan bringing up the rear. Moira had to trot to keep pace with her brother, but she didn't mind. If it got her to Russ a little faster, all the better.

A minute or two later, they reached the docks. Once again, Devon waved his press pass and the cop on duty let them through the barrier. There were a lot less people by the boats, since only the entrants, their families, and their friends were allowed in the area. And the press, of course.

"DEVON! HEY, FITZ!" a voice shouted. Devon waved and made his way toward a short, stocky man in his late thirties carrying a notepad and pen. "Where you been, man? You're late!"

"Got stuck in the crowd, Jim. This is my sister, Moira, and my friend, Jonathan Crenshaw. Jim Hennessey — he's a writer for the paper."

Jonathan shook hands with the older man while Moira merely nodded her head, her eyes raking the boat decks nearby, searching for a familiar head of dark hair. No luck. Devon swung his camera up and began taking pictures.

"Man, the light is perfect right now! These are gonna turn out great!"

"Good," Jim said. "Hey, listen, I just found out that one of the entrants in the Dart class is running for mayor — some banker guy named Desmond Baines. I wanna try to get an interview with him."

"Yeah, we know him. My mom works for him," Devon told him.

"Great! You can introduce me!"

Moira tuned out the men's voices as she continued looking for Russ among the many regatta entrants. Once she thought she'd seen him, but it turned out to be a very tall woman with short hair. A minute later she spotted the Tout À l'Heure pulling into a slip on the other side of the marina. Brody and Aunt Caroline waved to her as they clambered up onto the dock.

"Uncle Phil and Aunt Caroline are here," she told Devon. He nodded absentmindedly to her and continued taking pictures. Giving her absorbed brother a disgusted look, Moira wandered toward her aunt and uncle. Maybe she'd find Russ over there.

"Hi, Aunt Caroline...Brody," she called as she approached the sailboat.

"Hi, sweetie," Caroline called back to her niece as she tied off the bow line. "Hello, Jonathan. How are you?"

Moira spun around, surprised. She hadn't realized that Jonathan was shadowing her.

"I'm good, Mrs. Attison. Thanks for asking," he said, shaking hands with Uncle Phil. "Perfect day for the race, don't you think?"

"Where's Braidy?" Moira asked, suddenly realizing that her other cousin was nowhere to be seen.

"She was here just a moment ago," Caroline mused, glancing around. She shrugged. "Guess she's in the galley. She'll be up in a minute."

"ENTRANTS IN THE TWO-MAN DART CLASS EVENT, PLEASE PROCEED TO THE STARTING LINE!"

Moira jumped as the voice shouted over a loudspeaker nearby, giving Brody a good laugh at her expense. She chose to ignore him, concentrating instead on the numerous catamarans slowing working their way to the far end of the marina. She had no idea what Desmond Baines' boat looked like, but was hopeful that she'd see Russ nonetheless.

She was about to give up when...was it...? No, it wasn't....Yes, it was! There he was, adjusting the mainsheet on a green and blue catamaran with the name Sea Mist painted near the stern in white letters. She cupped her hands around her mouth.

"RUSS! HEY, RUSS!" she shouted, then waved frantically.

"Think he heard you?" Phil teased her. Moira gave her uncle a dirty look, quickly followed by a brilliant smile. Russ had seen her! He was waving back.

"GOOD LUCK!" she yelled. He gave her a thumb's up, then went back to work. Desmond, seated at the tiller, twisted around and waved as well, before heading the boat in the same direction as all the other racers. Moira sighed, a soft happy sound.

"You seem pleased to see him," Jonathan commented, smiling at her.

"Yeah...well...he's...um..." she stammered, turning pink. "He's a good friend," she finished, looking at Jonathan as if daring him to question her motives. He continued to smile.

"I'm sure he is."

Braidy stood at the top of the companionway steps, staring at Jonathan Crenshaw and her cousin. She'd only just worked up the nerve to make an appearance, having ducked into the galley the moment she spotted Jonathan walking down the dock toward them. And there he was, smiling tenderly at...*Moira?*

Braidy turned and climbed back down into the galley, her cheeks burning.

* * * * *

"Hand-a-lee, son! Ready to release the jib!" Desmond called.

They were nearly to the halfway mark of the race, cruising past the eastern shoreline of Georges Island as they tacked through the stiff breeze that was blowing from the southeast. They were out in front, part of a small pack of catamarans that had been in the lead from the start. Russ had been watching the other contestants closely. He figured they had a pretty good chance of winning. There were only two other boats that seemed to give any serious competition; a white and green Dart 18 called the Jersey Gull, manned by two men who appeared to be in their late twenties or early thirties, and a Dart 16 identical to their own in red and yellow, crewed by two young women who had named their boat the Sweet Dream.

Russ lowered the mainsail by nearly one third, then tightened the lower portion, tying the reef line off quickly. He sensed, rather than saw, Desmond shifting his weight slightly forward, giving the boat better trim as they tacked through the wind around the southeastern end of the island. The two men worked well in tandem, having years of practice behind them. Desmond had taken both of his children sailing before they could walk, and he and Russ had been regular entrants in the regatta ever since its inception six years earlier. They'd won the race easily two years ago, and had lost by inches the previous year. That particular opponent had already fallen well back in the pack, stymied by a problem with some tangled lines.

The white and green Dart 18 looked familiar; Russ was fairly sure they'd sailed in previous regattas. But the two women were strangers to him — new to the contest, and therefore, an unknown quantity. They certainly knew what they were doing, he had to acknowledge, as he watched them bearing away just ahead, the mainsail jibing quickly and efficiently as the women eased their way around the southernmost tip of the island. Spectators on the shore — and in boats floating well clear of the race course — cheered as the contestants sailed by, some more gracefully than others. Russ ignored them, concentrating instead on easing out the sails as Desmond shifted the tiller slightly, trying to take full advantage of the wind now coming across the stern at a forty-five degree angle. Both men knew that they had to catch the wind at just the right angle for a successful run — and any chance at winning the race. They completed their jibe as they rounded the southwestern shore and the Sea Mist leaped forward, the sails filling as Russ eased them out to their full capacity. Desmond leaned back once again as they began their run up the western side of the island, while Russ shifted back and to starboard, his hands firm on the reef line. The catamaran sped through the waves, gaining ground on their opponents.

Desmond laughed as they pulled away from the Dart 18.

"We'll show them!" he shouted, grinning widely.

Russ smiled at his father and gave him a thumbs up in return, exhilarated by the wind and the waves. Sailing was one of his favorite things to do. And he had certainly inherited enough of Desmond's ambitious nature to enjoy winning. Now all they had to do was catch up with the two women, and they were home free.

* * * * *

Moira, Devon, Jonathan and the rest of the family had managed to snag an excellent position on the northeastern shore of the peninsula, just past Marine Park, right at the finish line — thanks in good part to Devon's press pass. Jim Hennessey was nearby, interviewing a few of the spectators for his article. Devon was taking picture after picture, stopping only to switch media cards before clicking away again, oblivious to anything but what he saw in his viewfinder. Moira was monopolizing the binoculars, searching anxiously for the Sea Mist.

"Hand 'em over, Moir!" Brody protested. "I wanna see too!"

The two teens indulged in a momentary struggle — Moira won.

"Possession is nine-tenths of the law," she said smugly.

"Moira..." Caroline said, a warning note in her voice. Scowling, Moira handed the binoculars over to her cousin, who grinned triumphantly before scanning the harbor.

"Here, Moira," Jonathan said, "you can use mine."

Moira shot her own look of triumph back at Brody as she accepted Jonathan's offer.

"Why, thank you, Jonathan!" she said. "It's so nice to see that there are some gentlemen left in the world." Brody snorted in disgust.

"Want to see, Braidy?" he asked, holding the binoculars out to his sister after several minutes.

"No, thank you," Braidy said quietly.

"You okay?" Brody asked, noticing the grim set of Braidy's face for the first time.

"I'm fine!" Braidy said sharply, turning away. Brody stared at the back of her head for a moment, his enjoyment of the day dimming slightly. What was wrong with her? She usually loved these races, but today she wasn't paying any attention at all. Pensive, Brody turned back toward the water, handing the binoculars to his mother, who was also watching Braidy with a puzzled expression on her face. Mother and son exchanged a look, sharing their concern.

Braidy ignored them both, drowning in her own misery. Every minute seemed like an eternity as she was forced to stand by and watch Jonathan Crenshaw lavish Moira with his attentions. She felt humiliated, angry, jealous — and totally disgusted with herself. Why was she letting him get to her like this? It didn't make sense! Here she was, the most popular girl at Orleans High, pining away after some guy who hadn't even acknowledged her existence. What made him so special, anyway? She wasn't even sure she liked him.

And feeling jealous of Moira just made the humiliation even worse. Moira's feeble attempts at flirting with the young man would normally have sent Braidy into uncontrollable giggles. But today all she could do was fume. Jonathan should be talking to *her*, Braidy; not plain, dumpy, freaky Moira. It was so frustrating!

"Oops! Sorry!" Jonathan said as he stepped back onto Braidy's toes — the first words he'd directed toward her all morning. "I didn't see you there."

Braidy's jaw tightened. That was adding insult to injury. He hadn't even seen her! She moved away deliberately as he returned his attention to Moira, the two of them laughing companionably.

Suddenly someone to their right let out a shout.

"There they are!"

Moira squealed and raised the binoculars once again. Four tiny sails became visible in the far distance, about a mile out from the finish line. They were still much too far away to distinguish any clear markings, but Moira was convinced that Russ and his father were among them.

"C'mon, c'mon!" she muttered under her breath, staring across the waves as the boats gradually moved closer. Soon more sails could be seen as the other contestants hove into view. A few minutes later the frontrunners were close enough to determine sail colors and Moira's confidence was rewarded — the leading catamaran had green and blue wavy bars on the mainsail.

"It's the Sea Mist!" she shouted, jumping up and down in her excitement. "They're in the lead!"

It wasn't a clear cut lead, however. In fact, the race was extremely close. The Jersey Gull was running just to port of the Sea Mist, while the Sweet Dream was almost directly behind Russ and Desmond. The fourth boat in the pack — another Dart 18 — seemed to be falling back slightly. But any one of the three leaders could easily come in first.

Everyone on shore could see the sailors working the lines and tillers, trying to eke out the tiniest bit more speed from their vessels while avoiding the risk of a capsize. A difficult task, with the wind now having shifted a few degrees to the east, making it necessary for the helmsmen to tack downwind, handing the boom quickly across while their respective crewmen rapidly reset the jib. All of the catamarans now visible were taking a zigzag course across the water as the wind picked up slightly and the waves became rougher.

As the three leaders approached, it became obvious that the Sweet Dream was gaining on both the Sea Mist and the Jersey Gull, running to starboard. The larger Dart 18 seemed to be having some trouble with its trim, causing it to lose some of its momentum and fall back slightly. Nearing the finish line, the Sea Mist and the Sweet Dream were head to head. Everyone on shore was shouting and cheering, no one louder than Moira, when suddenly the Sweet Dream dipped forward and slowly somersaulted, stern over bow.

* * * * *

Russ ducked as the boom swung over him once again. They were tied for first place with the Sweet Dream, the finish line a few hundred yards away. He glanced back at his father, a big grin on his face — and froze.

Desmond was staring at the Sweet Dream, an intense expression on his face. He raised his right hand off of the tiller, waved it through the air, then clenched it in a tight fist. The two women on the other boat screamed.

"NO!" Russ yelled. His head whipped around. He watched in horror as the Sweet Dream pitchpoled, the bow of the catamaran digging deep into the waves, the mainsail dipping toward the water. The stern flipped over, almost in slow motion, as the women were tossed overboard. Their catamaran came down hard, right on top of them, as they both frantically tried to free themselves from the trapeze.

"Russ!" Desmond called out. "Release the jib!"

"WHAT?!"

"The Sweet Dream capsized!" Desmond replied as he put their boat onto a beam reach. "One of the crew is stuck underneath it. We're got to help those women!"

Russ stared at his father for a moment, totally confused.

"But didn't you just...?" he began. Desmond interrupted him.

"There's no time to argue, Russ! This is more important than winning some silly race, and you know it!"

Russ reacted automatically, releasing the jib & shifting his weight portside as the Sea Mist turned back toward the capsized boat. As they approached, Russ could see only one of the women in the water. She was swimming around the far side of the catamaran, searching the waves for her friend. He quickly dropped the mainsail.

"Take the helm, son! I'm going in after her!"

Before Russ could respond, Desmond had released his safety line and lowered himself into the cold Atlantic water. Russ repositioned himself at the tiller, his mind numb. Totally bewildered by what he'd seen his father do, unable to comprehend what Desmond's motives could possibly be, he forced himself to concentrate on the task at hand — rescuing the two women and righting the Sweet Dream. The race no longer existed for him.

Two or three other catamarans were heading in their direction, obviously intending to assist. Glancing toward the shore, Russ could see the Jersey Gull cross the finish line, the crew raising their hands in triumph, apparently unaware of the fate of their female opponents. But no one payed them any attention; everyone watching the race was mesmerized by the drama taking place out in the harbor.

Desmond dove under the capsized catamaran, searching for the missing woman. He came up a minute later, empty-handed.

"She's tangled in the lines!" he shouted. "I've got to cut her free!" He dove again, resurfacing a short time later just long enough to catch his breath before returning to the task. A crewman from one of the other catamarans joined him, pocket knife in hand. After what seemed an eternity, the two men's heads broke the water simultaneously, the woman's unconscious body held between them. Vaguely, Russ registered the sound of sirens. Turning his head, he saw a Coast Guard cutter heading toward them at top speed. It pulled up to the leeward of the various boats just as Desmond and the other man reached the Sea Mist, both women in tow. The girls were white as ghosts, but Russ saw with relief that the one who had been trapped under the waves was breathing regularly. Her friend was shaking, silent tears running down her cheeks.

"Everything's...okay," Desmond reassured her, gasping slightly from exertion. "Your friend is...going to be...fine...just fine..."

The Coast Guard rescue team quickly took charge, taking both women onto the cutter. Desmond clung to the side of the Sea Mist, as his breathing slowly returned to normal.

"Thanks for the help," he said to the other man, holding out his hand.

"No problem," the man said, shaking the proffered hand. "Just glad we were close enough to get here in time. What about their boat?"

"We'll tow it in," Desmond said. "Let's get it upright, okay?"

"I'll do that, Dad," Russ said quietly. "You've done enough already." Desmond gave his son a sharp look, not liking the tone in Russ's voice. Both men chose to let the double entendre slide, for the moment. Desmond scrambled back onto the Sea Mist and took the tiller as Russ joined the other man in the water.

They righted the Sweet Dream, attached a tow line, and clambered back into their respective catamarans. Russ let the sails out on the Sea Mist, Desmond pulled the tiller close, and they slowly returned to the marina, the Sweet Dream bobbing along behind them.

* * * * *

Devon took picture after picture of Desmond, the Sea Mist and the Sweet Dream as his colleague interviewed the hero, vying with a large contingent of reporters from throughout the area. The next set of contestants were lining up at the edge of the marina just behind them.

"So why did you turn back, Mr. Baines?" Jim Hennessey asked. "Standard procedure is to let every crew fend for itself."

"And normally, I would have followed that procedure," Desmond replied with a modest smile. "Believe me, I wasn't trying to indulge in histrionics or anything like that. But something caught my eye as we passed the capsize. Some instinct told me things weren't good. I felt it best we turn back and make sure the ladies were okay."

"But you lost the race as a result," another reporter stated the obvious.

"A life is much more important than any race, you know that," Desmond said. "I couldn't have lived with myself if anything had happened to either of those young women."

"So are you saying that the men on the winning catamaran, the Jersey Gull, were negligent?"

Desmond laughed. "Certainly not, Ken! You're trying to put words in my mouth — just like a sharp newsman." He clapped the reporter from Channel Three on the shoulder. "No, I doubt they even saw what had happened. They were running to port, while the Sweet Dream was on our starboard side. I'm sure, had they known what was going down, those men would have raced to assist the women as well. Please don't make me out to be a hero, folks. I merely did what anyone else would have done under the circumstances. All that matters now is that the crew of the Sweet Dream are going to be fine."

"This story certainly won't hurt your run for mayor, though, will it?" Jim asked slyly.

Desmond laughed again. "Well, now that you mention it...! No, Jim, one has nothing to do with the other. Today, I'm just an average guy who simply did what needed to be done. Nothing more."

Russ avoided looking in his father's direction as he finished lowering the sails of the Sea Mist. He tied off the stern, then double-checked the knot he'd used at the bow. Absorbed in his own troubled thoughts, he jumped when Moira hailed him.

"Exciting race, wasn't it?" she said, beaming up at him as he straightened. The second race began as he paused, not sure how to answer her.

"Yeah," he finally said, running his hand through his hair, his eyes narrowed as he finally glanced toward Desmond, who was still holding court, surrounded by reporters. "Real exciting."

"You okay?"

"Fine. Just fine." Russ sighed, his dark eyes reflecting the turmoil inside him.

"Don't look fine to me," Moira insisted, hands on hips. "In fact, you look pretty upset. What's up? You and your dad are heroes! That's pretty cool, isn't it?"

"Heroes?" Russ turned to stare at her. "You really think so, do you?" He laughed harshly, humorlessly. "Yeah, we're heroes all right!"

"I mean," Moira stammered, totally at a loss as to what was causing Russ's odd mood, "I know you must be disappointed that you lost the race, but..."

"I don't give a damn about the stupid race, Moira!" Russ hissed. "I wish we'd never entered the ignorant thing!" He strode off, quickly losing himself in the crowd.

Moira stared after him, openmouthed. Then shock gave way to anger; her eyes glittered, her mouth closed with a snap, her fists clenched.

"Fine!" she muttered through clenched teeth. "Don't talk to me! Don't tell me what the hell's going on! Who needs ya!" She walked off the dock and shoved her way through the crowd toward her family.

They were talking with Desmond — who had finally managed to free himself of the reporters — and a stunningly beautiful young woman. Devon quickly introduced her to Moira.

"This is Callista Baines, Moira," Devon said, "Mr. Baines' daughter."

The two girls exchanged a brief greeting. Moira noticed that every man within fifty feet, her uncle included, couldn't seem to take their eyes off the lovely Miss Baines. Every man, that is, except Jonathan Crenshaw, who was gazing out at the new group of racers.

"Where is Russell, Father?" Callista asked.

"I'm not sure, dear," Desmond replied, a small frown creasing his forehead. "He was tying off the boat..."

"He went that way," Moira stated blandly, pointing through the crowd.

Callista Baines looked down her nose at the much smaller girl.

"Do you know my brother?"

"Yeah," Moira muttered, "at least, I thought so...."

"Why didn't he join us, I wonder?"

"He didn't seem too thrilled with what happened out there," Moira said. "Took exception to me calling him a hero, for some reason."

Desmond's frown deepened. "Russ is a very modest person, Moira. I doubt he'd want to take credit for helping those women, any more than I..."

"He wasn't being modest, Mr. Baines," Moira interrupted him, her eyes flashing, "he was pissed. I guess he really wanted to win the race. You done, Dev? I'm ready to go."

"I've got to stay for the rest of the races, Moir! You know that," Devon told her, tearing his gaze away from Callista's face for a moment.

"But I'm tired! And it's hot! I want to go home!"

"I'm working," Devon stated the obvious.

"But...!"

"I can give you a ride, Moira," Jonathan offered. "I've seen all I want to. It was good to see you again, Mr. Baines. Nice to meet you, Callista."

Moira stuck her tongue out at Devon, who returned the sentiment, then concentrated once again on his camera. Moira turned to say goodbye to the Baines's, but paused, intrigued. Jonathan and Callista were shaking hands. Something in the way they looked at each other caught Moira's attention. She couldn't put her finger on it, but somehow she got the distinct impression that there was more there than met the eye. Then Jonathan turned away from the lovely Miss Baines, letting go of her hand, and the moment was gone. Moira wondered if she'd only imagined it.

"You ready?" he asked her.

"Yeah, sure. Bye, Aunt Caroline…Uncle Phil…see ya at home, Dev."

As they walked toward the parking lot together, two sets of female eyes followed them: Callista Baines' and Braidy Attison's. Neither one seemed particularly pleased with the situation.

* * * * *

July 23

WHAT IS HIS PROBLEM??!!!!!

Okay, that does it! I'm tired of duncing around with this guy! Talk about the moody type! And people complain about me?!

Damn! This really sucks! I was just starting to like him! Who am I kidding — I was really into him!

But what was bothering Russ so much? I can't believe he

was upset about losing the race. I mean, those women were really in trouble. He definitely seems to be the type who'd be more than willing to run to the rescue, especially of some damsel in distress. And not to show off. He definitely doesn't like the spotlight, like his dad. So what was up with him? He seemed really upset, but I don't think it was about losing. He gave his dad a really funny look, I noticed. I wonder if he thought his dad was capitalizing on the accident to get some free publicity, or something like that. And it bugged him. That might be it. But he could have told me that. Unless he was too embarrassed to talk about it. I guess if Mom or Andrew were acting like that, I wouldn't want to talk about it to anyone, especially some guy I was into.

Aw, hell! I'm not even sure Russ is into me! I mean, he seems to like me, as a friend at least, but he's never acted like he...well...wants me. Although I'm not sure I'd recognize it if a guy did want me! LOL Not exactly a ton of experience in that category. Although I must admit that I am pretty good at spotting when some guy is into some other girl...

Like that Callista Baines. Man, were all the guys checking her out or what?! Devon was practically drooling! Too funny. She seems pathetically stuck up, though — really full of herself. Not at all like Russ. He's so unassuming, so down to earth, so easy-going...most of the time. But something sure had his wand in a knot today. Wish he would call me...

Jonathan was really nice to me today. He's funny! I had a great time on the ride home. He's a little full of himself, too, but he's not so obvious about it. I wonder what that look was ...the one between him and Callista Baines. It was so quick, I'm not sure I didn't imagine it. It almost looked like they knew each other already. But from the way Jonathan talked, it sounded like he'd just met her today. Must have been my imagination. No reason for them to pretend not to know each other if they do, right...?

* * * * *

"I SAW YOU!!"

"What you saw, Russell, and what really happened are obviously two different things," Desmond replied, barely holding his anger in check. "Why would I do such a thing?"

"I don't know! I was hoping you could tell me!"

"Well, since I didn't do what you are accusing me of, I can hardly explain it to you, can I?"

"But I saw you, Dad!" Russ insisted, distraught. "You pushed their catamaran right into the waves, so they'd capsize."

"I did nothing of the sort! What possible reason could I have had for such an action?"

"I..." Russ paused, afraid to say what he thought. But he knew he had to get this out in the open. He took a deep breath and plunged ahead. "You wanted to win, and it looked like they were going to beat us, so you cheated. You used magic."

Desmond jumped up from his chair and strode across the room. For a moment, Russ thought his father was going to hit him.

"HOW DARE YOU! If you were anyone but my son....!" Visibly shaken, Desmond forced himself to calm down. "I would never cheat, Russell. You know that. Or at least, you should know that. And if that was my purpose, why did I insist on going back to help those women? Can you answer me that?"

"How should I know?" Russ sighed and turned his back on his father, staring out the window at the lights of the city. "Maybe, when you saw how bad the capsize was, and realized that one of them might be hurt, you had second thoughts?"

"Oh, please, Russell," Callista drawled from her seat on the sofa. Russ jumped. He'd almost forgotten his sister was still in the room; she'd remained silent up to that point. "You're making this up as you go along. You can't really think Father would stoop to such paltry methods simply to win a silly little regatta."

"Well, he sure managed to milk the situation for all it was worth when we got back to port!"

"I didn't ask all those reporters to come flocking around me!" Desmond protested. "They simply showed up! I did my best to downplay the entire situation, you know that!"

"Yeah, I guess," Russ sighed again. "I just..." He turned to face Desmond again, his face intent. "Do you swear to me, Dad, you didn't capsize those women?"

"I swear it, son." Desmond's expression was just as intent as his son's as he grasped Russ by the shoulders. "I would never cheat like that. I love to win, you know that, but I prefer to do so on my own merits."

Russ stared into his father's eyes as if he were trying to read the older man's mind. Finally, he nodded his head slowly.

"Okay, then?" Desmond asked.

"Yeah, okay," Russ said somewhat reluctantly. He scratched the back of his neck. "I'm pretty worn out. Think I'll get a shower and turn in early."

"Good idea. I'll probably do the same. Goodnight, son."

"Goodnight, Callista."

"Mmmm," she waved vaguely at her brother.

Desmond waited several seconds after Russ left the living room, then he walked over to the doorway and looked down the hall toward the bedrooms. Russ's door was closed. Desmond heaved a sigh of relief.

"Well." Callista raised an eyebrow. "That was special."

"We're going to have trouble with him," Desmond said, sitting next to his daughter.

"No, we're not, Father. Family comes first with Russell. You'll see. He'll come around, once you've won the election. He'll realize our plans are for the best."

Desmond grunted, obviously not convinced.

"Cheer up, Father," Callista drawled. "The plan worked perfectly. You're the talk of the regatta. You're a hero. Better still, according to the press, you're a modest hero. You completely snowed those brainless reporters."

"Yes," Desmond sighed. "I just hate having to lie to Russ like that. If only we could take him into our confidence..."

"He's not ready for that, and you know it, Father," Callista insisted, sitting up straight. She placed a calming hand on her father's knee. "That silly, over-active conscience of his would come up with all sorts of arguments against the agenda we've mapped out. He'd begin spouting on about the end not justifying the means, or some such nonsense, and we'd have a huge argument on our hands. We don't have the time for that. Nor do we need the distraction. No, it's best we leave Russell out of the loop for now. Once the election is over, and he can see how much good we can do for the community, he'll understand our motives."

Desmond nodded slowly, still frowning. He took a deep breath.

"Callista," he murmured, "we are doing the right thing, aren't we?"

"How can you doubt it, Father?!" Callista replied, her eyes boring into his. "We can do so much good, but only if we're working from a position of strength. You know it's the only way."

"Yes, I know, I know," Desmond said, his usual spark of determination returning. "It's just Russ...it's difficult to explain, Callista, dear. I know that for all intents and purposes, he's a grown man now, but a part of me still sees him as the little boy who always looked up to me. I'd hoped he'd always look up to me..." His voice faded away.

"He will, Father," his daughter reassured him, "as do I. Once we have everything in place, Russell will have no choice but to join us. It's the only logical decision."

"I hope you're right, my dear," Desmond sighed. "I sincerely hope you're right."

Chapter Eight:

Back To School

"The cafeteria is down that hall, across from the gym," Braidy said. "The computer lab, art room, and library are downstairs, to the left. All the senior lockers are along here. What's your number?"

"Six-five-seven," Moira replied, her head spinning. Braidy was giving her a quick tour of the high school before the first bell. The halls were filled with students talking and laughing, catching up on the events of the summer with their friends. Some of them stared at Moira while most of them ignored her completely. She wasn't sure which she preferred. Stumbling along in Braidy's wake she tried her best to absorb the information her cousin was imparting, but she was convinced she'd forget most of it and wind up lost for the greater part of the day.

"Here's your locker," Braidy said, coming to a stop and pulling open the metal door. "Got your schedule handy? I always make an extra copy and tape it inside my locker door. That way I don't have to search for it when I'm in a hurry."

"Um...yeah...I'll have to do that..." Moira mumbled. She dug through her backpack for the computer printout of her classes provided by the school secretary. Unsuccessful in her search, she dropped the backpack onto the floor in front of her locker and began pulling out notebooks, paper, a ruler, a calculator, several pens and pencils... "Damn! I know it's gotta be here somewhere!" she muttered under her breath. She could sense her cousin's impatience. It didn't help. Suddenly, a lightbulb went off.

"I remember!" Moira exclaimed, straightening up and reaching into her jeans pocket. Triumphant, she flourished a folded piece of paper. "I stuck it in there this morning before I left the house, so it wouldn't get mixed up with everything else."

Braidy managed to refrain from rolling her eyes. She even gave her disorganized cousin a small smile. "Okay, Moira, who's homeroom are you in?"

Moira glanced at the sheet, slight frown lines forming on her forehead. "Um...let's see...I know I saw it on here...there it is! Miss Kane, Room 206."

"You're in luck. That's right across the hall," Braidy smiled as she pointed to the classroom door directly across from where they were standing. Her smile was tinged with a fair smattering of relief — the two girls were in different homerooms. Moira followed Braidy's finger and sighed. One hurdle overcome.

"So what do you have first hour?" Braidy continued, looking down at Moira's schedule.

"Current Affairs." Moira groaned. "How do they expect anybody to be awake enough to discuss politics at 7:30 in the morning?"

Braidy stifled her own groan.Current Affairs was her first class, as well. Glancing down the sheet, she quickly ascertained that Moira would be present in at least six of her seven classes each day. The only time they weren't together was fifth hour, right after lunch, when Braidy had French IV and Moira was in Creative Writing. She sighed.

"I didn't know you signed up for Music," Braidy commented, trying to sound nonchalant.

"Yeah, well, it was that or Art," Moira said as she stuffed her supplies back into her bookbag, "and since yours truly can't draw a straight line with a ruler, I figured I'd better not torment the poor teacher." She tossed her bag over one shoulder, straightened, and slammed the locker door shut, securing it with the school's standard issue combination lock. Squaring her shoulders, she turned to face her homeroom door. "Okay, I'm ready as I'll ever be. Throw me to the lions."

Braidy smiled in spite of herself.

"You'll be fine, Moira," she said, patting her cousin on the back. "The teachers here are pretty cool, for the most part. Some of them are kind of strict, and they all expect you to pull your weight, but they don't usually play favorites or any crap like that. And if you have any trouble with the material, they're willing to help you out."

"It's not the teachers I'm worried about," Moira muttered, frowning at the waves of students making their way to class.

Braidy hesitated a moment, only too aware of what her cousin was referring to. Then she took a deep breath.

"There's tons of kids here, you're bound to have something in common with a few of them, at least. I'll introduce you around at lunch, okay? Get you started. Besides, you already know a few of them. You met them last summer, when you stayed with us, remember?"

"Yeah!" Moira brightened visibly. "I'd forgotten! Except...they didn't like me much, did they...." she raised an eyebrow at Braidy.

"Well," Braidy replied, grinning, "maybe you'll grow on them."

Moira snorted, partly amused, partly disgusted at the prospect. With that, the school bell rang. She jumped.

"That's the homeroom bell," Braidy told her unnecessarily. "Better get in there. You don't want to be late your very first day."

"Yeah..." Moira swallowed, her nerves returning with a vengeance.

"I'll see you first hour," Braidy called over her shoulder as she wound her way through the few remaining students toward her own homeroom. "Room 232...that way..." She pointed in the opposite direction. "Bye, Moira!"

"Bye," Moira mumbled, her mouth dry, her palms damp with sweat. "Okay, girl," she said to herself, "it's just school. Nothing new here. You've been doing this for fourteen years now, counting pre-school. Just walk through the door, find an empty desk, and sit in it." She took a deep breath, strode across the hall, a determined look on her face, and entered the classroom for the first time.

* * * * *

After homeroom, Moira slowly found her way to her first class. Once again, she hesitated outside the door, waiting for she knew not what. Several other students pushed past her to enter the room, their backward glances curious. Finally, when the hall was nearly empty, Moira forced herself to join them.

Twenty-two heads swiveled in unison as twenty-two pairs of eyes focused on her hair, her face, her clothes. Moira stared back, her stomach trembling, the faces a blur. Complete silence filled the room. She sincerely hoped her fellow classmates couldn't see how nervous she was, how her palms were sweating and her stomach was trembling. A lone empty desk beckoned from the third row, a mere ten feet away. It looked more like ten miles. Gulping hard, Moira set her mouth in a thin, hard line and forced herself to run the gauntlet.

Everyone in the room followed her progress and continued to stare as she threw herself into the seat, including Mr. Sumner, the Current Affairs instructor. At least the teacher's expression was open and friendly, unlike that of the students, most of whom appeared indifferent at best and downright hostile at worst. Moira took a deep breath, screwed up her courage, and glanced around the room, staring the others down. Braidy smiled slightly; her friend, Karen, didn't exactly smile, but at least she nodded in a somewhat friendly manner. The rest simply stared. One face in particular stood out: a boy, near the windows, with long blond hair and an expression of disgust on his face. Brody's friend, Jeremy.

"Brilliant," Moira muttered to herself, turning to face the front of the room again. "Just what I needed." She slid down in her seat, trying to make herself as small as possible, wishing she'd chosen a less noticeable shade of pink for her hair color that week. Catching Braidy's eye, Moira rolled her own. Braidy gave her a small, encouraging half-smile in return. The noise level gradually rose again, as the various conversations her entrance had interrupted picked up once more. No one spoke to Moira, although occasionally someone would glance in her direction. She noticed Jeremy whispering fiercely with the boy seated directly in front of him; both boys glared at her.

Moira sniffed disdainfully, tossed her head, and straightened up in her seat. Damned if she was going to let these dorks get to her! She was worth ten of them...put together! Moira directed her determined gaze toward the front of the room to discover that Mr. Sumner was looking right at her. He gave her a surreptitious wink.

"All right, everyone, your attention, please," he called out, glancing around the room. The talking and whispering slowly faded away. "Welcome to another year — the final year, for all of you — and welcome to Current Affairs. I am confident that, by the end of the year, this will be your favorite class."

Various groans and snorts of disgust came from the students. Mr. Sumner grinned.

"Put it this way, folks," he said, still grinning, "you want a good grade, you'd better at least act like it's your favorite class." He winked again, the gesture directed at the entire class this time. This elicited a laugh from the kids. He turned to the blackboard and started writing.

"For those of you who haven't had the extreme pleasure of meeting me before now...I saw that gesture, Mr. Grady...my name is Mr. Sumner. I teach American History, World History and Current Affairs. I've been at Orleans High for six years...graduated from here myself. I have my degree from Notre Dame — go, Irish! — and am currently working on my Ph.D from same...online, in my spare time." He stopped writing, dropped the chalk, and turned to face the class, brushing chalk dust from his hands. "Now, I know it's your first day back, and it's way too early in the day for this stuff, but I'm getting paid to teach you something, so...who can tell me the significance of these names?"

He pointed toward the scribbles on the blackboard. The students stared blankly at the words he'd presented them with.

"C'mon! This is an easy one!" Mr. Sumner insisted. "These were all mentioned in the news in the past week."

"We were supposed to be watching the news?" a tall boy at the back of the room called out. "During summer vacation?"

"It helps, if you want to know what's going on in the world," Mr. Sumner said.

"That's what I watch *Potato Brain* for," the same boy joked, eliciting a laugh from most of his classmates.

Mr. Sumner grinned. "We'll get to that. There's some rather interesting political and sociological parallels in the popular cartoons of the day."

The kids groaned.

"I hate those stupid *Adventures of Potato Brain* cartoons," Karen commented. "They're lame." Several other girls nodded in agreement.

"Typical," Jeremy said. "Girls never get *Potato Brain*."

"I like *Potato Brain*," Moira commented. Jeremy whipped around to stare at her. She gazed back blandly. "My favorite episode is the one where he got trapped in that french fry factory, and Fairy Farty and Steve had to rescue him."

The boys laughed, while most of the girls merely rolled their eyes.

"That's my favorite, too," Jeremy commented quietly. He gave Moira an odd look, then turned toward the front of the room. "Mr. Sumner, are those the names of the people who were involved in that Wall Street scam this week?"

"Good guess, Jeremy, but, no," Mr. Sumner told him. "Anyone else?"

"Are they senators?" Braidy offered. "Or state representatives?"

"Nope. You're close, though."

Moira studied the six names written on the board. There was something familiar about them, but she couldn't quite put her finger on it. Where had she heard them before? Suddenly, inspiration struck.

"Those are the names of the characters in that new series, *Capitol Hill!*" she cried out. "They were talking about it on the news last night! A bunch of senators are ticked off about it, 'cause it doesn't make them look too bright." She laughed.

"Very good!" Mr. Sumner praised her. "Give the pink-haired lady a cigar! I'm sorry, I don't know your name?"

"Moira," she replied, grinning back at her new favorite teacher, "Moira Fitzgerald."

"New to the school?"

"Yeah, we moved here from Quincy this summer."

"Gotcha."

"But, Mr. Sumner," Braidy questioned, "what does a television series have to do with Current Affairs? I mean, I know it's supposed to be about our government, but it's really fiction, right?"

"True, Miss Attison. But we can learn a lot about our society from all aspects of the media, not just the news...which is more often than not at least half fiction, anyway," he finished wryly.

"That's what my mom says all the time!" Jeremy's friend said. "She won't even watch the national news anymore. Says they're all a bunch of liars."

"What do you think about that, folks?" Mr. Sumner asked. "Is the news media lying to us?"

The discussion continued, becoming rather heated at times. Moira joined in gleefully; this sort of debate was right up her alley. Soon she found herself the undisputed leader of the liberal sceptics, while Karen headed the more conservative class members. To her surprise, Jeremy backed her up on more than one issue. The students were actually disappointed when the bell rang, signaling the end of class. Slowly, they filed out into the hall.

"Thanks, Mr. Sumner."

"Yeah, thanks! That was cool!"

"Told you it would end up being your favorite class," Mr. Sumner replied smugly.

The kids laughed. Moira waved as she walked out. She stopped in the middle of the hall, suddenly realizing that she had no idea where to go for her next class. She looked around for Braidy, feeling a small spark of panic deep in her stomach.

"Lost, little girl?" a voice said behind her.

She whipped around to find herself face to face with a smiling Jeremy. She gulped.

"Um...yeah...don't quite have my bearings yet," she admitted in a low voice.

"What's your next class?"

"Physics, I think."

"Me, too," he said. "C'mon...I'll show you where it's at."

"Um...thanks!" Moira replied, totally flustered by this new, friendly incarnation of the boy. They walked together to the Physics classroom, engaging in light chitchat along the way.

He is being nice, Moira thought to herself. *And he's kinda cute. I guess he's okay, after all.*

When they reached Room 214, Jeremy held back slightly to allow Moira to enter first. Brody, who was also in the class with them, glanced up. The greeting he was about to call to his friend died on his lips as he stared in shock at Jeremy and his cousin chatting away like old buddies. Moira merely smiled back and took a seat. As she settled in for the next hour, she thought, *This school might not be so bad after all.*

* * * * *

"Jonathan! Hey, man, wait up!"

Jonathan Crenshaw waited for Devon to catch up with him, gesturing for his other friends to go on without him.

"Yo, Dev. What's up?"

"Nothing much. Haven't seen you since the regatta."

"Yeah, I've been pretty busy. We had that big fund raiser for the station, took up a lot of time," Jonathan said

"I saw you on it. With that Melody Hammond." The two young men strolled across campus as they talked. "Is she as stuck-up as she appears to be?"

Jonathan laughed. "Unfortunately, yes. But she's got great legs!"

Devon laughed in response. "Well, at least you had something nice to look at. Man, that pledge drive goes on forever!"

"You're telling me!" Jonathan yawned. "By the third day, I was having a tough time just staying awake. You wind up saying the same stupid crap over and over, with those annoying fake phone calls in the background..."

"The phones are fake?!" Devon exclaimed. "I thought that was people calling in to make donations."

"Some of it is real," Jonathan grinned, "but they add the sound of more phones ringing to encourage viewers to call in."

"Does that really work?"

"Apparently, it does," Jonathan scratched his neck. "Makes people feel guilty for not making donations themselves when they think a bunch of others are. Some sort of electronic peer pressure, I guess."

"Strange..." Devon mused, a smile hovering around his lips, "didn't bother me in the least." He grinned at his friend.

"Yeah, well, that's because you're such a cheapskate," Jonathan grinned back. "So, what were you watching?"

"The Dark Harbor concert," Devon told him.

"That was my favorite night! Were they tight, or what?!" Jonathan opened the door to the Pewter Spoon, a diner that was a favorite lunch spot for many of the students. Both he and Devon were greeted with calls and waves as they worked their way through the crowd to an empty table.

"It would be so slammin' to see them in person!" Devon shouted over the noise of the other students.

"See who?" Jonathan shouted back.

"Dark Harbor, man! They were totally awesome!"

"Oh, yeah...right!" Jonathan laughed at himself. "This okay?" He indicated a small table near the back of the restaurant.

"Sure." Devon grabbed a chair and sat down just as a pretty, young waitress approached them. Her long brown hair swung freely across her back, her generous mouth outlined in bright red. She smiled at Devon.

"Hi, Devon!" she said brightly.

"Hey, Patti!" he smiled up at her, slipping one arm around her tiny waist and pulling her close. "How are you, sweetheart?"

"Better now," she replied, leaning down to kiss him full on the lips. "I've missed you," she whispered. "You haven't been around much lately."

"Sorry, love," Devon said as he tactfully extricated himself from her embrace. "I've been ridiculously busy, what with school and work... listen..." he added quickly, taking note of the small frown lines that appeared on Patti's forehead, "...you doing anything Friday night? I thought maybe we could catch a movie, or something."

Patti brightened up immediately.

"I'd love to! What time?"

"I'll pick you up around seven... sound okay?"

"Perfect!" She got back to business. "So, what do you want to eat?"

"Give me the Philly steak with a side of beans. You, man?"

"Same...no peppers on the sandwich, though. And a Sam Adams Light."

"Coke for me," Devon added.

"Got it!" Patti said. Devon gave her a light pat on the bottom as she turned toward the kitchen. She responded with a smile and a wink over her shoulder.

"What?" Devon grinned at the expression on Jonathan's face.

"How many girls you stringing along, dude?" Jonathan asked, shaking his head in mixed wonder and exasperation at his friend's cavalier dating practices.

"I don't know...four or five...so what?"

"What if they find out?"

"Hey, I make no promises...that way they can't accuse me of breaking any!" Both men laughed. "Although, I gotta tell ya, man...I'd give 'em all up for a chance with that Callista Baines."

"Who?" Jonathan looked away. "Oh...that girl we met at the regatta? The one whose father is running for mayor?"

"That's the one!" Devon sighed. "Man, was she amazing, or what!"

"Not my type," Jonathan dismissed her quickly. "An Ice Princess like her could freeze you out real fast."

"Yeah, maybe, but think how much fun you could have getting her to melt!" Devon laughed.

Patti returned with their drinks. The conversation paused as both men quenched their thirst.

"Our waitress reminds me a lot of that cousin of yours...what's her name? Brenda? Bridget?" Jonathan commented a moment later.

"Braidy," Devon supplied.

"Yeah! That one. Kinda pretty, but way too quiet for my tastes."

"Good! She's too young for you, anyway," Devon stated.

"How old is she?" Jonathan asked.

"Seventeen. She's a senior in high school."

"That's not that young." Jonathan glanced casually around the room, nodding at several familiar faces. "Just four years difference. Not that I'm interested, mind you," he hastened to assure his companion.

"You sure seemed to hit it off with my sister," Devon said quietly, staring down at the table. "She's the same age as Braidy...only seventeen." He deliberately placed extra emphasis on the word "only".

Jonathan laughed, ignoring Devon's guarded warning. "That girl sure is something else! Doesn't believe in pulling her punches, does she...she's a blast! Who's that guy she's so hot for? Russ something?"

"I don't know...Moira's not dating anyone right now."

"She was anxious enough to see him, though," Jonathan said. "Seemed pretty ticked off when he ignored her. I felt kinda bad for her."

"I didn't notice," Devon replied, relaxing a little. It seemed Jonathan's interest in Moira was merely friendly, not romantically motivated. "I was too busy taking pictures."

"Shame that cousin of yours is such a wallflower," Jonathan mused. "I mean, she's a pretty girl, but if she doesn't learn to come out of her shell, no guy's gonna give her a second glance."

Devon stared at his friend in disbelief for a moment, then burst out laughing.

"What's so funny?" Jonathan demanded.

"Braidy?! Braidy Attison, a wallflower?! You're joking, right?"

"No...why? What do you mean?"

"Braidy is the most popular girl at Orleans Senior High, dude. Always has been. She's beautiful, and she's smart, and she's talented. She goes on more dates than I do! She is most definitely not shy!"

"She barely said two words to me," Jonathan stated.

"Maybe because you barely said two words to her, man. Braidy is not accustomed to doing the chasing...hell, she's never had to. Boys flock around her like moths to the flame. You're probably the only straight guy who hasn't fallen all over himself to get near her since she was five years old."

"You said she's smart?"

Devon nodded, reaching for the sandwich Patti had just set down in front of him. "Thanks, love. Yeah, man, real smart. Straight A's. She'll probably wind up being valedictorian."

"Thank you," Jonathan smiled at Patti. "And talented?" He spooned a large glob of baked beans into his mouth.

"Mmhmmm...." Devon swallowed. "She plays flute and piano... and she's the star of the girls' volleyball team...might even be the captain…I forget. You'd have to ask my mom." He took another huge bite of his sandwich. "Moira 'ates 'er," he managed to say around the beef and bread in his mouth.

"How come?"

"Braidy's always been better at everything…smarter, prettier, nicer… they've been at each other's throats for years…although it has been better since last summer…"

"Why since last summer?" Jonathan asked.

"Ummm…" Devon hesitated, not sure how to answer. He took another bite of his sandwich to give himself time to think. He hadn't known Jonathan the previous summer, when Moira, Braidy, and Brody had been kidnapped and taken to New York City. Of course, the fact that the crime had been committed by magicals, using magic, for evil magical purposes, made it that much harder to explain. He decided to take the easy way out. "…they spent some time together during summer break… somehow they managed to come to some sort of agreement …figured out how to tolerate each other…at least, in small doses. Of course, now that they're going to school together, that might change."

"This Braidy sounds pretty full of herself," Jonathan resumed the conversation after several minutes of uninterrupted feeding.

"Naw, not really," Devon told him. "I mean, yeah, she's got a lot of confidence…it's not like she doesn't know she's beautiful and all…but she doesn't usually flaunt it. She's pretty cool."

"So, then, why does Moira hate her?" Jonathan asked, grinning.

"Because she's a girl? Hell, I don't know. You figure it out!" Devon laughed. Jonathan joined him before giving his food his undivided attention. Devon followed suit. Their lunches quickly disposed of, the two friends paid the bill and left the diner, both headed for their next class.

"So Moira's started at her new school now?" Jonathan asked.

"Today. I hope she does okay."

"What do you mean? She seemed pretty bright to me."

"Oh, yeah. Moira's smart enough. She just doesn't make friends that easily."

"Your cousins will help her out with that, won't they? Introduce her to their friends...take her along to their usual hangouts..." He paused, then asked nonchalantly, "Where do the kids hang out in Orleans, anyway? Can't imagine they have that many places to choose from."

"Don't know, really. There's the Mall, I guess, in Barnstable...the Christmas Tree Shop... they have a music store and a book store in East Orleans...there's the usual fast food joints, and a Starbucks...and there's always the beach. At least until the weather turns. It's not exactly Boston, though."

"She'll do fine, Dev. She's got a lot of personality. I wouldn't worry about Moira, if I were you." Jonathan gave his friend an odd smile. The inference was lost on Devon, who noticed nothing strange about either Jonathan's expression or his tone. He glanced down at his watch.

"Damn! I'm gonna be late for class. Gotta run, man." Devon waved as he broke into a jog.

Jonathan stood for a moment, gazing after his young friend.

"No, Devon, Moira isn't the one you should be worried about," he murmured to himself, the odd smile still in place. "Not at all..."

* * * * *

"C'mon, Moir!"

"No, Brody! Stop bugging me about it!"

"What's the big deal?" Brody insisted. "I just want to give the girl a call."

"Like hell!" Moira snorted. "I'm no fool...you want to give her a lot more than just a call!"

"Well, now that you mention it, there are a few other things I had in mind..." Brody grinned. "But only if it's okay with her, I swear! Please, Moira?"

"Why do you want to go out with my best friend, tell me that!"

"Because she's beautiful! D'uh!" Brody laughed.

"I knew that, stupid!" Moira punched her cousin in the arm. "But why does it have to be my best friend?"

"Hey, you're the one that invited her to the Fourth of July party."

"So, it's my fault, is that what you're saying?" Moira gave Brody a disgusted look. Brody merely grinned in reply. Moira sighed, exasperated. "Oh, all right! But I'm asking Lucia first. If it's okay with her, I'll give you her number tomorrow, okay?"

Brody dropped to his knees in the middle of the cafeteria, raised his arms up over his head, and bowed to the floor. "I worship you, oh great and powerful Moira! My fate is in your hands!"

Everyone around them burst into laughter. Moira rolled her eyes. "You are such a dork..."

* * * * *

"Don't be absurd!" Alex laughed, but there was no amusement in the sound. "Jonathan is totally trustworthy, I assure you."

"Then why has he not already delivered the Attison girl?" Morty asked petulantly. "She'll be eighteen in April...that doesn't leave us much time."

"Jonathan assures me that we will have the girl under our protection shortly," Alex reassured the other man. "This project requires patience and finesse. He can hardly barge in and simply kidnap the girl, now can he?"

"Why can't he?"

"What?"

"Why can't he?" Morty repeated. "Just kidnap the little brat. Sure would save a lot of time and trouble."

Alex's eyes narrowed. "We tried that last year, remember? It didn't exactly work like we'd planned, did it," he said, his tone heavy with sarcasm. Morty squirmed in his seat. "Besides, I've realized that the results will be much more positive if young Braidy can be persuaded to join us, rather than forced."

"How do you mean?"

"If she chooses to work with us, the experiment is much more likely to succeed than if I have to coerce her into using her powers."

"If she chooses..." Morty looked puzzled. "How the hell are you going to pull that off?"

"Simple," Alex stated. "Once she falls in love with Jonathan, she'll be putty in his hands. Girls that age always are. He will then convince her of the righteousness of our agenda, and she will gladly combine her powers with mine for the good of mankind. All to please the man she adores."

"What if she doesn't fall in love with him? What if he's not her type? What then?" Morty insisted.

Alex laughed again...this time with amusement. "My dear friend, Jonathan Crenshaw is exactly the type of young man a girl like Braidy Attison would fall for. Just because he's not your type..."

Morty turned bright red. "That's not what I meant..." he muttered angrily.

"Forget it." Alex waved his hand dismissively. "Don't worry about Jonathan. He'll do his part. He has good reason to."

"What do you mean?" Morty glanced up, suspicious.

"Calm down, old friend," Alex smiled reassuringly. "All I meant is that our Mr. Crenshaw will want to keep me happy, now won't he? Otherwise, certain...shall we say...perks might be withdrawn?"

"Oh...yeah...that..." Morty nodded in agreement. "Are you sure she doesn't mind being used like that?"

Alex's smile turned cold and icy. "*Used?*" he repeated quietly. Morty gulped. "Hardly. It was her idea in the first place. No, Morty, she doesn't mind at all."

"What if she falls for him, as well?"

"That's not likely to happen, now is it," Alex stated, one eyebrow raised. "She has never given her heart easily. In fact, I feel quite confident in claiming to be the only person she has ever truly loved... aside from herself, that is." He stood up quickly. Morty pried himself out of his own chair and followed Alex to the door. "Stop worrying, my friend. Everything is under control."

Alex walked Morty past his secretary's desk and waited until the elevator doors closed.

"Hold all my calls, Miss Shigati," he instructed his secretary, closing the door to his office. He strode over to the plate glass window and stared out at the Boston skyline, a frown darkening his handsome face.

"Yes, Morty, you can stop worrying," he murmured. "I'm worried enough for both of us."

* * * * *

"You can't be serious," Moira said into the phone. "You don't really want to go out with that loser cousin of mine, do you?"

"Why not?" Lucia replied with a giggle. *"I told you, I think he's cute. And nice."*

"Man oh man," Moira grumbled. "You're friends with someone for twelve years, think you know them inside and out, and then they go and dump a whammy on ya!"

"C'mon, Moir, what can it hurt? You've always liked Brody, haven't you? You've always said he's pretty funny."

"Yeah," Moira agreed reluctantly, "I guess so. It's just...hell, girl, he's my cousin! And you're my best friend!"

"So?"

"So...oh, all right! Just don't say I didn't warn you!" Moira stated, her tone dire. "I'll give him your number tomorrow."

"Thanks, chica! Hey, I gotta go. Gotta help Mama with supper."

"No problema, girlfriend. Call me tomorrow?"

"You got it! Adios!"

"Bye!"

Moira flipped her cell phone closed, stuck it in the pocket of her jeans, and pulled out her journal...

August 22

What a day! You know, it didn't turn out half bad. It was definitely better than I expected it to be.

Mr. Sumner seems pretty cool. He treated us like adults, not kids. He actually seemed interested in what we had to say. And Ms. Kane is great! Creative Writing is DEFINITELY my favorite class! She's actually been published! That is so cool! Okay, so it was some sort of lame poetry collection...I never have really gotten into poetry much...but, hey! Published is published...right? LOL Although, I guess song lyrics are a type of poetry, and I really get into those. At least, the ones worth listening to...

Mr. Knup is boring...but what can you expect from a Physics teacher? Mrs. Partridge looks like her name...short and fat! LOL Oops, better watch it...I don't have much room to talk. She's the perfect Home Ec teacher. She really gets off on cooking and cleaning and all that. Mr. Sinter was pretty quiet...the typical computer geek. Guess that's why he teaches computer classes! LOL I'm not sure about Ms. Brigham yet. She seems nice enough, but tough. Like when she was working with the soprano section and the guys in the tenor section were messing around, she came down on them pretty hard. I'm not too crazy about that song she's having us learn, but at least it's not something totally lame, like Handel's *Messiah*. Braidy said she's amazing on keyboards...

All in all, not a bad start. I missed Lucia and Leslie like crazy, but the day went so fast, I didn't have much time to think about them. And at least Braidy was trying to be helpful, showing me around and all. And what's up with Jeremy? I thought he hated me! He sure gave me a dirty look when I first walked into class. Okay, maybe, just maybe, I gave him good reason to. I wonder why he changed his mind about me? Was it just because I said I like *Potato Brain*? That would be a pretty stupid reason to start liking someone. But, you know, he is a guy...LOL

It felt so weird, telling Lucia all about my day, talking about teachers and kids she's never even seen, not to mention having her tell me what everybody I know was doing while I wasn't there. It's almost like being out sick for a day, except I know I won't have the chance to go back and catch up. The new school is okay...most of the teachers are all right ...even some of the kids seem kinda cool...but it's not the same. I miss my school, my friends, my world. Why do things have to change? And now, if Lucia starts dating Brody, things are gonna change even more.

I just don't get it. Why on earth would Lucia want to go

out with a dork like Brody? She's so pretty, and smart, and sweet...she could do way better than him. Although, he isn't all bad, I suppose. He is pretty funny...and his looks have improved, especially since he started wearing contacts instead of those awful glasses. And he's tall... Lucia likes 'em tall. But still...Oh well, no accounting for taste, I guess.

I wonder if Braidy is dating anybody. There's always plenty of guys hanging around her, but she doesn't seem particularly interested in any of them. It's kinda freaky, when you think about it. I mean, it's like she has to have the adoration of the multitude, but she's not willing to commit to any one of them. Granted, I wouldn't complain if I had dozens of guys falling all over themselves to get next to me, but I'd sure as hell go out with one or two of them...at least now and then. I can't remember Braidy ever having an actual boyfriend... just loads of admirers. Hmmmm...makes you wonder...is she really picky, or is she actually afraid of guys, deep down inside? Maybe I should ask Dr. Freud... yeah, like he had a clue! LOL

Oh well...time to get the homework done. At least the teachers took it easy on us today. Something tells me that won't last for long...

Chapter Nine:

Cupid's Dart

Desmond strode into campaign headquarters late in the afternoon.

"Hello, all!" he called out to the numerous workers scattered throughout the spacious office. "Hello, Kathy...How are you, Scott?... How's that thesis coming, Richard?" He greeted several individuals by name as he made his way to the small, glass-walled cubicle at the back of the room. Callista stood in the door of the cubicle, watching her father work the room, a small half smile on her lips.

"Hello, Father," she greeted him, reaching up to kiss him on the cheek. "Busy day?"

"Not as busy as yours, I would hazard to guess," he replied, returning the kiss. "Did the new numbers come in yet?"

"Half an hour ago," Callista told him, walking back into the cubicle and sitting down. "I've only just started going over them."

"Well, let's see what we've got." Desmond followed her, closing the door behind him. He took the chair behind the desk and reached for the latest poll. "Let's not overdo the loving, affectionate daughter act, shall we, my dear?" he said as he studied the poll sheet. "It's beginning to look staged." He glanced up sharply.

Callista raised an eyebrow. "Why, whatever do you mean, Father Dear?" she asked sarcastically. "Are you implying that I am not a loving, affectionate daughter?"

Desmond laughed, short and harsh. "Loving, perhaps, but hardly affectionate. You haven't kissed me in years."

"Perhaps I'm making up for lost time," Callista replied, a cold sneer marring her beautiful face. "Of course, you haven't kissed me in years, either."

Desmond laughed again. "Now, be honest, Callista — would you have wanted me to?"

Callista's sneer turned into a slightly more genuine smile. "Probably not," she admitted. "After all, public displays of affection are hardly your style. Or mine. So what do you think?" she asked, indicating the poll sheet.

"Looks good," Desmond commented, glancing down once again at the sheet of paper in his hand. "We've gained six points in the past month. Wellsley is barely four points ahead, with two months left before the election. We've been gaining on her steadily for the past three months. Looks to me like we have a good chance of winning this thing..."

"Of course we're going to win. After all, we have the contingency plan to fall back on."

"I'd rather not use that unless we have to," Desmond said. "I'd like to be elected without having to resort to magical means."

"Why?" Callista questioned, sincerely puzzled. "All that matters is that we win. How we make that happen is immaterial."

"Not for me," Desmond told her, standing up and turning his back to gaze out of the window. "It would mean so much more to me to know that the voters of Boston chose me for the job."

"What difference would it make? If we win, we win. Once you're in office, we can put our plans into action, and life will be better for everyone. We're doing this for their benefit, Father."

"I know, I know," Desmond sighed. "I'd simply feel better about it if we had the full support of the constituents."

"It will be for their own good," Callista dismissed the discussion with a wave of her hand. "Besides, there is no way to guarantee a victory without magic. You had no problem using magic to capsize those women at the regatta, merely to gain yourself some positive press time."

Desmond spun around. "And I've regretted it ever since! It could have been a terrible mistake, Callista!" he exclaimed. "If either of those women had been killed..."

"You were there to make sure that didn't happen," Callista stated blandly. "Everything was under control. Of course, it would have been better if Russell hadn't suspected anything."

"Don't remind me!" Desmond ran a hand through his hair, his expression troubled. "I truly wonder if he will ever understand what it is we are trying to achieve."

"He will, Father," she soothed him. "I've already told you, once he sees the good we can do for the community, he'll be eager to join us."

Desmond grunted, obviously not convinced.

"Come, Father, once you become mayor, none of this will matter. You know perfectly well, the end always justifies the means."

"Yes, you're right," Desmond admitted. He sat back down. "So, let's go over it once again. You're certain we have enough people on board to adjust the results, if it proves necessary?"

"Positive," Callista stated emphatically. "At least one election official at each polling place throughout the city. If you are more than five points behind in the exit polls at noon, each one of them will readjust the voting computers at their location."

"How much of a readjustment are we talking about? One for one?"

"No, that would be too obvious," Callista said. "Quinn and I thought every third or fourth ballot would be less conspicuous. We don't need Wellsley demanding a recount. That would merely complicate matters."

"So throughout the afternoon, every third vote cast for Wellsley will actually be recorded in my favor. In addition to my own votes, that is."

"Yes."

"Will that be enough to ensure the election?"

"It should be. We've run the numbers several times, under numerous scenarios. If voter turnout is consistent with past elections, that should give you a comfortable margin of approximately ten to fifteen thousand votes. Enough to win handily without raising suspicions of tampering."

"All right," Desmond leaned back in his chair. "I want it understood that we resort to this plan only if my numbers look bad, is that clear?"

"Of course, Father," Callista drawled. "Our people have very specific instructions, I've seen to that personally. Everything will go exactly as planned."

* * * * *

"Well, hello there!"

Braidy turned around — and momentarily forgot to breathe. Jonathan Crenshaw was standing directly behind her and her friends in line, smiling broadly, his hand held out in greeting. Numbly, Braidy shook hands with the handsome young man, praying desperately that he couldn't hear her heart pounding.

"It's Braidy, isn't it?" he said. "Braidy Attison? Devon's cousin."

"Yes," Braidy managed to reply, her voice low and husky. She swallowed nervously. Becky and Jan looked over at their friend, puzzled.

"Your change, Braidy," Becky murmured as the Starbuck's clerk held out her hand.

"What? Oh...yeah...thanks..." Braidy took the change and stuffed it into her purse.

"I'm Jonathan Crenshaw. We met on the Fourth...at that barbecue... remember?"

"Vaguely," Braidy replied, hoping she sounded as uninterested as she intended to. This time it was Karen's turn to stare at Braidy, as confused as the other girls by Braidy's tone.

"There were a lot of people there that day," Jonathan said. "I don't blame you for not remembering me. Anyway, it's good to see you again. How's it going?"

"Fine," Braidy stated shortly, turning her back to accept the cup of coffee she'd ordered from the clerk. "We ready, girls?" she asked her bewildered friends. "Goodbye, Mr...I'm sorry? What was your name again?" she asked, her head high, her back stiff.

"Jonathan...Jonathan Crenshaw," Jonathan replied, smiling, apparently not put off in the least by Braidy's attitude. "See you around, Braidy," he called after her as she practically ran from the store. The others scrambled to catch up.

"What the hell was that all about?" Karen demanded.

"Nothing," Braidy said coldly.

"You totally dissed that guy!" Becky said. "What's the problem? I thought he was pretty cute...and he seemed really nice!"

"I barely know him."

"You didn't even introduce..." Jan began, but Braidy interrupted her.

"Just drop it, okay?" Braidy rounded on her friends. "It's not important!" She marched to the car, her back straight as a board. Damned if she was going to give Jonathan Crenshaw the satisfaction of seeing how he had flustered her. She had her pride, after all. A pride that would have plummeted dramatically had she glanced back to see the triumphant smile spread across his face at that moment.

"Nice act, girl," he murmured to himself. "Phase Two begins."

* * * * *

"So...um...listen...the reason I was calling..." Brody stammered into the phone. There was a moment of silence.

"Yes?"

"I...um...I was wondering...that is..." he cleared his throat, "are you...um...doing anything Saturday night?"

"Well...Moira and I were thinking about getting together," Lucia replied. *"We see so little of each other these days, but..."*

"Oh...yeah...well..."

"What did you have in mind?"

"Oh, nothing much...I just thought you might like to catch a movie...grab a bite to eat... something like that..." Brody said. "But if you and Moira already have plans..."

"It's nothing definite," Lucia said. *"I'd like to go out with you."*

"Yeah?" Brody's tone brightened substantially. "Great!" He hesitated. "But what about Moira? I don't want her to get pissed at you...or me either, for that matter!" he laughed.

Lucia joined in his laughter. *"That's a given! Hey, what about a double date? Do you have a friend Moira might like to go with? It could be fun!"*

"Um..." Brody was very glad that he and Lucia were on the phone, so she couldn't see the expression on his face. The problem wasn't in finding someone Moira would want to go with; the problem was in talking one of his friends into going with Moira. Then a thought occurred — Jeremy had been almost friendly toward Moira that week. Perhaps he'd consider putting up with the girl for one evening — to help out a buddy. "Actually, there is someone I could ask. Can I get back to you tomorrow? Let you know for sure?"

"Okay! Should I say anything to Moira?"

"No, I'll talk to her at school — after I check with my friend."

"Fine. Well...um...I'd better get my homework finished. Talk to you tomorrow?"

"You bet! It was great talking to you!"

"You too! Bye!"

"Bye!"

Brody ended the call, then quickly dialed Jeremy's cell phone. A few minutes later, the plans were set.

"No problem, man," Jeremy assured him. *"I've been thinking about asking her out anyway. This gives me the perfect excuse."*

"You were?!"

Jeremy laughed. *"Don't sound so shocked, dude!"*

"This is Moira we're talking about, right? My cousin, Moira Fitzgerald?"

"Yes! Turns out, she's pretty cool after all. I mean, we're kinda getting to be friends, so..."

"Hey, whatever floats your boat!"

"So what's Moira's number?"

Brody rattled off the seven digits, then said goodbye. Tossing his phone onto his desk, he lay back on the bed, his fingers laced behind his head, feeling rather pleased with himself. Okay, so he hadn't exactly handled the Jan situation with the greatest tact, but that was over and done with. And now, one of the most beautiful girls he'd ever laid eyes on had agreed to go out with him Saturday night. So he'd have to put up with Moira as well…so what? Besides, she'd be Jeremy's problem, not his. He'd be focusing all of his attention on the lovely Lucia. He sighed happily, picturing himself sharing a particularly passionate goodnight kiss with his soon-to-be date.

"That's some cloud you're floating on, son," Phil commented, smiling in at the door.

Brody jerked out of his reverie, abruptly returning to terra firma. "Oh! Hi, Dad," he said as he sat up. "I didn't know you were home."

"Just got in,"

"How was practice?"

"Pretty good. I've got some really solid players this year."

"Great! Um…Dad?"

"Yes, son?"

"I hope you don't mind that I never went out for soccer. It's just…I mean…" Brody stammered, his face a little pink.

"That's okay, Brody," Phil said. "I know swimming is your thing. I never expected you to like everything I do. You're your own person."

"Thanks, Dad!" Brody breathed a sigh of relief. He'd never want to disappoint his father, but swimming was the sport he truly loved. He enjoyed soccer, but it could never be the same for him. He was relieved to know his father didn't mind.

"By the way," Phil continued, "did I just hear you talking to Jeremy about asking Moira for a date?"

"Yeah…why?"

"Jeremy…and Moira?" Phil asked skeptically. "I thought he hated her."

"He did," Brody told him. "But I guess, now that they're in school together, she's started to grow on him. You know, I think she may be growing on me as well. I mean, I know she can be a total pain, but she's a lot smarter than I thought. She's funny...and she stands up for what she believes in. That's pretty cool."

Phil smiled crookedly. "Will wonders never cease. I guess that means there's hope for her yet?"

Brody laughed. "Yeah, she's not half bad after all."

"Your aunt and uncle will be very happy to hear that," Phil called over his shoulder as he left the room. "Don't forget your homework."

"Already done!" Brody called back. He snapped his fingers and music blared from the computer speakers across the room.

"TOO LOUD!" floated down the hall. Brody rolled his eyes, wiggled two fingers in the general direction of the computer and the volume decreased substantially. Humming tunelessly, he closed his eyes and returned to his daydreams.

* * * * *

Braidy dropped her backpack onto the carpet and sat down at the large round table. The library was mostly empty at that time on a Saturday. Exactly the way Braidy liked it. She had a paper due the following Tuesday and couldn't afford a lot of interruptions. She pulled out her notebook, turned to a blank page, opened the large encyclopedia she'd taken from the shelf, and started reading, searching for the information she needed to complete the project.

She'd been at it for more than thirty minutes when a kink in her back forced her to straighten and stretch. Glancing around the library, she spotted an all-too familiar face bent over an impressive pile of books at a table nearby.

"Oh, no!" she whispered. Hoping he hadn't seen her, Braidy quickly began packing up her materials. But it was too late.

"What do you know...we meet again!" Jonathan said, smiling down at her.

Damn! He moves quick! Braidy thought to herself as she slowly gazed upward. “Hel... hello,” she stammered. “How...how are you?”

“Good!” Jonathan replied, sitting down next to her. “You mind?”

Braidy shook her head, torn between wanting him near and wanting to run away as fast as she could.

”What are you doing here?” Braidy asked. “Don’t you live in Boston?”

“Yeah, but I’m working part-time for the PBS station in Hyannis,” Jonathan informed her. “I fill in whenever one of their regular reporters wants a day off. They need me to cover for them fairly often, so I’m back and forth a lot. After I got here yesterday, though, I remembered some research I needed to do for a story I’m working on, so I decided it wouldn’t hurt to spend a couple of hours in the library. I’m not due on the air until eleven. What about you? What’s a beautiful girl like you doing inside a gloomy library on a gorgeous day like this?” he asked, reaching for a nearby tome. “*The Failure Of Desert Storm*,” he read the title aloud. “Sounds like some pretty heavy stuff! What’s this one?” Jonathan reached for a second book. “*Afghanistan And The Taliban...* studying Mideastern diplomacy, are we?”

“It’s for my Current Affairs class,” Braidy told him. “I have a paper due on Tuesday.”

“Current Affairs?” Jonathan sounded skeptical. “Didn’t all this stuff happen ten, twenty years ago?”

“The actual events, yes,” Braidy agreed, “but the effects are still being felt today, don’t you agree?”

“I suppose,” he said, pushing the books away, obviously uninterested in the political upheavals of the Middle East. He leaned in close, smiling. “Listen, you about finished here? I thought maybe we could get a cup of coffee. You know what they say — all work and no play...”

"No...um...no, thank you," Braidy stammered, flustered by his nearness. His aftershave smelled of lemons and spices, with just a hint of something sweet. She turned away, trying desperately to ignore her body's instinctive reaction to him. "I...I have to...to go."

"Right now? Why?"

"I...um...I have a date," she lied, silently cursing her cheeks for choosing that moment to turn bright pink. She never was a good liar.

"Well, in that case...You don't want to keep your boyfriend waiting." Jonathan moved even closer, whispering into her ear. "Guys hate that, you know."

His breath on her neck sent a shiver down Braidy's back. Almost against her will, she found herself staring into his eyes. He was so close that the slightest movement would have brought their lips into contact. A sigh escaped her. He held her gaze for one brief, excruciatingly lovely moment. Then he stood up abruptly. She blinked, crashing suddenly down to earth again.

"Have fun tonight," he said in a dismissive tone as he walked away.

Braidy didn't move for several seconds, trying to regain her composure. Then she leaped to her feet, grabbed her things, and ran from the library, her cheeks burning.

* * * * *

"That had to hurt."

Lucia's laughter rang out as Brody delivered the punch line of his joke, Jeremy joining in. Moira cracked a half-smile, trying to get into the spirit of the evening. After all, things weren't all bad. Brody and Lucia were obviously having a wonderful time. Brody was at his most witty and charming. He hadn't done or said anything remotely embarrassing all evening, and even Moira had to admit that he was looking rather handsome. An opinion that Lucia obviously agreed with — her eyes sparkled, her cheeks were flushed with excitement, and she hadn't stopped smiling since Brody had helped her into the car.

Lucia was happy, Brody was in his glory, Jeremy was being friendly, polite, courteous. So what was wrong with her? Moira frowned, exasperated with herself. She knew why she was uncomfortable — that was the problem. Had it been only a case of first date jitters, she could have dealt with it easily. After all, she genuinely liked Jeremy. He was turning out to be pretty cool — and he was kind of hot as well. For a guy with blond hair, that is. No, the only problem with Jeremy was that he wasn't Russ.

Moira gave herself a mental shake. *Stop that!* she thought. Russ had made it quite clear he wasn't interested. She hadn't heard a word from him since the fiasco at the regatta. *Good riddance! Who needs him? There's plenty more fish in the sea.* Moira forced a smile onto her face and joined in the conversation.

"How's your sushi?" Jeremy leaned over to ask.

"Good!" Moira replied. "So...um...you hear the new song by Roadkill?"

"No! I didn't know they had a new CD out!"

"Oh, man! It's killer!"

"No pun intended, right?" Jeremy grinned at her.

Moira stared at him, momentarily nonplussed, then burst into laughter as she realized what she had said. As they continued to banter back and force, she felt the tension in her shoulders slowly seep away. Maybe the evening was going to turn out okay after all.

* * * * *

Braidy walked slowly along the shoreline, her mind racing, her emotions in utter turmoil. All she could think about was Jonathan

Crenshaw — his face, his hair, his eyes, his hands, his...everything. A shiver ran through her. The guy had definitely gotten to her, but she couldn't explain why. Not even to herself. She'd never felt this way about any boy before. Oh sure, she'd had her share of crushes over the years — she smiled slightly at the memory of a certain red-haired boy she'd dated briefly two years earlier — but they'd all been short-lived, and easily recovered from. Something told her that whatever it was she was feeling for Jonathan was much more serious, more intense — and it scared her. He scared her.

Braidy sighed. Staring out over the dark, restless sea, she tried to think logically about the situation. What was it about Jonathan Crenshaw that had gotten so deep under her skin? Yes, he was very good looking — light brown curls that barely touched his collar, bright blue eyes, a slender yet muscular build...although he was rather short. He couldn't be more than an inch taller than Braidy herself. And his nose was slightly crooked, as if he'd broken it when he was younger. But his smile...Jonathan's smile could make her heart stop beating. It promised delights she'd only dreamed of up to now, while at the same time hinting at mysteries she could barely imagine. And when he looked at her, that enigmatic smile playing across his lips, it felt as if he was stripping her very soul bare. Her breath would catch in her throat, her heart would pound frantically, her knees shake, her stomach clench. Her mouth would go dry and every cohesive thought would fly out of her brain, irretrievable. She felt...she felt...helpless in his presence. As if she no longer had any control over her own actions. As if she was nothing more than a puppet — and he was the puppeteer. But why?!

The tears took Braidy by surprise, welling up without warning and pouring down her cheeks as she began to sob. Her desire — her need — for Jonathan was like a physical ache inside her chest. She wanted to be with him more than she'd ever wanted anything, and yet, she was afraid of him as well. She was afraid of the effect he seemed to have on her. She'd always prided herself on being in control...but when Jonathan was around, she lost all power over her emotions, her reactions, even her instincts...all of which told her to stay the hell away from the guy. She knew, somehow, deep down in her gut, that Jonathan Crenshaw was bad news. He had heartbreaker written all over him. She'd be a fool to get involved with him and she knew it. So try telling her heart that.

Angrily, she swiped at her wet cheeks, willing her sobs under control. She was not going to let this ridiculous obsession take over her life! Jonathan Crenshaw meant nothing to her! He was merely a passing fancy, a schoolgirl crush she would laugh about in years to come. She would get over this...she had to get over this...

"Lovely night for a walk, isn't it?"

Braidy gasped and spun around. Her resolutions of a moment ago melted away instantaneously. Giving in to the inevitable, she walked slowly across the sand to where Jonathan stood in the moonlight, smiling...

* * * * *

"You should have seen him! The ski went one direction, the rope went another, one leg went left, the other went right, and his arms were flailing around like a couple of windmills! It was the funniest thing I've ever seen!"

Moira was laughing so hard, she could barely breathe. Lucia was in a similar condition in the front seat of the car, sitting next to Brody.

"Yeah, well, you wouldn't have been exactly the picture of grace yourself, pal!" Brody laughed back at his friend. "I didn't have a chance against the wake from that damn cruiser! And it hurt! Like hell!"

"Aw, poor baby," Moira teased, wiping a pretend tear of sympathy from her eye.

"Did it?" Lucia asked, her laughter dampened slightly by concern. "Did you get hurt?"

"It was agony!" Brody exclaimed, playing it for all he was worth. "My whole left side was raw where the life belt scraped me...the water stung like crazy!"

"So what did you do?"

"I pulled the boat around," Jeremy told Lucia, "and picked him up." He started laughing again. "Remember how much trouble you had getting into the boat, man?"

"I remember!" Brody grimaced at the memory. "And you weren't much help!"

"Sorry," Jeremy grinned. "I was having too much fun watching you. It looked like you were auditioning for the Keystone Cops or something!"

"Why? What did he do?" Moira asked, still laughing.

"Let's see...he fell back into the water three or four times as he tried to climb up the ladder...then, when he finally got one foot over the gunwale, the other one caught on the top rung and he lost his balance... you tumbled into the bottom of the boat, arms and legs everywhere, yelling like a scalded cat!" Jeremy laughed.

"It wasn't that funny," Brody groused as the girls continued giggling at Jeremy's description. "Oh, yeah, and what does this genius do when we get back to the house?!" he continued, glaring at his friend through the rearview mirror. "He pulls out this can of Solarcaine and starts spraying it at me, right where the skin had peeled away! That crap is pure alcohol!!"

"I was just...trying...to help!" Jeremy gasped between laughs. "It says right on the can... that stuff is...supposed to be great...on cuts and scrapes...He started...jumping up and...down... screaming at the top... of his lungs...I had to chase him...all over the house!"

"Stop! Stop! My stomach hurts!" Moira begged, tears of glee running down her face. "Oh, man!" she sighed delightedly. "To have been a fly on the wall..."

"Moira!" Lucia cried. "He could have been badly hurt!" She slipped her arm into Brody's, all sympathy.

"I was lucky it wasn't much worse," Brody said, trying to sound serious. "I could have suffered permanent damage."

"Oh, so that explains it!" giggled Moira.

"I bet it was a long time before you went waterskiing again," Lucia said, giving the still giggling Moira a dirty look.

"Naw," Brody said, grinning, "we went back out the next day!"

Both girls squealed. Lucia punched Brody in the arm.

"And here I was, feeling all sorry for you!" she protested as she started to slide to the other side of the car. Brody grabbed her hand and pulled her back.

"Yeah, I kinda enjoyed that," he murmured, smiling at her.

Lucia blushed prettily, but stayed where Brody had placed her. Moira rolled her eyes, started to make a snide remark, then caught the look Jeremy was giving her. Blushing profusely as well, she shut her mouth with a snap and stared pointedly out of the window, trying to ignore her rapidly speeding pulse. A moment later, Brody parked the car in the driveway of Lucia's house.

"Here we are," he said, unnecessarily. All four teens suddenly felt shy and nervous. This was the moment on any first date when the boys were planning frantically...and the girls were wondering just what those plans might be...if they weren't making plans of their own, that is. The silence stretched awkwardly for several seconds, then Brody cleared his throat.

"I'll...um...I'll walk you up, okay?" he said to Lucia. She nodded, a small smile on her lips.

"Goodnight, Moir," she said softly, glancing back at her friend. "Call me tomorrow?"

"Yeah, 'night, Luce," Moira replied gruffly. Her nerves weren't eased any by the whispered instructions she overheard Jeremy give to Brody as the latter climbed out of the car.

"Take your time, dude..."

Moira stared out of the window, studiously avoiding Jeremy's gaze, which seemed to be burning a hole in the back of her head. Her heart was pounding, her palms were sweaty, and her stomach felt as if several dozen Mexican jumping beans were having a dance contest in it. But she was damned if she'd let Jeremy see that.

Jeremy slipped an arm around Moira's shoulders and pressed his thigh against hers. Her resolution of a moment before flew right out the window as he gently turned her toward him.

"This..." Moira's voice squeaked. Embarrassed, she cleared her throat and tried again, still not looking at Jeremy's face. "This was fun, wasn't it? I really liked the movie. We'll have to do this again some..."

"Moira," he interrupted her, smiling gently, "stop talking."

She finally looked up a split second before his lips met hers.

"Oh!" she sighed...and closed her eyes.

Brody returned to the car some time later, smiling broadly and whistling, obviously pleased with himself and the events of the evening. His grin grew when he saw what was happening in the back seat. Clearing his throat loudly to give the other couple warning, he pulled open the driver's side door and climbed behind the steering wheel, slamming the door loudly. Glancing in the rearview mirror, he saw that his arrival had had no effect whatsoever on the others' activities.

"Don't mind me," he said, still grinning.

Moira's voice floated up to him. "Shut up and drive, will ya..."

* * * * *

August 27

WOW!!!!!!!!!!!!!!!!!!!!!!!!!!!!!!!!!!!!!!!

* * * * *

"See you soon," Jonathan whispered, barely brushing the back of Braidy's hand with his lips.

Braidy shivered at his touch, his first of the evening. Smiling up at her from the bottom of the steps, he backed away, then turned, and disappeared into the darkness. She stared after him, more confused than ever. After a moment, she gave herself a little shake and went inside.

"There you are!" Caroline exclaimed when Braidy mounted the stairs to the family room. "I was getting ready to call out the Coast Guard."

"I just went for a walk, Mom," Braidy said softly.

"Did I hear you talking to someone?" Phil asked from behind the book he was reading.

"Um...yeah... I ran into Jonathan...he walked me home..."

"Jonathan..?"

"Jonathan Crenshaw...Devon's friend...he was here on the Fourth," Braidy reminded her mother.

"Oh, yes! Now I remember," Caroline said. "What was he doing here? I thought he lived in Boston."

"He does. But he also works for the PBS station out of Hyannis sometimes. Apparently, they needed him this weekend."

"I see. So, what did he want?"

"Nothing," Braidy said. "He saw me walking and decided to say hello."

"You're not thinking of going out with him, are you?" Phil asked, lowering his book. "I don't think your mother and I could allow that. He's too old for you."

"I just ran into him, Dad. He's never even asked me out. I'm tired. I'm going to bed. Goodnight," she ended the conversation abruptly, kissing her mother on the cheek. "Goodnight, Dad."

Phil returned to his book, satisfied. Caroline, however, watched her daughter closely as she left the room, a troubled look in her eyes.

"Phil."

"Hmmmm...."

"Does Braidy seem...okay to you?"

"What..." Phil glanced up, puzzled. "What do you mean?"

"She just...she doesn't seem herself lately."

"How so?"

"I don't know, exactly," Caroline admitted. "She seems...quiet... preoccupied...something ...I'm not sure...just different."

"She is seventeen, sweetheart. Don't most girls go through phases like this?"

"I guess," Caroline sighed. "Maybe that is all it is. I hope that's all it is..." she murmured to herself, not completely convinced.

* * * * *

August 28

Now that's what I call some serious suck-face!!!

Sorry I couldn't go into more detail last night...I had to

come back down to earth first! LOL

So that's what kissing is supposed to feel like. Not bad... not bad at all! I could get used to that real fast...And Jeremy was really cool about it...not all handsy like that turd Brad Mulligan...but a real gentleman. I mean, it was great! Sexy, and exciting, and all that. But not once did I have to worry about what he was doing. I was able to just relax and enjoy myself.

Jeremy asked me to go out with him again. I said yes. I know! I know! I still haven't resolved my feelings for Russ, but what the hell...a girl can't wait around forever, ya know? Besides, Russ has gotten me pretty ticked off these days. I mean, if he really liked me, if he really wanted to be my friend, why did he give me the brush-off at the regatta? And why hasn't he called me since? Okay, so I haven't called him either, but...

Besides, Russ and I are only friends. It's not like we're dating or something. I mean, I like him and everything, but it's no big deal. He's not even that good looking. He's just a guy...and there's loads of those around...Russ is just one of the many. Nothing special, just a guy, like all the others. I was getting pretty silly about him, I guess. Glad that's over now...

Chapter Ten:

Temptation Strikes

Devon strode into the noisy newsroom, his camera slung over his shoulder. Several feet away from the desk he shared with one of the junior reporters on staff, he came to an abrupt halt. In a chair in front of the desk, her long legs crossed gracefully at the ankle, her silky blond hair thrown over her shoulders, sat Callista Baines, utterly and disdainfully oblivious to the many stares of the surrounding men. Totally bewildered by her unexpected appearance, Devon stepped forward.

"Hel...hello?" he said hesitantly.

Callista spun around in the chair, looked up at him, and smiled. Devon forgot to breathe.

"Hello!" she greeted him brightly. "You're Devon Fitzgerald, aren't you? We met at the regatta."

"Um...uh...yeah...yes..." Devon cleared his throat, "yes, we did, Miss Baines. How...how are you?" He walked around to the other side of the desk and sat down himself, astounded that she had remembered him. Callista continued to smile. She turned sideways, draping one slender white arm over the back of the chair.

"I'm quite well, thank you. And you?"

"Good! Good…um…is there something I can help you with?"

"There certainly is!" Callista replied with a light, tinkling laugh. "More than one thing, I hope," she added, leaning forward slightly and staring into Devon's eyes. Devon gulped as he stared back, mesmerized. Her eyes were an amazing shade; from a distance, one would assume that they were blue, but up close, he could see that they were actually violet in color. He'd never seen anyone with violet eyes before. "As you know, my father is running for mayor…"

"I vaguely remember hearing something about that," Devon teased, his natural self-confidence beginning to reassert itself. Callista laughed again.

"Yes, well, a few evenings ago we were discussing the lack of attention our campaign has been receiving. We're not getting the space in the local newspapers we'd hoped for. Oh, yes," she waved a hand dismissively, "there have been a few stories, but nothing on the front page, not since the regatta. We need to make Father's face more recognizable. But we haven't been able to devise a plan for doing that. Then Father had a wonderful idea. Why not hire a photographer? Someone with connections to the local press, who could chronologize the entire campaign, create a photographic journal, as it were. And, hopefully, get some of the pictures into print."

"Well, there's probably several people around here who would fit the bill," Devon said, glancing around the room. "Of course, they won't necessarily come cheap. But I could put out a few feelers for you, see if anyone's interested…"

Callista leaned forward, placing one perfectly manicured hand on Devon's arm. A delicious shiver ran through him at her touch.

"I'm sure they would," she said softly, "but Father and I were rather hoping that you might be interested in taking on the assignment."

"Me?" Devon exclaimed, then burst into laughter. "You're joking, right? I'm just an apprentice! The lowest of the low! I'm still in college!"

"Yes, I know," Callista replied as she sat back, her tone cool. "But it was your photograph of Father that the editor of this newspaper chose to use for the story about the regatta. That says something about his opinion of your abilities. Besides," she smiled again, a rather wicked twinkle in her eye, "we were hoping, since you are still in school, that you might come cheap?"

Devon threw his head back and laughed again, even harder this time. Several of his colleagues stared, bringing him to his senses.

"Look, Miss Baines..."

"Callista, please."

"Callista," Devon continued, "this isn't exactly the best place to discuss this. Perhaps we could meet somewhere later...?"

"What time will you be finished here?" Callista asked as she stood up.

"Around eight."

"I'll meet you, then. Eight-thirty? At the Bay Tower Room?"

"Sounds great! I'll see you there."

Devon watched Callista leave the room, then leaned back in his chair, a self-satisfied smile on his face. The position of personal photographer for an up-and-coming politician would look fantastic on his resume — especially if Baines actually won the election. Of course, getting to spend time around Callista would be an extra added bonus.

"FITZGERALD!!!"

Devon jumped. "Yes, sir!"

"I'm not paying you to sit around, daydreaming about your new girlfriend!" his boss yelled from across the room. "Get back to work!"

"Yes, sir," Devon muttered, his face red. He did his best to ignore the scattered chuckles of his co-workers and follow his boss's advice.

* * * * *

"C'mon...c'mon!"

Moira was seated cross-legged on her bed several weeks later, muttering to herself as she pointed one index finger at a pencil lying on the desk across the room. The pencil wriggled back and forth a little, rose about two inches into the air, then dropped back down. It skittered behind a dog-eared paperback copy of *Hamlet* as if trying to hide from her.

"Aw, c'mon!" Moira groaned, disgusted. She flexed her fingers, cracking the knuckles loudly, then pointed toward the desk once more, a look of fierce determination on her face. "Come here!" she commanded in what she hoped was a forceful tone. Apparently, it was forceful enough because both book and pencil flew through the air, straight at her face. Moira squealed and ducked, covering her head with her arms. She felt the book hit her on the shoulder and fall to the bed, while the pencil landed on her head — and stayed there, perfectly balanced, the eraser end resting firmly on her spiked purple hair. Slowly, tentatively, Moira reached up to grasp the pencil. The pencil gave a little wriggle as it settled into her hand, then remained still. Moira sighed with relief.

"Gotta work on my technique," she murmured, smiling slightly as she bent over her homework.

"What are you doing?"

Moira jumped, turning to face the door.

"What are you doing up here?!" she demanded of her little sister. "This is my room!"

"I know that," Ainsley replied, giving her sister a bland look. "I heard you talking and wondered who was up here with you."

"Well, as you can see," Moira scowled, "there's nobody but me. Just the way I like it," she added pointedly.

"So who were you talking to, then?" Ainsley persisted.

"None of your business," Moira muttered, her cheeks red.

"Were you talking to yourself?"

"No...I mean, yes...I mean...What's it to you?" Moira glared at the younger girl.

"Nothing," Ainsley wandered over to one of the windows and gazed out at the rain falling softly on the sand and waves below. The horizon was barely visible, the sky and ocean blending together in one vast expanse of grey, the clouds barely a shade darker than the waves beneath them. Sharp gusts of wind hit the house from time to time, rattling the shingles and moaning through the eaves. Moira's aerie was warm and cozy in comparison, the soft glow of the bedside lamps gleaming on the polished wood floor, brightening the dark red walls, highlighting the gold threads in the duvet tossed across her bed. "It sounded like you were ordering somebody around," Ainsley continued. "Somebody...or something," she added sharply.

"What the hell is that supposed to mean?" Moira asked nervously.

"It almost sounded like you were trying to do magic," Ainsley stated, turning to stare straight at Moira. "I thought you hated magic."

"I do! I didn't! I wouldn't! I mean...oh, hell!" Moira threw down the pencil, which promptly jumped back into the air and tucked itself neatly behind her right ear. Both girls' eyes grew wide as saucers. After several seconds of complete silence, Moira took a deep breath and pointed her finger at the stairs. "Would you please get out of my room? Now," she said, her voice shaky.

"Sure...um...right..." Ainsley stammered, unable to look Moira in the eye. As she started down the stairs to the second floor, she called back over her shoulder, "Don't forget...It's Mom's late night, and it's your turn to make supper. You should probably get on it pretty soon... it'll take you close to an hour...since you don't use magic," she added, more than a touch of sarcasm in her tone.

"I'll be down as soon as I finish my homework," Moira replied, blushing again. "Damn!" she muttered, throwing herself back on the pillows. The pencil leaped out from behind her ear and flew across the room, landing on top of the wardrobe. Moira glared at it. "And good riddance to you!" she groused. "That'll teach me to mess around with this magic crap."

She rolled off the bed and went to the desk, where she pulled her journal out of the drawer...

October 8

When am I ever gonna learn...

Magic is nothing but trouble. Oh yeah, sure, it can come in handy from time to time, but at what cost? I mean, was that embarrassing, or what? And that was just a stupid pencil...witnessed by my stupid sister. What if it was something a lot more important, or even dangerous? For example, look what happened to Braidy, Brody, and me last summer. We were nearly killed...and for what? Nobody ever explained a thing. I never did find out what that Dumari crap was about. Mom never wanted to talk about it — she just changed the subject every time I mentioned it. I even tried googling the word "dumari" — all I found was some stuff about a place in Africa. Come to think of it, I never heard if they caught that Alex dude...the one that seemed to be in charge of the whole thing. He could still be out there, plotting and planning something just as nasty. I sure as hell don't want to go through THAT again!

Calm down, girl. They must have caught him. Mom is not the type to ignore a threat like that. In fact, she's more the type to worry about things that don't even exist. And she doesn't seem worried or uptight about anything these days...unless it's got something to do with the bank. Naw, if there was still a chance of some psycho grabbing me or Ainsley, she'd be a nervous wreck. They must have tracked him down, whoever he was. I wonder what they did with him? I mean, it's not like they could take him to court and have him charged with trying to take over the powers of the Dumari. The judge would have them all committed! And with good reason!

You know, that's something I've never thought about. How DO magicals keep each other in line? It's not like nonmagicals could keep them under control...they wouldn't stand a chance against some evil wizard with Matthew's powers, for example. Is there some sort of magical police force nobody else knows about? Are there magical lawyers and judges out there prosecuting these guys? Do they have a secret prison somewhere that they can send them to if they're convicted of some magical crime? And what if they commit some regular crime, like stealing or rape or murder? Could a nonmagical prison actually hold them? I greatly doubt it.

So how are magical criminals caught and punished, I wonder? I suppose it's handled by that convention thingy Braidy and Brody were talking about last year — that meeting Mom and Andrew supposedly went to during all that kidnapping mess. I should ask Andrew — or better yet, Matthew! Yeah! He'd tell me! In fact, I bet he's the president, or the chairman, or whatever they call their chief muckety-muck! LOL And if he asks me why I want to know, I'll just tell him...what? What excuse could I give him for being interested in the magical world after all this time? Idle curiosity? Nope, he'd never buy that. I'm doing research for a school paper? Yeah, right! Hmmmm...hang on, I've got it! I'm writing a story — a fantasy novel about...about... Jack the Ripper! Yeah! That's it! Only he's a magical, which is why the nonmagicals can't catch him. So eventually the magical police track him down and lock him away for life in the magical prison...I'll call it...um...Fort Pittsworth? No... Montanatraz? Stupid! Stop looking at the map for ideas! What about...Atlantisimo Bay!!! LOLOL

Hey, you know, that's not such a bad idea. Maybe I could write a story like that. I mean, that's what I want to be, right? An author? A novelist? Who says I have to wait until I'm finished with college to give it a try? Writing in my journal is good general practice, but writing fiction is totally different. If I'm gonna do this for a living, I'd better start getting some serious practice in.

And at the same time, maybe I can pry some info about the Dumari and the whole magical law enforcement scene out of freaky ol' Matthew...

"Moira!" Andrew's voice crackled over the intercom speaker. Moira jumped. *"It's almost 5:30..."*

"Damn!" Moira muttered, glancing at the clock. "I'll be right down!" she called to him.

Moira stuffed her journal back into the desk drawer and ran down the stairs to the kitchen.

"I know! I know!" she said as she passed Andrew in the hall. "I'm getting supper started now!"

"Is your homework finished?" he asked.

"Um...almost...just one more thing. I'll finish it after supper."

Muttering under her breath, she pulled Renatta's recipe file up on the kitchen monitor and got to work. Ten minutes later, the pork chops were in the oven, baking in a teriyake marinade, and Moira was peeling potatoes. She fought off a momentary temptation to slice them by magic... *No knives, fool! You're dangerous enough with a pencil!*...but couldn't resist summoning the spatula with a snap of her fingers. It popped out of the utensil drawer and soared obediently through the air, directly into her outstretched hand. Smiling smugly, she flipped the sliced potatoes neatly in the frying pan. Suddenly, she stopped in mid-flip, staring at the utensil in her hand, a troubled expression on her face. A few moments later, Moira sighed, shrugged her shoulders, and returned her attention to the potatoes...

Oct. 8, after dinner...

So...am I a gonna be a witch...or aren't I?

It's time to make up my mind, one way or the other. On the plus side: magic makes a lot of things way easier to do... housework, homework, cooking, avoiding traffic jams. On the negative side: it can put you in a lot of danger (although I wasn't even using magic when we were kidnapped and those jerks grabbed me right along with the twins anyway), you have to hide it from nonmagicals, and — in my case — it doesn't always work right.

Positive: I'd never have to scrub another toilet as long as I live;

Negative: I'd have to lie to Lucia on a regular basis (like I haven't had to do that already);

Positive: that combobulation thing could really come in handy, especially when I get hungry or thirsty up here;

Negative: with my aim, I'm bound to knock an eye out one of these days;

Positive: if Alex and his goons are still out there biding their time, I'd have a way of defending myself against them (although my boots worked pretty well the last time);

Negative: nonmagicals think all witches are evil...okay, sometimes they're right about that one;

Positive: Russ is a magi...

STOP THAT!!!

Negative: Jeremy is NOT a magical...someone else I'd have to be lying to;

Positive: no more sitting in traffic for two hours on a sweltering hot summer day;

Negative...aw, hell, I could go on like this forever! I just have to decide.

You know, thinking back, what did giving up magic get me in the long run, anyway? I mean, yeah, so I gave it up for Daddy. Did he come back? Nope! He didn't even know I'd stopped doing it. So what good did that do? Maybe Mom and Devon are right — maybe Daddy didn't leave because of the magic. Maybe he just...left. I mean, parents do just leave sometimes. It's pretty obvious he and Mom didn't get along at all anymore. It happens. Nobody's fault. Of course, that doesn't explain why he stopped coming to see me and Dev...I mean, even though Dad and Mom are divorced, he's still our father. He shouldn't have walked out on his kids like that. That was wrong of him.

God, did I just say that? I guess I am growing up a little after all. I've always thought Daddy was perfect — but I think perhaps I was just a wee bit prejudiced on that score. Maybe — MAYBE — Braidy was sorta right, about what she said that time... that Daddy wanted me to use magic to help him cheat on that ball game. Okay, so he needed a little extra cash right then, or something. No biggie. I mean, sure, it wasn't exactly a good thing to do, betting that the homerun king would strike out, then asking me to make sure he did just that. But it's not like it was murder. He made a mistake, that's all. He's human. It was the way Mom jumped on him about it that made him leave.

But I suppose that was sorta his fault as well — at least in part. Even if Mom shouldn't have come down on him so hard, he shouldn't have let it upset him so much that he stopped visiting me. I guess he just couldn't deal with her accusations anymore. And she couldn't trust him.

Love — marriage — divorce — I don't get any of it. If you don't love the person, why marry them? And if you love them one day, how can you not love them another day?

And if you don't love them anymore, why would you care about what they do or say? It's weird — I always thought growing up would solve all my problems. When I was little, grown-ups seemed to have all the answers. But the older I get, the more I realize how not true that is. The older I get, the more confusing it all seems. Go figure...

Moira sighed heavily...

...Oh well. Guess I'd better put off the life lessons until later. That essay Ms. Kane assigned me isn't gonna write itself. Till tomorrow, then...

* * * * *

Brody wove his way through the tables and chairs in the school cafeteria, his destination the seat right next to the blond in the tight red sweater. As he approached the table, she glanced up and smiled at him. He returned the smile, along with a wink. She giggled in response.

"This seat taken?" he asked.

"It is now," she said coquettishly. Two girls seated across from her stared.

Not bad...for a start, he thought as he folded himself into the chair. He popped open a can of Coke and took a sip.

"My name's Brody, by the way," Brody introduced himself, holding out his hand. "Brody Attison."

"Yeah, I know," the girl smiled, shaking his hand firmly. "My brother's on the swim team with you. Robert Romano. I'm Carla. This is Nancy and Jenny." She indicated her friends.

"Oh, yeah! I know Robert!" Brody said. "He's cool. Good swimmer."

"He's okay, I guess," Carla replied, rolling her eyes. "He's my brother."

Brody laughed. "Yeah, that's what my sister says about me."

The conversation lagged momentarily while they both concentrated on their food for several minutes. Brody watched Carla out of the corner of his eye. He liked what he saw. Quickly, he decided to follow through with his first inclination.

"So, what do you do to keep yourself busy? Play sports? Go to the movies? Hang out with your boyfriend?"

"I don't have a boyfriend," Carla told him. Nancy and Jenny watched, enthralled.

"You're joking! A beautiful girl like you? I don't believe it! What's wrong with all the guys around here?!"

When his female audience burst into giggles, Brody felt a momentary panic, afraid he'd laid it on a bit thick. But luckily for him, Carla seemed to lap it up. She blushed and smiled and looked up at him through her eyelashes.

"So what do you like to do, mon cher?" he asked again, leaning in close.

"Ooh, you speak French? That is so sexy!" Carla sighed, her eyes shining.

"Yeah, well..." Brody waved a hand nonchalantly, "when you're a man of the world, like I am..." He gave her a wicked grin. Carla giggled. He leaned even closer and murmured something unintelligible, but with vague pretensions of being French, in her ear. Carla's cheeks turned bright pink.

"What does that mean?" she whispered.

Brody thought fast.

"It means...it means that I can't wait to be alone with you," he whispered back. "Somewhere quiet...and private...and dark..."

"And just when do you plan this rendevous?" Carla smiled wickedly.

"The sooner, the better, girl."

The two teens gazed into each other's eyes, their attraction to each other palpable. Nancy and Jenny were forgotten, the noise of the cafeteria faded away...they were in their own little world, all alone. Until...

"Ahem!"

The sound came to Brody through a fog. He glanced up...and the smile on his lips froze. Standing not five feet away was Moira — hands on her hips, glare on her face, sparks shooting from her eyes. He moved away from Carla and cleared his throat nervously. Carla turned to see what he was looking at.

"Who's that?" she asked suspiciously.

"My...my cousin," Brody stuttered. "I...um...I promised to help her with her Spanish homework. Guess I kinda forgot. I...um...I gotta go..."

"Spanish? I thought you took French!"

By this time, Moira had her arms crossed and was tapping one foot impatiently.

"Yeah...well...um...I'll...uh...I'll talk to you later, okay?" Brody grabbed his things and stood up quickly, hoping against hope to stave off the explosion he knew was coming. At least until Carla was out of earshot.

"What the hell do you think you're..." Moira began as he joined her.

"Not here!" Brody hissed as he grabbed her by the arm and spun her around, forcing her to walk double-time out of the cafeteria. Spluttering furiously, Moira had no choice but to go along. But the moment they reached the hall, she turned on him.

"YOU STUPID, IGNORANT, EVIL...!"

"Calm down, Moira..." Brody interrupted her — not the wisest move he'd ever made.

"Calm down! Calm down?!" You're dating my best friend and I catch you hanging all over some blond bimbo and you have the nerve to tell me to calm down?!!!" She punched him as hard as she could. Brody dropped his bookbag and grabbed his arm where Moira had hit him.

"Ouch! Knock it off! It's no big deal!"

"No big deal! I oughta..." Moira punched him again.

"Will you stop hitting me?!"

"No! Lucia really likes you — don't ask me why! — and here you go and hit on someone else behind her back..."

"I'm sure as hell not gonna do it in front of her back!" Brody's attempt at levity failed miserably. Moira's eyes narrowed dangerously. She glared at him in silence for a full count of ten, then punched him twice in quick succession.

"HEY!" The shout took them both by surprise. The boys' gym coach strode down the hall toward them. "No physical stuff allowed!"

"He's my cousin! And he deserved it!"

"I don't care if he's your long lost twin brother, missy. No hitting! You'll have to come to the principal's office with me."

"It's okay, Coach Fitz. She really is my cousin. We'll stop. It won't happen again," Brody quickly reassured the muscular black man. "Just a little family thing."

"I don't know..." Coach Fitz hesitated, not completely reassured. He frowned down at Moira, who attempted to appear appropriately contrite, while still fuming on the inside. Apparently, her performance was convincing enough. After several moments, Coach Fitz relaxed slightly. "Very well. Consider this a warning, young lady. Next time, it's straight to the principal's office. Understood?"

"Yes, sir," Moira muttered. She waited until the coach turned the corner, then rounded once more on Brody.

"You...you...!" Moira was so angry, she was actually lost for words.

"C'mon, Moir! We're just dating! It's not like we're engaged, or something!"

Moira glared. "Thank God for that! What Lucia ever saw in you..."

"She likes me! And I like her! What's so strange about that?" Brody demanded.

"If you like her so much, why are you hitting on somebody else, then?!"

"I...I...aw, hell! I don't know!" Brody's shoulders slumped. "I'm sorry, okay? Is that what you want to hear?"

"I'm not the one that needs to hear it," Moira pointed out.

"You're not gonna tell Lucia about this!" Brody gasped, aghast. "Are you?"

"I should!"

"No, please! You can't!"

"She has the right to know, Brody! I'm not gonna lie to her...she's my best friend!"

"Aw, c'mon! It was just a little harmless flirting..."

"You were all over that girl! You practically had your tongue in her ear! I'm not gonna cover for you, Brody. You will not do this to Lucia," Moira hissed. "Got it?"

"What do you want me to do?" Brody asked resignedly.

"Make up your mind, stupid! Either end it with Lucia, or stay the hell away from Little Miss Red Sweater. Got it?!"

"Got it," Brody mumbled.

"And make it up soon! I don't want this hanging over me!"

"All right! All right! I'll get it sorted out by this weekend."

"Fine!"

"Fine!"

Moira stormed back into the cafeteria, leaving Brody to face his conscience.

He really did like Lucia — she was sweet, and gentle, and very pretty — but he liked Carla, as well. What was wrong with that? Like many boys his age, he just could not understand why girls insisted on monogamous relationships. It would be different if they were older and considering the possibility of marriage. But not at his age. He was still in high school, with at least four years of college ahead of him. Settling down was the farthest thing from his mind. So why couldn't they both see other people? As long as they were honest with each other about it — he squirmed a little at that thought, knowing full well he'd had no intention of telling either Lucia or Carla about each other — what difference would it make? He was perfectly okay with Lucia seeing someone else as well (he pointedly ignored the Big Green Monster flexing its muscles in his guts). That was fine with him, he assured himself firmly.

Okay, that's what I'll do, then, he thought. *I'll tell Lucia I really like going out with her, but I want to go out with other girls, too. And that she's totally free to date other guys if she wants to. That should work.*

Feeling rather complacent about his decision, he made sure the coast was clear, then snapped his fingers. His bookbag slowly rose into the air, floating effortlessly right at shoulder height. Brody slipped his arms into the straps and made his way to his next class.

* * * * *

Lucia sat crosslegged on the floor of Moira's room that Friday evening, her lovely dark eyes red-rimmed.

"I thought he liked me," she sobbed softly. "I thought he really liked me."

"He did," Moira assured her. "He's just a ho."

Lucia sniffed. "A guy can't be a ho."

"Sure he can," Moira stated firmly. "Brody's dated three different people in five months. If a girl did that, everyone would call her a ho. So why can't he be?"

"I get the point," Lucia said with a small smile. "But there must be another word for it."

"Dork? Jerk? Loser?" Moira suggested wryly. "Take your pick."

"Jerk works for me." Lucia straightened, stretching her arms over her head. "I can't believe Brody actually thought I'd agree to him dating some other girl while he was still going out with me. What's wrong with him?"

"He's a guy," Moira said disgustedly.

"I wish..." Lucia mused as she wiped her cheeks and lay back on the floor, "I wish I had a magic wand I could wave at him and turn him into a toad, or something. That would make me feel loads better, I'm sure."

"Hmmmm..." A wicked gleam came into Moira's eyes momentarily, then disappeared as fast as it had appeared. *Nope, not humanly possible, even for us,* she admitted to herself. *But it was a nice thought.* She lay down and wrapped comforting arms around her friend.

* * * * *

Braidy sipped her coffee slowly, trying to make it last for as long as possible. The longer she stayed, the better her chances of meeting up with Jonathan.

She had no idea if he would be down this weekend or not. She'd neither seen nor heard from him since their walk on the beach. But hope springs eternal. Especially when you're seventeen — and well on the way to being in love.

Not wanting to get sidetracked by any of her friends, Braidy had chosen her seat with care. She was sitting at a table in the back corner of the coffee shop, out of sight of most of the patrons, but with a clear view of the door. That way she could see before being seen.

She'd come to town on the pretext of doing some early Christmas shopping. Not wanting to lie to her parents, she had indulged in some cursory window shopping before heading for Starbuck's. She'd even made a purchase — a red leather-bound journal for Moira, with brass-tipped corners and parchment pages edged with gilt. She'd briefly considered having the face of the book embossed with Moira's initials — until she inquired as to the cost. The journal was expensive enough without personalizing it.

The fact that she spent that much money on a present for her least favorite relative was a good indication of how far gone Braidy was. She blushed at the thought, her face warming at the memory of Jonathan's last visit. He hadn't touched her until he said goodnight, when he'd merely kissed her hand, but his presence alone was enough to make her tingle. Even just the thought of him sent butterflies swooping through her stomach.

The bell over the door jingled. Braidy's head came up quickly — and the butterflies started doing cartwheels. It was him.

Braidy averted her head, not wanting to seem too anxious, too eager. She managed to watch him, though, out of the corner of her eye, as Jonathan walked to the counter and placed his order. A totally unreasonable jealousy churned inside her at the smile he bestowed on the clerk who took his order. She continued to observe him, as surreptitiously as possible, as his own gaze wandered the room. He acknowledged an acquaintance from the station with a slight nod of the head, accepted a steaming coffee cup from the clerk and moved through the tables to join the other man. Several paces from the table, Jonathan finally glanced in her direction. He paused in mid-stride, then continued toward his original destination. Braidy noticed that he refrained from sitting with the man, although obviously invited to do so. After a minute or two, he waved goodbye and headed toward her.

Her nerves suddenly getting the better of her, Braidy stumbled to her feet and slung her purse over her shoulder.

"You leaving?" Jonathan asked, his voice soft in her ear.

She promised herself to always remember how quickly and quietly he could move.

"I...um...yeah...yes..." she mumbled, her head lowered, her hair mercifully falling forward to hide her red cheeks. "I've got some shopping to do. Christmas shopping."

"Bit early for Christmas shopping, isn't it?" he smiled, following her to the door.

"I like to get a head start," she replied, forcing herself to look him straight in the eye. "That way I beat the crowds."

"I prefer to do mine on Christmas Eve," he told her, still smiling that beautiful, wonderful, infuriatingly smug smile. "I like all the hustle and bustle of the last-minute rush."

"I'm not surprised," she finally smiled in return. The bell jingled as they left the coffee shop together.

"Why not?"

"You don't strike me as the type to plan ahead."

"Au contraire, my dear," Jonathan grinned, "I have all sorts of plans for the future." He winked at her.

Braidy blushed even deeper and lowered her head once again. Had she not, she might have been surprised by the rather calculating look in Jonathan's eyes at that moment. He kept pace with her as she wandered down the sidewalk, pausing now and then to glance in a shop window, pretending interest in things she didn't even really see. Jonathan commented from time to time on a particular item, but for the most part, they walked in silence. When they reached the corner, Braidy paused, uncertain. Jonathan slipped one arm around her waist and kissed her softly on the lips. She sighed and leaned against him. His arm tightened.

"So when are you going to go out with me?" he whispered in her ear.

"When are you going to ask me?" she whispered back.

Jonathan laughed softly. The sound sent shivers down her spine.

"I'm asking you now."

Braidy hesitated, torn. This was what she wanted, what she'd been waiting for. But she knew her parents would never approve. They thought Jonathan was too old for her. She hated the thought of going behind their backs, but her attraction to Jonathan was too strong to deny. She sighed.

"Well?" he asked, a note of impatience creeping into his voice. "Do you want to go out with me, or don't you?"

"I do! Oh, I do, Jonathan!" Braidy exclaimed. "It's just...my parents...they won't like it...they think you're too old for me."

Jonathan frowned. "So who's living your life? You or your parents? Aren't you old enough to make your own decisions?"

"Well...yeah...I mean...I am seventeen..." her voice trailed off. At the moment, seventeen sounded desperately young.

"Well, then," Jonathan tilted her chin up. "I'd say it's time to stand on your own feet. You're not a little girl anymore." He kissed her again, harder this time. Braidy's knees seemed to melt right out from under her.

"I won't be down again until the weekend after the election," he said. "Will I see you then?"

"Yes," she breathed, her eyes half-closed.

"Good. Meet me Saturday night at seven."

"Where?"

"Club Ving."

"You have to be twenty-one to get in there! They won't let me in!"

Jonathan smiled. "Don't worry. I'll get you in. Just be there."

He turned and walked away, leaving her standing alone. And utterly confused.

Chapter Eleven:

Election Results

"How do the numbers look?"

"Not bad," Quinn stated, checking through the latest report, "but not good either."

"What the hell does that mean?" Desmond snapped.

"It means you're about two points behind...as of an hour ago."

"Well, that's all right," Desmond relaxed. "It's not even eleven o'clock yet. Plenty of time to catch up. Think I'll go by the bank. I've got some work to do. I'll check back in after lunch." He clapped his old friend on the shoulder, gave his daughter a confident smile, and headed out the door.

Callista watched her father leave, then returned to the office, beckoning Muldoon to follow her. Muldoon closed the door and sat in the chair Callista indicated. The two sat in silence for several minutes, Callista gazing blankly into space, her fingers drumming a tattoo on the desk. Muldoon kept his head down, his mouth shut. He knew better than to interrupt his companion when she was thinking. He'd been on the receiving end of Callista Baines' temper before. He had no intention of repeating the experience. Finally, Callista seemed to make up her mind about something. She turned to face Quinn, all business.

"As you may have noticed," she began, "my father has unfortunately decided that he must win this election fairly. He seems to think that only if the voters actually elect him, will he be justified in carrying out our plans. Of course, as you and I both know, how he wins is a moot point. All that matters is getting him into office."

"I totally agree," Quinn nodded.

"I rather thought you would," Callista said blandly. "I see no point in waiting until the last minute to rectify the mistakes of the voters. Father must win this election. Our plans will benefit everyone in the community, not just ourselves and our fellow magicals. Therefore, I feel we are fully justified in enacting the contingency plan immediately."

"Without your father's approval?"

"Without my father's knowledge, Mr. Muldoon. He approved the idea weeks ago. We are simply anticipating the necessity of...shall we say, adjustments to public opinion? The voters are not aware of the situation. We were unable to apprise them of all the facts, therefore they are unable to make a fully informed decision. We, however, know what is best for the community. And it is requisite that we act on that knowledge. Don't you agree?"

"Of course," Quinn smiled. "Shall I give the word then?"

"Yes, I think so," Callista replied. "Notify our workers at the various polling locations. Have them start with every fourth vote for now."

"Every fourth vote? I thought we'd agreed to go with every third vote."

"We don't want anyone to become suspicious. Especially this early in the day. We'll keep an eye on the numbers and if necessary, make further adjustments this afternoon." She stood up. "You may use this office. I will see to it that you are not disturbed."

Callista left him alone. Muldoon settled himself into the chair she had vacated a moment before and began making calls.

The door to campaign headquarters opened, admitting Russ and Dan along with a blast of cold air mingled with a few snow flurries. Spotting his sister across the room, Russ wove through the various campaign workers scattered about, shaking a few hands, acknowledging the smiles, Dan trailing in his wake.

"Hey, Sis!"

"Don't call me that, Russell," Callista replied sharply. "You know I hate it."

"Sorry. How's everything going?"

"The latest exit polls have Father behind by two points."

"That's pretty good!" Dan smiled eagerly.

"Hardly," Callista deigned to look at her brother's friend, whose smile disappeared immediately at the contempt in her voice. "If this trend continues, Father will lose. There is no prize for second place in politics."

"Um...uh...yeah..." Dan muttered, his face burning. "I just meant... well...that's much better than when your dad started his campaign. And it is still early in the day. He can easily catch up, can't he?"

Callista gazed at Dan appraisingly for a moment. "Yes, he can," she finally replied with a slight smile. Dan's face lit up. "And he will."

"You sound pretty confident, Callista," Russ commented, watching his sister closely. Ever since the incident at the regatta, Russ had had the feeling that there were things going on between Callista and Desmond that neither of them wanted him to know about. His unvoiced suspicions had kept him tense and irritable for weeks. The knowledge that, whatever his sister and father were up to, there was nothing he could do about it, hadn't helped his mood. Especially since there was no one he could discuss the situation with. There was no point trying to voice his concerns to Dan. The moment Callista's name was mentioned, her not-so-secret admirer would go into a complete fog. Nor could Russ bring himself to call Moira, ashamed to tell her he couldn't trust his own family. He also had the sneaking suspicion that he had once again hurt her feelings, so he wasn't even sure she'd be willing to talk to him in the first place.

"You know I have great confidence in Father's abilities, Russell," Callista said. "I always have. Besides, he is obviously the best candidate for the position. I'm certain the voters have realized that. I won't be the least bit surprised if Father has taken a commanding lead by mid-afternoon. Now, if you'll excuse me, I have a luncheon date. Will you be at the victory party this evening?"

"Of course," her brother said. "Six o'clock at the Lenox, right?"

"Yes. Don't be late. And please, Russell..." she added, "wear a suit and tie, won't you? And decent shoes."

"Don't worry, sister dear. I promise not to embarrass you."

"See you tonight!" Dan called after her as she left them. Callista ignored him. "There's gonna be a band there tonight, isn't there?" he asked Russ.

"Yeah, I think so."

"Good!"

"Why?"

"I...um...I just thought I might ask Callista to dance with me," Dan said, his face burning once again. Russ shook his head.

"Good luck with that," he muttered to himself.

* * * * *

Moira climbed out of the car and followed her mother into the lobby of the Lenox Hotel. It promised to be an exciting night. Not only had Moira never been to an election party before, the results posted so far had the two candidates locked in a very close race. Desmond Baines had a small lead over his opponent, incumbent mayor Monica Wellsley, but there was still a chance she could catch up before the night was over. The polls had just closed and a number of precincts north of the Common had reported trouble with the voting computers, so their final totals would most likely be delayed by an hour or two. It was quite possible that the election would go right down to the wire.

Of course, the fact that Russ Baines was certain to be at the party had nothing to do with the knots in Moira's stomach. Or so she insisted to herself. The extreme care she had taken with her appearance that evening was in no way due to Russ's probable presence at the Lenox. There were bound to be reporters and news cameras there, she'd told herself. Might as well look her best, just in case she wound up on the eleven o'clock news. That was the excuse she'd given herself for dying her hair a deep, rich burgundy the night before — and for wearing her best outfit, a bright blue sweater with three-quarter length sleeves and a short denim skirt that ended in a wide lace ruffle several inches above her knees — and for exchanging her usual hiking boots for relatively tasteful black clogs. She'd spent a considerable amount of time on her makeup as well, actually lightening up on her usually heavy black eyeliner and wearing dark red lipstick instead of one of her less traditional shades. Russ or no Russ, Moira wanted to make a good impression. And if her appearance just happened to give the young Mr. Baines something to think about as well, all the better.

The ballroom at the Lenox was filled to capacity when they arrived. Victory was in the air, bringing with it the normal phalanx of sycophants, hoping to cash in on Desmond Baines' success, as well as Desmond's numerous legitimate supporters and campaign workers. The candidate himself was holding court center stage, surrounded by news reporters and their cameramen. Just outside the crush, Devon was taking pictures, the lovely Callista by his side. Glancing up momentarily, he spotted his family in the doorway of the room and gave them a hearty wave. Moira waved back, grinning. Devon was obviously having the time of his life.

"He's certainly in his element," Andrew commented, smiling. He had to raise his voice to be heard over the cacophony of sound beating against them from all sides.

"That he is," Renatta agreed. "I'm amazed that Desmond chose Devon for the job."

"He's a good photographer, Mom," Moira shouted over the noise.

"Yes he is, but he's still so young and inexperienced. I certainly would have expected Desmond to hire someone with more credentials."

"Well, it's probably like Devon told us — they wanted someone good — and cheap!" Andrew laughed. "Can't get much cheaper than a student looking for car money."

"And Mr. Baines had seen his photos from the regatta, so he knew Dev was good," Moira added.

Renatta nodded her head in agreement, not bothering to reply. The noise level was so high, it was nearly impossible to carry on a conversation. There was a five piece band set up on the far end of the room, but for all the music anyone could hear, they might as well not have been playing.

Holding one hand out toward Ainsley, Renatta stepped forward into the crowd, but stopped a moment later when she realized that Ainsley hadn't taken the proffered hand. Glancing over her shoulder, Renatta raised an eyebrow at her daughter.

"I'm thirteen, Mother!" Ainsley stated.

"And your point would be?"

"Don't you think I'm a little old to hold your hand?"

"I don't want to lose you in this crowd."

Ainsley rolled her eyes. "I can handle myself. Besides, all you have to do is look for the bright red hair."

Renatta and Andrew exchanged an amused glance.

"She has a point, Mom," Moira put her two cents' worth in. "Plus, she's taller than I am now. You're more likely to lose me."

"Is that a promise?" Ainsley muttered. Luckily, Moira didn't hear her.

Renatta hesitated for a moment more, then shrugged her shoulders.

"All right, just stay close, you hear?"

As they worked their way toward Devon, Moira kept a surreptitious lookout for Russ, but he was nowhere in sight. Andrew and Renatta were greeted by several people, some of whom Moira knew, many of whom she'd never seen before. Finally, they reached Devon.

"Hi, folks!" Devon shouted, kissing his mother on the cheek. "Quite a blowout, wouldn't you say? Mom, Andrew, this is Callista Baines. Callista, these are my parents — Andrew and Renatta Collins. And my little sister, Ainsley. You've met Moira — at the regatta."

Callista held out a slim hand. "Pleasure." She spoke in normal tones, yet, in spite of the noise around them, they were able to hear her clearly. Moira had the feeling Callista Baines never bothered to raise her voice. When she spoke, people would always listen — not necessarily because what Callista had to say was that important, but simply because she expected them to. And Callista Baines was definitely the type of woman who always got what she expected. The thought only increased Moira's instinctive dislike.

"Actually, we have met before," Renatta pointed out. Callista raised a perfectly arched eyebrow. "I work for your father, at the bank. I manage the Orleans branch."

"You must forgive me," Callista said, her voice cool and detached. "I'm afraid I have a terrible memory for faces." She gave Andrew an appraising glance. Moira managed to refrain from bursting into laughter at the dumbstruck expression on her stepfather's face, but when Renatta gave him a pointed nudge in the ribs, she couldn't help it — a giggle escaped her.

"Where...where's your brother?" Andrew stuttered, shooting Moira a dirty look.

"Late...as usual," Callista stated, sounding bored. "I'm sure he'll turn up at some point. Senator Compton just arrived, Devon," she added, laying her hand on Devon's arm. "We must have a photo of him with Father."

"Well, we'd better let you get back to work, then," Renatta said as Callista began to move away.

"I'll catch ya later," Devon called back, following Callista through the crowd. Moira couldn't help but notice that Andrew's eyes weren't the only ones following Callista as well. Renatta gave her husband another nudge in the ribs — a bit harder this time.

"Ouch! What?!" he exclaimed.

"Hello? Remember me? Your wife?"

Andrew had the decency to look ashamed. Moira snorted.

"That's quite enough from you, young lady," Andrew muttered. Moira opened her mouth, ready to give him a piece of her mind, but closed it with a snap. Russ Baines had just entered the ballroom.

Moira's stomach clenched at the sight of him. Why did he have this affect on her? Even now, when she had a steady boyfriend, she couldn't see Russ without her mouth going dry and her pulse racing. Even when she was furious with him for not contacting her in several months. Disgusted with herself, and overwhelmed by a sudden desire to avoid Russ altogether, Moira looked around the room, searching for a suitable distraction. Her gaze came to rest on the band.

"I think I'll go listen to the music for a while," she said to no one in particular.

"All right," her mother replied. "Don't wander off."

The band was good — not exactly Moira's favorite type of music, but at least they were playing some decent classic rock. And the bass player was hot — a definite plus. Moira stood nearby, nodding her head in time to the beat, exchanging an occasion smile with the bass player. Oblivious to the crowd around her, she jumped when a hand touched her elbow.

"You look very nice tonight," Russ said in her ear.

Moira allowed herself several deep breaths before turning to answer him.

"Why, Russell!" she said with all the nonchalance she could muster. "I didn't know you were here."

Russ barely managed to suppress a grin. Moira's voice reminded him exactly of his own sister at her most haughty and disdainful. While somewhat disappointed that Moira would take that tone with him, he had to acknowledge that she had every right to be upset with him. At least she hadn't yelled at him — *or punched me*, he thought wryly.

"How are you?" he asked.

"Lovely! Simply lovely! And you?" Moira frantically searched her brain for an excuse to get away. She didn't think she'd be able to keep up the calm, cool act for very long — not with him standing so close.

"Oh, okay, I guess. Busy." Russ took a deep breath. "Actually, not that okay. Listen, could we go somewhere a little more quiet? I really need to talk to you."

Moira had every intention of blowing him off, but then she looked up into his face. Something in his eyes gave her pause. Russ didn't usually let his emotions show. But tonight, in those enigmatic blue depths, Moira saw confusion, worry...even fear. Dropping her Ice Princess imitation immediately, she placed a hand on his arm.

"What's wrong, Russ?" she asked, frowning. "Are you afraid your dad is going to lose the election?"

Russ laughed, but there was no humor in the sound. "No," he said. "Just the opposite. I'm afraid he's going to win."

Moira's frown deepened.

"Look," Russ reached for her hand. "We can't talk here. Let's go out to the lobby, okay?"

Silently acquiescing, Moira followed him out of the ballroom and into the main lobby of the hotel.

The large, luxurious lobby was both quieter and cooler than the ballroom. Aside from two clerks on duty at the main desk, and an elderly gentleman reading the newspaper in a secluded corner, they were the only people to be seen. Russ led Moira to a cozy alcove on the far side of the lobby, away from both the entrance to the ballroom and the check-in desk. He waited for her to sit down on the tan suede loveseat, then took a seat next to her.

Moira squeezed herself into the corner of the loveseat, trying to appear relaxed, one arm thrown across the back of the sofa, her legs crossed, attempting to keep some space between her and her companion. She needn't have worried. Russ obviously wasn't interested in anything of an intimate nature. He sat hunched forward, his hands clasped between his knees, his head bowed. After several minutes of silence, punctuated only by Russ's sighs, Moira forgot both her indignation and her nerves. Shifting position, she sat up straight, moving closer to Russ. But not too close.

"Um...Russ?" she asked quietly. "You wanted to talk?"

"Yeah, I did." Russ kept his head lowered as he spoke. "I'm just not sure where to start."

Moira shrugged. "Then start at the beginning."

Russ shot Moira a look of exasperation. "I don't think I know where the beginning was."

"O...kay." Moira thought for a moment. "Does this all have something to do with your dad running for mayor?"

"You could say that," Russ replied, his voice dripping with sarcasm.

"You're having a problem with a magical being elected to non-magical government? You're not alone, pal. I've had my doubts, too."

"That's part of it, yeah, but there's more to it than that. I mean, magicals have held office in the past and done a good job. It's just..."

"Just...what?" Moira prompted.

Russ twisted around to face her. Hesitant at first, his words gradually came faster and faster, as if it was a relief to finally express the worries he'd held in for so long. "Something's going on, Moira. Something my dad and sister aren't telling me. They keep talking about these plans they have...but they won't tell me what they are. They're keeping me totally in the dark."

"Plans? What kind of plans?" Moira asked. "Some way of fixing the election?"

"No...well, yes, maybe...that could be part of it." Russ ran his hand through his hair. "But it's not just about winning the election, it's about what Dad will do once he's in office."

"I don't get it." Moira frowned. "What do you think he's going to do? Use magic to run the city?"

Russ hesitated before answering her, then looked up, staring straight into her eyes. "Yes, Moira, I'm beginning to think he might do just that."

"But...that's not allowed, is it? I mean..." She swallowed hard. "Russ, even if he does use magic while he's mayor, you don't think he'd do anything...bad, do you?"

The combination of concern, fear, and something akin to despair in Russ's eyes made Moira's breath catch in her throat. "That's exactly what I'm afraid of, Moira," he whispered.

"But...but, Russ, your dad's a good man, isn't he? My mom has worked for him for years and she has only good things to say about him. He's been friends with my Grandpa Matthew for ages...now, I grant you, Matthew is a pretty freaky guy, but they don't come any more honest. He wouldn't be friends with anyone who would consider doing something...witchy. And he helped save me and my cousins... you know...when we met..." her voice faded away.

"I know all that, Moira," Russ said quietly, his head bowed once again. "He's my dad, remember? It's just this feeling I've got...kind of like the one I had last year...when you'd been kidnapped."

"You knew we'd been kidnapped?!" Moira's eyes widened. Russ had never told her that.

"No," he shook his head, smiling slightly. "I didn't know what was happening. I just knew something evil was going down."

Moira stared at him in shock. "Are you...a Seer?"

"I wish!" Russ groaned. "Then maybe I'd know what the deal is, instead of being totally lost here."

The two friends sat in silence for several seconds, then a thought occurred to Moira.

"Russ...what makes you think that whatever your dad might have planned is going to be gormy? Couldn't he be planning to do good things? I mean...okay...he shouldn't be using magic even if it is for everyone's benefit, but...why do you think he's planning something evil?"

"Because..." Russ cleared his throat. Moira could tell that whatever he was about to say was very difficult for the young man. She reached over and took his hand in hers. "Because of what he did at the regatta."

Russ explained what he'd seen — or thought he'd seen — that day in Boston Harbor. Moira tried to hide her shock and disgust, but it wasn't easy.

"He denied it, of course," Russ said after telling her the details, "but I've wondered ever since if he wasn't lying to me."

"But, why..? I mean, you went back to help the women who capsized. You lost the race."

"Free publicity," Russ explained, looking disgusted. "Saving those women made him look like a hero — got him on the front page of the Globe, didn't it?"

"That's a lousy thing to say about your own father," Moira said, staring at Russ. "You can't really think he would have risked lives just to get on the front page of the newspaper!"

"I don't know! I don't know!" Russ exclaimed. "Believe me, I don't want to be thinking this stuff! It's been driving me crazy for months!"

"Did you...did you try talking to him about it?"

"Yeah...that was a lovely conversation," Russ grimaced.

"I bet!" Moira muttered. "So, what did he say?"

"What you would expect. He didn't do anything of the kind, he was appalled that I would even suggest it, how could I think such a thing of him."

"But you still think he had something to do with that catamaran capsizing."

"I know what I saw, Moira."

There was silence between them. Eventually, Moira took a deep breath.

"Why are you telling me all of this? Why not talk to Dan…or your sister…or…"

"Because if I don't talk to someone about it, I'm gonna burst! I can't say anything to Callista because whatever's going down, she's in the thick of it. I can't talk to Dan — although God knows I've tried — because the moment Callista's name is mentioned, he goes completely moony on me. And there isn't anybody else. Besides," he added after a moment, "I knew I could count on you to hear me out, and then give it to me straight. You're not the kind of girl who sugarcoats everything, just to make a guy feel better. You tell it like it is. A guy needs that."

Touched by his confidence in her honesty, Moira immediately forgave Russ for any and all transgressions, real or imagined. She squeezed his hand.

"Why didn't you tell me all of this sooner, Russ?"

"Why do you think, Moira?" Russ said with a mirthless laugh. "You think it's easy for me to admit that I think my dad is a liar and a cheat? Or that he might have some sort of nefarious plans in store for the city of Boston? He's my dad! I love him! And I've always been really proud of him. I mean, I know he has his faults. He's a businessman, and he can be ruthless when necessary, but I've never known him to do anything…anything really bad…or…or illegal…" Russ's voice trailed away. "I don't know what to do," he whispered.

Following an instinct she didn't even know she had, Moira reached out and pulled Russ close. He responded immediately, wrapping his strong arms around her, laying his head on her shoulder. They sat like that for several minutes, neither of them saying a word…neither of them needing to say anything. Shivers ran down Moira's spine as his warm breath tickled her neck.

"Moira…" he breathed, gently turning her face to his.

"There you are!"

Moira jumped and spun around. Ainsley was standing there, a mixture of jealousy and triumph on her face.

"What do you want, Ainsley?" Moira tried to keep her tone civil, but it was difficult. Ainsley's timing had never been worse.

"Mom was looking for you," Ainsley said. "And didn't you tell Jeremy you'd call him tonight?"

"Jeremy..." Moira's face was a blank.

"Yeah, Jeremy...you remember him, don't you?" Ainsley shot a look at Russ. "Your boyfriend?"

Moira felt Russ stiffen. At that moment, she would have gladly strangled her little sister.

"Whatever. Tell Mom I'll be right in," Moira muttered, glaring at Ainsley, who looked positively delighted with herself as she pranced back into the ballroom.

It was Moira's turn to hang her head.

"You have a boyfriend." It was a statement, not a question. Moira sighed.

"Um...yeah...yes, I do."

"That's great." Russ sounded as if he'd swallowed something the wrong way. "Nice guy?"

"He's okay..."

"Great...just great...Listen...about...what happened...or almost happened...um...a minute ago...you know...no big deal...I mean..." Russ stuttered.

"I was gonna mention it," Moira interrupted, feeling desperate. "Jeremy, I mean. It just didn't seem like a good time, you know?" She gazed up at Russ, her eyes begging forgiveness.

Russ smiled slightly and shrugged his shoulders. "I know, Moira. It's okay. Stupid of me to assume you weren't dating someone...a hot girl like you."

Moira's cheeks turned bright pink. "You…you think I'm…hot?" she whispered, her eyes gleaming.

"Well…yeah," Russ stated, as if this fact should be common knowledge.

"Most guys think I'm a freak."

Russ shrugged again. "Most guys don't have my good taste," he said with a wink.

Moira grinned with delight. "Thanks! Um…" she hesitated, her grin fading, "we're still friends, aren't we? I mean, my dating Jeremy won't change that, will it?"

"As long as it doesn't bother him any, I'm okay with it. Besides," he added wryly, "I need all the friends I can get right now."

Moira slipped her hand back into his. "Well, you definitely have this one!"

Russ smiled and squeezed her hand in response. "C'mon, we'd better get back in there before your mom calls the cops."

Russ stood up, pulling Moira up with him. Moira held him back a moment.

"Russ…about your dad…maybe you should try talking to him again. Tell him how you feel, what's got you worried…let him know you support him and want to help him, you're just afraid he's gotten too caught up in the whole election thing. I really can't believe he'd want to do anything to hurt anybody. He might just need to get his priorities sorted out. God, now I sound like my mother." She pulled a face, making Russ laugh.

"You're probably right," he said, still smiling. Moira's heart whimpered at the sight. "I'm probably just overreacting. Too much stress. I never realized what a pain an election can be. I'll be so glad when this night is over."

They headed back into the ballroom. It saddened Moira that Russ dropped her hand, but she knew it was only right. She'd barely gotten used to having one boyfriend. Having two at once was definitely biting off more than even she could handle.

As soon as they reached the door of the ballroom, Russ and Moira could tell that something momentous was about to happen. Desmond and Callista were standing on the dais at the far end of the room, beaming, while Quinn Muldoon waved his arms for attention. He tapped the microphone with his finger.

"Is this on?" they heard him say.

"I'd better get up there," Russ said. "Talk at ya later."

Moira spotted her family nearby and joined them. There was a crackle or two from the PA system as the noise in the room decreased drastically. Desmond stepped up to the mike.

"I have some important news for all of you. Russ!" he called as he spotted his son making his way through the crowd. "Get up here, son! Ladies and gentlemen, friends and neighbors, I have an announcement to make..." Desmond paused, waiting until Russ joined the group on the dais. "I just got off the phone with Mayor Wellsley. Although a few precincts have not quite finished tallying all the votes, most of the results are now in. After reviewing the numbers, Mayor Wellsley has accepted the inevitable, and has graciously conceded the election! We did it, folks! We won!"

The collective cheer that followed Desmond's statement made the entire room shake. Moira clapped her hands over her ears as balloons and confetti showered the ecstatic crowd. Quinn grabbed the microphone once again.

"Ladies and gentlemen!" he shouted. "I am proud to present the next mayor of the fine city of Boston, Desmond Alexander Baines!" and he laughed.

Moira's head came up sharply as goosebumps erupted on her arms. What did that laugh remind her of? Instinctively, she moved closer to her parents.

"Thank you, Quinn! Thank you!" Desmond clapped his toady on the back. "Well!" He threw his head back and laughed, a strong, hearty sound. "I gotta tell you, folks, this is an amazing feeling!" More cheers. "And I owe it all to you! If not for your hard work and dedication during these past months, we never would have made it this far. So give yourselves a round of applause!" His listeners willingly obliged. "And, of course, my deepest thanks go to my family — my son, Russ, and especially my lovely daughter, Callista, who has been my secretary, my campaign manager, my chief cook and bottle-washer..." laughter broke out... "in short, the glue that held this campaign — and this candidate — together. We have some wonderful ideas to bring this great city back to the forefront of our country, and now, thanks to all of you, we can begin to implement those plans. But no more work tonight! Tonight we celebrate!" More cheers, in particular from the younger crowd. Desmond gave the crowd a big wave, then pulled Russ and Callista up next to him, grabbing their hands and raising them in triumph. Moira noted that Russ's smile appeared rather fixed. She could only hope that his suspicions were unfounded — for all their sakes.

* * * * *

It was nearly midnight, but the party was still going strong. Several couples were on the dance floor, gyrating to the over-loud music, while many others sat or stood throughout the ballroom, attempting to carry on conversations over the excessive noise around them. Desmond was telling jokes to an admiring group of young female supporters, Callista was dancing with Devon, and Russ was sitting alone at the back of the room, having just said goodbye to Moira and her family. He'd had no further chance to talk with Moira alone, but at the moment he was rather glad of that.

Russ had never been able to figure out what his feelings for Moira actually were — until tonight, that is. When she pulled him into her arms and he held her close, a fire began to burn deep in his gut, unlike anything he'd ever known before. He wanted nothing more than to keep on holding her, feeling her warmth, breathing in the scent of her. He'd been an instant away from kissing her when Ainsley had interrupted them. Hearing that Moira had a boyfriend had been like having a bucket of ice water thrown in his face. But even that news hadn't extinguished the new feelings he felt for her — if anything, it had only made them stronger.

He wanted her. More than that, he cared about her, he was jealous of anyone who had a claim on her time or her affections. He sensed that perhaps he even needed her. It was thrilling and terrifying all at the same time. And completely, totally, utterly frustrating. His timing had never been worse.

Russ was broken from his reverie abruptly when Dan plopped down in the chair next to him. The normally cheerful young man was looking somewhat less than happy at the moment. Russ sighed. He was pretty sure he already knew why.

"Hey, man," he said.

"Hey," Dan muttered. "What's up?"

"Not much. You okay?"

"Great! Just great..."

Russ sighed again. *Might as well get it over with,* he thought.

"That sounded convincing," he said.

It was Dan's turn to sigh. "I'm wasting my time, aren't I…tell me I'm wasting my time." He stared at the dance floor, where Callista and Devon were dancing cheek to cheek.

"You don't need me to tell you that, Dan," Russ replied, as gently as he could. "You've known it for years."

"Yeah, I know. Damn it! Why can't I get that girl out of my head?! I know I'm not good enough for her!"

Russ felt a surge of anger at his friend's blindness. Sitting up straight, he grabbed Dan by the shoulder, forcing him to turn around and face him.

"You idiot!" Russ growled. "When are you gonna realize that Callista's not good enough for you?!"

"But…but…" Dan stuttered, astounded at Russ's reaction. "She's beautiful! She's intelligent! She's so incredibly classy! And she's your sister! How can you say that about her?!"

How many more people was Russ going to have to diss his family to tonight?

"Yeah, she's beautiful, all right. On the outside. And she's smart and elegant. But she's cold, man. Cold, calculating. Hard. Callista has never loved anyone, Dan. At least, no one but her precious self."

"She cares about you…and your dad…doesn't she?"

"Callista doesn't give a damn about me. Never has. And as for my dad…well, I guess she does care about him a little…at least for as much as she can get out of him. No, man, my beautiful sister doesn't love people…she uses them. And then she discards them."

"Well, it looks like that's about to change," Dan gestured toward the dance floor. "She's all over that photographer guy she hired."

Russ stared at the couple, his eyes narrowed. "She's just using Devon, too. Keeping him happy while he records Dad's campaign for posterity."

"Um...Russ? Campaign is over...remember? So why's Callista still messing with the dude?"

Russ frowned. "Good question..." he mused.

"Oh well," Dan continued after a moment of silence, "won't make any difference to me, one way or the other." He stood up. "Listen, I'm going home. Wanna spend the night at my place?"

"Yeah," Russ stood as well. "Yeah, I do. Thanks."

The two friends left together, both glad to put the evening behind them.

* * * * *

Nov. 5

I'm gonna kill her! Ainsley did that deliberately...interrupting us like that! And mentioning Jeremy! Just when Russ was about to...

Aw, hell! What difference does it make?! I am dating Jeremy...I have no right to start something up with Russ, too. Damn, my timing sure does suck. I mean, I like Jeremy — a lot! — but I really like Russ as well. Jeremy and I have a lot in common — I have a great time when we go out together — he's a REALLY good kisser — but Russ — Russ is just — he makes my knees melt just looking at me — my heart beats faster — my stomach gets all woogly — if I don't watch it, I may actually start drooling whenever he comes near me! Oh, yeah, that would be attractive...

LOL!! If someone had told me a few months ago that I'd have to choose between two guys, I would've LMAO!!! Russ actually thinks I'm hot! Be still my foolish heart! I have to be fair to Jeremy, though. He's a good guy, and a lot of fun. What's that old saying? A bird in the hand is worth... something lame. I guess what it means is better hang on to what you've got instead of trying for something you may not like if you did get it. Although, I am pretty sure I'd like hanging onto Russ if I got the chance...*wink wink*. Forget it, girl! Dealing with one guy full time is complicated enough. The last thing you need to do is start acting like Brody. Besides, men are much more territorial than women. They don't like to share. And since Russ already knows about Jeremy (damn it, Ainsley!), it's probably a moot point, anyway. Oh well...not bad for the ego, though...having two guys wanting me at the same time. So there, Princess Braidy! LOL

I'm pretty worried about Russ, though...this whole thing with his dad. And now that Mr. Baines is gonna be the mayor, what happens? I wonder if I should say something to Mom or Andrew about what Russ thinks? No, I can't do that. Russ told me in strictest confidence. I suppose I could just mention it, kinda like the thought had just occurred to me...no, that wouldn't work either. I barely know Mr. Baines. Where would I get the idea that he was up to no good? Man, what if he is?! This could get really gormy! Like, in an extremely nasty way! Mr. Baines seems like a pretty powerful dude. What if it came down to some sort of fight? How could we stop him? This all goes back to what I was wondering about before...how do magicals punish other magicals for breaking the law? There's gotta be some sort of rules in place, or we'd have total chaos. I've gotta talk to Matthew about this...if anyone knows, he would.

In the meantime, not much point worrying about it. Russ could be totally off-base about the whole thing. Mr. Baines will probably turn out to be a great mayor. I have noticed that Russ doesn't tend to be exactly a ray of sunshine on a general basis...he's probably just overreacting to something that ice-blooded sister of his said. Man, is she a glacier, or what?! I thought Braidy was a princess, but Callista Baines is in a class all by herself! And cold! I got shivers just being in the same room with her! I sure hope Devon isn't falling for her. Something tells me she's the love-'em-and-leave-'em type...I'd hate to see him get hurt like that. Oh well, he's a big boy...he'll just have to handle it himself.

It's late, and I've got school tomorrow. Better call it a night...

* * * * *

Jonathan sensed he was pushing his luck. His companion was not the type to allow a man to take advantage of a situation, but he couldn't resist the temptation. He'd seen her so seldom lately, and the complete privacy of the moment was a rare luxury. Closing his eyes, he leaned in for another kiss, pulling her tighter at the same time, and allowed one hand to wander a little. He then made an attempt to nibble on her ear, and was immediately rebuffed.

"Stop it, Jonathan! You know I don't like that!"

"Sorry..."

"Besides, we need to talk." She pulled away from him completely and reached for her drink. "I'm concerned about your lack of progress with the Attison girl. We need to get this situation resolved. Alex is getting impatient."

"Don't worry. I have everything under control."

She raised an eyebrow. "Do you?"

"Yes," he replied, rather peeved. "I'm seeing her on Saturday. Our first date," he grimaced.

"What?" she asked, the second eyebrow joining the first. "You don't find her attractive?"

"A bit overdone, for my tastes. Typical Barbie doll type. I prefer a woman with subtlety ...one who's got some mystery to her." He tentatively slipped one arm around her shoulders. She allowed it.

"I wouldn't mention that to her, if I were you," she commented.

Jonathan laughed. "Don't worry. I know how to handle a little girl like Braidy Attison."

"So you'll be confirming the presence of the Mark on Saturday, then bringing her to us immediately afterwards, correct?"

"No..."

"No?"

"Remember, this isn't just about getting physical control of the Dumari. I...we...have to win her confidence as well. Convince her that our plans are for the best. She's too old to browbeat. Otherwise, Alex would have simply ordered another kidnapping. I have to be subtle, elusive, ambiguous...make her want me so badly she'll do anything to get me while at the same time holding her at arms' length. Nothing is more attractive to girls like her. Our date Saturday night is merely the next step in the process."

"We're running out of time..."

"We still have time," Jonathan interrupted. "Braidy doesn't turn eighteen until April. That's five months from now. I should have the job finished before the end of the year." He risked pulling her closer, close enough to murmur in her ear. "I'll be using my incomparable charms to make her fall madly in love with me. Think I can do it?"

She laughed, but didn't push him away. "I'm sure you'll have no problem with a brainless little chit like her. Those kind of girls are always falling for the 'bad boy' types — think they can reform them, or something."

"I'm not a 'bad boy'," he protested.

She laughed again. "You're hardly good, my dear!"

"I didn't hear you complaining a few minutes ago," he whispered, nuzzling her neck. She allowed the intimacy for a moment or two, then stood up abruptly.

"I'm tired, Jonathan. It's very late. It's time I went home."

Jonathan sighed. He knew from past experience that there was no point arguing. He walked her to the door.

"Make certain you have the Attison girl under control soon, Jonathan. Everything hinges on her cooperation."

"I know," he replied. "She'll be fully submissive by Christmas, at the latest."

"I certainly hope so," she said, allowing him a perfunctory goodnight kiss. "Goodnight, Jonathan."

"Goodnight, Callista."

Chapter Twelve:

Ainsley's Revenge

Braidy stood in the doorway of The Christmas Tree Shop, across the street from Club Ving in Hyannis. The store was closed for the evening, its windows dark. Blending in with the shadows, the hood of her coat hid her bright hair. She shivered, more from nerves than the cold night air.

She'd been having second thoughts about this date all week long. Yes, she had very strong feelings for Jonathan, more than she'd ever felt toward any boy she knew. She found him handsome, intelligent, sexy... and dangerous. It was this last that made her shiver — that, and the knowledge that she was here without her parents' permission. They weren't even remotely aware of her actual plans. That was something else that bothered Braidy. She'd lied to her mother and father about her intended destination...and her intended companion. She'd told them that she was meeting Karen at the movie theater in Barnstable. Karen wasn't even on Cape Cod. She and her family had gone to New York for the weekend, so there was no danger of Karen calling the house in Braidy's absence and giving her away. The chances of anyone in her family finding out what she was up to were very slim, but deception didn't sit well with Braidy. It never had.

She had just about made up her mind to forget the whole thing when a silver Solus pulled up and parked right in front of her. Jonathan Crenshaw climbed out of the driver's side, glancing casually up and down the street. Braidy held her breath, waiting for him to turn toward her. He did a moment later, and a slow, lazy smile crossed his lips as he spotted her standing in the shadows. Braidy froze, a deer in the headlights, as Jonathan approached.

"You were going to leave," he said, still smiling.

"How did you..?" Braidy gasped. Could he read her mind?

"I could tell by the look on your face. You're having second thoughts. Fine with me. Go home, little girl. I'm not interested in babysitting." Jonathan's smile had become a sneer. He turned his back on her.

"No!" Braidy exclaimed, grabbing his sleeve. Jonathan stopped, looking back at her over his shoulder. "Don't go! I...I..."

Jonathan scowled. "Make up your mind, girl. I haven't got all night."

Braidy swallowed hard. She knew her parents didn't approve of her dating Jonathan, but she wanted to so badly. He haunted her, day and night. Of course, his "babysitting" comment had really stung. Braidy prided herself on being mature for her age. The last thing her ego could tolerate was for Jonathan to think of her as a "little girl". She had to prove herself to him.

Besides, he wasn't that much older. Her parents were totally out of line on that. Jonathan was, what, twenty-one? Twenty-two, at most? Braidy was eighteen — well, seventeen-and-half, at any rate. There was only four or five years' difference in their ages. Not that much. Dad was three years older than Mom. And Grandpa Matthew was almost ten years older than Grandma Priscilla. So what was the big deal?

Of course, deep down inside, Braidy knew exactly what the big deal was. She was still in high school, while Jonathan was almost finished with college. It wasn't the years, it was the mileage. Jonathan had seen and experienced so much more than she'd had the opportunity to. As grown-up as she liked to think she was, Braidy knew that basically she was still a girl, while Jonathan was most definitely a man. Braidy sighed. Why did life have to be so complicated?

"I...I want to go out with you, Jonathan," she said softly. "You know I do! It's just...my parents..."

Jonathan's face grew hard. "We've already had this conversation. Go back to your playpen, Braidy." He pulled away from her and strode toward his car.

"NO! Wait!" Braidy cried, running after him. "I...I want to go...I do, Jonathan! Really!"

Jonathan stared at her in silence for a full minute, by which time Braidy was nearly in tears. Finally, he nodded his head.

"All right, then." He took Braidy's hand and dragged her close, kissing her hard. "Just don't disappoint me again, got it?"

Braidy nodded, her mouth too dry to speak. Jonathan kissed her again, more gently this time, then led her across the street to the dance club.

* * * * *

Brody stormed in the front door of the Bed and Breakfast, slamming the door behind him.

"Goddam! Son of a ..! This is so frickin' ignorant!"

He banged his way toward the kitchen, stomping his feet and crashing through doorways. Luckily, no one else was home. Phil and Caroline had gone out to dinner, while Braidy was at the movies with Karen. It was a slow time of year, tourist-wise, so the Bed and Breakfast was unoccupied. No guests to complain about the string of obscenities echoing through the house.

Brody hadn't expected to be home this early himself. He'd planned to take his latest girlfriend (Miss Red Sweater) out for dinner and a movie. They'd gone to the restaurant and were having a great time — until, that is, Brody made the mistake of flirting with the waitress. They barely made it to the car before Carla went ballistic. Crying and screaming, she'd gone on and on about how insensitive he was, how he never paid any attention to her, how she couldn't trust him. Brody had stared at her in shock, unable to get a word in edgewise. When Carla finally ran out of breath, Brody foolishly suggested, in a futile attempt to make peace, that they go ahead with their plans for the evening. Carla replied with an icy stare.

"You haven't listened to a word I said," she declared.

"Yes, I did!" Brody protested. "I..."

"No, you didn't," Carla interrupted him. "You just think you did. You don't understand at all!"

"Got that right!" Brody muttered under his breath.

"Take me home, please."

"Wha...what?"

"I said, take me home. I never want to see you again."

Brody protested, he argued, he begged — to no avail. Carla was adamant. In silence, he drove her home. When he pulled into the driveway, she jumped out and ran to the front door, not waiting for Brody to escort her. He made a halfhearted attempt to follow her, thought better of it, and left. During the drive home, the anger began to build, until by the time he reached home, he was steaming.

"All I did was talk to the waitress a little! I was just being nice! What the hell's wrong with that?! So what if she was hotter than Scarlett Johansson?! Is that my fault?! Girls are so...so...arghhhh!" he ended his diatribe with a roar of frustration. His expletives were interrupted by the sound of the phone ringing. Taking a deep breath, Brody forced himself to calm down...at least momentarily.

"Hello?"

"Brody? It's Karen. Is Braidy there?" Karen's voice sounded hoarse, as if she, too had been crying.

"Um...no!" Brody frowned. "Isn't she with you?"

"Me? No! We're in New York City for the weekend, but...but things kinda...oh, Brody! I need to talk to Braidy! Right now!"

"I'm sorry, Karen. She's not here. I thought she was going to the movies with you. What's wrong?"

Brody heard Karen sniff. *"We..my family and I...were going to spend the weekend in New York, go to see a Broadway show, do the tourist thing at the Statue of Liberty...but this afternoon, my parents got into this terrible argument! Dad got so pissed he walked out of our hotel and he hasn't come back!"*

"Wow! That's a bummer!"

"What if they decide to get a divorce?!"

"You don't think it's that bad, do you?"

"I've never heard them fight like that, Brody. It was scary! Mom's been crying for hours. Damn! Where is Braidy when I need her! I tried texting her, but she hasn't answered me!" Karen broke down completely and began crying in earnest.

For the second time that evening, Brody had a sobbing girl on his hands, without a clue how to deal with the situation. He made a few soothing, unintelligible noises in an attempt to ease Karen's distress. To his utter amazement, his efforts eventually paid off.

"Tha...thanks..." Karen finally said, with a sniff and a hiccup. *"I really appreciate you listening, Brody. You're the greatest! Have Braidy call me tomorrow, okay?"*

"Sure." Brody hung up the phone and leaned against the kitchen counter. "So I'm the greatest, am I? Try telling Carla that..."

He was halfway up the stairs before it hit him.

"Where *is* Braidy, anyway?"

* * * * *

"I'll just be a minute, Jeremy."

Moira gave her boyfriend a quick peck before running up the stairs to her bedroom. They had a big test in Physics on Wednesday, and Moira had promised to share her notes with Jeremy.

Jeremy waited in the foyer. The house was silent. Moira had mentioned that her parents were having dinner out with her aunt and uncle, and of course Devon was away at college, so the only other person in the house was Ainsley, who was currently nowhere in sight. Jeremy briefly considered following Moira upstairs, a wicked grin on his face, but wisely thought better of it. Ainsley was somewhere on the premises. Being interrupted by a curious little sister was not what he had in mind at all. He'd just have to wait until later, when he and Moira were alone in his car, somewhere quiet...and dark.

The wisdom of his decision was made evident moments later, when he heard Ainsley calling to her sister.

"Moira? That you? Russ called..." Ainsley appeared in the doorway from the living room. "He wants you to...Oh! Um...hi, Jeremy! I didn't know you were here." Although Ainsley's smile was as bright as ever, Jeremy detected an uncharacteristic tenseness about her. And who the hell was Russ?

"Hi, Ainsley. Moira went upstairs. She's getting some class notes for me," he explained. "So who's Russ?"

"Oh...um...nobody..." Ainsley blushed, increasing Jeremy's suspicions. "Just...just a friend...no one special. Moira hasn't mentioned him?"

"No."

"Oh...um...well, no biggie...I'll just...I'll tell her later. See ya, Jeremy." She left him alone, puzzled and decidedly jealous. It was obvious that Ainsley had not told him everything about this Russ character — and Jeremy was less than happy about how his imagination was filling in the details. Something was going on. And he was going to find out exactly what that something was.

Several minutes later, Moira came down the stairs, a bright red spiral notebook in hand.

"Sorry that took a while," she said. "I couldn't remember where I'd left it." She handed it to Jeremy with a smile — a smile that quickly faded at the expression on his face. "You okay?"

"Yeah...fine," he replied, not very convincingly. They stepped out onto the porch and headed back to the car. Halfway down the sidewalk, Jeremy halted in midstep.

"Who's Russ?" he demanded.

Moira stared at him, momentarily nonplussed. "Who...what..? Where'd you hear..?"

"Ainsley was looking for you. She said he'd called you. So? Who is he?"

"Russ Baines. He's...he's just a friend." Unfortunately, the blush spreading across Moira's cheeks only served to confirm Jeremy's gut feeling. His heart sank.

"Funny," he said coldly. "That's not the impression I got."

"Well, it's true!" Moira's embarrassment increased. "We're friends, that's all."

"That may be all he is, but is that all you want him to be?" Jeremy asked astutely. Moira's look of chagrin told him volumes. "I see. Goodbye, Moira." He held out the notebook.

"What do you mean?" Moira's confusion was quickly turning to anger. "Are you dumping me?!"

"I'm not going out with a girl who'd rather be with some other guy. Or worse, who's yo-yoing me behind my back."

"I am not a yo-yo!" Moira stomped her foot. "So I like him, so what? We're just friends! You telling me there aren't any other girls you like?"

"No, there isn't."

"Ha! Yeah, right! Guys are always checking out other girls. It's okay for you, but not for us, right? I don't think so!"

"That's not true! Not all guys are like that!"

"Oh, yeah?! What about Brody? He's been jumping from one girl to the next..."

"I am not Brody!" Jeremy shouted.

"Really?" Moira was on a roll. "Then what about that magazine you two were drooling over at school? It sure as hell wasn't the latest issue of Popular Mechanics!"

"I...that...we..." Jeremy stuttered, turning red himself. "That's just a guy thing."

"Bull!" Moira stated succinctly. "If it's okay for you to be drooling and dreaming over some supermodel in a skimpy bikini, it's okay for me to be friends with another guy."

"It's a totally different thing!" Jeremy insisted. "I'll never even meet that girl!"

"But if you did," Moira continued, her eyes narrowed, "you'd be all over her in a heartbeat, wouldn't you."

"I...we...that's totally beside the point!" Jeremy realized that he'd somehow lost control of the argument, but had no idea how.

"I think not," Moira stated. Spinning abruptly on her heel, she stalked back to the front porch. "Haven't you ever heard?" she flung back over her shoulder. "It's the thought that counts!" She ran up the steps and into the house, slamming the door with all her might.

"But...! I...!" Jeremy sputtered, furious. "That was exactly MY point!" he shouted. Flinging Moira's notebook onto the porch, he stormed back to his car and peeled off down the street, his tires squealing.

Moira found Ainsley spying through the dining room window, an ugly expression of triumph and glee on the young girl's face.

"You...you...!" Moira was so angry, she couldn't speak at first. Taking a deep breath, she brought herself back under control. "You did that deliberately."

"Did what deliberately?" Ainsley asked blandly.

"You made Jeremy think I was going out with Russ Baines behind his back!"

"I said nothing of the kind," Ainsley replied smoothly. "I just mentioned that Russ had called you, that's all."

"It wasn't what you said, chit! It was the way you said it!"

"Is it my fault that your boyfriend has a suspicious nature? I can't help it if he inferred more than I meant."

"You made sure he did! You must have! Jeremy had no reason to suspect there was anything between Russ and me!"

"Ha!" Ainsley crowed. "So you admit it! There is something between you and Russ! I knew it! I saw it in your face the night of the election!"

"That's not true! He was upset about something and I was just trying to help him work it out!"

"Oh, please! I'm not an idiot! I saw the way you two were looking at each other!"

"But nothing happened! And besides, it was none of your business! Why did you have to say anything to Jeremy?!"

"Payback's a bitch, ain't it, dear sister," Ainsley said coldly, her normally warm green gaze suddenly sharp and icy as a glacier. "'Bout time I got you back for burning me with Jason Hicks."

Moira stared at the girl in shock. Then something inside of her snapped.

"YOU WITCH! YOU COW! YOU HO!!!" she screeched at the top of her lungs, her hands forming into tight fists at her sides.

"LOOK WHO'S CALLING THE KETTLE BLACK!" Ainsley shouted in return. "YOU'RE THE WITCH!"

"I AM NOT!"

"YES YOU ARE! YOU'RE MEAN...AND SELFISH...AND... AND...MEAN!" Ainsley repeated herself, too upset at the moment to come up with a more original insult.

"YOU SPOILED ROTTEN LITTLE BRAT!"

"I AM NOT SPOILED ROTTEN!"

"You are, too! You get away with murder around here! Anything Ainsley wants, Ainsley gets! Daddy's precious little girl!" Moira shouted, waving her fists in the air. The tablecloth on the dining room table flew up into the air and dropped in a heap on the floor on the other side of the room. Both girls completely ignored it. "Just because you're the *baby*!" Moira sneered.

"Well, you..." Ainsley paused, wracking her brain for a truly cutting reply. "You... you're FAT! And...and UGLY! And...and...!"

"WHY, YOU LITTLE...!" Moira raised her hand and took a menacing step forward.

"WHAT THE....?!"

A strong hand grabbed Moira's uplifted arm and held her firmly. Trying her best to pull free, Moira fought against her stepfather's grip. Her parents had arrived home just in time.

"What on earth is going on?!" Renatta demanded, stepping between the girls. "Stop that, Moira! What are you two fighting about?!"

Ainsley glared at her older sister, her face flushed with fury. Moira was breathing hard, her eyes glittering with anger and her teeth bared. Pulling free of Andrew's restraining hand, she straightened her shoulders and pointed an accusing finger at Ainsley.

"She..." Moira began, her voice shaking with hatred and disgust, "...she made Jeremy think I was moonlighting on him, and he broke up with me because of it!"

"Moonlighting?" Andrew queried.

"Cheating on him," Renatta explained quickly. "Were you?"

"NO! And that's beside the point! She had no right to say anything like that to my boyfriend, true or not! It's none of her business! She was just being evil!"

Both parents turned to gaze at their younger daughter.

"Ainsley," Andrew said, "is this true?"

"I...I..." Ainsley's eyes widened at the expression on her father's face. The enormity of her deed suddenly came crashing down upon her. "I didn't *exactly* say..."

"You implied it!" Moira interrupted.

"I...I didn't..."

"Yes, you did! You wanted revenge! For that stupid Jason Hicks! Like it was my fault you screwed that up!"

"It was!" Ainsley cried. "You made me think he was just using me, and I got all jealous, and...and..." she burst into tears.

"Ainsley Marie Collins." Moira jumped. She'd never heard Andrew use that tone of voice before — certainly not to his precious baby girl.

For a moment, Moira almost felt sorry for Ainsley. Almost. "Did you lie to Jeremy about Moira?"

"I..." Ainsley stared up at her father, terrified.

"Did you make him think that she was seeing someone else behind his back?"

"I..."

"ANSWER ME, YOUNG LADY!"

All three females took a step back in shock. Ainsley gulped.

"Yes," she whispered, hanging her head with remorse.

"Moira, I would appreciate it if you would go to your room," Andrew said, not looking at her. "Your mother and I need to have a talk with Ainsley. You," he jerked his head at Ainsley, "in the other room. Now!"

Ainsley scuttled toward the living room, her parents right behind her. When he reached the doorway of the dining room, Andrew turned back to Moira.

"Moira..." he said, the anger in his tone palpable, "for the record... I ever catch you raising your hand to your sister again, you will be grounded for a month. Is that clear?"

"Yes, sir," Moira replied softly. She'd never seen Andrew this furious before. Something told her he meant every word he said.

"Good!" He joined his wife and daughter.

As Moira slowly climbed the stairs, suddenly exhausted by all the drama of the past hour, she heard Andrew's voice floating into the foyer, punctuated by quiet sobbing and sniffling from Ainsley.

"I cannot begin to express how disappointed we are in you, Ainsley. What you did to Moira was unconscionable. Worse than that, however, is what you did to Jeremy — a perfectly innocent bystander, whom you used to hurt Moira. That was cruel, Ainsley, terribly cruel..."

Moira didn't stay for any more. She'd heard enough. When she reached her bedroom in the attic, she kicked off her shoes, flung herself across the bed, and let the tears flow.

* * * * *

Braidy couldn't stop giggling. Nor could she walk a straight line. That second margarita had done her in. Although not exactly drunk, she was seriously tipsy. Her behavior seemed to amuse Jonathan, judging by the smile hovering around his lips.

"Time for some coffee, young lady," he said, steering her in the direction of an all-night diner a block away, "or you'll have a difficult time driving home."

"I'm fine," Braidy insisted, pulling herself up regally. Unfortunately, the image was ruined when she lost her footing and stumbled over the curb. Once again, she broke into helpless giggles as Jonathan grabbed her arm to steady her.

"Sure you are," he said, chuckling. He found a booth near the back of the diner, settled her into a seat and quickly ordered coffee for them both. He didn't allow Braidy to add any sugar or milk when the waitress brought two steaming cups. "Black," he insisted. "Now drink."

Braidy wrinkled her nose, but she did as Jonathan instructed and drank the entire cup. Halfway through the second cup, her giggles had subsided. Two cups later, she was mostly sober, and in desperate need of the ladies' room.

Once Braidy felt a bit more put together, Jonathan walked her back to her car.

"When will I see you again?" she asked shyly.

"Hard to say," he replied. "I'm not sure when I'll have time."

"Oh..." Braidy whispered, trying not to sound disappointed. Something told her that Jonathan would not be interested in the clinging type. "I...um...I had a really good time tonight, Jonathan."

"Me too." Jonathan leaned her up against the car and kissed her. Braidy gasped. She'd never been kissed like that before — as if the kiss involved not only their lips, but their entire bodies. It left her trembling. Jonathan chuckled softly as he stroked her cheek lightly with his fingertips, his torso molded to hers. He claimed her mouth again, leaving her breathless. Without warning, he let go of her and stepped back. Braidy had to grasp the door handle to keep herself steady.

"I'll let you know when I can see you again," he said casually, almost flippantly. He walked away without a backward glance.

Braidy inhaled deeply, letting the air out slowly as she fought back the tears that had sprung to her eyes. She watched Jonathan walk away, her pulse still racing. When he disappeared around the corner, she sighed, climbed into the car, and slowly made her way home.

* * * * *

Russ slammed the door to his bedroom, furious with his father, his sister...and the weather. In that order.

The Baines family was spending the weekend on the Cape, away from the noise of the city, and the never ending stream of meetings for the soon-to-be mayor of Boston.Russ had been looking forward to some peace and quiet, planning a long walk on the beach...with the extra bonus of possibly running into Moira. Instead, he was trapped in the house by a wicked Nor'easter. And he'd just had a horrible fight with Desmond and Callista.

What were they thinking?! How could they possibly justify their actions?! Russ's worst nightmares had come true. All his apprehensions of the past several months hadn't been so unfounded after all. He threw himself across the bed, covering his eyes with one long arm, his head spinning. Going over the argument in his mind wasn't going to make things any better, but he couldn't help himself...

They had just finished breakfast when the bombshell was dropped.

"How have your meetings been going, Dad?" Russ had asked.

Desmond shrugged. "As well as can be expected, I suppose," he replied.

"What do you mean? Isn't being the mayor-elect all you thought it would be?" Russ teased lightly. Desmond responded with a half-smile.

"Actually, it's pretty much what I'd expected. I merely find it frustrating — too much talk, not enough action. I'm not used to having my hands tied like this."

"Your hands tied?"

"I'm only the mayor-elect, Russ, not the mayor. Not yet, anyway. All I can do at this point is listen...and make a few suggestions from time to time. I can't actually get anything done until I've been sworn into office."

"Patience, Dad," Russ counseled. "It won't be long."

"I know, son. I just hate this feeling of impotence. There's so much that needs to be done — will I have enough time to get to all of it?"

"You'll have eight years, Father," Callista said coolly.

Russ gave his sister a sharp look. "Dad was elected for four years, Callista. He'll have to run again if he wants a second term. And win again."

"I know that, Russell," she replied. "That won't be a problem."

"How do you know? No offense, Dad, but what if the people of Boston decide four years from now that they'd rather elect someone else?"

"Then we'll simply convince them otherwise," Callista said, in an infuriatingly superior tone.

Russ's eyes narrowed. "Convince them? How?"

"The same way we did this time," she replied.

"Callista..." Desmond's voice held a note of warning.

"Oh, please, Father! Russell is a big boy. He might as well know the truth...he'll need to if we're going to bring him into the loop anyway." Callista stood up and walked to where her father was seated, resting one hand on the back of his chair. Russ's heart began to pound. He had a feeling he wasn't going to like what he was about to hear.

"What are you talking about, Callista? Dad?"

"Simply that we know what's best for this city...and its citizens. Both magicals and non-magicals. And we know what has to be done to achieve the necessary results," Desmond began to explain.

"So of course we had to make certain that Father was elected," Callista continued for him. "Regardless of how the ballots were actually cast."

"What did you..?" Russ gasped, aghast.

"Callista and Quinn merely used a little magic to tweak the numbers a bit, Russ," his father tried to reassure him. "Without my permission, I might add..."

"You had approved the plan in theory prior to the election, Father," Callista pointed out.

"In theory, Callista. I distinctly remember telling you and Muldoon to hold off on implementing it. But as you know, Russ, your sister is even less patient than I am. She became a bit anxious and jumped the gun. As it turned out, however, the procedure wasn't even necessary. I would have won anyway."

"But that's...that's illegal!" Russ jumped to his feet, horrified. "You tampered with election results! You could both go to jail!"

"Oh, grow up, Russell!" Callista rolled her eyes. "All's fair in love and war — and politics most definitely fall under the war category. Besides, how could anyone prove anything? We used magic...there's no physical evidence to use against us."

Russ paced back and forth like a caged animal, running his hand repeatedly through his hair. "That makes it even worse! You broke the first rule of magicals — we're not allowed to use magic to interfere with the lives of non-magicals, remember? You abused the privilege!"

Callista laughed. "Please, Russell! Spare me the empty platitudes! What is the point of being magical if we can't use our abilities to get what we want?"

Russ suddenly felt sick to his stomach.

"You can't mean that. Tell me you don't mean that."

Desmond held out his hand. "She didn't mean it the way it sounded, Russ. You know your sister better than that. What she meant is that we should use our talents, whatever they may be, to make the world a better place for everyone. That's what we want. Isn't that what you want as well?"

"Of course, but..."

"Then we're on the same wave length — the betterment of our society. I have so many plans, Russ! I can't wait to tell you all about them. I want you in on things as soon as possible..."

"What you did was wrong!" Russ interrupted his father, his eyes blazing. "I don't care how good your intentions were, it was still wrong! You broke the law!"

"The end justifies the means, son," Desmond said, his voice cold and hard. "I'll be able to do a lot of good for Boston, and you know it."

"Not like this! Not with magic!" Russ shouted. "You took unfair advantage of your opponent, Dad! What else have you used magic for that I don't know about? Is that how you've managed to be so successful in business all these years? What other lies have you told me?!"

Desmond jumped to his feet. "That's enough! I won't be spoken to that way by my own son!"

Russ's breakfast had turned into a lump of lead in his stomach. He stared at his father in silence for several moments. Something very basic had changed between them. He felt as if he was going to cry.

"The end does not justify the means," he said sadly, "and we are definitely not on the same wave length. I can't even begin to comprehend where you two are coming from right now, so if it's all the same to you, I'd rather you cut me out of your plans." Russ moved slowly toward the doorway, wanting nothing more than to be alone. Silently, he cursed the weather that prevented him from escaping outside — escaping from the house, from his family, from the disappointment burning in his throat.

"You'll understand some day, Russ," Desmond pleaded, his hand held out.

"No, Dad, I don't think I will. Any more than Mom would have." And he left the room.

The tension in the room was nearly tangible. Desmond slowly sat down, his body slumped forward, his head in his hands.

"Damn it!" he whispered.

"I'm sorry, Father," Callista said, moving back to her own chair. "I'm afraid I've underestimated the strength — and irrationality — of Russell's romantic nature. He still believes in the luxury of seeing everything in black and white. I was certain once the election was behind us, he'd be more than willing to come on board."

"Well," Desmond replied, raising his head, his eyes cold and hard, "we'll have to find a way to convince him we're right. I need his help. I can't do this alone."

"You're not alone, Father," Callista insisted, her tone slightly hurt. "You know that I'm with you one hundred percent."

"Of course, my dear," Desmond soothed her. "Your support means the world to me, you know that. But I need Russ as well. How am I going to convince the world that our goals are for everyone's good if I can't convince my own son?"

For once, Callista had no answer for her father.

Half an hour later, sprawled across his bed, Russ groaned. What was he going to do? What could he do? Nothing, really. Who could he tell about Desmond and Callista's activities? Who would even believe him? No one. Tears came to his eyes and he buried his face in his pillow.

* * * * *

November 10

GOD! WHAT A NIGHT!!!

If I got two hours of sleep last night, it's a miracle. All I could think about was the expression on Jeremy's face. He looked so hurt, so disappointed, so depressed. God! I'm crying again! What the hell is the matter with me?! I never cry!

I guess I really care about Jeremy. Not like I'm in love with him, or anything like that...but he's definitely turned out to be more than just a good time. I really enjoy spending time with him. He's my friend...correction, he WAS my friend.

Okay, maybe I should have told him about Russ. But what could I have told him anyway? It's true, I've been kinda crushin' on Russ, but I hadn't done anything about it, had I?

And I really do like Jeremy! I mean, after that conversation at the election party, I could have broken up with Jeremy and tried to get things going with Russ. After all, he did seem really interested in me that night. But did I make a move? NO! And why didn't I? Because I wanted to be with Jeremy, that's why!

Ainsley had no right to stick her stupid little turned-up nose into my business! I hope Mom and Andrew really gave it to her, the little witch!! I hope they grounded her for the rest of her life, locked her in her room, put her on bread and water rations...too bad the rack is illegal these days! Who am I kidding! They're not gonna do anything to her ...their Little Princess! They probably just gave her a good talking to...as if any kid ever listens to that crap! Although, from the look on Andrew's face last night, he wasn't exactly planning to be easy on her. I was really glad it wasn't ME he was so pissed at...he was actually pretty scary! I've never seen him so angry. He's always been so laid back, so calm, cool and collected. I had no idea he had that kind of temper. Not like Ainsley didn't deserve it, the stinking little...

So, what do I do now? Do I try to make it up with Jeremy? Would he even want to talk to me? Or should I write him off as a lost cause and just go for it with Russ? What if I read Russ wrong? What if he was just needing a touch of comfort that night and that was it? It's not like he's ever shown any real interest before...beyond being friends, that is. If I approach him, and he's not interested, I'll look like a complete dork...that would be incredibly harsh! But if I don't try, I'll always wonder...

Okay, you know what I need to do? I need to make up my mind! Who do I like more ...Jeremy or Russ? And then whichever one I decide on, I need to just give it everything I've got. Either beg Jeremy to take me back (Me? Beg? Gag me!) or lay it on the line with Russ and let him take it from there. God, this is really scary...putting myself out there like that. But they're both good guys...they're worth it. I think...

* * * * *

"Good work," Morty grinned at Jonathan. "You've practically got the girl eating out of your hands."

"That was the whole point, wasn't it?" Jonathan smiled coldly. "Make Braidy fall in love with me, get her so obsessed that she'll do anything for me, including go along with our plans willingly, thereby making Alex's job much easier...and negating Matthew Collins's protective shield in the bargain."

Morty cackled. "Couldn't have set it up better myself. The stupid little chit won't know what hit her. Alex will have her wrapped around his little finger in no time. And then we can finally get to work." He took a swig of beer and wiped his mouth. "So when do you plan to make your move?"

"Christmas Eve."

"Christmas Eve?! That's more than a month from now!"

"I'm well aware of that, Morty. Just the right amount of time for her to pine after me... without risking any loss of influence."

"You sure about that?" Morty asked.

"Positive. Girls like Braidy Attison are pathetically predictable. She'll spend the next two weeks waiting eagerly for me to call...then she'll get angry..."

"Angry with you? We don't want that, do we?"

"Don't worry, it won't last. Besides, she won't just be angry with me for not calling," Jonathan explained, "she'll be furious with herself for hoping. And that will lead to Step Three."

"Which is?"

"Depression," Jonathan stated, "and resignation. She'll give up on ever seeing me again, she'll tell herself that she wasn't good enough for me, that I was bored with her, that I've moved on to someone else...so, of course, when I do appear again, she'll be ripe for the picking."

"Of course," Morty grinned maliciously. "But why Christmas Eve?"

"Braidy mentioned that she and her friends have a tradition of going ice skating on the cranberry bogs every Christmas Eve, right after dark. I'll show up, unannounced, and sweep her off her feet. So to speak." Jonathan leaned back in his chair, looking rather pleased with himself.

"You're going to do this in front of a bunch of kids? Are you crazy?!"

"Morty, the bogs are out in the middle of nowhere. It will be a piece of cake to get her off alone. Besides, what do you think I'm going to do to the girl?" Jonathan laughed.

"What are you going to do to her?" Morty asked, a nasty gleam in his eyes.

"Down, boy," Jonathan warned him. "Remember, Alex wants her unharmed...and untouched. My job is merely to convince her to talk with him. He'll take it from there."

"So you intend to get her away from her friends and bring her to Alex, is that it?"

"That's the plan." Jonathan stood up, stretching. He tossed his empty beer bottle into a nearby trash can. "He'll be waiting for us at the lighthouse. He likes the idea of not having to risk another kidnapping. In fact, if Braidy is as malleable as I think she'll be, we won't have to worry about keeping her hidden away at all."

"What do you mean?" Morty sat up straight. "Alex isn't considering the possibility of letting her continue to live with her family, is he?"

"Don't be absurd!" Jonathan scoffed at the older man. "No matter how cooperative Braidy is, we'll need to keep a constant eye on her. She'll merely tell her family that she's moving out."

"You're going to have the girl living with you?"

"Correct. At least, that's the way it will look to her family and friends. But, as you know, she will actually be spending most of her time with Alex."

"Will you keep up the pretense of a relationship with her?" Morty asked.

"Only for as long as is necessary to insure her complete cooperation," Jonathan said. "Once she is fully under Alex's control, I won't need to be involved with her at all."

"That should make Callista happy," Morty grinned wickedly.

"Callista knows that whatever I do with the Attison girl is strictly business. She knows she has nothing to be jealous of...not that Callista is petty enough to be jealous in the first place. She knows how superior she is to any other woman."

Morty shrugged and refrained from commenting on Callista's superiority.

"Sounds like you've got everything worked out then," he said, adding his own empty beer bottle to Jonathan's. "Let me know if you need a hand with anything."

"Don't worry," Jonathan smiled coldly as he left the room. "My plan is foolproof. Braidy Attison will be ours by Christmas morning."

Chapter Thirteen:

Revelations

Brody slipped into the family room, glancing down the stairs to make sure the coast was clear. He was in luck. Phil and Caroline were nowhere in sight. Tiptoeing to Braidy's bedroom door, he knocked softly.

"Bray?" he whispered. "You up?"

There was no response. Brody knocked harder.

"Braidy? It's me...we gotta talk."

"Go away!" Braidy replied with a groan. "I'm sleeping."

"If you were sleeping, you wouldn't have answered me," Brody pointed out, grinning. "C'mon, Bray! This is important!"

"Oh, all right!" Brody heard his sister cussing softly as she stumbled out of bed and across the room. The door was flung open abruptly to reveal a much disheveled Braidy, glaring bleary-eyed at her unwelcome twin.

"You better mean life-and-death important," she grimaced, "or I'm never speaking to you again!"

Braidy turned her back on Brody and returned to her bed. Flinging herself down on the mattress, she winced at the sharp throbbing behind her eyes. Braidy was not camping happy. Having never had more than a few sips of watered-down wine before, she was suffering quite a bit from the after-effects of two giant margaritas. If only the room would stop spinning...

"Never again!" she muttered to herself as she tried to get comfortable. Unsuccessfully.

Brody sprawled in the overstuffed chair near the window. His grin had faded at the sight of his sister. He had a sinking feeling this conversation was going to be even worse than he'd anticipated. He hated having to ask Braidy what had happened the night before, but he had to know. It wasn't like Braidy to lie to everyone. It wasn't like her at all. And that worried him.

After more than a minute's silence, Brody cleared his throat and plunged in.

"How was the movie?"

"The movie? Oh, yeah! The movie!" Braidy rolled onto her back and covered her eyes with one arm. "Good! Real good!"

"What did you see?"

"Um... *The Edge Of The Universe*...you should go. I think you'd like it."

"What's it about?"

"Um...you know...space travel stuff. Why are you asking me? You saw the trailer on the internet."

"Yeah, well...you can't always tell much just from trailers and commercials..." Brody forced a casual tone. "Did Karen like it?"

"Yeah...yeah...she liked it a lot." Braidy lifted her arm and scowled at him. "Is this what you woke me up to talk about? 'Cause if it is, you're an idiot."

"Braidy..." Brody hesitated, a part of him not wanting to know what his sister had really done. He leaned forward in the chair, his hands clasped between his knees. "...Karen called here last night, looking for you."

"What?" Braidy's eyes widened briefly, but she immediately tried to cover her surprise with a half-hearted laugh. "Oh, yeah...I forgot. We got our signals crossed at first. I thought we were meeting at the theater, but she thought I was picking her up. We got it sorted out. How'd you know she called here? Did she leave a message on the machine?" She stood up and walked to her desk, her fingers nervously fiddling with a pen and some paper. Braidy's body language belied her casual tone. Her shoulders were tensed and she pointedly refrained from facing her brother. Brody sighed.

"I talked to her," he told her.

Braidy spun around. "What?! I thought you had a date!"

"I did. It ended early. Braidy..." Brody stood up, moving closer to his sister, "Karen wasn't with you last night. She was in New York City, with her mom and her sister."

"How...how do you know that?"

"She told me. Her family went for the weekend, but her mom and dad had a big fight...she wanted to talk to you because she was really upset, and you weren't answering her texts."

"Oh!" Braidy whispered, biting her lower lip. Jonathan had made her turn her cell phone off early in the evening. She hadn't even thought about it since.

"Braidy..." Brody grasped Braidy's shoulders gently. "What did you really do last night?"

Braidy twisted away. "That's none of your business."

"I'm your brother! It damn well is my business; you lie about where you're gonna be and who you're with, you wake up this morning with a major hangover...don't deny it! I know the symptoms! And you can bet Mom and Dad will recognize them as well!"

"They won't! Not if you don't tell them!" Braidy yelled, immediately regretting it. She groaned and grabbed her head with both hands.

"Don't be a ditz! Of course they will!" Brody yelled back. Braidy winced.

"Not so loud! Can't you just leave me alone in my misery?"

"No!" Brody grabbed her by the shoulders again, harder than before, forcing her to face him. "This isn't like you, Bray! I won't let it rest until you come clean...I can't! Where the hell were you?"

"All right! All right! I'll tell you!" Braidy replied, tears in her eyes. "But you have to promise to cover for me with Mom and Dad."

"I..."

"Promise! Or I don't tell you a thing!"

"Okay! I promise! Now come clean. Where were you?"

"I was..." Braidy gulped. "I was at Club Ving."

Brody stared at Braidy in shock. "But...you're underage! How'd you get in there?"

"Jonathan got me in."

"Jonathan Crenshaw?!" Brody squeaked, his voice shooting up an octave. "Mom and Dad told you not to go out with him! He's too old for you!"

"He's not even twenty-two yet! He's still in college!"

"His last year!" Brody turned away, running his hands through his hair in exasperation. "And you're still in high school!"

"I'm nearly eighteen!"

"Not for five months! He's more than four years older than you!"

"That's not that much. Dad is older than Mom..."

"Barely three years! Besides, they're adults...there's a difference."

"Oh please!" Braidy scoffed. "Four years is four years...whether now or a decade from now."

"No, it's not, Bray, and you know it," Brody insisted. "Jonathan's an adult. We're still kids."

"That's not what you said when you were trying to talk Dad into letting you go on that overnighter with Glen and Jeremy," Braidy pointed out sharply.

"That was different. We were just three guys hanging out together. This is you and an older guy...a guy who obviously wants you to act older than you are," Brody said coldly.

"What do you mean by that?" Braidy shot back.

"He got you drunk last night," Brody growled.

"He didn't get me drunk!" Braidy protested weakly. "I chose to have one drink, that's all. I was curious." She had chosen to have one drink. The second one was Jonathan's idea.

"One drink? Looks to me like you had a bit more than just *one* drink," Brody raised an eyebrow.

"Jonathan saw how much I enjoyed the first one, so he got me another," she admitted, her face red. "And I wasn't drunk...just a little tipsy."

"So what else did Jonathan do?" Brody asked, his eyes narrowed.

"Nothing! He was a perfect gentleman. He even made sure I had a bunch of coffee, so I could drive home okay."

Brody's hands formed into fists. "That stinking little freak got you drunk and then let you drive yourself home?! All the way from Hyannis?! Why, I ought to...!"

"I told you! He made sure I'd sobered up before he let me drive! And I was very careful! I kept the speedometer at ten miles an hour the whole way, because that was as fast as I could see."

Brody didn't laugh. He didn't even crack a smile.

"Oh, Brody, just stop this!" Braidy dropped her head into her hands. "I'm a big girl," she muttered through her fingers. "I can take care of myself."

"I'm not so sure of that," Brody stated blandly. "I don't get what you see in the guy, in the first place."

"Well, I don't get what you see in most of the girls you go out with!" Braidy flared up. "What have you got against Jonathan?!"

"I...I..." Brody hesitated, not sure how to answer her. "I don't know, exactly...I just don't trust him, for some reason."

Braidy laughed harshly. "Well, that's a definitive answer, I must say."

"Knock it off! There's something about him...he's...he's just...too slick, ya know? And he has no business messing around with a high school girl! Besides, what do we know about this guy? He shows up out of nowhere, and you start drooling all over him..."

"I do not drool!" Braidy cried indignantly. "And he didn't show up out of nowhere — he's friends with Devon, remember?"

"My point is," Brody continued, "you shouldn't be going out with a guy you know virtually nothing about, that Mom and Dad don't approve of, and that is way too old for you. It's one thing to lie to them about what we do from time to time...but when you have to lie to me, as well?" Brody raised an eyebrow. "Not a smart move, dear sister. Just think about it, okay?" With that parting shot, he left.

"Oh, go away!" Braidy threw herself across the bed and screamed into her pillow in frustration. "He doesn't understand!" she whispered to herself. "No one does."

* * * * *

"It's time, Renatta."

"No, Matthew! Please!" Renatta begged her father-in-law. "Things were going so well — both girls have settled into their new schools, Moira was dating that nice boy, Jeremy — she'd begun to open up to both of us..."

"Until the fight with Ainsley, that is," Andrew said dryly.

"Exactly!" Renatta said. "Now we're practically back to square one with her. For weeks now, Moira has spent all her free time up in her room. She barely says a word at the supper table...and she won't even look at Ainsley. We tell her the truth now, she's liable to withdraw from us completely! I couldn't bear that! We'd come so far with her this past year..."

"We can't keep putting it off, Renatta," Matthew said gently. "Moira and the twins will be eighteen in a matter of months. They will come into their full powers and they have the right to know what those powers are."

"But it may not even be one of them," Renatta said. "It could be Ainsley, and she won't reach maturity for years yet..."

"But that's the problem, sweetheart," Andrew put in. "We have no idea which one of them it is, so there's no way to prepare them properly. We need to know. And they have the right to know...all four of them. We have to tell Moira and the twins, at least — and the sooner, the better."

"Tell us what?" Moira asked, stepping into the living room. She was greeted with an awkward silence. None of the adults had heard her approach. "Tell us what?" she repeated impatiently. "Is this about that lame Dumari crap?"

Matthew and Andrew both glanced at Renatta, who had eyes for no one but her daughter. Two pairs of bright green eyes met and held — Renatta's worried and loving, Moira's confused, yet determined to get to the truth at last. Finally, Renatta sighed and looked away.

"You tell her," she murmured. "I can't."

"Dad?"

"Gladly." Matthew took Moira by the elbow and steered her out of the room. "Why don't we go upstairs? I've been wanting to see that aerie of yours for some time."

Moira trotted to keep up with Matthew's long strides. Her stomach was twisting and turning with excitement...and a little fear. A quick glance over her shoulder gave her a brief glimpse of her mother enfolded in Andrew's arms. Moira felt a slight pang on Renatta's behalf, but Matthew and Andrew were right. It was time she knew what the score was.

Two flights up, Moira ushered Matthew into her private domain. She quickly scooped a pile of dirty clothes up off the floor, threw the covers haphazardly across her unmade bed, and grabbed her bookbag from the rocking chair, dumping it unceremoniously onto the floor near her desk. Matthew bowed his thanks before taking the proffered seat. Moira ensconced herself on the bottom of the bed, her legs crossed underneath her.

"So...um...what's up?" she asked with a nervous smile.

Matthew replied with a small, slow smile of his own. He leaned back comfortably in the rocking chair, his long legs stretched out in front.

"Don't be too hard on Ainsley, Moira," he said.

"Wha...who...oh...um..." Moira stammered, momentarily wrong-footed. Then her anger flared. "She had no right to do what she did! It was totally ignorant!"

"Yes, it was," Matthew agreed, throwing Moira for a loop once again. "But we all make mistakes, don't you agree? It's how we learn."

"Yeah...well...I suppose..." Moira muttered grudgingly. "I just hope Ainsley's learned from her mistake!"

Matthew raised an eyebrow. "Oh, she has. Have you?"

Moira chose to ignore Matthew's question, responding with one of her own. "So, is that what you wanted to talk about?"

"No, Moira, it isn't." Matthew paused, took a deep breath, then plunged in. "You were correct, Moira. What I have to tell you is about the Dumari."

"I knew it!" Moira's stomach tightened a bit more. "Are you finally gonna tell me what the hell was going on last year? When those dillweeds kidnapped us?"

"Yes. At least, as much as I know. Exactly who ordered the abductions, and what their true purpose was, I can only guess. But I can tell you why you, Braidy, and Brody were the targets."

"Lay it on me!" Moira's eyes gleamed. Matthew couldn't help but smile at her enthusiasm.

"You may not be so excited once I've given you the details," he said. "It's not an easy burden."

"I just want to know the truth, Grandpa," Moira replied. "I need to know the truth. Whatever this is, it nearly got me killed last year. I'd say that gives me as good a reason as anybody to know what the score is, don't you?"

"I agree totally, Moira. I would have told you much sooner, but your mother..."

Moira rolled her eyes. "Mom's a wuss."

"Renatta is much braver than you give her credit for, Moira. Her one weakness is her children. She would do anything to protect you, but the time has come for her to let you face your destiny on your own. She can shield you no longer."

Matthew gazed at Moira in silence for several seconds, as if assessing her. Moira stared back, trying not to squirm with impatience. Finally, the old man nodded.

"Yes, it's time. It's past time." He leaned forward, propping his elbows on his knees, his hands clasped. "Renatta has never told you the Legend of the Dumari, has she..."

"No, but Braidy and Brody were talking about it, when we were in New York. It's some sort of really powerful magical, right?"

"In part. The word Dumari comes to us from the Egyptians, who were the first to recognize and name this special person. Originally, the title was Dewah Meri, which roughly translates as 'Beloved Morning', but over the millennia the pronunciation has been bastardized down to what we know today. The Egyptians honored and revered these personages, recognizing their extraordinary ability to give to the world of their talents and abilities. There can be only one Dumari alive at a time, and there have been long years when there was none at all. Most of them have lived quiet, unassuming lives, but a few have made enough of a mark to be noted by historians — not as magicals, of course, but as strong and influential people..."

"Who?" Moira asked eagerly. "Who were some of them?"

"Merlin, of course..." Matthew told her.

"Of course," Moira grinned.

"...Leonardo Da Vinci, Benjamin Franklin..."

"Are they always good guys?"

"First of all, they're not always guys," Matthew corrected her. "Elizabeth Tudor was one of the strongest Dumari ever known."

"Queen Elizabeth?!" Moira whistled. "Wow! Impressive! No wonder she ran circles around all those dorky men trying to run her country for her. She was really cool!"

Matthew smiled again. "Yes, she was. Although she very nearly wasn't. She had a difficult childhood, and she sometimes allowed her childish worries and fears to control her. You see, that's the risk for the Dumari. They are essentially good, but they are also incredibly powerful. And if, at a young age, the Dumari comes under evil or selfish influences, they can wind up taking a very dark path. Luckily, it seems that when that happens, the lifespan of the Dumari is drastically shortened."

"Do we know who any of these bad Dumari were?"

"There are only two that are known to history — the person that is commonly referred to as Jack the Ripper..."

"Ha!" Moira crowed, startling Matthew. "Whaddaya know! He *was* a magical! I wasn't too far off the track after all!"

"Developed a sudden interest in magical serial killers, have we?" Matthew asked dryly.

"Um...sorta," Moira mumbled, chuckling to herself. "No biggie. Who else?"

"Alexander of Macedonia."

"Alexander the Great! That's intense! Although what could possibly be considered great about some jerk who murdered and raped and pillaged his way across the entire known world is beyond me," Moira observed. "Sounds to me like he was nothing more than a conceited bully with delusions of grandeur."

"I couldn't agree more, Moira. That's exactly what he was."

"But, Matthew, what does all this have to do with me? With us? You don't really think that one of us is..." she hesitated for an instant, then stumbled ahead "...the...the...Dumari, do you? I mean, I know those yahoos who kidnapped us thought so, but..." Her voice trailed away.

Matthew closed his eyes for a moment. "No, Moira, I don't think it is one of you children ...I know it is." He opened his eyes and looked straight at her, his brown eyes filled with concern ...and love.

"How do you..?" she whispered, her own eyes wide with shock.

"When your mother was pregnant with Devon, Meredith had a vision. A Seeing. Sean, your grandfather, came to her. He had been dead many years by then, but in the vision, he looked as young as the day they met. He told her that one of their grandchildren would be the new Dumari."

"Is Grandma sure it was a real Seeing, not just a dream?"

"Positive."

"Freaky!" Moira whistled softly. "So it's true? One of us — Braidy, Brody, Ainsley, or me — is gonna be this super-duper powerhouse?"

Matthew smiled at her description. "Something like that."

"Grandpa Sean couldn't have mentioned which one of us it would be, while he was at it?" Moira said wryly.

"None of you were born yet, your identities were as yet unknown," Matthew pointed out. "Even an essence from the other side can only See so much."

"Yeah, well, that doesn't really matter does it?" Moira cocked her head. "Doesn't take a genius to figure out which one of us it is." Matthew cocked his head. "Oh, c'mon, Grandpa! It's obvious, isn't it? Who's the most beautiful, the most intelligent, the most talented one of the bunch? Christ! Braidy really *is* a goddess — or the next closest thing, anyway. Figures!"

"Don't be so sure, Moira. The Dumari is not necessarily beautiful, intelligent, or talented — except magically, of course. The attributes of the Dumari are a bit more subtle than that."

"Then how do we tell which one of us it is? Do we have to take some sort of test, or something?"

"No test, Moira. We will know by the Mark."

"The what?"

"The Mark of the Dumari."

"The Mark of the Dumari," Moira repeated. "What's that?"

"It is the symbol of our kind. We often refer to it as the Wellspring of Life."

"Hang on!" Moira snapped her fingers. "Is that that kind of bowl-shaped thingy with the two lines sticking up through it? Looks like the euro symbol turned on its side? Andrew has one on his keychain. And I think Mom has a necklace or something..."

"Yes, that is the Mark." Matthew pulled a keychain out of his pocket to show her. "Andrew and Renatta received theirs on their eighteenth birthdays — the day they reached adulthood."

"But if you can just be given this...whatever you called it..."

"The Wellspring of Life."

"Yeah, that. If you've got one, and Mom and Andrew, how can you tell which one of us kids might be the real Dumari?" Moira asked, puzzled.

"What is sometimes given to young magicals as a present is nothing more than a symbol, a reminder of what we hold dear...and a means of recognizing each other. The Dumari will have the true Mark. It appears somewhere between the twelfth and sixteenth birthday...right behind your ear, under the hairline." Matthew pointed to Moira's right ear. Reflexively, she covered the ear with her hand.

"What? Like a...like a birthmark, you mean?"

"Exactly like a birthmark, Moira. It will be light brown in color, and rather small in size, making it difficult to detect."

"Why? Why difficult, I mean? Don't we want to know who this Dumari is? Not just now, for our own sakes. Wouldn't we — all magicals, I mean — have always wanted to know who it is?"

Matthew shook his head. "Over the centuries, we have found it best to keep the identity of the Dumari quiet. There are, as you found out last year, some magicals who would try to exploit the powers of the Dumari for their own purposes. That is why you children were abducted — somehow, someone discovered our secret. They wanted to control your powers...to what end, I dread to think," he sighed.

The old man suddenly looked every bit his age...and bone-tired into the bargain. Moira found herself realizing for the first time that Matthew wasn't ageless. Or invincible, as she'd always assumed.

"Grandpa," she said softly, hesitantly. "Grandpa...you're the most powerful magical I've ever seen. Or heard of. Are you telling me that one of us...one of us kids...is even more powerful than you?"

Matthew looked Moira straight in the eye. "Yes, Moira, that is exactly what I'm telling you. And it could just as easily be you as Braidy. You both have talents and abilities far above the norm. As do Brody and Ainsley as well. It could be any one of you."

"So why haven't you guys been checking behind our ears on a daily basis?!" Moira exclaimed, rubbing her scalp vigorously. She knew it was her imagination, but now that she was aware of the possibility of the Mark being there, her skin tingled and burned.

Matthew laughed. "Honestly, Moira, would you have let us?"

Moira gave him a half-smile. "Probably not. But you should have told me — us — sooner. Why didn't Mom want me to know?"

"When you were young, we all felt it best not to burden any of you with the knowledge. By the time the Mark might have first appeared, you had turned your back on magic — and on your mother. She was afraid the information would drive you further away. She couldn't bear the thought of that. And it wouldn't have been fair to tell the twins, but not you. So we continued to keep it a secret...or so we thought."

Moira hung her head, her cheeks red. She really had been too hard on Renatta all those years.

"You mean more to Renatta than you could possibly know, Moira," Matthew said gently. "She loves you very much."

"Yeah..." Moira cleared her throat and sniffed, "...me too." Standing up, she walked over to the window and gazed out at the ocean. "So, we should be able to see the Mark on whichever one of us it is now, right?"

"Yes. Unless it's Ainsley. She may have the Mark already, but she may not. It might not appear for a few more years."

"But..." Moira mused, frowning. "If there's no Mark on Braidy, Brody, or me, it has to be Ainsley, right? By process of elimination?"

Matthew smiled. "Very good, Moira. Yes, that would seem to be the case." He joined her at the window. "Would you like me to look for you?"

Moira suddenly felt shy and self-conscious. "Um...well...would you mind if...if I looked for myself, Grandpa? It's just...it's a pretty big moment, ya know? Finding out I'm some sort of omnipotent being — or not. I think I'd rather check it out for myself. Besides, I'd like a little time to adjust to the idea first."

"I understand, Moira," Matthew said, placing a comforting hand on her shoulder. "I'll leave you to it, then."

When he reached the stairs, Matthew turned back, giving Moira a sharp look.

"You will tell us if you find anything, won't you?" he asked pointedly.

"You don't really think I'd keep something like this to myself," Moira gave him a wicked smile, "and miss out on the opportunity to lord it over Braidy, do you, Grandpa?"

Matthew laughed loudly. "I knew I could count on you, Moira." He gave her a wink as he left the room.

* * * * *

Dec. 23

IT IS FRICKIN' IMPOSSIBLE TO SEE BEHIND YOUR OWN EARS!!!!

I twisted every way humanly possible...no luck! Practically gave myself whiplash in the process...

Yes, I know, I told Grandpa I wanted to wait a while before looking, that I needed some time to adjust to the whole thing...you didn't REALLY believe that, did you? LOLOL

I know! I need a little hand mirror! I bet that would do the trick! Do I have a hand mirror? Of course not...maybe Ainsley has one. I'm not asking her! I'm not even talking to her! Maybe Mom...naw, she'd want to look with me.

I don't know why I want to be the only one to know at first. It's not like I expect it to be me...I don't care what Grandpa said. Seems pretty obvious to me who's the most likely candidate here. God, there'll be no living with Braidy after this. Oh well, she'll be good at it...better than I could be, that's for sure!

God, this is sooooo freaky! To think, one of us is gonna be powerful enough to change the course of history...if we wanted to, that is. Although it sounded like a bunch of these Dumari haven't bothered to do much of anything fantastic. They just went on with their lives as if there was nothing out of the ordinary about them. But some of them...

How would that feel, knowing you had that kind of power? I feel woogly enough, just knowing that there's even the slightest possibility it could be me. But if it IS me...*shudder*...Who am I kidding? Moi? The most powerful magical of the age? Hell, I can't even call a pencil across the room without nearly taking my eye out! LOL

But if, by some strange twist of fate, it does turn out to be me...what do I do then? How do I handle it? A year ago, I wanted nothing to do with magic. Even now, I'm not sure where I'm at with it. I mean, I know I've been trying a few things lately, but is that what I really want? To be a magical again? Granted, it can come in handy sometimes, but it can also cause some serious headaches. And it's a total pain to have to hide it from all the nonmagicals — especially my friends. Do I really want to mess with all of that?

It would definitely be easier to just forget about it. But can I? Forget about it, I mean? After all, it's a part of me. If I choose to ignore it, that would be the same as if I had a beautiful singing voice but refused to open my mouth. Or was an amazing artist, but never picked up a paintbrush. It would be wasting my talent, my gift. Is that right? Can I do that? SHOULD I do that...?

* * * * *

Braidy strode toward the cars, her skates slung over her shoulder, fuming. At the same time she was on the verge of tears, as so often these past several weeks. The glow from the bonfire near the frozen cranberry bogs slowly faded, as the darkness enveloped her.

Karen was totally out of line. Who was she to tell Braidy that waiting for Jonathan Crenshaw was a waste of time? Hadn't she moaned for weeks — months, even — over that boy visiting from Brazil in sixth grade? Karen didn't even know Jonathan. She had no idea how special he was, how exciting, how mature. He was completely, totally, utterly different from the boys they usually hung out with. They weren't even in the same league as Jonathan.

"You've been what?!" Karen had squealed a few minutes earlier, when Braidy had confessed all to her and Becky during a break from the skating. "Why haven't you told me?!"

"I...I wanted to keep it to myself for a while," Braidy said. "It was so new, so unexpected, I guess I didn't quite believe it myself."

"Ooh, an older man! When are you seeing him again?" Becky asked excitedly. "Is he coming here tonight?"

"Um...no...I don't think so," Braidy muttered, her head lowered. "I...I haven't heard from him...recently..."

Karen's eyes narrowed. "When did you see him last?"

"Um...about six weeks ago."

Karen and Becky exchanged a look.

"And when was the last time he called you?"

"He hasn't," Braidy whispered.

"I didn't catch that."

Braidy raised her head, defiant.

"He hasn't."

Karen stared at Braidy in shock for a moment. Then she exploded.

"He hasn't bothered to call you or see you in six weeks?! Six weeks?! What the hell kind of boyfriend is this?!"

"He's busy!" Braidy defended Jonathan. "He goes to school full time, plus working as an apprentice at the PBS station. And I think he has another job, as well."

"You think?" Karen said pointedly. "He didn't bother to tell you what he does?"

"Not exactly...Look, what difference does that make? I know what he wants to be, what he's training for. And, more important, I know him. He's so...so...Oh, Karen! What if he never calls me again? What if he thought I was boring? Or stupid? Or...or...childish?" Tears welled up in Braidy's eyes as she confessed her worst fears.

Karen snorted. "When have you ever cared what some dork thought of you? What's gotten into you?"

"Yeah, Braidy," Becky said, "that's one of the things I've always envied about you — your self-confidence. You weren't going to change yourself for anybody — they had to accept you exactly as you are. I've always wished I could be that strong."

"Yeah, well, maybe I never met a guy worth changing for before," Braidy replied sadly.

"No guy is worth changing for!" Karen insisted. "And you know it! You've always said that! I can't believe you're doing this to yourself! Twisting yourself inside out for some loser who can't even be bothered to call you now and then!"

"Jonathan is not a loser!" Braidy cried, her anger flaring. "He's smart, and hot, and...and so much more interesting than any of the dweebs we know! He could have any girl he wants!"

"Well, looks to me like he doesn't want you anymore," Karen said in disgust. "But here you sit, waiting like a lost puppy for him to throw you a bone. I never thought I'd see the day. C'mon, Becky. I've heard enough of this." Karen took Becky by the arm and turned her toward the bog.

"You don't understand!" Braidy insisted.

"If you ask me," Karen replied, spinning to face Braidy, "you're the one that doesn't understand! He was playing with you, Braidy! Guys like that eat high school girls for lunch! When you didn't give him what he wanted fast enough, he decided to move on!" She returned to the ice.

"He didn't even ask!" Braidy shouted after them, not sure if she was more insulted or relieved by that fact. But Karen didn't hear...or chose not to.

Plopping down on the snow-covered ground, Braidy wrenched her ice skates off, thrust her feet into her shoes and took off into the darkness. Light snowflakes fell gently from the overcast sky, as they had all day. The night air was cold and crisp, with no wind. Gotchalk's Farm stretched off into the distance, silent except for the cries and laughter of the skaters. The warmth of the bonfire they'd built near the cranberry bogs was quickly lost to Braidy. As was her anger at Karen, which soon turned to the despair she'd been feeling for more than a week. Every night she'd gone to sleep filled with disappointment at Jonathan's silence, and every morning she'd made up new excuses for him. But deep down inside, Braidy knew the real reason he hadn't called her again — he didn't want to. He wasn't interested. Karen was right — he had been playing with her.

Braidy stopped in the middle of the field, her body bent double, sobbing as if her heart would break.

"What's this? Won't the other kiddies let you play?"

Braidy straightened and spun around all in the same motion.

"Jonathan!" she gasped. There was just enough light from the distant fire for her to see his features. He was smiling.

"Don't cry, Princess," Jonathan said softly, wiping the tears from her cheeks.

With one last sob, Braidy threw herself into his arms.

"Why didn't you call me, Jonathan? I thought..."

"I've been busy, girl. But I'm here now." Jonathan turned his head to kiss her. He stepped away, holding his hand out to her. "Come with me."

"But..." Braidy hesitated. Jonathan merely looked at her, waiting. Slowly, she placed her hand in his and followed him to his car.

* * * * *

"Braidy? Braidy! Where are you? Has anyone seen Braidy?" Brody scanned the group of faces in the light of the bonfire, but there was no sign of his sister. "Karen, where's Braidy? Have you seen her?"

"We were talking about half an hour ago," Karen replied, "but I haven't seen her since."

"Maybe that Jonathan guy she's so hot on actually bothered to show up," Becky giggled, "and she went off with him."

"Jonathan? You mean Jonathan Crenshaw?" Brody exclaimed. "He was here?!"

"No idea," Karen said. "But it sure is about time the jerk bothered to show up for her. Did you know he hasn't even called Braidy in, like, six weeks? If I were her, I wouldn't give him the time of day even if he did call me!" Karen flipped her hair over her shoulder and skated away. "Don't worry, Brod. She's probably over by the cars, pouting. She'll be back when she gets cold enough."

Brody gazed into the darkness surrounding the parked cars, but couldn't see anything clearly from that far away. He didn't like the strange feeling he was getting in his gut, but what could he do? If Jonathan had arrived, and Braidy had left with him, what could Brody do about it? Call the cops? Hardly! Braidy had every right to go out with the guy if she wanted to — regardless of what Brody thought of him.

"Brody!" Amber said, skating up and slipping her mittened hand through Brody's arm. "C'mon! Did you ask me here to skate or just stand around freezing?" She smiled up at him and tugged him toward the middle of the bog.

"Yeah...um...right! Right..." With one last glance over his shoulder, Brody returned his attention to his latest girlfriend.

* * * * *

"Let's take a look, shall we?"

Braidy stiffened, not quite sure she was ready for this, but not wanting to disappoint, either. She took a deep breath and started to turn. "All right."

"No, no...stay just as you are," Jonathan murmured. They were on the beach, overlooking Nantucket Sound, an old lighthouse barely visible on the ridge behind them. Jonathan was leaning up against the hood of his Solus, Braidy's back to him, his arms wrapped around her. The snow flurries had stopped, the clouds had drifted northward, and a bright moon glowed on the water in front of them. There was not another soul in sight.

Jonathan reached up to remove Braidy's hat — an old, oversized, hand-knitted tam — and dropped it on the ground. Then he tilted the side of her head toward the moonlight, bending the soft part of her ear forward with one hand while pulling her hair out of the way with the other.

"Jonathan, what..?" Braidy started to ask, totally puzzled by his actions. This was not what she had expected at all.

"Be quiet, girl! And hold still!" Jonathan angled her head farther, then swore. "Dammit! I can't see a thing in this light!"

Braidy heard a sharp, snapping sound next to her ear. Immediately, the beach was flooded with light — from the headlights of Jonathan's car. Braidy gasped and tried to pull away.

"What did you...?! How did you...?!"

"I told you to shut up!" Jonathan growled, pulling her tight against him. He pushed her head sideways again, tugging on her ear. She could feel his hot breath on her neck. "Wrong side, apparently," he commented casually as he twisted her head around and peered behind the other ear. Braidy felt him stiffen momentarily. Then he forced her onto the ground, directly into the beam of the lights. Braidy screamed. Jonathan ignored her. Grabbing her by the hair, he shoved her head around as he searched behind both ears. Then he straightened, leaving Braidy on the ground.

"Nothing!" he said, staring down at her, his face inscrutable. "Nothing!" He turned away and started laughing harshly. "All this time...all this effort...for nothing!" he shouted. "You're not it," he commented, turning back to face Braidy.

Braidy stood, shaking slightly. Something very strange was going on. She tried to hide her fear. "I'm not what?"

Jonathan stared at her, his eyes dark with anger and frustration.

"The Dumari."

Chapter Fourteen:

Believing Is Seeing

Ainsley sat curled up on the window seat of her bedroom, staring pensively through the glass at the swirling snowflakes falling outside. The house was silent; Devon was on a date, Andrew and Renatta were at a party, and Moira was ensconced in her housetop aerie, an area Ainsley knew was completely off limits to her. The girls might as well have been on two different planets.

Moira hadn't spoken to her sister since the night of their big fight. Ainsley's half-hearted attempts at reconciliation had been abruptly and rudely rebuffed. After three or four tries, the young girl had given up. She'd done all she could; the ball was in Moira's court now.

As Ainsley continued to gaze at the winter landscape, she couldn't help but think about what she'd done. A single hot tear rolled down her cheek. Ainsley was a soft-hearted girl; she couldn't bear to witness anything in pain, human or animal. Knowing that she was the one to have inflicted the pain herself was almost more than she could bear. What had she been thinking? How could she have done that to Jeremy, an innocent bystander? Even worse, how could she have hurt Moira like that, her own sister? A small sob escaped her.

Ainsley's tears slowly eased. The falling snow had an almost hypnotic effect on her, calming her, lulling her into a near trance, her mind's eye focused vaguely on the velvety darkness punctuated by the lacy white flakes floating and swirling outside the glass. Her body relaxed and she felt herself drifting, drifting, drifting on the winter wind...

Gradually, a new image superimposed itself over the falling snow — a dark, cold room, high in a tower, the wind whistling and moaning, rattling the glass in the old windows. Braidy lay huddled on the floor, tied and gagged, two menacing figures standing over her. Ainsley gasped. The heavier of Braidy's captors had his face turned away, the shadows hiding his identity. But the face of the other showed plainly, illuminated by what Ainsley immediately recognized as magically produced lighting. It was Jonathan Crenshaw. Ainsley could see his lips moving as he spoke, but all she could hear over the cold winter wind was a word here and there. Those few scattered words, however, were quite enough to send a chill down her spine.

"*...get rid of her...*" Ainsley heard the larger man say.

"*...useless...dead...police...Damn it, Morty!*" was all she caught of Jonathan's reply. But the expression on his face spoke volumes. He stared down at Braidy with such utter loathing, it made Ainsley wince.

For the next several seconds, Ainsley strained to hear their voices, with no luck, until her efforts were finally rewarded with three final words, spoken coldly by Jonathan's accomplice.

"*...her* body*...suicide...*"

Moments later, the two men headed for the metal staircase. Jonathan snapped his fingers and the tower room went dark. With that, the vision shifted. The small dark room receded as Ainsley seemed to float through one of the windows to the outside. The snow had stopped falling, giving her a clear view of a stone lighthouse rearing up against the black sky. There was no welcoming beam visible through the windows, just a glimmer of moonlight reflecting off the glass. Ainsley shivered...and was back in her bedroom.

Breathing fast, her entire body shaking, Ainsley slowly stood. It took barely a moment for her to decide what to do. She headed for the doorway — and the stairs to the third floor.

* * * * *

"Are you mental? I'm not going over to the dork's house and beg him to take me back! I already apologized to him. If that wasn't good enough, then to hell with him! He's not the only guy around. It's not like I was in love with him, or something."

"Then why do you keep talking about him?" Lucia's voice sounded distinctly skeptical, even over Moira's cell phone.

"Hell, girl...I don't know! I liked him. We had some really good times. And it was pretty cool, talking about 'my boyfriend'," Moira admitted sheepishly. "Ridiculous how much social standing that gives you. Like suddenly I was more important, just because some dillweed liked to slobber all over me on Saturday night." She laughed sharply. "Okay, yeah, before you say it, I kinda liked slobbering all over him, too!"

Lucia giggled. "I wasn't going to say that!"

"No, but you were thinking it!" Moira laughed harder.

"Moira! Moira!"

"Hang on, Luce." Moira turned toward the stairs leading down to the rest of the house. "You aren't allowed up here," she said coldly, as Ainsley bounded into the room.

"But it's an emergency, Moira!" Ainsley insisted. "Braidy is in danger!"

"Huh?"

"She's being held captive by...by Jonathan Crenshaw and some other guy...in some old lighthouse!"

"What the hell are you on about?" Moira hissed, covering her cell phone with her hand. "And keep your voice down! I've got Lucia on here!"

"But Braidy's in terrible danger! They were talking about kill... killing her!" Ainsley gulped.

Moira rolled her eyes. "Braidy and Brody went skating on the cranberry bogs tonight. Ol' Man Gotchalk isn't gonna kill them for that. Hell, he's been letting 'em go out there every Christmas Eve for years."

"It wasn't Mr. Gotchalk! I told you, Moira! It was Jonathan Crenshaw!"

Moira laughed, dismissing Ainsley's story. "That just proves how stupid this is! Jonathan Crenshaw isn't a killer! He's a really nice guy — smart, cute, hot. And he's Devon's friend. Why on earth would he want to kill Braidy? He barely even knows her! Go back to dreaming, little girl."

"It wasn't a dream, Moira! It was a Seeing!" Ainsley cried.

"Yeah, right...whatever."

"It was! Just like those times I saw you...in New York...when you were kidnapped!"

"Oh, please! Not that again! I'm telling ya, kid, you dozed off and had a bad dream, that's all. Now, get out of my room!"

"Fine! I'm going to Aunt Caroline's — we'll see if she believes my dream!" Ainsley shot back as she ran down the stairs.

"You're not supposed to go anywhere!" Moira yelled after her. "Especially by yourself! You're still grounded!"

"Then come with me!" Ainsley pleaded, sticking her head back up into the room.

"I'm not about to go running around in the dark and cold for some stupid nightmare!" Moira scowled.

"IT WASN'T A NIGHTMARE!!!" Ainsley shouted. "It was a Seeing, a true Seeing! I swear!"

"Yeah, right," Moira replied sarcastically. "And I'm the Dumari."

"The what?"

"Never mind. Forget it. Go back to your room."

"I'm going to Aunt Caroline's...with or without you," Ainsley stated firmly.

"Fine! Just don't blame me if Andrew grounds you for life when he finds out!"

"He won't do that," Ainsley's voice floated up the stairs along with the sound of her feet tumbling down the wooden steps. "He'll understand why."

"And then you woke up," Moira muttered dryly. She sighed before bringing the phone back to her ear. "Sorry about that, Luce. Ainsley had some stupid nightmare. I had to calm her down. What were we talking about?"

Moira resumed the conversation with her friend, deliberately ignoring the tight, nagging feeling in the pit of her stomach.

* * * * *

Braidy lay on the cold wooden floor of the lantern room, shivering, as Jonathan and his companion discussed her fate. It was obvious that the lighthouse had not been in use for years, although someone had obviously attempted a few renovations recently. The former location of the light was marked by a patch of paler wood planking in the center of the floor — nothing of the light itself remained. The eight windows spaced evenly around the circular walls were still intact, but the only evidence of human occupation was an old sea chest, a metal step ladder, a small work bench with a tool box and several tools laying around it, a pile of scrap lumber, and a few painting supplies, including two filthy drop cloths and several open paint cans — although even that much information barely registered. Braidy felt numb all over. Her brain seemed incapable of functioning properly. One lone thought raced through her mind over and over: *Jonathan is a magical...he thought I was the Dumari...Jonathan wasn't interested in me, just the Dumari... the Dumari... the Dumari...*

"What do we do with her now?"

Jonathan's voice cut through Braidy's pain.

"We get rid of her, of course," the other man replied. "She knows too much. She can identify both of us, for one thing. All these months wasted...Now it's back to square one again."

Braidy realized that she recognized the other man's voice. He was the same man who had argued with Lorena Lewis outside that horrible attic in New York City eighteen months earlier. He was Morty.

Jonathan ran a hand through his hair. "And I'll be totally useless to the project. This stupid little chit probably told all her friends she was dating me. When she turns up dead, I'll be persona non grata with her family, the police, the press...Damn it, Morty!"

"You'll have to go into hiding for now, until we can regroup and sort this mess out. Once we have things under control again, you'll be contacted. It won't be long...we don't have much time left..."

"I'm beginning to wonder if it's even worth it. Perhaps we should simply go ahead with the plans without the Dumari. Hell, it could be any one of the other three!"

"We can't make this happen without the Dumari, you know that!" Morty insisted. "We need that power! We can't give up now!"

A small part of Braidy's mind began working again. If the other man was Morty, did that mean that Jonathan was the one they all called Alex? Could he be the mastermind behind all the terrible things that had been happening to her family over the past two years?

"We were so sure Braidy was the right one! How are we going to figure out which one of the other three it is? And how will we even get to them, at this point? Once Braidy's body is found, the protections around the others will be tripled, at least!" Jonathan turned away, disgusted.

"We'll find a way, don't worry," Morty reassured him with an evil grin. "Besides, who said her body would be found?"

Jonathan looked over his shoulder at the older man. "What do you mean by that?"

"The plan was to make her look like a runaway, right?"

"I know that! We would have made her tell her family that she was living with me. Can't exactly do that now, can we?" Jonathan sneered.

"No...but what says she had to run away with you? Kids run away from home all the time. She'll just become another statistic. We make her write a note — something pathetically sappy, about how she felt trapped and stifled at home — then we get rid of her, and her family none the wiser. They won't have a clue her disappearance has anything to do with the Dumari."

Jonathan stood silent for a moment, tapping an index finger against his lips as he searched through the possibilities.

"We handle it that way, I may not have to go into hiding after all," he said finally. "What's to say she took off because of me? After all, as far as anyone knows, I haven't seen her or spoken to her in weeks." His face brightened.

"The police ask any questions, you can just tell them you broke up with her," Morty chuckled. "That way, if her body is found later on, it'll look like a suicide. In fact, that might be the best way, after all. The poor kid killed herself because you dumped her." He laughed again. Braidy's stomach churned sickeningly.

"No way, man! The less involved I appear to be, the better!" Jonathan argued.

"Yeah, you're probably right. Better stick with Plan A. Let's get to it, then. There are some details to work out if we expect to pull this off." Morty headed for the stairs.

"What about her?" Jonathan jerked his head toward Braidy.

"What about her? She ain't going nowhere," Morty laughed.

Jonathan gave Braidy a long inscrutable look, then he followed Morty, snapping his fingers to extinguish the light, leaving the terrified girl alone in the cold, dark tower room.

As the sound of their footsteps on the metal stairs faded, Braidy wriggled her hands back and forth, trying to loosen the ropes around her wrists. Her efforts did no good, however. The knots were tied too tight. After several minutes of increasing frustration, she gave up, laying back and closing her eyes in despair. The past thirty minutes raced through her memory in a confusion of growing terror...

"Wha...what do you mean, I'm not the Dumari?" Braidy had gasped half an hour earlier, standing in the glare of the magically illuminated headlights. "How do you know about the Dumari? And how did you turn those lights on?"

"How do you think, little girl?" Jonathan had sneered at her. He yanked his cell phone out of his pocket and flipped it open, his fingers dialing quickly. His call was answered immediately. "We have a problem...She's not it...That's what I said....Yes, I looked behind both ears, you idiot! What do you take me for?... Yes, I've still got her here...

Not easy to hide my intentions, digging around under her hair. Hardly standard make-out fare...So what the hell do I do with the stupid chit now?..."

There was a long pause on Jonathan's end as he listened intently. Taking advantage of his temporary distraction, Braidy slowly inched toward the darkness beyond the glare of the lights. She had no plan formulated — she only knew she had to get away.

"All right, I'll bring her in...Ten minutes, right...Don't worry, I will..." Cursing vehemently under his breath, Jonathan shoved the phone back into his jeans pocket. Braidy knew it was now or never. She turned and ran.

"Not so fast, girl!" Jonathan yelled. He flung a hand up sharply, as if he was cracking a whip. Braidy screamed and fell headfirst into the sand and snow, her calves burning where Jonathan's spell had wrapped around them. Weaving his hands over her, he quickly conjured ropes out of the cold air, tying her tightly at the wrists and ankles. He left her lying as he began to pace back and forth beside her.

"Why are you doing this, Jonathan?" Braidy cried, managing to roll onto her back. "Who are you, really?"

"Shut up."

"The Dumari is just a legend, an old witch's tale. It has nothing to do with me!"

"Obviously. And I told you to shut up."

"Let me go, Jonathan! Please! I just want to go home! I won't say a word to anyone! I promise!"

Jonathan laughed. "What do you take me for, girl? I'm no fool! I set you free, you'll go running to Mommy and Daddy with the whole story! I have no intention of doing any jail time. Your's truly don't like small spaces. Now shut up!"

"No, Jonathan, I swear! I won't say anything! I don't know why you want the Dumari. I'm not even sure I know what the Dumari is in the first place!"

That got his attention. Stopping in midstride, he stared at her in amazement. "Do you mean to tell me that after what happened to you in New York, your parents still haven't told you? I don't believe you!"

"It's true! I swear! They didn't tell us anything! Not me or Brody! Not about the Dumari, anyway. They said that was just a bunch of old fairy tales."

"So what reason did they give you for the kidnapping, then?"

"Mom said they didn't know for sure, but they assumed it was some sort of ploy to get at Grandpa Matthew...to blackmail him somehow."

Jonathan stared at her for a moment longer, then burst out laughing. "And you believed that lame story? God, you're even more pathetic than I thought!" He resumed pacing. "Matthew Collins may be one freakin' powerful wizard, but he's nothing compared to the Dumari."

"But why do you want the Dumari so badly? What are you going to do?"

"We're going to take control."

"Control? Of what?" Perhaps if she kept him talking, he'd be distracted enough for her to make another escape attempt. It was a long shot, she knew, but it was all she could think to do.

Jonathan came to a stop near her head. "Of everything, of course! The world's been screwed up for too long. It's time someone took charge...somebody who has a plan. There's going to be some organization for a change...and some justice."

"And you think you can do this?" Braidy forced as much contempt into her voice as she could muster. "You? Mr. 'I'm going to be a TV news anchor because I'm so good looking'?" She laughed derisively. "Sounds like delusions of grandeur to me."

"Not me alone," Jonathan said.

"Then who else? More of those freaks who kidnapped us? They didn't exactly seem like the brightest stars in the universe to me. If you really want to fix the world, you're going to have to do better than that!"

"Don't worry," Jonathan grinned nastily. "Those dillweeds were merely convenient, expendable...and cheap. Most of them didn't even know the blueprint. They were just looking for an easy score."

"So, that's what this is all about — money. I should have known," Braidy sneered. But it was all bravado. Inside, she was trembling with fear. She knew too much already...and Jonathan knew that. "Some stupid get-rich-quick scheme."

Jonathan leaned down, grabbing her sharply by the arm. Braidy cried out.

"This is not about money!" he hissed at her, his teeth bared. "This is about order, and discipline, and harmony. We have great improvements in the works!"

"Then why don't you just tell everybody else about them?!" Braidy screamed at him. "Well? Answer me that! Why can't you share your ideas and let us all help?!"

"Because most of you are too stupid or sanctimonious to want to help! People like Matthew Collins, Leo Radcliffe, your parents...you think you're better than the rest of us! That you have all the answers! That your way is the only way! You go on and on about making changes, improving the quality of life, helping the unfortunate, but you're not willing to do the work! You don't want to get your hands dirty."

"That's not true! We do want to help! We try to!"

"Is that so?" He shook her roughly. "THEN WHY DON'T YOU DO SOMETHING?!" Jonathan flung her back onto the sand

and turned away. "All you hypocritical types do is talk about making changes. You never actually DO anything!"

"Kidnapping me isn't going to improve anything for anyone."

"Not true, my dear. Once we have the power of the Dumari on our side, we'll be able to do anything we want."

"Neither my brother nor my cousins will be any more likely to go along with your ignorant plans than I am!" Braidy cried.

"Don't worry," Jonathan glanced over his shoulder at her, "we'll find a way to persuade them."

"But..."

"That's enough. I'm sick of your whining, little girl." He twirled one index finger in a tight circle next to his ear. A thick rag appeared out of nowhere and forced itself into Braidy's mouth, gagging her. As Jonathan glanced at his watch, Braidy's eyes filled with tears once more, only this time for herself.

How could she have been so blind, so stupid? Why had she allowed herself to become obsessed with Jonathan Crenshaw — a man she had apparently known next to nothing about? Why had she defied her parents, lied to them? Everything involved in her relationship with Jonathan — her actions, her thoughts, her feelings — had been totally alien to her true nature. She'd found herself inordinately attracted to him from their first meeting, and had lost sight of everything else in that one, overwhelming desire. She'd sacrificed her intelligence, her self-respect, her pride, her very being to him. And now it appeared that she would be sacrificing her life, as well.

A short time later, lying alone in the cold, dark lantern room, she faced the fact that the two men had no choice but to kill her. And there was no escape. Terrified, she struggled again with her bonds, to no avail. All she could do was lay there — and wait for the end.

* * * * *

Caroline was just putting the last of the pies for Christmas Day dinner into the oven when the front doorbell rang. She straightened, brushed her hair off her forehead, and sighed.

"Who the hell could that be?" she muttered, wiping her floury hands on a dishtowel and quickly setting the small timer she had clipped to her waistband. "Phil...? Oh, never mind! I'll get it myself."

Her husband was upstairs in their bedroom, wrapping Christmas presents. He probably hadn't even heard the bell ring. The pies would have to take care of themselves for the moment. Caroline tossed the towel onto the counter and headed for the main part of the house.

By the time she reached the foyer, their visitor was pounding frantically on the door.

"I'm coming...I'm coming!" Caroline called. "Keep your bloomers on!" She threw open the door and found herself gazing at her shivering, wild-eyed young niece. "Ainsley! What are you doing here? Are you okay?" She drew the shaking girl into the house. "What's going on? Why aren't you wearing a coat?"

"I for...forgot it. Is...is Braidy...here...Aunt...Caro...Caroline?" Ainsley stammered, her teeth chattering with cold. Caroline grabbed a sweater from the coat rack and threw it around Ainsley's shoulders.

"No, Ainsley. She and Brody went ice skating tonight with their friends...like they do every Christmas Eve."

"They're not...not home yet?"

"I wasn't expecting them for at least another hour. They usually stop off at the Lobster Claw for hot chocolate afterwards. Why?"

Ainsley dropped onto a nearby bench and slumped forward, her hands clasped between her knees.

"I...I Saw her, Aunt Caroline. She...she wasn't with Brody and her friends...She was with ...Jonathan Crenshaw..."

"What?!" Caroline gasped. "We told her not to see him! She promised us! I can't believe she went back on her..."

"That's not important now!" Ainsley cried. "She's in danger, Aunt Caroline! Terrible danger! Jonathan can do magic! I saw him! He had Braidy tied up, and gagged...and there was another man there — I couldn't see his face — but he and Jonathan were talking like they were going to...going to..."

"Going to what?" Caroline asked, wrapping her arms around herself, suddenly chilled.

Ainsley gulped. "They were talking about killing her..." she whispered. "I couldn't hear everything they said, but..."

"Ainsley, sweetheart, are you sure this was a true Seeing?"

Ainsley looked up into her aunt's worried eyes. "Yes, Aunt Caroline. I'm positive."

"Phil!" Caroline ran for the back stairs, Ainsley just steps behind her. "PHIL!!!" As she skidded into the kitchen, she flung her hand out wildly. The phone flew off of the wall and into her hand. "Dial Braidy's cell!" she snapped at the phone. "PHILLIP!" she yelled up the stairs. "I NEED YOU! NOW!! Damn! No answer...call Brody's cell," she instructed the phone.

Ainsley heard her uncle clattering down the stairs from the third floor at top speed.

"What's up? What's going on?" he demanded as he took the last three steps in one bound.

"We may have a problem," Caroline said gruffly. She held up her hand to fend off his next question. "Hang on...Brody? It's Mom. Is Braidy with you?...I see. How long ago?...And you have no idea where?..." Caroline gave her husband a despairing look. "Have you checked with the others?...What about the car? Could she be waiting for you there?...All right, Brody. Listen, we need you to come home. Right now...I'm not sure, but there could be a problem... Ainsley has had a Seeing...Just come home, Brody! Please! And be careful!" She tossed the phone into the air, not bothering to watch as it floated back to its place on the wall. Facing her husband squarely, she took a deep breath. "As you just heard, Ainsley Saw Braidy...She was with Jonathan Crenshaw..."

"Jonathan Crenshaw! We told her..."

"It wasn't a date, Phil. He's a magical. It looks like he's kidnapped her. And there was another man with them."

"Oh, God!" Phil groaned. "Not again!"

"Ainsley..." Caroline walked over to the trembling girl and gently rubbed her arms. "Sweetie, what exactly did the men say?"

"I...I couldn't hear them very well..." Ainsley said, her eyes filling with tears. "But I think Jonathan said something about her being useless, and he mentioned the police. And I know I heard the other man say *'...get rid of her...'* It was hard to catch their words, because the wind was whistling really loud through the windows."

"Who was this other man?" Phil asked.

"I don't know, Uncle Phil. I never saw his face. Only Jonathan's... and Braidy's. She looked so scared!" Ainsley burst into tears. Caroline pulled her niece into her arms and held her tight. "Jonathan called him Morty..." she added, her voice muffled against Caroline's shoulder.

Husband and wife stared into each other's eyes, aghast.

"It must be..."

"What do we do now?" Phil said, slumping against the kitchen wall. He looked all of his forty-two years in that moment...and then some.

"We contact the family. Ainsley, where's Moira?"

"She's at home."

"Good. She'll be safe there. You stay here with us for now. Phil, use the phone to call Mom. Have her get hold of Matthew, so our line stays free. I'll reach Renatta."

Phil nodded his head and picked up the phone.

"Ainsley, with me," Caroline said, starting up the stairs. As Ainsley followed her aunt, she heard Phil beginning to explain the situation to his mother-in-law. Ainsley shuddered; what if they weren't in time?

Caroline didn't pause at the second floor landing, but continued on to the third floor. When she reached the top of the stairs, she went directly to the large bay window overlooking the ocean and pushed the curtains out of the way.

"It's not absolutely necessary," she said softly, "but a clear view does help." She placed her hands together as if in prayer, directly in front of her face, her eyes closed tight. "Renatta, it's Caroline. I need you. Braidy is missing. Come home now," Ainsley heard her aunt murmur. She held her position, repeating the exact same words twice, each time slower and softer, until her voice was barely more than a whisper on the third time. A moment later, Ainsley heard her mother's voice floating eerily through the air.

"We're on our way."

Caroline sighed and lowered her hands. "They'll be here as soon as they can, I'm sure."

"I wish I could do that," Ainsley said.

"You'll learn," Caroline said with a small smile. "It just takes practice."

"What do we do now, Aunt Caroline?"

Caroline sighed again. "We wait." She dropped onto the sofa, pulling Ainsley down next to her and holding the frightened girl close. Phil joined them a few minutes later.

"Meredith is on her way. She said she'd let Matthew know before she left the house."

"Good."

"Caroline...?" Phil knelt down in front of them and reached out toward his wife.

"I know, Phil. I know!" Caroline whispered, hanging onto his hand like a lifeline.

The three of them stayed that way for some time, the silence stretching between them. Finally, Phil straightened up and began pacing the room. They all jumped when the timer on Caroline's waistband beeped insistently.

"Damn!" Caroline muttered. "The pies!"

She went back to the kitchen, the other two following. As Ainsley helped her aunt take the pies out of the oven, the doorbell rang.

"I've got it," Phil said, heading for the front hall. Within moments, he had returned, followed closely by Meredith.

"Mom!" Caroline cried, throwing herself into her mother's comforting arms.

The next ten minutes were filled with chaos as the rest of the family arrived, everyone bursting with questions. Renatta made a beeline for Ainsley the moment she entered the house, pulling her young daughter close.

"Ainsley! What are you doing here? Are you all right?"

"Just worried, Mom," Ainsley reassured her. "I'm not the one in danger, Braidy is."

"Where's Moira?"

"At home," she said flatly.

"What's happened?" Matthew asked. With that, Brody walked in.

"Thank God!" Caroline exclaimed, tossing her arms around her son's neck and nearly strangling him.

"Mom!" Brody choked, extricating himself. "Let a man breath, will ya? Any word?"

"Nothing."

Brody muttered something unprintable under his breath.

"I repeat," Matthew said, "what's happened? Your message said Braidy is missing...?"

"We were ice skating at Gotchalk's, like we do every Christmas," Brody explained. "But about an hour ago, Braidy disappeared, and no one's seen her since. A couple of her girlfriends thought she might have met up with this guy she's been sort of dating lately."

"Jonathan Crenshaw," Phil provided.

"Devon's friend?" Renatta was understandably puzzled. "What's wrong with that?"

"Aside from the fact that we'd forbidden her to see him, you mean?" Caroline said, her tone bitter. "And rightly so, it appears, seeing as he's not only been hiding the fact that he's a magical from everyone but has also apparently kidnapped my daughter."

"What on earth makes you think...?" Andrew began.

"I had a Seeing," Ainsley announced suddenly. Her father's mouth shut with a snap as everyone's attention focused on the young girl. "Jonathan and some guy named Morty had Braidy tied up and gagged. They were talking about...about..." The enormity of the situation suddenly crashed down onto Ainsley and she burst into tears. Andrew drew her into his arms, rubbing her back. The adults exchanged worried glances.

"Morty..." Brody whispered, his eyes wide with fear.

"Yes."

"Crap!"

"Ainsley told me that it sounded as if they were planning to..." Caroline gulped, "...kill her."

"Renatta, call Moira," Andrew said, his voice hoarse with worry. "Make sure she's safe. And tell her to stay put!"

Meredith turned away from the others, closing her eyes and breathing deeply. The others waited in silence. After more than a minute, Meredith sighed.

"I can't find her," she told them sadly. "I'm being blocked." She gazed at Ainsley with an odd expression in her eyes. "Ainsley, are you certain it was a true Seeing?"

Ainsley looked her grandmother straight in the eye. "Yes, Grandma. I'm positive."

The two women, young and old, gazed at each other intently for several seconds. Then Meredith nodded.

"I believe you. Tell us everything you can remember."

* * * * *

Dec. 24

I'm really surprised Lucia thought I should try to get Jeremy to take me back. I mean, he broke up with me, for what? — just because I sometimes kinda fancied another guy. A guy, by the way, who hasn't even called me in ages! What is it with Russell Baines?! Does he want to be friends with me, or doesn't he? The last time I saw him, at his dad's victory party, it seemed like he wanted to be close — really close! But I haven't heard from him since. Of course, that was when he found out I was dating Jeremy. Maybe he's jealous...or doesn't want to interfere...hmmm, I like the idea that he might be jealous...

But back to Jeremy. I apologized to him, I asked him to

> reconsider, but he's so stubborn and pigheaded! And I will not beg!! It's true, I miss him, but I'm not so hard up that I need to go groveling on my knees to any guy! I wouldn't even do that for Russ...or Ben Branson, for that matter! LOL... Nope, best just write that one off as a lost cause and move on...What was Russ's phone number? *teehee*
>
> Can you believe Ainsley? What a load of waffle — like I'm gonna believe that a cool guy like Jonathan Crenshaw would be so lame as to kidnap Braidy! Why would he want to, in the first place? He barely knows she exists! He's met her, what, a total of maybe two or three times? What possible reason could he have...

The ring tone of Moira's cell phone went off suddenly. She glanced at the display; her mother's cell number flashed back at her. Moira picked it up and pushed the talk button.

"Yeah?"

"Are you okay? Are you at home? Has anyone been there?" Renatta asked in a rush.

"Whoa, Mom! Slow down! Yes, I'm fine, I'm home, and no one else is here. What's up?"

"Braidy is missing. It appears that she's been abducted by Jonathan Crenshaw and is in serious danger. We're at Caroline's, trying to figure out what to do. Did you have any idea that he's a magical? And that Braidy's been dating him secretly?"

"No! Is this about that stupid dream Ainsley had earlier? Mom..."

"You knew about that? Why didn't you come here with her?"

"It was just a nightmare, Mom. I didn't think..."

"It wasn't a dream, Moira. It was a Seeing. Believe me, she's telling the truth. And Braidy is definitely missing. She left Gotchalk's over an hour ago without a word to anyone and hasn't been seen or heard from since."

"But Jonathan never said anything about being a magical! Why would he want to kidnap Braidy?" Moira insisted, still reluctant to believe. "And how could Ainsley have a real Seeing? She's just a kid!"

"She Saw you and the twins in New York last year," Renatta stated. *"She can See. Just stay where you are, Moira. Do not leave the house and do NOT answer the door!"* The connection went dead. Moira stared at her phone for a moment in shock, then dropped it on the bed as if it burned her hand.

"Oh God!" she moaned.

* * * * *

"But I don't understand," Priscilla said when Ainsley had finished her story. "How could Jonathan have taken Braidy from the cranberry bogs? That's less than ten miles from here — the new Protective Shield you created after we got them back last year would have kept her safe, wouldn't it, Matthew? You made it so much stronger than the original one, I would have thought..."

"If Braidy has been dating this young man, my love," Matthew explained, "she would most likely have gone with him willingly — to begin with, at least. Once he got her to his intended destination, which may very well be outside of the range of the Shield, he could quite easily have overpowered her, especially as he seems to have had assistance. My shield can't protect against that. It can't stop the children from making their own choices." He turned to Ainsley. "You say Jonathan and this other man were holding Braidy in a lighthouse, correct?" Ainsley nodded. "Could you see the lighthouse? The exterior, I mean. Do you know what it looked like?"

"A little bit, Grandpa. Enough to know it wasn't any of the ones near here."

"Tell us."

Ainsley searched her memory, her eyes closed tight. "The tower was round, with sloped sides, made of stone," she murmured, "unpainted... the lantern room wasn't all glass, like the lighthouses around here. It had walls covered with wooden shingles, and there were a bunch of narrow windows in it. There was no light in the lantern room..."

"Decommissioned, then," Andrew commented. "Probably one of those privately owned places."

"That would make sense," Matthew agreed. "They wouldn't want to risk being seen by a keeper. I expect Jonathan — or more likely whomever he's working for — owns the property. Ainsley, do you think you could recognize it if you saw it again?"

"I...I think so. It was dark, but there was some moonlight reflecting off the windows. I remember thinking it was really different from all the other lighthouses I've seen."

"Brody, get that book your Aunt Pat sent you...*Keepers Of The Light.*" As Brody raced for his room, Caroline explained to the others. "It's a history of lighthouses on Cape Cod and near Boston. If this lighthouse is anywhere nearby, there should be a picture."

"Here." Brody tossed the book in Ainsley's direction as he skidded around the corner from the hall. Ainsley caught the book in midair and quickly began paging through it. She stopped at page forty-two.

"This is it!" she cried.

"You're sure?"

"Positive! Point Gammon Light." She flipped through the remaining pages. "It's the only one that looks like that. This must be it!"

Phil took the book from her. "It's located just the other side of West Yarmouth. It says here that the property has been privately owned for more than one hundred years...but nothing about the current owner." He handed the book to Brody. Holding his hands out helplessly, he appealed to the others. "What do we do now?"

Matthew stood, his face set. He exchanged a glance with his son, who nodded briefly in reply. Then the old man turned to Phil, his eyes bright and fierce. "We find my granddaughter and bring her home."

Chapter Fifteen:

At The Lighthouse

Brody paced the floor of the dining room, needing to be alone, but wanting to stay close to the women as well, just in case they got word. Andrew, Phil, and Matthew had left a short time before, their destination Gammon Point. His mother, aunt, and grandmothers were in the kitchen, trying to keep busy while they waited. Ainsley had fallen asleep on the futon in Caroline's office, exhausted by the evening's drama. The old house seemed eerily quiet, the only sound the soft murmur of the women's voices seeping through the kitchen door. Now he understood what his parents and the others had suffered the year before, when he, Braidy, and Moira had been abducted and taken to New York.

"I ever get my hands on Crenshaw, I'll...!" Brody muttered, slamming a fist into the palm of his other hand. It was the waiting that was the worst. He'd wanted to go with the men, but they had insisted he stay at home.

"We need to know you other three are here, close to home, safe and sound," Matthew had said when Brody had begged to go along on their search. Brody had opened his mouth to protest further, but his father shortstopped him.

"Please, Brody!" Phil had interrupted, his voice hoarse. "Braidy missing, in danger, is horrible enough. I don't need anything happening to you as well. Stay here, look after your mother and the other women. We'll find her, son...I promise."

"But you're not even a magical, Dad!"

"Do you really think that's gonna stop me from tearing that stinking little worm apart when I get my hands on him?" Phil had replied, his blue eyes blazing. "Let's go!" He'd kissed Caroline, clapped Brody on the back, and climbed into the back of Matthew's car. Moments later, they were gone.

It hadn't occurred to Brody until later to question Matthew's statement. What other three? His cousins and himself? But that would be four, if you counted Devon. For that matter, they had no idea where Devon was at the moment. Nor did Brody have any idea why Jonathan Crenshaw would want to harm Braidy in the first place. Unless...Brody ran to the kitchen.

"Does this have something to do with that ignorant Dumari legend again?" he demanded as he burst through the door.

The four women stared at him, their conversation interrupted in mid-sentence. Caroline turned her gaze toward Renatta.

"Well?"

Renatta nodded her head. "Matthew told Moira last night."

"Finally! Would you explain it to Brody, Mom?" she requested. "Please? I don't think I'm up to it at the moment."

"Of course. Brody, the legend of the Dumari is not simply a children's fairy tale..." Meredith began, "it is based on the truth. Do you remember any of the legend?"

"A...a little," Brody said. "The Dumari is a really powerful magical, right?"

"An extremely powerful magical, with the ability to do a great deal of good for mankind," Meredith said. "A great deal of good...or a great deal of harm, depending on what influences come into play. Which is why we have been so careful to protect you children all these years..."

"So you're telling me that those freaks that took us last year were on the right track? That one of us is..." he gulped, "the Dumari?"

"Yes, Brody."

"But how the hell can you know that?"

"Your grandfather came to me," Meredith told him, "in a Seeing, before Devon was born. He told me one of our grandchildren would be the next Dumari."

"Which one of us?"

"He couldn't tell me that. None of you were born yet."

Brody resumed pacing. "So it's Braidy, then? That's why Jonathan took her tonight?"

"He apparently thinks that it's Braidy, but we don't know for sure."

"Well, it must be! Otherwise he wouldn't have bothered to take this risk. But how did he find out? I mean, if you didn't even know..."

"He must have looked for the Mark," Meredith said. "You said they've been dating, correct?"

"Um...well...yeah...Braidy mentioned something..." Brody avoided his mother's eye.

"Then at some point, he must have found the Mark on her."

"Mark? What Mark?"

"The Mark of the Dumari."

"What's that?"

"It's a birthmark of sorts," Renatta explained. "It looks like this..." She lifted the delicate chain hanging around her neck, holding up the golden pendant dangling from it. It was exactly like the keychain Matthew had shown Moira the evening before.

"The Wellspring. You've got one of those, too, don't you, Mom?" Brody asked.

"Yes," Caroline said. "It was a present from your grandmother for my eighteenth birthday."

"So where is this birthmark? And why didn't you look for it on each of us when we were born?" Brody demanded.

"It only appears sometime after the Dumari turns twelve," Meredith told him. "Although by your age, it would definitely be visible."

"Where?" Brody asked. "Where would it be?"

"Behind the ear, beneath the hairline."

"Hell, Jonathan probably spotted it when they were making out," Brody muttered, again avoiding his mother's gaze. It didn't work.

"You knew," Caroline stated. "You knew Braidy was seeing him, after we'd told her not to."

"She...um...might have mentioned it," Brody said, his face red. "I couldn't tell you, Mom! I promised her! I didn't like it either, but she wouldn't listen to me. It was like he'd hypnotized her or something. She was totally unreasonable about the jerk. Besides, she hasn't seen him in weeks. I was hoping it was over between them."

"Apparently not," Caroline sighed. "I understand, Brody. You couldn't betray a confidence like that. I just wish..."

"Me too!"

"I'm still confused about all of this," Priscilla suddenly chimed in. "If this young man wants to use Braidy's powers for his own purposes, why was he talking about killing her? What use will she be to him when she's dead?"

"You know, Priscilla, you're right," Renatta mused. "That makes no sense."

"Unless he needed her powers for only one task," Meredith pointed out, "and he's already accomplished whatever he'd abducted her for."

"Seems like an awful lot of trouble to go to," Priscilla commented, "for just one thing. I mean, this isn't the first time he's tried to take over the Dumari. What about last year, in New York? Wasn't that more of the same?"

"You have a point," Caroline said. "And didn't Ainsley say that both Jonathan and the other man holding Braidy seemed angry? Why would they be angry? They've gotten what they wanted, haven't they?"

"Not if she's refusing to cooperate," Meredith said.

"Or if Jonathan was wrong...if she's not the one after all," Caroline whispered, staring into space. Slowly her gaze focused on Brody.

"Don't be ridiculous, Mom! It has to be Braidy. You can't possibly think it could be me?" Brody laughed

"Why not?"

"Because...well...just because! This is Braidy we're talking about, remember? It's always Braidy! She's always best at everything!"

"Oh, son, don't underestimate yourself," Caroline said with a sad smile.

"Okay, fine! Let's settle this right now, then!" Brody stated vehemently, turning his back on his mother and folding his earlobes forward. "Go on...look! I want to know!"

The four women exchanged glances. Caroline shook her head, so Meredith stepped forward. Gently, she brushed Brody's hair out of the way. After examining both sides of his head, she patted him on the back.

"Nothing. It's not you."

"See! I told you it was Braidy!"

"Not necessarily, Brody," Meredith said. "It could be Moira..." Brody snorted. "Or Ainsley," Meredith continued, giving her grandson a sharp glance.

"Yeah, I guess it could be Ainsley," Brody agreed. "But then why would Crenshaw have bothered to take Braidy? Don't you think he would have checked first?"

"Most likely," Renatta admitted. "I would think he was threatening Braidy simply in order to coerce her into going along with his plans."

"Could be," Caroline agreed, slumping against the counter. "I'm beginning to think you were right, Renatta. This whole Dumari thing is a curse..." She closed her eyes, trying desperately to hold back the tears.

"I swear, he hurts one hair on her head..." Brody left his threat unfinished, but the others got the gist. An uneasy silence descended as their vigil continued.

* * * * *

"Come here, woman."

"Devon, please! Someone might be home." Callista pushed Devon away, gently but firmly. He grabbed her by the arm and pulled her close again.

"No one's here," he murmured, burying his face in her neck. "We're all alone." He nibbled on her ear, then moved to her mouth, kissing her hard and deep. Callista allowed the intimacy for a moment or two, then extricated herself.

"You don't know that for certain," she said, moving quickly to the other side of the living room. "I would prefer not being introduced to your family in the middle of a passionate embrace, thank you very much."

"You haven't complained about my passionate embraces before now," Devon inched toward her, a wicked grin on his lips.

"That was different," Callista stepped back, trying to keep a respectable distance between them. "We were alone then."

"We're alone now."

"That's not necessarily true. It's a big house — your parents or your sisters could be upstairs." She stepped behind the sofa. Devon continued his pursuit.

"Even if they are, it's a big house, like you said," he teased. "They wouldn't even know we're here." He slipped around the end of the sofa.

"Devon...!" Callista said, holding out one hand to ward him off. With that he pounced. Callista squealed, making a dash for the door. But Devon caught her before she could escape. Laughing, he fell onto the sofa, the beautiful blond wrapped tightly in his arms, and quickly stopped her half-hearted protests with kisses. Neither one of them heard Moira running down the stairs.

"Devon?" she called as she entered the room. "Dev, is that...Oh!" Moira skidded to a halt when she spotted the couple entwined on the sofa. Blushing furiously, she looked away. "Sorry. I didn't know you had company."

Devon reluctantly untangled himself and stood up. "I didn't think anybody was home. You remember Callista, don't you? What's up?"

"I...um..." Moira shot a quick glance at Callista, who had already managed to recover completely and stared coolly at the younger girl. Moira decided to ignore her. "I need to talk to you, Dev. It's important."

"So talk."

"In private. Family stuff."

"Moir, Callista is my girlfriend now. And she's a magical, remember? Whatever is going on, you can say it in front of her."

Moira gave Callista another look, obviously skeptical. "Whatever. It's your funeral. It's about Braidy."

Callista stiffened slightly. Neither Devon nor Moira noticed.

"What about Braidy?"

"She's missing."

"She's what?"

"Missing. She was skating at Gotchalk's with a bunch of friends, but then she took off and they can't find her. Did you know she was dating Jonathan Crenshaw?"

"What?! You're joking!"

"Nope. Apparently she's been sneaking around with him for months. Anyway, she left with Jonathan hours ago and they can't find her. Oh, and by the way, he's a magical."

Devon laughed. "Don't be ignorant! Of course he's not!"

"He certainly appears to be," Moira said. "And it looks like he may have kidnapped Braidy. Mom said they think he's holding her in one of the old lighthouses."

"This is totally lame!" Devon ran a hand through his hair. "This is completely ridiculous! I've known the guy for more than a year — I think I would have noticed if he was a magical!"

"Not if he didn't do any magic in front of you, pinhead," Moira sneered.

"What are they planning to do? To find Braidy, I mean," Callista asked. Moira stared at the other girl. What did she care?

"I don't know. Mom said they were trying to figure that out and told me to stay put. They're at Aunt Caroline's," she added for Devon's benefit.

Devon sighed. "I'm sorry, Callista. Looks like I'd better cut our evening short."

"That's all right, Devon. I understand."

"I'll take Callista home, then go straight to Aunt Caroline's. Will you be okay here, Moira?"

"Yeah, sure."

"Might I use the restroom before we go, Devon?" Callista asked. "I'll just be a moment."

"Sure. It's down the hall." Devon pointed his date in the right direction, then returned to the living room to wait.

"Don't worry, Moir," Devon said. "I'm sure it's all some stupid misunderstanding. Jonathan is not a magical, I'm sure of it — and he's no kidnapper, either. You'll see."

"God, I hope you're right!" Moira murmured. "But Mom seemed so sure..."

"She's wrong!" Devon insisted in a low voice. "She has to be! Jonathan's my friend...he's a good guy..." Shaking his head, he fell silent.

Callista closed the bathroom door quickly, locked it, and turned the faucet on full blast. Taking a deep breath, she placed her hands together in front of her face and closed her eyes.

"Jonathan, they know...The family knows you've got the girl... They're looking for you...," she whispered three times, then waited for his response. Nothing. She tried again. "Jonathan, they've found out about Braidy...We've been betrayed...Get out of there!" Again, she waited, but again there was no response. She cursed. "The shield is too strong! I can't get through!" She pulled her cell phone out of her purse, dialing quickly. It was answered on the second ring. "Dawson... Callista Baines...We have trouble...No, I don't have the time to explain now. Meet me at the beach house...Yes, as quickly as you can. I'll be there in five minutes..." She pushed the end button and tossed the phone back into her purse. Turning off the water, she rejoined Devon.

"I'm ready," she said unnecessarily.

Devon escorted Callista to the front door. As she stepped outside, he looked back at his sister. With a wordless gesture of frustration, exasperation, and utter bewilderment he left, leaving Moira alone again.

* * * * *

Matthew, Andrew, and Phil moved quietly toward the Point Gammon Lighthouse. The old tower loomed above them, the natural stone gleaming in the moonlight, the outline sharp against the velvety black winter sky. They'd left the car parked at the entrance to the Great Island peninsula, not wanting to alert anyone to their approach, and hiked as quickly as possible through the snow. When the lighthouse came into view, they paused.

"All right, then," Andrew said, his voice barely above a whisper. "Obviously they'll have a shield up around the place..."

"I'm actually rather surprised we haven't encountered it already," Matthew commented.

"Are we sure they even bothered with a shield?" Phil asked.

"Meredith couldn't get through," Andrew reminded him. "She was blocked, remember?"

"So what do we do, then? If Meredith couldn't get around it, how will we?" Phil's voice cracked with strain.

"Don't worry," Matthew reassured him, "there are ways to get past things like this. It all depends on what type of shield they're using. My main concern is that they have it set to warn them in case of a breach. Depending on how far out from the lighthouse they've placed it, we could be giving them too much time..."

"Too much time?"

"Advance warning...time to escape," Andrew explained.

"But we can see the damn place," Phil said. "They leave, we go after them...simple as that."

"It's not escape I'm most concerned about," Matthew frowned, "but rather what Jonathan and this Morty might do to Braidy if they realize they've been discovered. Once we break through, we'll have to move fast." He sighed. "I don't move as quickly as I used to, I admit."

"Just get us through that shield, Dad," Andrew smiled grimly. "Phil and I can take it from there."

"Need I remind you that you will be facing at least two magical opponents in there, son? And Phil is not a magical."

"I don't need magic for what I intend to do to those two," Phil stated coldly.

"I'm sure you don't," Matthew placed a calming hand on Phil's shoulder, "but I guarantee they'll be using magic against you."

"I can hold down the fort until you manage to get in there," Andrew said. "Phil, you concentrate on finding Braidy and getting her out. I'll distract Jonathan and Morty until you join me, Dad, then between the two of us, we can restrain them. Once Braidy is safe, and we have the situation under control, we'll contact Leo. The authorities can take care of the rest."

"Meredith was going to alert Leo, ask for assistance. Perhaps it would be better to wait for them..."

"We have no idea how long it will take for them to arrive, Dad. We're the only magicals on the Cape. They'll be coming from Boston, or farther."

"Please!" Phil pleaded. "We're wasting time as it is. I can't bear to think what those jerks might be doing to my little girl..." His voice failed him.

"Phil's right," Andrew said. "We need to find Braidy now."

Matthew nodded. "True enough. All right, then. Andrew, use whatever powers you have to...Phil, stay out of the line of fire as much as possible...and both of you, keep your heads down! Let's go."

The three men moved forward cautiously, one step at a time. They'd gone only a few feet when Phil, slightly ahead of the others, came to a dead stop. The snow he was tramping through suddenly seemed to have taken on the consistency of quick-drying cement. He tried to lift his foot, but it wouldn't budge.

"What the...?!"

"Don't move!" Matthew warned.

"As if I could," Phil muttered.

"I'd say we found the shield," Andrew commented dryly. "Dad?"

"Working on it." It was too dark to see Matthew clearly, but both younger men could feel the waves of power emanating from the old man. "It's strong," he gasped after several seconds, "very strong."

"I wonder if they've made Braidy use her powers to reinforce it for them," Andrew said.

"What if we can't..." Phil began, but with that there was a loud cracking noise and he stumbled forward, falling onto his knees in the snow. At the same moment, they heard a loud clanging sound emanating from the lighthouse.

"They know we're here!" Andrew reached down and pulled Phil to his feet. "Let's go!"

The two men sprinted across the snow-covered grass at top speed, leaving Matthew behind. The old man bent over, breathing hard, then straightened and followed the others slowly.

"I'm getting to old for this," he muttered as he gradually picked up speed.

* * * * *

"We've been breached!" Morty yelled over the sound of the alarm, racing for the window. He peered out into the darkness. "There's two of them, headed this way! Go upstairs and get rid of the little chit...I'll hold them off down here."

Jonathan leaped up the stairs as something hit the door with a bang, shaking the old wooden timbers. He glanced over the bannister as the second impact blasted the door off its hinges and across the tower, the force of the power burst flinging Morty off his feet and sending him flying. Andrew Collins ran through the doorway moments later, followed closely by Phil Attison. Phil looked up and his eyes met Jonathan's.

"WHERE IS SHE?!" Phil shouted. "WHERE'S MY DAUGHTER?!"

Jonathan raced for the lantern room, Phil right on his heels. At the second-level deck, the younger man waved his hand and sent a rusty metal spike lying on the floor straight at Phil's head, then pelted upwards, not waiting to see if he hit his target.

"LOOK OUT!" Andrew yelled from below. Phil ducked just in time; the spike flew through the air and embedded itself in the stone wall behind him.

"Damn!" he breathed. "This kid's playing for keeps!"

"Stay behind me," Andrew said, joining Phil on the narrow staircase. They climbed cautiously, following the sound of Jonathan's footsteps on the metal steps.

"What about the other guy?"

"Out cold."

"Did you recognize him?"

"Couldn't see...he was face down on the other side of the tower, half covered by the door — or what remains of it. Matthew will deal with him, whoever he is."

They were halfway up the second flight when they heard a dull thud above them.

"Trap door."

"He doesn't really think that will stop us, does he?" Phil said.

"No, but it will buy him some time," Andrew replied. Taking two steps at a time, they quickly reached the top. Both men pushed at the trap door together, but it didn't budge.

"Blocked," Andrew said, "magically. Step back."

Moving down several steps, Andrew braced his feet and raised his arms high above his head, his palms facing upwards, his fingers curled slightly. Taking a deep breath, he bent his elbows fractionally, then thrust upwards. The trap door didn't move.

There was a muffled scream from above.

"BRAIDY!!" Phil called. "I'M HERE, PRINCESS! DADDY'S HERE! Hurry up, will ya!" he urged Andrew.

Concentrating with all his might, Andrew pushed up again. The trap door lifted several inches, immediately dropping down again. With the third thrust, Andrew shouted inarticulately, his face red with strain. They heard Jonathan cry out and the door burst into pieces. Protecting their heads and faces from the falling splinters, Phil and Andrew jumped up onto the deck of the lantern room.

Braidy lay against the wall on the other side of the tower , still tied and gagged, her eyes wide with fear. Jonathan was raising himself from where he had fallen in the middle of the room, his face twisted with pain. Andrew advanced toward him as Phil ran to Braidy.

"You're strong, Jonathan," Andrew said, "very strong. But not quite strong enough."

"I could have been," Jonathan responded, his tone bitter, "if she'd been the Dumari, like we thought." He stood slowly.

"Braidy would never have used her power for anything evil," Andrew told him. "If you thought she would, you didn't know her at all. Anyway, it doesn't matter now. It's over. Let's go." He turned slightly and gestured toward the stairs, then froze as he saw the head peaking into the room from below.

"Muldoon? Quinn Muldoon? What are you doing here? How did you get here so fast?" Then realization hit. Andrew's eyes narrowed. "*You're* Morty?! Why, you stinking, filthy..."

Jonathan took advantage of Andrew's momentary distraction. He flung his hand out, sending a streak of white-hot energy straight at Andrew's head. Andrew caught the movement out of the corner of his eye, and threw himself behind the step ladder. He immediately whipped his right hand around the legs of the ladder and pulled Jonathan's legs out from under him, causing the young man to tumble to the floor between the tools and the pile of wood.Meanwhile, Muldoon slipped past them and stalked toward Phil, who was attempting to untie his daughter, his back to the rest of the room. Luckily, he had at least managed to remove the gag from Braidy's mouth.

"DADDY!!" she screamed as Muldoon approached them. Phil spun around, saw Muldoon raise one hand, and threw himself in front of Braidy, trying to protect her. With that, Muldoon cried out; he stumbled sideways, nearly falling to his knees. An energy burst had clipped his shoulder. Matthew had arrived.

"Get Braidy out of here, Phil!" Matthew called from the top of the staircase. Muldoon recovered quickly and waved a hand at the lumber, sending one large plank at Matthew. Andrew jumped up to protect his father, but Matthew stopped the wood in midair, letting it drop harmlessly to the floor. He approached his opponent.

"So you're behind these attacks, are you, Quinn?" Matthew said, his tone almost conversational. "Why does this not surprise me..." He waved his hands gracefully, conjuring ropes and sending them toward Muldoon.

"You don't really expect me to give up that easily, do you, Matthew?" Quinn grinned nastily, sweeping one hand through the air. The ropes bunched up into a tight ball, then burst into flames. Muldoon pitched the fireball back at Matthew. The old man ducked, throwing his arms over his head to deflect the attack. The fireball sailed past him and landed on one of the drop cloths; it quickly caught fire, the flames fed by old paint and turpentine splatters. Matthew staggered and nearly fell. Braidy screamed. Phil grabbed her under the arms and dragged her behind the sea chest.

"We'll be safer over here, Princess," he tried to calm her, far from calm himself, "out of the way, while I get these off of you." Kneeling down next to her, Phil pulled out his pocket knife, flipped it open, and began sawing at the ropes around Braidy's ankles.

Andrew ran toward the burning cloth, but before he could act, his father cried out in warning.

"Andrew! Down!"

Glancing up quickly, Andrew saw a large hammer sailing directly toward his head. He dropped to the deck. The hammer Jonathan had thrown flew past him at top speed, flying into the window behind him and smashing the glass with a crash.

"DAMMIT!!" Jonathan yelled.

"FORGET THEM! GET THE GIRL!" Quinn shouted, running to the work bench. Jonathan went airborne, somersaulting over the wood pile. Andrew jumped up, spread his arms wide, then moved them together, cutting off the oxygen to the fire and putting it out. He had just turned to help Phil and Braidy when Quinn grabbed a handful of nails and sent them whizzing toward Andrew and Matthew. Matthew spun in place, whirling faster and faster. The nails bounced off of the old man's force field, shooting upwards to embed themselves in the roof. Matthew advanced on Quinn, his face set with steely determination.

Phil had managed to cut through the bonds around Braidy's ankles, and was working on the ropes around her wrists when the knife suddenly flew out of his hand. Spinning on his heels, Phil watched the knife drop into Jonathan's waiting grasp.

"Stupid old man," Jonathan sneered. "As if you stand a chance against magicals."

"Who you calling old, pipsqueak?" Phil growled. With that, Jonathan threw the knife straight at Braidy's heart. Braidy flung herself sideways, her hands still tied. Instinctively, Phil reached for it barehanded.

"NO!"

Luckily Andrew spotted the glint of the knife blade from across the room. The lid of the old sea chest sprang open, nearly banging Phil in the nose. The point of the knife hit the wood with a soft thunk and remained there, quivering.

Phil took a deep breath. An anger unlike any he had ever known burst inside him. With a roar, he leaped out from behind the chest and launched himself at Jonathan. A moment later, he was lying on the floor, stunned, his head throbbing where it had slammed into the corner of the sea chest.

"DADDY!" Braidy screamed. Frantically, she fought with the ropes still knotted around her wrists, trying desperately to free herself and go to her father's aid.

Jonathan laughed nastily, then ducked quickly as a screwdriver sailed past his ear. Quinn was throwing every tool on the work bench at Matthew, but the old wizard wasn't fazed in the least. He continued to walk straight at his attacker, deflecting one tool after another. Several more screwdrivers, a couple of pliers, and a small hand saw littered the floor around him.

"Give it up, Quinn," Matthew said. "You can't win, and you know it."

As Andrew moved toward Jonathan, a monkey wrench skittered across the deck and stopped at Jonathan's feet. Desperate, wanting only to escape now, Quinn pushed the work bench at Matthew and ran for the ladder. Side-stepping the bench, Matthew lost his balance momentarily.

"KILL HER AND GET OUT!!" Quinn yelled at Jonathan as he climbed to the top of the ladder. He leaped, flipped sideways and landed on the stairs, grunting with pain as his ankle twisted under him. Regaining his balance, Matthew took off after him.

Jonathan sent a blast at the paint cans near the stairs, knocking them over, spilling paint across the floor at Andrew's feet. Andrew slipped, skated a few feet, and landed hard on his back, the breath knocked out of him. Jonathan snapped his fingers; the monkey wrench flew up into his hand. He advanced on Braidy, smiling an evil smile.

"Goodbye, little girl," he said, raising his arm high.

Using every ounce of strength she had left, Braidy wrenched her hands free of the ropes and thrust both of them forward with a loud cry.

Jonathan was lifted off his feet and thrown across the room, crashing into Matthew. The monkey wrench sailed out of his hand and clattered down the stairs, barely missing Muldoon. Both men went down in a jumble of arms and legs. Smaller, younger, and quicker, Jonathan broke free first. Before Matthew could react, Jonathan punched him in the nose, jumped to his feet and sprinted for the stairs. Reaching blindly across the floor, Matthew managed to raise the partially burned drop cloth and fling it over Jonathan's head. Blinded, Jonathan staggered backwards, fighting the thick cloth as it wrapped itself around him.

Seeing that Jonathan had failed, Quinn made one final effort to kill Braidy. Wincing as he put weight on his twisted ankle, he leaned over the edge of the trap door opening and flung a killing surge directly at the young girl where she huddled over her dazed father. Then he ran.

Andrew, still shaken by his fall, heard the hiss of the surge as it soared over him. Desperately, he clapped his hands and flung a protective shield in front of Braidy and Phil a split second before the surge reached them. It crashed against the shield in a blaze of bright green light, bounced off, and sailed back across the room, hitting Jonathan squarely in the chest. Once again, the young man was lifted off his feet, his slight figure eerily illuminated by the spell. He hung in midair momentarily, then, as the others watched in horror, he fell back through the broken window behind him. Seconds later, they heard the sickening crunch of his body hitting the ground twenty feet below.

Chapter Sixteen:

Accusations And Protestations

"I can't believe it."

"You'd better believe it!" Matthew snapped. "He nearly killed Braidy. Hell, he nearly killed me!"

"Quinn...Quinn Muldoon...I thought I knew him better than that," Desmond shook his head. "How could he be so stupid!"

"You tell me," Matthew said, his tone suspicious and accusing. The two men were in Desmond's office on the top floor of the Commonwealth Bank Building in Boston. Desmond stood at the plate glass window, staring blindly at the excellent view of the Charles River. Matthew was seated straight and rigid in a chair in front of Desmond's desk. At Matthew's accusation, Desmond spun around.

"Just what is that supposed to mean?"

"No one knows Muldoon better than you, Desmond...no one is closer to him. Can you tell me how he could have been planning all this time, plotting these attacks on my family without your knowledge?"

Desmond's eyes narrowed. "If we weren't such old friends, Matthew, I'd take exception to those words." He strode to his desk and slammed his fist on the granite top. "How could you possibly think I'd have anything to do with such a ridiculous, hare-brained scheme! Kidnapping an innocent young girl? Getting that young man...what was his name?... killed? Why on earth would I risk everything...my fortune, my business, my political career? You'd have to think I was insane!"

"That would be a given," Matthew said, his voice as cold as his eyes.

"How long have you known me, Matthew?" Desmond asked. "Can you really think that of me?"

The two men stared at each other long and hard. Finally, Matthew sighed and lowered his head.

"Of course not, Desmond. Forgive me. What happened to Braidy the other night has me so rattled, I'm not thinking straight."

"I understand, Matthew," Desmond sat down, slowly shaking his head. "If I were in your shoes right now, I'd go ballistic."

"Believe me, Desmond, if I could find Muldoon, I would!" Matthew stated fiercely. "He has a lot to answer for!"

"I have a few questions for him myself," Desmond said dryly. "This has me more upset than you could possibly imagine. Quinn wasn't only my friend, he was my colleague, my employee...practically my partner. I thought I could trust him with my life. Hell, I did trust him with my life! Or at least, my livelihood. For him to have screwed up like this isn't only a shock — it's a reflection on me. My one consolation is that none of my nonmagical constituents will know anything about it. How would it look if their newly elected mayor was linked to a kidnapper and murderer, I ask you? I'd have to resign before I was ever sworn in!"

"I will confess, Desmond, that is the least of my worries," Matthew commented sharply. "I'm rather more concerned about the safety of my family at this point."

Desmond replied with a wry half-smile. "Of course, of course! Please don't think that's not of the utmost importance to me as well, Matthew. I'll be happy to help in any way I can." He fiddled with some papers on the desk. "How is the young lady, by the way? Is she recovered?"

"More or less," Matthew told him. "She's very strong...resilient... but this has been quite a shock to her. It's going to take some time for her to get over it."

"She wasn't hurt...physically, I mean?"

"Nothing major. A few bruises. It's the emotional trauma that's of most concern right now. But Braidy has a good head on her shoulders — although her lack of judgement in this case wouldn't exactly bear that out, I grant you. However, I'm sure she'll bounce back quickly. She'll be all right."

"Resilient, like you said." Desmond stood and returned to the window, his back to the room once more. "So did Quinn or the young man tell her anything? Their reasons...motivations ...plans...?"

Matthew hesitated before answering, not sure how much to tell Desmond. Finally, he settled for a partial truth.

"Nothing substantive. Apparently, they were hoping to channel Braidy's powers with their own in some way — the Crenshaw boy claimed they wanted to take control of society in order to improve it. By force, apparently." Matthew shook his head sadly. "When are people going to learn..."

"I did some checking into who owns the Point Gammon property..."

"And?"

"No luck. The title is held by a dummy corporation that is obviously just a screen for the real owners, but there's no information about who they are."

"Nor would there be," Matthew sighed. "Muldoon would make sure they covered their tracks well. Thanks for trying."

"If there's anything else you need," Desmond turned, one hand held out to Matthew, "just let me know."

Matthew shook the proffered hand as he stood. "Thank you, Desmond. If you think of anything Muldoon said to you that might have bearing on this — anything at all — let me know."

"I will, old friend, I will."

Desmond slowly closed the door to his office as Matthew walk to the elevators, his face a mask.

* * * * *

Phil entered the library, carrying an armload of firewood. He set it down on the hearth, then straightened and stretched his back. Glancing around, he spotted Brody ensconced in the overstuffed armchair near the bookshelves.

"Where's Braidy?" Phil asked. Since the near disaster on Christmas Eve, he'd found himself coping with a desperate need to know where his daughter was at all times. He knew it was unreasonable, but he couldn't help himself. He only hoped it might ease with time.

"She's out on the deck," Brody replied without raising his eyes from his book.

"What's she doing out there? It's freezing!" Phil began to stride toward the door.

"Mom's with her," Brody said.

"Oh..." Phil stopped in his tracks. "Well, then..."

Caroline and Braidy sat snuggled together under a warm fleece blanket on the deck, slowly swinging back and forth in the glider. Occasionally, Caroline would reach over and gently wipe the tears from her daughter's cheeks, but she let the girl cry in silence. She was patient enough — and wise enough — to wait for Braidy to start the dialogue in her own time.

When the men had brought Braidy home, shaken, bruised, traumatized, every maternal instinct in Caroline had clamored to wrap her daughter up in her arms and hide her away from everyone. But, as Matthew had pointed out, it was best for Braidy to tell her story immediately, while it was still fresh in her memory. Then the healing process could begin in earnest. So Caroline had forced herself to stand by, her heart aching, while Matthew gently questioned Braidy about the circumstances of her relationship with Jonathan Crenshaw, her abduction that night, and the conversation between Jonathan and Quinn Muldoon.

Discovering that Muldoon was the man who called himself Morty — the same Morty who had been involved in the kidnapping of the twins and Moira the previous year — hadn't exactly surprised anyone; Caroline couldn't help but remember her own suspicions at the time. But the confirmation of those suspicions had still come as something of a shock, especially for Renatta, who had worked with and for the man for years. Of course, along with the outrage of Muldoon's betrayal was the concern that his employer might also be involved. Desmond Baines was one of the most powerful and influential magicals on the East Coast — for that matter, in the entire country. Caroline knew that possibility had Matthew disturbed enough to confront his friend with his misgivings.

However, Braidy's supposition that Jonathan Crenshaw was the mastermind behind both of the attacks on the kids had done much toward easing the adults' worries. If Jonathan had been the man both Lorena Lewis and Quinn Muldoon had spoken of as Alex, most of their problems should have ended with his death. The one thing that still had them uneasy was the fact that Muldoon remained at large

— even more dangerous now that his true colors had been revealed; he no longer had anything to lose. Although if the man had any brains left, he'd stay well clear of the men of the family. The glint in their eyes whenever Muldoon's name was mentioned sent chills down even Caroline's spine.

Braidy reached for the box of Kleenex and blew her nose. Taking a deep, shuddering breath, she straightened slightly, pulling away from her mother's embrace.

"I feel like such a dork," she said, her voice low. "I thought he cared about me. I thought he wanted to be with me. How could I have been so stupid..."

Caroline tucked a stray strand of hair behind Braidy's ear. "You cared about him, sweetie. And from what you've told us, he did pursue you. Had someone acted that way with me, I would have thought the same thing."

"But did I care, Mom? I mean, did I even know Jonathan well enough to be able to truly care about him? Obviously not. And as far as him pursuing me is concerned...well, we know why he did that, don't we. And it wasn't like he acted as if he couldn't stand to be away from me. I'd go weeks without seeing him, or hearing from him, or... I'd never put up with that kind of treatment from any of the other boys I know. Why did I let him get away with it? Why didn't I just tell him where to shove it? What did I see in him?"

Caroline sighed. "Well, he was quite handsome...and intelligent... and charming. I have to confess, a good look into those big blue eyes of his gave even me a cheap thrill once or twice..."

"Mom!"

"What?" Caroline blushed slightly at the look of horror on her daughter's face.

"You're...you're married! And way older than...than Jonathan was!"

Caroline smiled a little. "I may be married...and you may think I'm over the hill...but I ain't dead yet. You'll understand someday," she assured her still appalled daughter. "The point I was trying to make is that your infatuation for Jonathan was totally understandable. He was the type of young man that, you might say, has a way with women. I would think almost any girl would have had a difficult time resisting his allure. And the fact that he was totally different from all the other boys you've known had to have been a huge part of his attraction. He was exciting... magnetic... dangerous."

"Got that right!" Braidy sighed. "From now on, I'm only going out with dull, boring types...if I date at all, that is."

"You will. Give your heart — and your pride — time to heal. Just don't be in such a hurry to fall in love next time, all right? And please, please don't lie to me again."

Braidy nodded, her cheeks red. She quickly changed the subject.

"It's so freaky, that the whole Dumari thing is for real, and not just a fairy tale like I thought."

"What's really freaky is the possibility that it might actually be Moira," Caroline said dryly. Braidy grinned slightly.

"Don't forget, Mom, it could be Ainsley."

"Not with our luck!" Braidy's smile widened at her mother's tone.

"Do you think she's found the Mark yet?" she asked.

"I would think, if she had, we'd know about it. Moira isn't the type to keep something like that to herself."

"Yeah, you're probably right. She'd love to lord it over me." Braidy sighed again. "Oh well. At least I don't have to worry about it anymore."

"All these years, I thought it would be you," Caroline murmured, her eyes lowered. "You seemed to be the obvious choice..."

"I'm sorry, Mom," Braidy whispered. "I never meant to disappoint you."

Caroline's head came up quickly. "Oh no, sweetie! I didn't mean that! You have no idea how proud I am of you!" She slipped an arm around Braidy's shoulders and pulled her close. "It's my own fault. I guess Renatta was right about me. I was being vain. I thought if you — or Brody — turned out to be the Dumari, that would make me important as well. Stupid, really. Like I had anything to do with it. The selection of the Dumari is purely random. And I think I finally understand what both Renatta and your grandmother have been trying to explain to me. Although being the Dumari is certainly a great honor, it is also a terrible burden. And I have to confess, now that I've seen what can happen when people are blinded by power and greed, I'm very relieved that neither of my children will have to carry that load."

Caroline planted a soft kiss on Braidy's forehead. They rocked on in silence, watching the waves hit the sand.

* * * * *

"That's it, then." Devon tossed the *Cape Cod Times* onto the sofa and turned toward the window. The headline of the article he'd been reading stared up at Renatta: "Local PBS Intern Dies After Drunken Fall."

"That's it," Andrew replied. "At least as far as the police and the newspapers are concerned."

"So the police bought the story. That Jonathan and some unnamed friends were having a party in that old lighthouse, he got drunk, and fell through a window, breaking his neck, and the other guys made tracks," Devon's voice was low, harsh. "Not a word about what happened to

Braidy — no mention of you, Matthew, Uncle Phil — nothing about that weasel, Muldoon."

"No. How could there be? Can you imagine the uproar if the general public — the nonmagical public — were told that Jonathan was killed during a battle between several magicals? They don't even know we exist!" Andrew said.

"We're a legend, a fairy tale to them..." Renatta added, "and that's just the way it needs to stay. You know that."

Devon acknowledged his mother's statement with a shrug.

"We can't tell the truth, Devon. Not in this case." Andrew sighed. "Believe me, I like having to lie no more than you do, but if word got out that magic is real, we'd have a riot on our hands. Fabricating the story about a party that got out of hand was the only way. Anything closer to the truth could have raised suspicions, which would have only led to more questions. More questions would have led to more suspicions, and in no time the conspiracy theorists would have jumped all over it. We couldn't let that happen. The world is not ready to accept our talents. It never has been, and I suspect never will be. No one must ever deduce that magicals really are living among the general population, or that Jonathan Crenshaw was one of us."

"Was he?" Devon asked pointedly, shooting his stepfather a sharp glance. The mood in the room suddenly turned icy.

"You doubt us?" Andrew asked, his eyes narrowing. "After seeing the condition Braidy was in when we brought her home that night?"

"Sweetheart, I'm sure Devon didn't mean..."

Andrew raised his hand, stopping Renatta in mid-sentence. "Do you?" he demanded.

Devon closed his eyes tightly, his face a picture of misery and grief. "I...hell! No! I don't know! It's just..." he spun around to face his parents, crying out in anguish,"why didn't I know?! Why couldn't I see that Jonathan was a magical?! I've lived with magicals all my life! How could I not have known?!"

"None of us knew, Devon," Renatta pointed out gently. "He was obviously very good at dissembling."

"But none of you were as close to him as I was! You only saw him a couple of times. I thought I knew him. I thought we were friends. Instead, all along he was just using me to get close to Braidy."

"I imagine Jonathan Crenshaw used a lot of people in his lifetime," Andrew said tartly.

"Yeah, and I was the perfect tool, wasn't I," Devon continued, sounding more cynical and self-pitying with every word. "I can just imagine the conversation between him and Muldoon. 'Let's use Devon to get to Braidy!' 'Yeah, he's just a stupid nonmagical. He'll never catch on.'"

"Devon!" Renatta protested.

"That's what I am, aren't I, Mom?" he insisted. "Just a stupid nonmagical. An idiot in a family of geniuses."

"Stop it!" Renatta walked over to her son, grasping him by the arm. "You are not an idiot! Not having magical abilities..."

"Makes me a freak!" Devon interrupted her. "I'm a freak in my own family!"

"That's not true!" Renatta cried. Devon ignored her.

"I'm the only nonmagical in the entire family! What else does that make me?!"

"Uncle Phil is a nonmagical..."

"That's different, and you know it! He married into it...I'm your son! Why didn't I inherit any magic from you?!" The sheer agony on Devon's face brought tears to Renatta's eyes.

"You know your father wasn't..."

Devon didn't bother to let her finish the sentence. "He was Moira's father, too. Why is she a magical, and I'm not?" He laughed harshly. "It's actually quite ironic, you know. Moira's got all this frickin' magical power, but wants nothing to do with it. I'd give anything to be a magical, and I can't even turn the damn TV on without a remote. It is so not fair."

Renatta stared at him. "Have you always felt this way?" she whispered.

"What do you think?" Devon replied sarcastically, avoiding her gaze. "It's not your fault, Mom," he continued, softening his tone for her sake. "I know there's nothing you could have done. It just hasn't been easy, always feeling inadequate around the people I love the most. I wish..." His words faded away.

"Oh, Devon." Renatta slipped her arms around her son. "I've never wanted you to be anything other than what you are."

"Of course you haven't," he said with a wry smile, hugging her in return. "You're my mom. The problem is that I've always wanted to be something else...something more. But I can't be. I'm stuck with what I am."

"Devon..." Andrew shook his head, at a loss for words. "I don't know what to say."

"There's nothing you can say, Andrew. It is what it is." Letting go of his mother, Devon turned back to the window. "Damn it, Andrew, did you have to kill him?" he added gruffly.

Renatta stiffened. "Andrew didn't kill Jonathan," she said, her face flushing with sudden anger, "it was an accident! He was trying to protect Phil and Braidy! He would never have deliberately...!

"I know...I know!" Devon cut her off. "I didn't mean...forget it." Staring out of the window, he cleared his throat. "I've been thinking... maybe it's time I go my own way...get out on my own..."

"What do you mean?"

"You have been on your own!" Renatta sounded worried. She didn't like the direction the conversation was taking. "You've been living in the dorm for more than a year now..."

"That's not the same, and you know it, Mom," Devon said, turning to face her. "Besides, I've been back here at least once a month, and every one of the holidays, plus all last summer. Don't you think it's time I learned to do my own laundry?"

"I could teach you here," Renatta said in a small voice.

"Mom...!" Devon ran a hand through his hair, somewhat exasperated. "You know what I mean! I've got to do this, Mom. I've got to come to terms with things on my own. I've got to start finding my own way."

"I understand, Devon," Andrew said, his eyes filled with sadness... and resignation. "You're right. It's time."

"But where will you live?"

"I'll camp out at the dorm for now, until I can find a cheap apartment. There's always somebody looking for a roommate...that's an option I can explore once everybody's back on campus."

Renatta sighed. "All right. It's obvious you've made up your mind and I'm not going to change it. At least wait until after the holidays to leave, okay? We can't have our New Years Eve party without you here."

"All right, Mom. I can wait a few more days." He headed for the stairs.

"Devon," Andrew called to him. "Never forget...this will always be your home."

Devon nodded his head. "Thanks. I won't forget."

Moira was waiting at the top of the stairs.

"You have got to be the biggest dork I've ever seen," she commented flatly.

"Leave it, Moira!" Devon growled. He entered his bedroom and flung himself on the bed.

"I mean, I know there was a time not too long ago that I was the resident idiot around here," Moira continued with a grimace. "There's some who might say I still am...but in my opinion, you just took the prize, dear brother."

"Why? Because I want to get out on my own? Everybody does that eventually."

"Not that!" Moira shot him a disgusted look. "Because of the whole magical thing. Who cares if you can do magic or not? Nobody in this family does, especially me! I couldn't care less! You're my brother...that's all that matters."

"That's not all that matters, and you know it!" Devon snapped. "I've never fit in around here! I've always been different!"

"You wanna see different? Look at me! Talk about not fitting in!"

"That's because you choose not to! You could be exactly like the rest of the family if you wanted to be. Me — I can't even come close! Believe me, I've tried!"

Moira frowned. "You have? When..."

"Drop it, Moira! It's not important. The point is, I've never felt like I really belong around here. All the magicals in the family try to act like it's no big deal, but I know they think less of me because I don't have the same abilities they do."

"I'm a magical too, Dev," Moira said softly. "Do you think I feel that way?"

"Of course not! Don't be stupid! Besides, you gave up magic, right?"

Moira shrugged her shoulders. "More or less. Doesn't matter. What does is that you're acting really stupid about this."

"It's the way I feel, stupid or not."

"Devon, don't leave. Please."

"I have to, Moir," Devon stood and placed his hands on Moira's shoulders. "I've got to get away from all of this. It's just...it's too much, ya know?"

Sadly, Moira nodded her head. She'd sensed a restlessness, a dissatisfaction in her brother for months. He'd been drifting further and further away from her — and now he was leaving.

"I need some fresh air," Devon said with a sigh. "I'll see you later."

"You will keep in touch, won't ya?" Moira tried to keep her tone light, but feared her success was minimal. "After you move, I mean."

"Yeah, sure." Devon leaned down to give his sister a one-armed hug, then strode out of the room and down the stairs.

"Stupid dork," Moira muttered. "I hope he knows what he's doing."

The front door slammed, and Devon was gone...

December 29

Happy Frickin' New Year...

Devon is being such a pinhead! What's his twist, anyway? I don't care that he's not a magical...hell, I'm still not completely sure I want to be one myself. And nobody else in the family cares that he's not. It doesn't matter to them at all. They like him loads better than me — with or without the magic crap! Why can't he see that?

So has he been jealous of the rest of us all these years? Has he been jealous of ME?! That is so freaky! I had no idea. Devon has always seemed so sure of himself, so confident, so comfortable in his own skin...I really envied that. I guess it just goes to show you can never really know a person completely. All this time he's been envious of our abilities, and none of us guessed. Hey, I wonder if Uncle Phil feels that way too? And Grandma Priscilla...naw, not her! She's too frickin' happy all the time.

I wish Dev wasn't going to move out. I mean, I know he's been living at the dorm a lot of the time, but he's been home a bunch too. He still had his room here. And most of his stuff. Now, who knows when I'll see him again? Guys aren't exactly the greatest in the correspondence area, ya know? WHY ARE GUYS SO STUPID?!!!!

I never thought I'd say this, but I feel so sorry for Braidy. I mean, it was harsh enough when it was the three of us together in New York, but at least none of us had to go through it all alone. But she was all by herself this time. And as if that wasn't bad enough, the guy dissing her was somebody she liked — jeez, he was her frickin' boyfriend! As ignorant as Jeremy was about dumping me, at least he didn't try to kill me! She's got to be totally messed up right now. And she doesn't even have the consolation of being the Dumari...

The Dumari...

God...

This is for real. One of us really is the most powerful magical of the age...

And it's not Braidy...

Or Brody...

Which means...

It's Ainsley...or ME! Now *that's* a scary thought!

Crap — Ainsley. I really screwed that up, didn't I — ignoring her like that. If she hadn't gone running to Aunt Caroline's.... oh man, I can't go there!

But I have to go there. I can't pretend it didn't happen. I was totally out of line. Okay, yes, Ainsley had no business messing me up with Jeremy...but I did screw with her head about that Hicks kid last spring. That was wrong, too. So I guess I started it. And Andrew did punish her pretty good, and she did apologize for what she did...hell! I shouldn't have held a grudge like that. Besides, one had nothing to do with the other. Regardless of how pissed I was at Ainsley, I should have listened to her. I mean, I know she's got a lot of magical talent. And I knew she'd had some Seeings, like Grandma. What if she had just stayed home, like I told her to? Braidy could be...GOD!

I guess Devon isn't the only idiot in this family. You know, I really need to learn to control that temper of mine. It's gonna get me in some serious trouble one of these days. Yeah, like nearly getting my cousin killed isn't serious enough...

* * * * *

"You can't blame yourself..."

"Can't I? If it weren't for me, for my actions, that young man would still be alive, Renatta! I certainly can blame myself for his death! Devon was right about that."

"No, he wasn't!" Renatta insisted, grasping her husband by the arms and forcing him to face her. "You were trying to protect Phil and Braidy. If anyone is to blame, it's Quinn Muldoon — and Jonathan himself."

"Are you saying he had some sort of death wish?"

"No, of course not. But he created the situation. His actions forced you to react the way you did. He attacked first. You were simply attempting to stop him."

"I know that, Renatta," Andrew sighed, dropping onto the sofa. "I simply can't help wondering if I might have handled the situation differently."

"How? Both Jonathan and Quinn were trying to kill all of you! What else could you have done? I think you acted admirably — you and Matthew both." Renatta joined Andrew on the couch. "You both took a purely defensive stance — not once did either of you use your powers to assault, only to protect. Remember, it was Muldoon's surge that killed Jonathan, not yours. All you did was shield Braidy and Phil from it — it was a complete fluke that it then hit Jonathan."

Andrew leaned back and closed his eyes. "But could I have changed it somehow?"

"Changed it?"

"Sent it in a different direction...diffused it instead of deflecting it...blasted the damn thing out of the air...I don't know! Something! Anything..." He opened his eyes and stared at his wife, his distress nearly choking him.

"You barely had time to do what you did, Andrew," Renatta soothed him. "I'm amazed you were able to throw that shield up in time. You didn't have the luxury of considering other options."

"You're right. I know you're right." Andrew sat forward, his hands clasped between his knees. "It's just...I never dreamed I'd kill anyone,

Renatta. Accidental or not, defensive or not, I still have to accept some responsibility for Jonathan Crenshaw's death. The question is, how do I live with myself after this?"

"By accepting the fact that you had little or no control over the situation — that Quinn and Jonathan attacked you, not the other way around. A war can be started by only one side. Everyone has the right to defend themselves."

"Do we? Or will that line of thinking merely take us back to the old eye for an eye and tooth for a tooth mentality?"

"That's not self-defense, that's revenge!" Renatta replied angrily. "Andrew, you know all of this. We can't just stand by and allow people like Quinn and Jonathan to take over. They'd destroy everything we believe in! I know society is far from perfect — but what they wanted to do is so far wrong, it's off the charts! Who are they to decide they have all the answers? Why should they be allowed to force their choices and beliefs down everyone else's throats? And since when has violence been a solution for anything?"

"Whoa, girl!" Andrew smiled slightly, holding up his hands. "You don't have to convince me. What they were trying to do goes against my very being. I only wish I hadn't been the one to be involved."

"I wish none of us had to be involved!" Renatta whispered fervently. Andrew slipped an arm around her shoulders.

"Have you talked to Moira yet?"

"No," she admitted. "I'm a little afraid to, I admit. And a part of me keeps hoping that she'll come to me."

"It could be Ainsley, you know."

"Don't say that! Don't even think it!" Renatta cried, horrified. "She's my baby, my little girl! The thought of Ainsley being in the kind of danger Braidy was..." she shuddered, leaving the sentence unfinished.

"But it'd be okay if that happened to Moira?" Andrew asked with a wry glance.

Renatta couldn't help but laugh a little. "Of course, it wouldn't be! Don't be silly. It's just...Moira's older, more resilient, more self-sufficient. She could handle it better."

"True. Although I'm beginning to get the impression that our little girl is a lot tougher than she appears..." It was Renatta's turn to look askance. Andrew chuckled at her expression. "Don't get me wrong, punkin. If anything like that happened to Ainsley, I'd be a basket case. But I sure as hell don't want anyone messing with Moira, either."

"Well, hopefully, we won't have to worry about that anymore. Whoever was involved in these attacks has now lost their leader. Jonathan must have been the one the kids heard them all referring to as Alex. And Quinn was obviously going by the name of Morty. He may still be out there, but we can protect ourselves from him now. We know the face of the enemy." She shuddered again.

"Never did like that jerk, Muldoon, did you."

"No," Renatta stated flatly. She took a deep breath and stood up. "Enough of this. The worst is over, the kids are all safe, none of you were seriously hurt...and Devon will straighten himself out in time. His friend's death was quite a shock. But he'll get over it. And perhaps it is time for him to have his own place. He's old enough. And he has a good head on his shoulders. He'll be fine. It's just the hardest thing a parent has to do...letting them go, I mean," she sighed.

"I know, punkin. But it's also the most important thing parents have to do."

"I know." She leaned down and kissed her husband. "Time to make supper."

Andrew watched Renatta leave the room, somewhat surprised at her matter-of-fact attitude toward the situation. Knowing what a worrier she tended to be, he suspected she was putting a brave face on things for his sake. But he decided not to call her on it.

"Maybe you're right," he murmured to himself. "Maybe the worst is over..." He rolled his eyes as reality reared its ugly head, "...and then we woke up."

* * * * *

"Can I come in?"

"Of course, Devon," Callista said, hiding her surprise beneath her usual cool demeanor. She held the door of her father's beach house wide for him.

"I'm sorry I didn't call," Devon apologized, heading for the living room. "I needed to get out of the house. I didn't know if you would be here or at the penthouse for New Year's, but I decided I might as well give this place a try."

"What's going on?" Callista asked.

Devon flopped down in a chair. "I'm moving out. Permanently. For good. Right after the holidays."

"I take it your decision was not greeted with enthusiasm?"

Devon shrugged. "Mom wasn't exactly thrilled with the idea, but Andrew understood, I guess."

"And what brought this decision on?"

"I've been thinking about it for a while," he said. "I'm too old for my mom to still be making my bed. I've got to start doing things for myself. But it's not just that..."

"Then what?"

Devon sat forward, his hands clasped between his knees. "Have you ever felt totally out of place...completely out of your element?"

"No."

He smiled slightly. "Of course not. Not you. You're perfect, exactly as you are, so you're bound to fit in anywhere you go."

Callista acknowledged the compliment with a slight nod. "I take it you don't feel that way."

"Not with my family, no."

Callista waited patiently for him to elaborate. He took a deep breath before continuing.

"Now, don't misunderstand what I'm going to say, Callista. This has nothing to do with you."

"I didn't think it did," she stated coolly.

"It's just...they're magical. I'm not. Do you have any idea what it's been like, growing up knowing you don't belong in your own family? That you're the oddball, the sore thumb, the freak? They were always making excuses for me, pretending it didn't matter, telling me I had other talents...yeah, right! Like I didn't know the only talent that really mattered to them was being a magical. I was never good enough. Man, I would have given anything to be a magical! But I'm not, so I'll never fit in. Not with them."

"I certainly hope we don't make you feel that way as well, Devon."

"Mr. Baines!" Devon jumped to his feet at the sound of Desmond's voice. "I mean, Mr. Mayor, that is..."

Desmond smiled and waved his hand in dismissal. "No formalities here, Devon. After all, you are dating my daughter." He joined Callista on the couch. "You haven't answered me yet. Do we make you feel that way? As if you're not good enough, simply because you don't happen to be a magical?"

"No, sir. Of course not." Devon sat back down. "But...there's still a difference. Do you understand, sir? Callista? I know I can't do the things you can, and it makes me feel...inadequate, somehow. It's so frustrating! I'd learn it, if I could...but last time I checked, they weren't offering Spells and Enchantments 101 at the university yet."

Desmond chuckled. "No, I don't suppose they could. So, did I hear correctly? You're leaving home permanently?"

"Yes, sir."

"Do you have a place to stay?"

"The dorm, I guess. For now, anyway." From Devon's expression, it was obvious that he wasn't overly thrilled at the prospect of living at the college dorm full time.

"Sounds thrilling."

"It's a place to sleep, at least. I guess it will do until I can afford a place of my own. Or find someone to room with."

"As I recall, living in the dorm is not only rather noisy and uncomfortable, but can prove to be fairly expensive," Desmond commented.

"That it can, but it's still cheaper than an apartment," Devon replied. "I can't afford one by myself. You were most generous during the campaign, Mr. Baines, but that gig's over now...and they don't pay much more than pennies down at the newspaper — not to a newby like me."

"I wouldn't think so," Desmond said. "However, in my opinion, a bright young man like yourself needs some peace and quiet in order to realize his full potential. I like you, Devon. I think you have a lot of talent. I'd hate to see that wasted in the noise and distraction of dorm room life."

"What did you have in mind, sir?" Devon asked, sitting up eagerly.

"Now mind you, this would only be a temporary solution, just until you finish your training and establish your career — but you might want to consider living with us for a while. Until you can get on your feet, that is."

Callista gave her father a sharp glance.

"Really?! You mean it?!" Devon broke out in a wide grin. "That would be so cool! I'd really appreciate it, Mr. Baines. I'd be no trouble,

I promise. I don't stay out late — well, not too often, anyway — and I don't eat much..."

Desmond smiled and raised his eyebrows. Devon laughed.

"Okay, maybe I do eat a fair amount," he admitted, "but I'll try to restrain myself. And I insist on paying you something for room and board."

"Of course. This is, after all, a business proposition. I'm certain we can agree on a reasonable amount." Desmond leaned forward, holding out his hand to Devon. "We have a deal, then?"

"We sure do! I can't thank you enough, sir," Devon grasped Desmond's hand and shook it vigorously. "I really appreciate this."

"My pleasure, Devon," Desmond assured him. "By the way, Devon...regarding your... education...perhaps I could help you out a bit there as well."

Devon frowned, momentarily perplexed. "I don't understand...my education?"

"Your...shall we call it...specialized studies?" Desmond said.

Devon's eyes widened. "What do you mean, Mr. Baines?" he asked, his heart suddenly pounding.

"Let's just say there may be some things you could pick up," Desmond replied enigmatically, "if you're willing to work hard enough. Things you can't learn in any classroom. I'm not promising anything, mind you," he warned, "but it might be worth a try."

"Wait a minute. Are you saying it might be possible for me to learn how to do magic?"

"Well, theoretically..." Desmond waved a hand vaguely. "A person can learn how to draw, or cook a gourmet dinner, or throw a football, correct? Magical ability is a skill, just like those. So if you could learn to perform other skilled tasks, why not magic?"

"Oh, man! That would be brilliant! I wouldn't be the family oddball any more!" Devon jumped out of his chair and began striding back and forth. He laughed. "Can you picture Moira's face if I walked in some day and started sending stuff flying around the room?!"

"Calm down, Devon," Desmond smiled. "This is only theoretical, mind you. I don't know for certain if I can teach you anything."

"But it's possible, right?"

"It's not necessarily probable," Desmond hesitated for an instant, "...but, yes, it could be possible. In theory, at least."

"That's good enough for me! I never thought there'd be a chance... Thank you, Mr. Baines!"

Callista stood suddenly. "I'm hungry. Buy me dinner, Devon."

"Yeah, sure...we can celebrate!" He took her by the arm, but she pulled away.

"I'll meet you at the car. I need to ask Father something about the inauguration."

The moment Devon left the room, Callista turned to her father, her gaze bemused.

"Is this wise? Having him live with us?"

"Trust me, my dear." Desmond smiled coldly. "This couldn't be working out better if I'd planned it myself."

Chapter Seventeen:

Breathing Space

"Okay...so I just dial Russ's number and ask him to come to the party tonight. No biggie. Just a friendly little invitation to a New Year's Eve party, that's all."

Her decision made, Moira reached for her cell phone. But then she paused, a troubled expression crossing her face. Slowly, she sat up, her legs hanging off the side of the bed. She stared at her reflection in the mirror above her dresser. "Braidy. Damn. What the hell am I going to say about that? He'll want to hear the whole story. I'll have to tell him about Ainsley's Seeing, but then he'll probably ask why I didn't go with her to Aunt Caroline's. Yeah, he's gonna love that answer! But I can't even begin to describe what happened that night without mentioning what Ainsley Saw...it wouldn't make any sense. Crap! As soon as Russ finds out what a witch I was to Ainsley about the whole thing, he isn't going to want anything to do with me! And rightly so!"

Moira stood and began pacing back and forth. "God, I'm such a freak! Why didn't I just help Ainsley?! Why did I have to be so...so..." she couldn't finish the sentence. She stopped pacing and faced herself in the mirror. "You know what you are, girl? You are one total, verifiable head case! A complete ditz! Ainsley has been trying to make things up with you for weeks, and you just blew her off! When the hell are you gonna get over it, and forgive her, for christ's sake?!" She glared angrily at herself for several moments before a look of determination replaced the anger. "Right now, that's when!" she said fiercely. "You've got to face the facts — take responsibility for your own actions — admit you were wrong. And then you're going to be straight with Russ about the whole thing — even if it does totally turn him off. If you're going to have a relationship with the guy, you can't start it out by lying to him. It's time to do some major growing up!"

Taking a deep breath, Moira squared her shoulders and marched down the stairs to the second floor. As she approached Ainsley's bedroom, she hesitated slightly, but with a mental shake forced herself forward.

"It's now or never, kid," Moira whispered, her eyes steely with resolve. She knocked on the open door. "Anybody home?"

Ainsley was sitting in her window seat, reading a book. She lowered the book and looked up, an odd expression in her eyes as she gazed at her sister.

"What do you want, Moira?" she said quietly.

"Got a minute?"

"I suppose."

Moira slowly entered the room, unsure of how to start. Giving herself another shake, she plunged in.

"I...um...I wanted to talk to you about..." she coughed, "about what happened...you know ...Christmas Eve."

Ainsley waited.

"Actually, I wanted to...well...apolo..." Her voice caught on the word. She swallowed hard, "...apologize for the way I acted. It was really stupid of me. I mean, I know you can See, and I knew you wouldn't make up something like that, but I was still so pissed about the whole thing with Jeremy, that I wouldn't even listen to you."

"I know."

"Yeah...well...um...I just wanted to say I was sorry," Moira continued, forcing herself to ignore Ainsley's less than positive reception, "and that I realize how wrong I was. About everything. If you'd stayed home like I told you to, if you hadn't gone to Aunt Caroline on your own, Braidy would probably..." she gulped again, "...probably be dead right now. And it would be all my fault." Moira's voice faded away. The enormity of her childish behavior had finally hit home. Dropping down onto the bed, she buried her face in her hands. "I can be such a bitch."

Ainsley watched Moira for a moment or two, then moved next to her on the bed. Tentatively, she reached out and patted the older girl on the back. "Not all the time."

Moira twisted her head around. "Huh?"

"You're not a bitch all of the time," Ainsley replied with a distinctly pragmatic air. "Just some of the time. Sometimes, you're actually kinda nice."

Moira's eyebrows went up.

"Gee, thanks!" she said tartly.

"I'm just agreeing with you," Ainsley pointed out.

"I...! You...! Aw, nuts!" Moira chuckled. "Yeah, you're right. So am I forgiven?"

"Yeah. Am I?" Ainsley asked in return.

Moira shrugged her shoulders. "Yeah. I mean, I liked Jeremy, but it's not like he was the love of my life, or something. It probably wouldn't have lasted much longer anyway."

"And now you're free to pursue other possibilities," Ainsley pointed out shrewdly.

Moira looked away, a small smile hovering around her mouth. "Yeah, well...I might. If I can find the time."

Ainsley grinned.

"So!" Moira stood abruptly. "We're good, then?"

"Yeah." Ainsley nodded. "We're good."

Moira nodded in return and left the room. Halfway up the stairs to her eagle's nest, she paused, drew in a deep breath, and let the air out slowly.

"That wasn't so bad. One down...two to go."

With a sudden burst of energy, she raced up the remaining steps. Her cell phone flew into her outstretched hand before she reached the top and flipped itself open. Her fingers shaking slightly, she punched in the numbers as fast as she could.

"Um...yeah...could I...uh..." Moira took a deep breath. "Could I speak to Russ, please?"

"This is Russ."

"Oh! Um...Hi!" she giggled. "It's Moira."

"Hey! How are you?"

"Good! Um...actually, just sorta okay, I guess. You heard about my cousin?"

"Yeah, I heard. That was totally harsh. How is she?"

"Decent, considering. She's a lot tougher than she looks. Listen," Moira paused, crossed her fingers, then continued, speaking very fast, "we're having a little New Year's Eve party... nothing fancy, just family and a few friends...and I was wondering...well...if you might want to stop by." There! She'd done it.

"Oh! Um...well...I usually spend New Year's with my friend, Dan..." his voice trailed off.

"Oh...okay..." Moira's heart fell. She uncrossed her fingers. "That's cool. I just hadn't talked to you in a long time, and I thought...no biggie..."

There was an awkward pause as both of them searched for something to say.

"Well," Russ finally broke the silence, *"there'll be a lot of people there, I imagine — your family, all your friends, your boyfriend. We wouldn't have much chance to talk anyway."*

"My family will be there, of course," she said. "But none of my friends can make it — and I don't have a boyfriend anymore."

There was another pregnant pause.

"You don't?" Russ asked, the tone of his voice distinctly warmer.

"Nope. We broke up a few weeks ago."

"I'm sorry." He didn't sound sorry. Moira grinned and hugged herself.

"That's okay. It was kinda going nowhere, ya know?" She wasn't about to tell him the real reason Jeremy had broken up with her. Not yet, anyway.

"Yeah. I've been there before." Russ cleared his throat. *"So what time is the party?"*

"Anytime after eight."

"Well...would it be okay if Dan tagged along?"

"Sure! No problem!"

"I'll see what he says. Maybe we'll stop by for a few minutes, if that's all right."

"Great! I'll see ya then, I guess?"

"Yeah...sounds good! See ya tonight! Bye!"

"Bye!"

Moira shut off her cell phone and tossed herself across the bed, grinning from ear to ear. The new year had just gotten decidedly brighter.

* * * * *

Ainsley gulped, her eyes wide with a mixture of wonder and fear. "You're sure about this, Mom?"

"Yes."

"And it's either Moira or me?"

"Yes," Renatta said with a sigh.

"Whichever one of us has the Mark, right?"

"Correct."

"Has Moira looked yet?"

"I don't know," Renatta admitted. "I didn't want to push her on it, with the way she feels about magic in general."

"I don't think she's so bent about it anymore, Mom," Ainsley commented. "In fact, I think she may have been practicing some lately."

"I'd wondered that myself. At least she hasn't blown up over this Dumari business. I'm just grateful for that much right now."

Ainsley scooted closer to her mother's side. "This is so freaky. Mom..." she hesitated, then gathered her courage and said what was on her mind. "Mom, I don't want to be the Dumari. I'm not strong enough, or brave enough, or...anything enough! If I'd had to go through what Braidy just did, I'd be a total screw case right now! Just Seeing what happened to her has me freaked enough — in fact, being able to See anything has me pretty twisted! I'm still not sure how to deal with all of that. And I hate that I can't control it...that it just happens to me, without any warning. Like I can't control my own thoughts, or something."

"Grandma can help you with that," Renatta soothed her. "She wasn't too much older than you are now when her Seeings began, so I'm sure she understands exactly how you feel. Mention it to her tonight — she'll be glad to teach you how to control your talent and use it properly. But as far as being or not being the Dumari is concerned... I'm afraid none of us has any say over that. I'd hoped it wouldn't be one of my children..." she smiled sadly, "but my wishes weren't at issue. It is who it is."

"Which one of us do you think it is?"

"Honestly, Ainsley, I have no idea. You're both strong — yes, you are, whether you realize it or not — and brave, smart and talented. Not too long ago I assumed it couldn't be Moira because of her attitude toward magic, but that really has nothing to do with it. And she has been more open to it lately. Hell!" Renatta's shoulders slumped forward. "I'd really hoped it would be one of Caroline's kids — then I wouldn't have to worry. Well, at least not as much."

"I'm sorry, Mom," Ainsley whispered sadly.

"Oh, sweetie! It's not your fault!"Renatta reassured her. "It's nobody's fault, really. It just is, that's all."

"Do you..." Ainsley gulped again, "do you want to look?"

"Do you want me to?"

"I'm...not sure, actually. If it's me, I don't know if I'm ready to deal with it all yet. But if it isn't me, it would be nice to have the suspense over with." She took a deep breath and turned her back. "Go ahead. Look. I'll deal with it, whatever."

Renatta swallowed hard, her mouth suddenly dry. Reaching out, she brushed Ainsley's hair out of the way, first on one side, then the other. She sighed and leaned back.

"Nothing."

"Nothing? Wow!" Ainsley breathed a sigh of relief. "Then it *is* Moira!"

"Not necessarily."

"But you said the Mark appears by the time the Dumari is twelve. I'm almost fourteen, Mom! If it were me, the Mark would be there."

"I said the earliest it appears is at twelve. It's been known to show up as late as sixteen. It could be two more years before you have it."

"Well, that sucks!" Ainsley frowned. "So I may have to wait two more years before I know?"

"Don't worry. I greatly doubt Moira will want to wait that long to find out. I'm sure she'll be ready to face the facts soon. I just don't feel right pushing her on it."

"No, you definitely don't want to do that," Ainsley stated dryly. "She's liable to push back!"

Renatta laughed softly. "We'll know soon, sweetie."

"And then?"

"And then..." Renatta gave Ainsley a big hug, "...we deal with whatever comes."

* * * * *

Brody stuck his head in Braidy's open bedroom door.

"You ready?"

"Just about." Braidy was slipping into her shoes. She was dressed in a simple forest green dress with long sleeves and a hem that reached mid-calf. Brody was in his usual jeans and a warm, thick pullover. Both twins had instinctively chosen dark, subdued colors for their attire. They seemed to feel it best not to draw attention to themselves — even among their own family.

"You...um...you doing okay?" Brody asked hesitantly.

Braidy looked up at him. They hadn't spoken alone since the disaster on Christmas Eve. She'd assumed Brody was too angry with her to want to discuss what had happened. Nor had she herself been eager to open the subject. She knew how wrong she'd been to leave with Jonathan — she didn't need her brother reminding her.

"Yeah, I guess. Sort of," she replied, shrugging her shoulders. "It'll take a while, I suppose, but I'll get over it. Eventually."

"Good thing Dad made me stay here that night," Brody continued, his voice rough. "If I'd gotten my hands on that jerk, I would've..." His hands balled into fists.

Braidy stared at him.

"I thought you were mad at me," she said.

"Why would I be mad at you?" Brody stared in return. "It's not like you wanted them to kill you, is it?"

"No, but I went with Jonathan," she said, fiddling with her dress, unable to meet his eye, "when I knew Mom and Dad didn't want me to. Even you warned me off him — and Karen, too. But I wouldn't listen to anybody. I was so stupid."

Brody shrugged. "You liked him. It was your call. Besides, none of us thought he'd turn out to be a total slimeball. We just thought he was too old for you." He walked over to his sister and placed a hand on her shoulder. "Look, Bray, you made a mistake. We all do, now and then. I'm just glad you're okay. I...I would have missed you," he ended quietly.

Braidy fought back tears. "Thanks," she whispered.

They stood in silence for a moment, then both twins moved forward at the same moment. Brody wrapped his arms tight around his sister, her head resting on his broad shoulder.

"Just be more careful from now on, okay?" he whispered. "I kinda like having you around, ya know?"

"I will," Braidy sniffed, holding on for dear life.

* * * * *

Moira was trying desperately to keep her cool, but a silly little grin appeared on her face every time she looked up to see Russ standing in the living room...every time she heard his voice...every time someone said his name...every time she felt his eyes on her. Which was deliciously often.

Russ, too, was rather more jovial and ebullient than usual. Although still sparing with his smiles, his eyes were sparkling and he was a good deal more talkative than she'd ever known him to be. He was actually giving Dan — never exactly the silent type — quite a run for the money in the volubility department. Of course, the looks her family members were exchanging didn't help any. It seemed everyone was in on her secret.

Russ and Dan had arrived around eleven o'clock, just as Moira had given up on them. After politely making the rounds, Russ had joined Moira near the front window.

"Thanks for the invite," he said, toasting her with his beer bottle.

"I was beginning to think you weren't gonna show," Moira replied. *Damn! Did that sound whiny?*

"Dan's mom wouldn't let us leave any sooner," Russ explained. "She had a big cake for me and insisted I had to make a wish and blow out the candles first."

"Blow out..? Is it your birthday? I didn't know!"

"Tomorrow, actually," he told her.

"So you're a New Year's baby," Moira grinned up at him. "Were you the first baby of the year?"

"Naw. Dad's always complained about that...he had to wait a whole year before he could claim me on his taxes and they didn't even get the freebies for having me before anyone else that day."

Moira laughed. "You might have been a bit more considerate of your parents, Russ."

"Yeah, well, I've always had lousy timing," he grinned.

Moira's breath caught in her throat. She'd almost forgotten how his smile transformed his face. She realized she was staring at him, and blushed.

"Well...um...happy birthday, then. An hour early, that is." She held out her hand. Russ set his beer down and enveloped Moira's little hand in both of his big ones.

"Thanks," he murmured. They stood in silence, the rest of the room forgotten. Eventually, Russ cleared his throat.

"You said on the phone you wanted to talk," he said. "What about?"

"Wha...? Oh! Um...yeah." Moira glanced quickly around the room. "Not here. Too many ears, ya know?" She jerked her head toward the front hall. "C'mon!"

Still holding Russ's hand, Moira led the way to her attic retreat, the noise of the party slowly fading behind them.

"Wow!" Russ exclaimed as he entered the room behind her and gazed around. "What a slammin' room!"

"Yeah," Moira smiled, pleased that he liked it, "Andrew really nailed it when he came up with this idea."

"It's like a...like a treehouse...or an eagle's nest," he enthused. "Up here all by yourself. It owns!"

"I kinda like it," Moira beamed.

Russ wandered over to one of the window seats.

"You look really nice tonight, by the way," he said. "Not that you don't always look nice, I mean," he added, his face red, "but you look particularly good tonight."

"Thanks," Moira murmured, her own cheeks turning pink. "You... you look good, too."

"Thanks." Russ sat down, resting one hand on the window seat next to him, an obvious invitation in his eyes. Moira joined him, holding her breath, praying she didn't seem too eager.

"It is okay for us to be up here alone, isn't it?" Russ asked softly, leaning toward her.

"Oh! Yeah...sure...I mean...I can trust you, can't I?" she glanced up archly with a half-smile.

"More or less," he murmured, his breath warm on her face. Shifting slightly, he slipped one arm around her waist, pulling her close. Their lips barely an inch apart, he paused.

"No boyfriend, right?" Russ said firmly.

"No boyfriend," Moira shook her head vigorously. "Do you have a girlfriend?" she asked in return, her pulse racing.

Russ smiled slightly. "I'd say that's up to you..." He didn't bother to wait for her reply.

Several minutes later, as Moira slowly returned to earth, she snuggled up against him, smiling complacently.

"If you only knew how long I've wanted you to do that," she said.

"If you only knew how long I've wanted to!" Russ replied, feeling rather smug himself.

Moira laughed. "Yeah? Really?"

Russ kissed her again. "Yeah...really," he whispered in her ear. Nuzzling her neck, he continued, "So is this what you wanted to talk to me about?"

Moira stiffened slightly. "Um...yeah...well, partly, that is."

Russ leaned back. "What's up?"

"I...um...I really debated whether or not to tell you," she said. "I mean...I don't want you to change your mind...about going out with me, I mean."

"Sounds serious."

"It...um...you could say that," Moira murmured, her head lowered.

"Moira..."

"The thing is, I've got to grow up sometime, don't I? I mean, a person has to take responsibility for their own actions, right? Or their own inaction, as the case may be. I can't keep pretending this stuff is everybody else's fault, can I? I mean, okay, what Ainsley did was really grody, but that doesn't justify the way I acted, does it? After all, Braidy was in some seriously deep crap and..."

"Whoa, Moira!" Russ held his hands up to slow her down. "What exactly are we talking about here?"

Moira gazed up at him, the tears in her eyes surprising them both. "Don't hate me, please!" she whispered. "It's my fault Braidy almost got killed."

Russ frowned. "What do you mean?"

"I was pissed at Ainsley about...about something, something that happened weeks ago, so when she told me she'd Seen Braidy with Jonathan Crenshaw, I just blew her off and told her to go back to her room!" Moira cried. "If she hadn't gone to my aunt's house on her own, Braidy would be dead right now! And it would be all my fault!" She buried her head in her hands and let the tears fall, certain that Russ would want nothing to do with her after her confession. But in some strange way, she still felt better for having admitted her transgression to him. No one in the family had accused her, but deep inside she knew she'd been terribly wrong to ignore Ainsley that night. And the silent guilt had been wearing on her.

Russ let Moira cry for a minute or two, mulling over what she'd told him. Finally, he pulled her hands away from her face and tilted her chin up, forcing her to look at him.

"Now you listen to me, Moira Fitzgerald," he stated. "What you did was wrong, yes...but you are not responsible for what happened to your cousin. That blame belongs solely to the two men who kidnapped her and tried to kill her. I've known Quinn Muldoon for years. He's a complete jerk. He's quite capable of something evil all on his own, without any help from you or anybody else."

"But..."

"Don't beat yourself up over this, Moira," Russ said, placing one finger across her lips to silence her. "I'm not sure anything you could have done at that point would have made much difference. Events were already in motion. Besides, from what I've heard, Braidy has to bear at least some of the responsibility for what happened herself. She wasn't supposed to be going out with that Crenshaw dude, was she?"

"No. Uncle Phil and Aunt Caroline thought he was too old for her. But she really got him. I don't blame her for wanting to be with him."

"I don't either. But she obviously didn't know him very well, did she? I mean, she didn't even realize he was a magical, right?"

"None of us did. Did you know Jonathan?"

"No. I'd only met him a couple of times. You?"

"A little. He was friends with my brother. I talked to him a few times. He seemed nice enough." She shrugged her shoulders and stared out of the window. "No telling, huh?"

"Apparently not."

"So..." she sniffed. "I really screwed up, I know."

"It wasn't a smart move, no, but you didn't intend any harm. Seems to me what you need to do is apologize to Ainsley for not believing her..."

"I already did that," Moira interrupted him.

"Okay...then you should probably apologize to Braidy for not trying to help quicker," he continued.

"I was planning to..."

Russ turned Moira's face up to his again and gently wiped away the tears "Then all you have left to do is find some way to forgive yourself."

Moira nodded, then gasped as Russ kissed her. Tears filled her eyes again.

"What?"

"I thought you wouldn't want to go out with me after learning what a witch I'd been."

It was Russ's turn to shrug his shoulders. "Yeah, well...everybody makes mistakes. And I've already seen that temper of yours in action, so I kinda know what to expect. Besides, what's wrong with being a witch? My sister is one...and so was my mom," he grinned.

Moira swatted him on the shoulder. "That's not what I meant, and you know it!"

Russ chuckled and silenced any further protests with another kiss.

"You complaining?" he asked when he finally let her up for air.

"Not at all!" Moira said. She closed her eyes and rested her head on his shoulder, breathing a silent sigh of relief. Two down...

"It's almost midnight," Russ murmured softly. "Maybe we should go back downstairs."

"If we must."

"The last thing I want to do is get on your parents' bad side before we've even had an actual date, girl!" he chuckled. "If we don't show up soon, they're gonna send out the posse!"

"Yeah, you're probably right," Moira agreed reluctantly. "Mom's been even more over-protective than usual the past few days. We'd better get down there."

Which is why, fifteen minutes later, Moira was bouncing around the living room, unable to sit still, and trying her best to ignore the knowing looks everyone was giving both her and Russ.

"I swear, if Andrew winks at me one more time..." she muttered as she handed Russ another beer. Russ just grinned.

"Hey, everybody! It's almost time!"

Everyone gathered around the big screen in the family room as the crystal ball in Times Square began to drop.

"Ten...nine...eight...seven...six...five...four...three...two...one... Happy New Year!"

"Happy New Year, Moira."

"It certainly is!" Moira sighed, raising her lips for her first New Year's kiss. "And happy birthday!" she added, pulling Russ's head down for another, longer lip lock.

"The best one I've had in a long time," Russ smiled, and held her close.

* * * * *

Devon lay sprawled across the bed in the Baines' guest room, humming tunelessly to himself and occasionally bursting out with a drunken, "Happp-ee New Year!" Callista scowled at him, her violet eyes full of contempt.

"Lovely house guest you've saddled us with, Father," she said, her inflection frosty at best. "Why not dump him into a taxi and send him home?"

"We can't do that, Callista. Think how it would look to his parents."

"So instead we have to deal with it? I hardly think that's fair. We didn't exactly force him to drink all that champagne."

"He's had a bit too much to drink," Desmond soothed her ruffled feathers. "Like thousands of others tonight. He'll sleep it off and be fine in the morning."

"Not likely! Besides, that's not all I was referring to. Why on earth did you invite him to move in with us?"

"Why, Callista dear, I thought you'd be pleased! He is your boyfriend, isn't he?" her father teased.

"I refuse to dignify that question with an answer."

Devon snored. Desmond chuckled as he closed the door to the bedroom, shutting his guest inside alone.

"How can you laugh, Father!" she exclaimed, striding back to the living room. "This is utterly ridiculous! You know the only reason I ever wasted a single moment of my time on that...*boy*...was because you thought it would be wise to have another connection to his family." She threw herself onto the sofa.

"As it has proved to be," Desmond pointed out. "Having this young man under our influence may just make it possible for us to retrieve something from that disaster the other night." He poured himself another glass of champagne. "How could Muldoon have been so stupid! He knew secrecy was of the utmost importance."

"Why didn't he leave the lighthouse with you — before Jonathan brought the Attison girl in?" Her voice caught ever so slightly as she mentioned her former boyfriend's name.

"He wanted to oversee her termination personally."

"Then why didn't he simply get rid of her immediately?" Callista asked. "What on earth was he waiting for? They could have eliminated her, tossed her body into the ocean, and been done with it — no one would have suspected a thing. And Jonathan might still be alive."

"I know, my dear, I know. Quinn assured me that he would take every precaution. But, as so many times before, he dropped the ball. I promise you it will be the last time." Desmond raised his glass in a mock toast, his face grim.

"So you plan to get rid of Muldoon as well?"

"As soon as I find him, yes."

"That may not be the best plan, Father," Callista said reluctantly. "Believe me, I'd like nothing better myself, but he may still be of some use to us."

"How so?"

"Devon has informed me that his family now believes that Jonathan was in actuality the elusive Alex," she replied. "They are, of course, aware of Muldoon's pseudonym. They seem to think that Muldoon — Morty, that is — was taking his orders from Jonathan, or at the very least was in partnership with him. Therefore they assume that with Jonathan's death the operation has lost its leader. If Muldoon turns up dead, however, they may rethink that theory."

"Quinn's sudden demise might have them wondering if Alex is still alive, you mean? That he would have been the one to order Muldoon's execution?"

"Exactly. Which he — you — would have."

"Good point," Desmond stated, tapping his lips with one long finger. "We must keep them in the dark — lull them into a false sense of security — while at the same time making sure that they don't get a chance to question Muldoon." He sat down, resting his head on his hand. "I was so certain that Braidy Attison was the Dumari."

"She certainly seemed to be the most likely candidate."

"Has Devon given you any hints?"

"Apparently, no one is certain."

Desmond rolled his eyes. "I find that hard to believe at this late date. He must be holding out on us. You'll have to persuade him to confide in you, dear."

Callista gave her father a sharp glance. "I've done more than my fair share of persuading him, Father. All he could tell me was that they are positive neither one of the Attison twins is the Dumari. But whether it is Moira or Ainsley, he had no idea. Actually, he didn't seem to place much credence in the entire story. He's still reluctant to acknowledge Ainsley's magical talent, and he swears that Moira won't have a thing to do with magic."

"Interesting," Desmond mused. "Although, it is obvious that our young Devon carries a rather large chip on his shoulder where his family is concerned, particularly in regard to their magical abilities. It appears to me that he is terribly jealous of them all, and greatly resents his own lack of magical talent."

"What was your first clue?" Callista asked caustically.

Desmond smiled. "That resentment may just come in handy. At the very least, you need to encourage him to keep in touch with them. He's rather close to Moira, isn't he?"

"Apparently."

"Good. As long as he remains in contact, we'll have an inside track."

"What about Matthew Collins? He considers you to be a friend, doesn't he? Can't you pump him for information?"

"Ah, I'm afraid dear Matthew isn't that trusting," Desmond said with an exaggerated sigh. "Or that gullible. He has not been as open or forthcoming with me as I had hoped. No, my dear, Matthew is playing his cards close to his chest — very close indeed. As he always has. It looks as if our drunken house guest is our best bet right now."

"Wonderful," Callista muttered.

"Cheer up, my dear. At least he's relatively attractive."

"He's not Jonathan," Callista murmured softly.

Desmond stared at his daughter, surprised by her pensive tone. "I'm sorry, Callista. I didn't realize you'd cared that much."

Callista waved him off. "Don't be ridiculous, Father! I merely enjoyed Jonathan's company. We had a great deal in common. And he had certain...ah...talents, shall we say?"

"Please don't elaborate. As your father, I'd rather not know the details."

Callista smiled slightly. "Suffice to say, I shall miss him. I have every intention of making Andrew Collins pay dearly for his death." Her eyes sparked with an unaccustomed intensity as she contemplated her revenge. "Devon Fitzgerald isn't half the man Jonathan Crenshaw was."

"No, he isn't. I will agree with you there. I must admit, I find myself missing Jonathan a bit myself — for different reasons, obviously."

"Obviously." Callista took a sip of champagne, making a face at the taste. "Warm. Top me off, won't you, Father?"

Desmond obligingly retrieved the champagne bottle and refilled her glass, draining the last few drops into his own glass.

"Thank you." She drank deeply. "So, what are your thoughts?"

"Hmmm?"

"Which one of the girls do you think it might be? Moira...or Ainsley?"

"I've been thinking about that," Desmond replied, sitting back down. "Originally, I wrote Moira off because of her attitude toward magic in general. But I now wonder if I might have been too hasty in that assessment."

"In what way?"

"Discovering that you are the Dumari can be rather daunting, especially for a young girl like Moira. I wonder if her rejection of magic is actually a rejection of her destiny."

"Out of fear, you think?"

"Perhaps. A knee-jerk reaction, as it were. With time she will probably come to welcome her endowments and enjoy making use of them."

"But do you think she has the qualities of a Dumari?" Callista asked, obviously skeptical. "From what I've seen of her, she's nothing more than a snotty little brat."

Desmond laughed. "Don't care much for our little Moira, do you, my dear?"

Callista gave him a withering glance, not bothering to reply.

"In answer to your question, yes, I think she does have those qualities," Desmond continued. "Some of them, at least. She's bright, inventive, feisty...and, most important of all, strong. I also recall that when she was young, she was quite talented magically. Renatta used to brag about her all the time."

"So you think we should concentrate our efforts on Moira, then?"

"I think we'd better. From a purely logistical viewpoint, if for no other reason. We're running out of time. She'll be eighteen next summer. If we don't have her under our control by then, we'll be screwed."

"Assuming that she is the one. But if she's not..."

"We'll have only lost a few months. And Ainsley is several years younger than her sister. We'll have plenty of time to work on her.

Although, the more I think about it, the more convinced I am that Moira is our girl."

"Wonderful," Callista said, disgusted. "You realize how difficult it will be to convince someone as stubborn and obstinate as Moira is to go along with our plans...for that matter, to even perform magic in the first place?"

"Don't worry. We'll find a way. Find her weak spot, and capitalize on it. Much as I intend with young Devon. I'm sure you noticed how he lit up when I mentioned the possibility of teaching him magic..."

"But you can't do that. Everyone knows a person has to be born with the aptitude for magic...it can't be acquired unless the talent is there to begin with."

"You know that, and I know that, but if Devon ever did, he's so desperate to become a magical that he's chosen to forget it. Which plays right into our hands. By the time he realizes that I've been merely stringing him along, we'll have what we want, and will no longer have any use for him. You'll see, by this time next year, we'll be in control of the entire east coast...then the whole country..."

"And then the world..." Callista breathed, her eyes gleaming. She raised her champagne glass. "To you, Father — the future ruler of the world!"

"And to you, my dear," he toasted her in return, "the power behind my throne!"

* * * * *

January 1

SQUEEEEE!!!!!!!!!!!!!!!

This was the best — the absolute BEST! — night of my

whole entire life! It's like, what, three in the morning, and I'm not even tired! If I were any happier, I think I'd burst!

I wonder why Devon never came back. He promised he and Callista would get here before midnight. Andrew said he called at least, but it was still ignorant of him not to show. Granted, I didn't much mind not having the Ice Princess chilling the air — how the hell can she and Russ be brother and sister! — but it seemed totally weird to have our party without Devon. And I missed our annual New Year's dance. But having Russ here instead sure made up for it. I am soooooo glad I worked up the nerve to ask him.

Dan's cool, too. He's really funny! He even got Braidy laughing...which, considering what she went through a few days ago, is quite an accomplishment. I'm glad I made the time to talk to Braidy tonight, instead of putting it off till tomorrow. You know, she's not half bad after all. I mean, she's still a little princess, but she's liveable. I guess finding out that she's not the Dumari has knocked her ego down a bit. And she was really nice about what I'd done. She even said she understood, that she might not have listened to Ainsley either! And that it didn't matter, 'cause the whole thing was her own fault in the first place. Although, if you ask me, the whole thing was Jonathan's fault, not Braidy's.

Man, how wrong was I about him! He seemed like a pretty nice guy — not my type, of course, but cool. Who'da thunk the guy was not only hiding the fact that he was a magical, but was actually the mastermind behind all of this Dumari crap?! Learning Mr. Muldoon was in on it isn't quite as much of a stretch, ya know? That guy always gave me the willies. Now I know why Morty's laugh sounded so familiar to me last year in New York. I'd heard it dozens of times before.

So. The Dumari. Yeah, I know, I gotta get my head around that. I'm not sure why I didn't tell Russ. Sure, Grandpa Matthew said we still need to keep it as secret as possible, at least until they find Mr. Muldoon and find out who else he might have been working with. But I can trust Russ, can't I? I mean, I'm dating him...I should be able to trust him. But then again, this may not be about me. It could just as easily be Ainsley. In fact, now that I think about it, it probably IS Ainsley. Isn't the Dumari supposed to be one of those philanthropical types? That definitely fits Ainsley better than it does me! LOL

I should just let Mom take a look behind my ears and be done with it. But for some reason, I still feel kinda freaky about it. What if, by some miracle, it is me? What the hell do I do then? I'm still not that crazy about the whole magic thing as it is. One step at a time, girl. Get straight about being a magical first, then figure out how to deal with being a powerhouse — if I am, that is.

Man, it will be so much simpler if Ainsley is the Dumari! Then I can just get on with my life — finish high school, go to college, get to know Russ much, MUCH better...

But what if it IS me? What do I do then?

This is ignorant, you know that? What am I afraid of? If I am the Dumari, I am! If I'm not, I'm not! Wouldn't it be better to just know? How can I expect to get on with my life if I don't know what that life might entail? What was it I was saying earlier today about growing up and facing things straight on? I can't just keep wondering...

Moira slammed her journal shut. Moving quietly so as not to wake the rest of the house, she made her way to the bathroom on the second floor. After searching through several cabinets and most of the drawers, she finally found what she was looking for — a small hand mirror. Walking on her tiptoes, she returned to the attic, went into her bathroom, and closed the door.

"Okay, here goes," she whispered, tilting her head and pulling her ear forward with one hand, while holding up the small mirror with the other. "God, I'm trembling!" she laughed shakily. She squeezed her eyes shut for a moment, then opened them wide and leaned forward, angling the hand mirror for a clearer view.

She peered at the reflection closely for several moments, then moved the mirror to the other ear. Again, she stared intently, her entire body tensed. Slowly, she placed the mirror on the sink counter, walked back to her desk, and sat down. After staring blindly into space for several minutes, Moira flipped her journal open once again...

Man...

Well, now I know...

I suppose I should feel a little sorry for Ainsley, but it's like I said...

The pen slipped from Moira's fingers as she drew in a ragged breath, and finished the sentence in a whisper...

"...better her than me."

Printed in the United States
137643LV00002B/2/P

9 781440 109911